WESTON FIELDS

The Guardians of Kawts

Sign up for my newsletter at weston-fields.com to receive regular updates on future titles and get a free copy of the previously unreleased short story "Crystal Clear."

Chapter 1

"Attention all students - your school day has begun," a robotic voice crackled over the intercom. Timothy sat down at his desk, along with the twelve other students in his class. Under the table, his leg bounced up and down as he strained to hear what the voice would say next.

"Today's lunch is pink glop," the voice continued. "Seventh level students wanting to go on the tour of the food production plant must have their permission slips turned in to the Council by the end of the day."

The voice paused for a moment, and Timothy's heartbeat quickened. *Please don't be today. Please don't be today. Please don't be-*

"Today, the fifth level students will be running The Race. This is the final week of school for the twelfth level students. Good luck to all!" the voice concluded.

Timothy shared a glance with his friend Aksell as the tension drained from the room. He sagged forwards in his chair.

Just another day of training, he thought, a smile slowly spreading across his face. *We're safe. For now.*

Timothy's teacher, a smartly dressed woman named Emily Louise, walked up to the front of the class, the heels of her shoes clacking on the tiled floor.

"Good morning, class," she said pleasantly. The class mumbled an acknowledgement, and after a brief pause, Mrs. Louise continued. "Today, you will take your final history exams, followed by practice for The Race. Lunch will be available whenever we finish."

Mrs. Louise reached into her desk drawer and pulled out a packet of papers, setting them on top of the nearest table. Timothy reached into his bag and pulled out a pencil, tapping it idly against the top of his desk as Mrs. Louise took attendance. His eyes wandered around the room, finally coming to rest on the Kawts flag that hung in the front of the classroom.

Twelve years of incessant history lessons had drilled the symbolism of the flag into him - the five interlocking rings represented the five cities, while the ring of twelve stars around them stood for the twelve Council members, the guardians of Kawts. The stars, Timothy knew, were a relatively recent addition to the flag, having been added in response to Milkop Quawz' rebellion several generations prior.

Timothy's reflections were interrupted as a loud bang suddenly echoed through the room. He spun toward the source of the sound, terror surging through him.

It's the anarchists! It has to be-

The tension slowly drained out of him as he realized what had caused the noise. Standing in the doorway were two of his classmates, identical twins Crystal and Jewel. Jewel still had one hand on the doorknob, wincing a little as she eased the door away from the wall.

"Sorry we're late," she said with an apologetic smile, brushing a stray lock of her raven-colored hair out of her face.

"We had to take an unexpected detour," Crystal said. Her own hair was shorter, and had been dyed a brilliant shade of bright red for as long as Timothy could remember. Both twins had the same piercing blue eyes.

Crystal raised an eyebrow. "Apparently, MacGregor Street is *still* an active crime scene."

Mrs. Louise gave them a disapproving frown. "We were about to begin our history exam," she said, a steely tone in her voice. "I trust you're prepared to join us?"

Jewel nodded, quickly taking her seat. "Of course. Sorry."

Mrs. Louise turned away from the twins back to the rest of the class. "You will now take your final history exam," she said, quickly masking her irritation. "You all know the rules. No notes are allowed. Fill in the blanks with your answers, and try to complete as much of the test as you can. Your score will determine which jobs you are eligible for, so do your best. Are there any questions before we begin?"

Near the back of the room, a hand shot up. Mrs. Louise sighed, and Timothy knew without turning around who it was.

"Yes, Edwin?" Mrs. Louise asked, pinching the bridge of her nose. "What is it now?"

"On a scale of one to ten, how mandatory is it?"

"How mandatory is what, Edwin?"

"The test."

Mrs. Louise sighed again. Somewhere in the room, someone unsuccessfully tried to suppress their laughter. In the front of the room, Larnell turned around in his seat.

"'Every twelfth level student must take the Kawts History Exam in order to graduate. Those who do not graduate are ineligible for future employment, and may be considered anarchist sympathizers,'" he said. "Kawts Student Handbook, Revised and Expanded Edition."

"Thank you, Larnell," Mrs. Louise said with a weary smile. "Does that answer your question, Edwin?"

"Guess so," Edwin muttered, rolling his eyes. Timothy suppressed a smile. As amusing as Edwin's antics often were, it was even better when someone called his bluff. Especially when that person was Larnell.

"If there are no further questions, I will begin handing out the exams,"

Mrs. Louise said, her face strained. "You may begin as soon as you receive your test." She walked down the rows of desks, passing out the exam packets. Soon, the only sound in the room was the scratching of pencils on paper.

Timothy looked down at his test, skimming through the questions. Slowly, a smile broke out across his face.

This'll be the easiest exam ever! It's the same stuff they've been teaching us since we were first level students!

Timothy sped through the test, finishing it in a little under half an hour. He set down his pencil and flexed his fingers. Then he picked up the test again, double, triple, and even quadruple-checking his answers.

I have to make sure I get this absolutely right, he thought as he scribbled out part of his answer and reworded it. *I need to get at least a ninety-eight percent to get the library job.*

Finally, satisfied with his answers, Timothy walked to the front of the room to turn in his test. He stared listlessly at the clock on the wall for a few minutes, then pulled a book from his backpack and began to read. The book had been a recommendation from Samuel, Kawts' head librarian. He had an excellent track record when it came to recommending books, and this one was no exception. After a few minutes, Timothy was completely engrossed in the story, hardly noticing the rest of his classmates getting up one by one to turn in their tests.

Long before the hour time limit had passed, Mrs. Louise cleared her throat, bringing Timothy back to reality.

"If everyone has finished, we will now go over to the track to practice for The Race," she said, looking around to make sure that all the exams were turned in. Satisfied that she had them all, she motioned for her students to stand, leading them across the street to the track.

"Good book?"

Timothy turned around to see Aksell standing behind him, a goofy grin on his face. Timothy laughed, nodding. "Samuel's latest recommendation. It's about a guy who gets lost in the woods outside of Kawts and has to try to make his way back to civilization."

"Sounds riveting."

"It's more exciting than it sounds," Timothy said. He sighed. "Although I'm pretty sure I can guess how it ends right now. It's always the same."

They walked in silence for a moment, then Aksell said, "Did you hear about the attack on the Security Force building last night?"

Timothy's stomach flip-flopped. "How many died?"

Aksell shook his head. "I don't know. I don't think it was too many. Just about everyone had already left for the night. Most of the casualties were Blanks who were guarding the building."

Timothy shook his head, his frown deepening. "I don't know how the Council keeps fighting them off," he said. "The anarchists are really good at what they do."

"So are the Councilmen," Aksell said, his hazel eyes shining with pride.

"I can't argue with that," Timothy said. A smile tugged at the corner of his lips, and he added, "I bet you can't wait to take your dad's place."

Aksell lifted his hand, pretending to smack Timothy. "You have no idea how often he brings that up!" he said, shaking his head. "'There has been a Deogol leading Kawts ever since its founding, Aksell,'" he said, mimicking his father's stern tone. He sighed. "I'm just not the warrior type. I wish I could convince him to let me work for Samuel or something instead."

"Hey, who knows? You might be able to-"

"Hey! You two! Quit dawdling and get over here!" the track manager, a gruff, middle-aged man named Taranis, shouted.

Aksell rolled his eyes and jogged the last few yards to the track,

Timothy right behind him.

"Today," Taranis barked as they arrived, "you are going to run a practice Race. This is your chance to re-accustom yourself to the track and practice setting your speed." He looked at the students assembled in front of him, a malicious gleam in his eye. "And, just for fun, you can all run it twice!"

His impressively large mustache quivered with what Timothy took to be rage. Taranis glared at each of the students, as if he was scrutinizing their very souls. Timothy shifted uncomfortably under Taranis' gaze, but he knew better than to react. Bitter experience had taught them that Taranis was liable to double that number if they complained, a trait for which many of the students had taken to calling him "the Tyrant."

Finally, Taranis leaned back, his eyes narrowed. "The Race will begin... NOW!" he bellowed.

The class took off down the track like startled hares. For the first few meters, the run was easy, but then the track turned towards a large grove of trees. Football-sized rocks littered the path, barely visible in the minimal light that filtered down through the dense canopy overhead. Twined between the rocks were massive old tree roots, some of which were nearly as old as the track itself. Timothy noted some particularly dangerous tripping hazards as he ran.

It won't end well for me if I trip on the day of The Race.

It has to be coming up soon, he thought as he ran, a cold pit of fear forming in his stomach. *There aren't that many classes left who haven't run it yet this year.* He ducked under a low-hanging tree branch. *I just wish they would tell us the date in advance. The not knowing when it's coming is almost as bad as actually running it.*

He shook his head. *What am I saying? The Race itself is still much worse.*

I guess I get why it's necessary. Between the anarchists and those nomadic raiders, the Council has to make sure that everyone can pull their own weight.

Still, a small voice in the back of his mind nagged, *there's got to be a better way to do that than killing the loser.* A picture of Quill's smiling face flashed before his eyes, and he shook his head, clearing his mind of both the treasonous thought and the sorrow it threatened to dredge up.

No, he thought. *Not now. I can't deal with this right now.*

The trees around Timothy thinned out as the finish line came into sight. He broke out into a sprint, pulling ahead of his classmates with ease. As he crossed the finish, he slowed back to a walk, gasping for air. Once his breathing had returned to normal, he walked over to Aksell.

"I can't wait until we're done with this."

Aksell looked at him, a glimmer of sadness in his eyes. "Me too, man. Me too."

Chapter 2

Timothy turned back toward the track, watching as his classmates crossed the finish line one after another. As the last person finished, he couldn't help but remember all the people they had lost to The Race over the years. A lump formed in his throat, and he quickly pushed the thoughts aside. Even so, he couldn't quite quell the churning in his stomach as he followed his classmates back to the cafeteria for lunch.

This could be the last time I see one of them, and I'd never know it. A wave of sadness threatened to overwhelm him, and he quickly switched his attention to the plate of pink glop in front of him.

He poked at it with his fork, debating with himself whether he was really that hungry. The pink food had a gelatinous, almost oozy texture that made it seem a little too slimy to be edible. Its taste was little better - although its slight sweetness made it widely regarded as the best food in all of Kawts. In Timothy's eyes, though, it was just as nasty as everything else, a sentiment he had in common with Aksell. A smile tugged at the corner of Timothy's mouth as he remembered all the times he and Aksell and Quill had debated whether pink glop was actually even food.

Timothy choked down the last bite of the glop on his plate and set down his fork, grimacing.

"I think Ives and Larnell are going over to the library to hang out for a bit," Aksell said, standing up. "I might go over there and join them."

Timothy shook his head. "Have fun with that. I promised my dad I would help Maurice in the shop while he's delivering that batch of chairs to Aria."

"That's right! I keep forgetting he's out of town. Do you guys know when he'll be back?"

Timothy nodded. "As long as the weather stays good, he should be back by tomorrow night."

"Good," Aksell said. "Well, I'll see you tomorrow, Tim."

"Yeah. See you." They parted ways at the door, Aksell walking over to the library and Timothy making his way over to his father's carpentry shop, a sizable room attached to the front of their house.

He stepped into the workshop, the door swinging open with a bang. A shaggy blond head looked up at him from the back of the store.

"Hey, Tim!" his brother Maurice shouted, waving at him with one sawdust-covered hand.

At eighteen, Maurice was two years older than Timothy. He had been apprenticed to their father for only a few months, ever since he was excommunicated by the Reporters Guild. It didn't surprise Timothy in the slightest, knowing all too well his brother's fondness for crazy theories and borderline traitorous ideas.

"Hi, Maurice," Timothy said, nodding to his brother and stashing his things in the corner of the workshop. "What are we working on today?"

"Mrs. Taylor stopped by earlier today to order a new dresser. I've been working on that for the last few hours."

Timothy craned his neck to see around his brother. He raised an eyebrow. "That does not look like a dresser."

Maurice grimaced. "Yeah. I may have gotten a little distracted. And anyway, woodworking is Dad's thing, not mine."

Then what is your thing? Timothy wondered with a slight shake of his

9

head. *Getting kicked out of places for being a suspected anarchist? Hanging out with your friends way past the Council's curfew on Sunday nights?*

"Woah! Take it easy, Tim!" Maurice exclaimed, and Timothy flushed, realizing that he had spoken his thoughts aloud. "I'll admit that some of my ideas are a little... controversial. But people will come around eventually."

Timothy bit his tongue, holding back any further accusations. The silence that followed stretched out uncomfortably long.

"Well." Maurice looked over at Timothy, rapping his fingers on the misshapen dresser. "Why don't you take over working on the dresser? I've got some bookkeeping stuff to catch up on, anyway."

Timothy watched Maurice leave with a twinge of regret. Then he sighed and turned toward the workbench, taking in the haphazardly arranged mess of tools. He stared at them for a moment, then began to move them around, organizing them by function.

I don't understand how Maurice ever manages to find anything, he thought, shaking his head.

Absorbed in his work, Timothy hardly noticed the time passing. It was nearly nine o'clock when Maurice returned, a smudge of ink across his forehead.

"I think it's about time we call it a night," he said, stopping a few feet away from Timothy.

Timothy glanced down at his Council-issued watch and nodded. "I'm surprised mom hasn't come looking for us yet."

A smile tugged at the corner of Maurice's lips. "She did. That's what reminded me."

Timothy set the tools back on the shelf and stepped back, taking a moment to admire his handiwork.

"You know, if that whole library thing doesn't work out, you'd be an excellent carpenter," Maurice said.

"It's not quite there yet," Timothy said, squinting at the dresser.

"There are still some things I need to tidy up."

"If you say so, Tim," Maurice said, patting Timothy on the back. After checking to make sure that the shop was all locked up, Maurice and Timothy made their way to the side door that led into their house, flipping off the lights.

Timothy's mother was waiting for them in the dining room when they emerged. She had the same brown eyes and brown hair as Timothy, although Timothy's was considerably messier.

"What were you boys working on in there that took you so long?" she asked as she handed them each a bowl of grey glop.

"It was nothing," Maurice said. "We just lost track of time."

His mother raised an eyebrow at him. "Maurice, you lose track of a lot of things, but dinnertime isn't one of them."

"I was working on a bit of a… special project," Maurice said, studiously avoiding eye contact. "It's a surprise."

"This had better not be another pamphlet suggesting that the Council arrange peace talks with the raiders. You remember what happened last time. It's a good thing the editor caught you before you went and got yourself arrested!"

Maurice set down his fork and raised his right hand. "I promise that I am absolutely, one hundred percent, not making any pamphlets. About anything whatsoever."

His mother stared at him for a moment longer, and Timothy could tell she wasn't entirely convinced. Maurice smiled, and she shook her head. "Just don't tell your father that you were working on this 'secret project' of yours during shop time." She glanced up at the clock on the wall. "I have some spelling tests I need to grade," she said, pushing back her chair. "Make sure you two clean up after you're done."

With that, she disappeared into the back room of the house, which her husband had converted to an office for her when she had taught eleventh-level students. A few years ago, she had switched to teaching first-level students, a change she never regretted. Except on Race day.

Timothy and Maurice stayed at the kitchen table for some time, Maurice furiously scribbling something down on a napkin.

By the time Timothy finally got up to his bedroom that night, it was nearly ten o'clock. He slid his history textbook onto his bookshelf, the worn cover standing in stark contrast to the neat spines of the ex-library books that surrounded it. He sat down on his bed, reflecting on all that had happened that day. As his thoughts turned once again to The Race, the faint smile on his face faded.

Who's going to lose this year? he wondered, feeling slightly guilty for hoping that neither he nor Aksell would be the unlucky student. He was fairly confident in his own abilities, but the fact remained that either he or one of his twelve classmates would not live to see their graduation.

As it often did, reflecting on The Race brought his thoughts back to Quill. He and Timothy and Aksell had been inseparable ever since they were first-level students. Until last year. The year Quill lost The Race.

Timothy stood and retrieved a box from his shelf. It was beautifully carved, crafted out of what seemed to be some kind of wood. It had been a gift from Quill on the day before their last Race.

* * *

"Hey, Tim," a voice said behind him.

Timothy turned to see Quill standing in the entrance of his father's workshop, his lanky frame filling the doorway. Timothy stood, leaving the project he was working on behind on the floor. His hands were covered in sawdust, and he brushed them off on the front of his shirt.

"Hey Quill," he said, walking over to his friend. "What's up?"

"I have a favor to ask you," Quill said in a quavering voice, glancing over his shoulder. He seemed nervous about something, although what it was, Timothy couldn't guess. Timothy stared at the space behind Quill, hoping to see something that would tell him the reason for his friend's odd behavior. The street behind him was completely empty except for a pair of Blanks marching past on their regular patrol.

"Sure. What do you need?" he asked, still trying to figure out why Quill was so jumpy.

"Keep this safe," Quill replied, handing him a strange wooden box that Timothy had not noticed until now.

"Okay…" Timothy said, raising an eyebrow. "Do you mind if I ask why I'm doing this?"

"Just trust me," Quill said. "Someone needs to keep this safe, and you're the only person I trust right now."

"Woah, slow down," Timothy protested, raising his hands in an effort to calm his friend. "Start at the beginning. What's going on?"

"I can't tell you," Quill said, with another glance behind him. He turned back toward his friend, and Timothy could see the tears in his eyes. "If anything happens to me, promise me you will keep this safe."

"Quill, what's this all about?" Timothy asked, but his friend was already gone, having disappeared down a narrow street across from the shop.

* * *

Timothy turned the box over in his hands, his thoughts on Quill's last few days. He set the box right side up again, tracing his finger over the series of strange symbols carved into the lid.

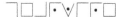

On the front of the box was a combination lock. Timothy idly spun the dials, trying a dozen different combinations before lowering the box once more.

I should have asked him what the password was when I saw him the next morning, Timothy thought, shaking his head. He twirled the dials again.

"What's the password, Quill?" he whispered to the ceiling. He fiddled with the box for a few minutes longer. Then, sighing, he returned it to its place on the shelf and fell asleep.

Chapter 3

Timothy was running. He tried to catch a glimpse of who or what was chasing him, but his attacker was always just out of sight. He tripped over something and fell forward, catching himself just in time. Timothy forced himself to return his attention to the path in front of him. The road came to a sudden stop only a few meters further on, hanging over a massive expanse of nothingness. He skidded to a halt, but not fast enough, falling into the endless abyss below.

* * *

Timothy awoke with a start. He looked around, re-assuring himself that he was safe. He glanced at his watch.

6:00 in the morning.

It isn't really worth going back to sleep now, he sighed, doing the math. He groaned and rolled out of bed, wandering downstairs to grab a breakfast cube from the cupboard.

As he passed by Maurice's room, he slowed to a stop, listening. He leaned closer to the door, straining his ears in hopes of hearing his brother's muffled snoring. No such sound greeted him, and he slowly eased open the door. Just as he had feared, the room was empty.

Timothy dashed down the stairs, frantically checking each room for his brother.

Was he here when I went to bed last night? He had to have been! Did he sneak out after the Council's curfew? If anyone sees him, they'll think he's working for the anarchists! What if someone already HAS seen him? I have to find him before he gets himself killed and-

Timothy stopped short as the familiar sound of sawing reached his ears. His concerns melted away as he opened the door to his father's workshop, revealing Maurice desperately trying to saw a plank in half without making too much noise. He yelped and started violently when he saw Timothy watching him.

Quickly regaining his composure, he whispered, "Good morning, Tim! I didn't wake you up, did I?"

Timothy shook his head, stepping into the workshop. "You didn't wake me up," he said. "Although you did make me think you'd snuck out after curfew again."

Maurice looked chagrined, rubbing the back of his neck. "Sorry about that. I couldn't exactly have told you what I was up to. Because you were asleep."

"What are you working on down here so early?"

Maurice avoided making eye contact. "I might have fallen a little behind on a few projects last night. I was hoping to catch up before dad got back from his trip."

Timothy frowned, his suspicion growing. "How far behind?"

"Ah... Let's just say that I didn't really get a lot done after you got back yesterday. I'm almost caught up now, I promise," he added quickly.

"If you weren't working on shop stuff yesterday, what were you doing?"

"Don't worry about it."

Timothy sighed. "Maurice, that just makes me more concerned about what you're up to."

"It's just a little project that Ally and Maverick and I are working on,"

16

Maurice said. "We're doing some research about Kawts' early history."

"This isn't another one of your conspiracy theories, is it?"

Maurice feigned shock. "Me? Never! I'm just curious - I want to know the parts that they don't teach you in school."

"They teach us pretty much everything there is to know," Timothy said. "Trust me - I just took the final exam yesterday. You already know everything important."

Maurice dismissed Timothy's objection with a wave of his hand. "There's always more to the story, Tim. First rule of being a reporter."

Timothy sighed and shook his head. "Well, good luck with your... project," he said. "I'm going to go have breakfast."

With that, he turned and went back into the kitchen, making his way to the cupboard where they stored their supply of breakfast cubes. He frowned as he noted the dwindling number of the small, dice-shaped cubes remaining.

Must be almost time for our monthly food delivery. Maybe they'll actually send something worth eating this time, he thought. *They did say that they invented a new flavor of glop last week.*

He held his nose as he quickly swallowed the small cube, which looked like a compressed conglomeration of slightly burnt scraps of leftover scrambled eggs. He washed it down with a glass of water, using up a good portion of his water ration for the day.

The city's primary source of water - the river that ran along Kawts' southern border - had become contaminated several years ago, poisoned by the anarchists in an attempt to throw the city into chaos. Fortunately, a team of scientists had been quickly drafted to find a way to purify the water, led by Councilman Simms and the late Howard Kolt. Before long, they had found a solution, but it was inefficient and expensive, only barely able to produce enough drinkable water to keep the city hydrated.

Timothy glanced at the clock on the wall.

If I leave now, I could stop by the old watchtower before school, he thought, grabbing his things and stuffing them into a worn backpack. He swung his bag up onto his shoulder and started out the door, meandering through the streets of Kawts, and enjoying the cool morning air. Attack drones buzzed quietly overhead, patrolling the streets for anarchist activity. As Timothy reached Franklin Plaza, a squadron of Blanks trooped past on their daily rounds.

Memories flooded him as he saw the ramshackle watchtower rising out of the corner of the plaza.

I don't think I've been back here since Quill died, he thought, staring frozen at the crooked spire. He stood there in silence for a few moments before moving over to the tower and ducking inside.

A plaque on the back wall explained the history of the tower, marking it as the site of the final skirmish of Milkop Quawz' rebellion. Timothy ignored the sign and kept walking, climbing the spiral staircase to the lookout post at the top. From his perch at the top of the tower, Timothy could see almost all of Kawts and much of the landscape surrounding it.

Quill would have loved this, he thought as he watched the sunrise over the Blanks' quarters. In the streets below, he could see the Blanks milling about in the streets, displaying no more emotion or signs of humanity than the attack drones.

Beyond the Blanks' quarters, the food production plant stood as a dark mass against the sky, concealing most of Kawts' eastern wall. The wall protected the city on three sides, the southern border being protected by a river too deep and too wide to walk across. Timothy turned to look at the river, his eyes being drawn to the dense forest beyond. He squinted at the tree line, hoping to spot something moving.

Edwin's always saying that the forest is inhabited by bloodthirsty tree-people, he thought, shading his eyes against the rising sun. A smile tugged at the corners of his mouth.

But then again, Edwin is hardly a reliable source.

Far to the north, Timothy fancied he could make out the southernmost edge of the Bearded Mountains on the horizon, the boundary of the territory of a mysterious race of giants. Nearer to Kawts, on the west side, was another mountain, Mt. Elbrus, which served as a natural defense mechanism for the smaller cities that also relied on the Council for protection and guidance.

At the risk of being late to school, Timothy lingered in the tower a little longer, enjoying the view and the sunrise. Finally, with a contented sigh, he climbed down and jogged over to his school, the largest and most centrally located of several school buildings throughout the city. He made it there with only seconds to spare, ducking into the room just as the voice came on over the intercom.

"Attention all students. Your school day has begun." The chatter died away as everyone moved to their seats. "Today's lunch is orange glop. The school trip to the food plant will be next Thursday. The twelfth level students will be running The Race today."

Timothy's heart started beating faster, the announcement about The Race awakening a cold pit of dread in his stomach. The announcement was hardly a surprise, but he had to admit that he had still harbored the hope that maybe, just this one time, they would forget about The Race.

It's hard to believe Quill's been gone a whole year already.

A faint smile stretched across Timothy's face as he remembered the jokes Quill had been cracking before The Race had begun.

That was such a Quill thing to do, he thought, shaking his head. *I think he would even find something clever to say about the apocalypse.* His smile was replaced by a frown as other memories took over. *I should have known something was bothering him even before The Race. He had been so jittery - I should have talked to him about it while I had the chance.*

"I am now going to read through the rules of The Race," Mrs. Louise announced, interrupting Timothy's reflections. "Once I have finished, we will all walk over to the track and begin the countdown for the commencement of The Race."

Mrs. Louise glanced down at the piece of paper in her hand, although in reality, there was no need to. Everyone in the room had memorized the instructions years ago.

"The Race is a one-and-a-half-mile race on the designated track. The Race will begin on the word 'go,' following a ten second countdown. Starting before the word 'go' will result in a sixty-second penalty for the offending student. Leaving the track is an automatic disqualification. Any student who is disqualified will be ranked in last place, regardless of their actual time. The first person to cross the finish line today will be granted the first choice of jobs tomorrow. After The Race, you are free to leave, although you may return here for lunch if you wish."

Mrs. Louise looked up from the paper. "Good luck to all," she said, her lips pressed together in a frown. She set the paper down on her desk, then motioned for the class to exit the room.

Timothy followed along with the anxious crowd as they left the school building and walked across the street to the track. He lagged behind the others, weighed down by memories.

"Thinking about Quill?" Aksell asked quietly, coming up beside him. The look on his face made it plain that he was, too.

"Yeah," Timothy said with a sad smile. "How could he have lost? He won the previous two Races by a landslide!"

"I don't know," Aksell said. "Maybe he left the track."

Timothy shook his head. "He was already really far ahead of us. Why would he have tried to cheat if he was basically guaranteed first place anyway?"

"I don't know, Tim. But it's the only explanation that makes any sense." Aksell's words hung in the air for a moment. Then he forced a smile. "We'd better hurry or we'll lose The Race before we even get there!"

Timothy laughed as he increased his pace, but his laughter wasn't heartfelt. Aksell's poor attempt at a joke reminded him too much of Quill.

They walked a little ways in silence. Then Aksell said, "Do you think he could still be alive?" The question hung heavily over them. There was no need for a reply. They walked the rest of the way without saying a word.

Chapter 4

"Now that we're all here," Taranis began, glaring pointedly at Timothy and Aksell as they arrived. "The Race will begin in ten seconds. Ten! Nine!"

Timothy jogged over to the starting line.

"Eight!"

He bent over, touching his fingers to the dirt.

"Seven! Six!"

Timothy closed his eyes. He took a deep breath, then slowly exhaled.

"Five!"

Timothy opened his eyes. His heart pounded in his chest.

"Four! Three!"

He glanced around at his classmates.

Goodbye, he thought. *I'm sorry.*

"Two!"

Timothy turned his focus back to the path in front of him, every muscle in his body tense.

"One. GO!"

The thirteen students took off like their lives depended on it. Aksell and Timothy quickly advanced toward the front of the group, the distance between them and the rest of their classmates gradually lengthening. As the track turned towards the trees, the rest of the group began to gradually drop out of sight, until eventually, Timothy and Aksell were alone. They rounded the corner into the deepest part of the forest, where the trees were more densely packed. Out of the corner of his eye, Timothy saw Aksell suddenly go down, tripping over an exposed root. He skidded to a stop, turning back to help.

"Keep going! I'm fine!" Aksell yelled, but Timothy could hear the fear and pain in his voice.

"No, you're hurt and you'll lose The Race!" Timothy shouted back, terror surging through him.

Just like Quill.

"Let me help you!" He had reached Aksell now. "Can you stand?"

"I can try," Aksell said with a weak smile. He started to get up, but his leg buckled underneath him and he collapsed back onto the ground with a cry of pain. "My ankle," he gasped. "I think I sprained it."

A grim silence settled over the pair - with his injured ankle, there was no way Aksell could run.

Even if I help him walk, there's no way we'll get to the finish line in time.

One of their classmates ran past them, then another, then another. The lead that they had built up was already beginning to crumble.

I can't just leave him here! Timothy thought as he watched the rest of the class vanish around a bend in the track. His heart raced as he desperately tried to think of a solution, the nagging knowledge that they were falling further and further behind only making it harder to concentrate. He was painfully aware of the fact that, unless they came up with something soon, it would be too late.

No. Focus on helping Aksell. Don't worry about everyone else right now.

Timothy took a deep breath, steadying himself. Several potential solutions came to mind, but he discarded them all in rapid succession.

If only I could make a cart, he thought. Then his eyes widened.

That's exactly what we need - a cart! Timothy looked around at the surrounding trees, an idea forming in his mind.

"Aksell! I have a plan!" Timothy shouted as he scrambled up a nearby tree.

I guess I'm technically leaving the track right now, he realized. Then he shrugged. *We're dead anyway. At least this way, we have a chance.*

Scanning the treetops, he selected a medium-sized branch and broke it off. A larger branch would work better for what he had in mind, but he simply didn't have the time or tools to collect one. As the first branch thudded to the ground, he called down to Aksell.

"Aksell! Try to find four large rocks of about the same size!"

"I'll try," Aksell called back. Timothy scrambled up the tree, searching for another branch of a similar size. He soon found what he was looking for, and before long, a second branch thudded to the ground beside the first. Timothy slid down the trunk of the tree, gathering a few thick twigs and some rope-like plants on his way. He began building a vaguely cart-like structure, thankful for all the hours he had spent helping his father make carts in his shop.

"Aksell! Tie those rocks you found to the ends of these large twigs!" Timothy said, tossing his friend a handful of the rope-like plants. Aksell nodded, and Timothy started on the next step, tying more of the plants to the front ends of the branches, securing them behind a pair of smaller branches that jutted out from the side. As Aksell finished his task, Timothy balanced the branches on top of the thick twigs and used the last bit of the rope-like plants to tie them loosely together. The result was a makeshift cart - if a cart had no sides or bottom and could fall apart without warning.

"Aksell, get in between the two branches!" Timothy said quickly. "Grab one with each hand. Put your feet on top of them, too. You'll have to hold yourself up off the ground."

"What are you going to do?" Aksell asked as he quickly maneuvered himself into position.

"I'm going to pull you," Timothy said, picking up the ends of the ropes attached to the long branches.

"That's crazy!" Aksell protested. "You'll never be able to catch up while you're pulling me in this thing!"

Timothy stared at him coolly, his determination to save his friend eclipsing his fear. "Either we try this now, or I stay here until we come up with a better idea. I'm not leaving you behind."

"Alright," Aksell conceded quickly, realizing that they'd both be dead if he kept arguing. Gripping the branches as tightly as he could, he hoisted himself up off the ground.

"Ready?"

"I'm ready when you are," came Aksell's nervous reply. Timothy nodded and took off running, fueled by pure adrenaline.

Their progress was painfully slow at first, Timothy struggling to build up the momentum to get the cart rolling. But before long, they were moving at a rapid pace, the thought of how much ground they had to make up spurring Timothy on. Part of him felt uneasy at running so fast so early on, but he quickly silenced the voice.

At this point, I'm going to have to sacrifice stamina for speed, he thought, straining forward with every ounce of strength he had.

Fortunately for both of them, Timothy was fast. Although he'd never won The Race himself, he'd come extremely close several times. With the possible exception of Quill, he also had the most endurance of any of his classmates.

Timothy stumbled as he rounded the corner ahead, encumbered by the rickety contraption he was pulling. As he regained his footing, he saw another runner in the distance. A few precious seconds later, they were traveling even with him. He had slowed to a walk, confident that his place in the top twelve was secure. He started violently when he saw Timothy and Aksell, and he broke into a run once more.

But Timothy was faster, despite the fact that he was beginning to tire. His initial burst of speed had dwindled, and panic began to set in. He shoved the feeling aside, urging his tired muscles to keep going.

His throat was dry and his breath was coming in ragged gasps, but still he kept running.

They could not come in last.

They would not come in last.

With this mantra echoing in his head, Timothy found a fresh burst of speed and redoubled his efforts. Before long, the others came into view. He strained forwards, passing his classmates one by one. Only a few people were still ahead of him as the finish line appeared in the distance.

"Tim? We might have a problem," Aksell called from behind him, a note of panic creeping into his voice. Timothy risked a quick glance backwards and saw at once what Aksell was referring to. On one side, the vines holding the axle in place had snapped, worn through by the friction.

"Hold on tight!" Timothy shouted as he threw himself forward across the finish line, Aksell clinging to what remained of the makeshift cart. He flew across the finish half a second before anyone else, his momentum carrying him forward several paces before he collapsed onto the grass, too winded to get up.

Chapter 5

I t took several minutes before Timothy had recovered sufficiently to stand, the vague beginnings of a headache gathering behind his forehead. He limped over to the record keeper for this year's Race, a kindly, balding man named Edward. He looked up as Timothy approached.

"It seems you've created quite an uproar with that little contraption of yours," he said as Timothy approached. "Some are saying that Aksell's finishing shouldn't count because he didn't actually run The Race." He glanced to the side, then he added in a whisper, "I think they're really just upset because Edwin came in last."

Edward's words hit Timothy like a sledgehammer. He felt a familiar wave of sadness wash over him, and his headache intensified as he tried to hold back tears.

This is my fault, he thought, remembering the runner they had passed. *It should have been me and Aksell.* He blinked rapidly and looked up at the sky, licking his lips. *Edwin was - well, Edwin. And now he's just... gone.*

"Aksell didn't run The Race, so he didn't finish! He's disqualified!" someone shouted.

Timothy snapped back to the present, his concern for Aksell cutting through his grief.

And... since Edwin was arguably the most popular person in the school, that might make people a little upset about the cart, Timothy realized with a growing sense of dread.

Murmurs of agreement rippled through the cluster of students. At any moment, the situation could escalate, creating a dangerous situation for both Timothy and Aksell.

With his injured ankle, he won't stand a chance if they decide to take matters into their own hands. And I'm in no state to stop them, Timothy thought uneasily, still winded from his desperate sprint. He glanced around the street for Aksell, but he was nowhere to be seen.

"Where's Aksell?"

"Relax," Edward replied, unflappable as always. "Doctor took him to the hospital to check out his foot. I'd say your concern is well-placed, though. Nothing I say seems to calm these folks down." He looked back toward the crowd, a pained frown flickering across his face.

"That's hardly reassuring," Timothy shot back, instinctively retreating a step.

Just then, Mrs. Louise strode out onto the track, scanning the volatile scene with a disappointed frown.

"What is the meaning of this?" she demanded, staring down the angry group of students.

"Aksell didn't actually run The Race! Timothy pulled him across the finish line!" someone yelled. The rest of the group growled their assent.

"He hurt his foot! He couldn't run!" Timothy shouted back in his friend's defense. The crowd began to shout at him, all talking over each other in their grief and their anger.

"QUIET! All of you!" Mrs. Louise shouted. "It's perfectly legal." Timothy looked up at her, surprised. "There's nothing in the rules that says *how* you must complete The Race. Although I don't doubt that there soon will be," she added with a stern glance at Timothy. "I read the rules aloud at the beginning of The Race. You know just as well as

I that there was no rule that says you must actually *run*." Slowly, the crowd's rage dissipated like air from a leaky balloon as they came to their senses. A few of the students still grumbled, but their neighbors quickly shushed them.

"Lunch will be available in the cafeteria until noon," Mrs. Louise continued. "You have a rest period until then, and I recommend you take advantage of it. Job selections will occur first thing tomorrow morning." She turned to Timothy. "Congratulations. You will receive the first pick of jobs tomorrow." With that, she turned and walked briskly away.

Timothy stood there for a moment as his teacher's words sunk in. Between the news of Edwin's death and worrying about Aksell's safety, he hadn't yet registered the fact that he had won The Race. He stood there, stunned, as his classmates dispersed.

Finally, he forced himself to move, walking over to the makeshift cart, which was lying near the track where he had dropped it after crossing the finish line. He started to untie the plants holding it together, but then he stopped. Glancing around to make sure that no one was watching, Timothy dragged the cart behind some shrubs that grew alongside the track. He gathered some brush and scattered it over the top of the cart, concealing it. Once he was satisfied that it wouldn't be noticed by any casual passerby, he hurried off to the hospital, hoping that Aksell was okay.

It took him only a few minutes to get from the track to the Kawts hospital, an ancient brick building within easy walking distance of both the police station and the school. The hospital was rumored to be the oldest building in Kawts, built hundreds of years ago - even before Milkop Quawz' rebellion. Some said that the ghosts of Milkop Quawz and his lieutenants haunted the old place, telling stories about screams and ghastly moans coming from the basement.

One guy even thought he heard his dead son, Timothy remembered, shaking his head as he rounded the corner. *If there even are any noises, it's probably just the furnace or some other malfunctioning piece of machinery.*

He came to a stop in front of the imposing building, feeling a shudder run through him.

But ghosts or no ghosts, there's definitely something kind of creepy about it. Stifling the slight fear he always felt when he entered the building, Timothy pushed open the door and stepped inside. He walked up to the receptionist at the front desk, passing a pair of Blanks who were marching in the opposite direction.

"I'm here to see Aksell Deogol," he said, craning his neck to see down the hallway. "Which room is he in?"

The receptionist scanned a list on her desk. "Room 105. Third door on the left."

"Thanks!" Timothy said, speed-walking down the hall towards Aksell's room. As he got closer, he heard voices drifting out into the hallway. The door was slightly ajar, and Timothy ducked inside. Aksell was lying on the hospital bed, his foot already in a cast.

Two men stood over him, discussing his injuries. Timothy instantly recognized the short brown hair and sharp hazel eyes of Aksell's father, Ethos. Timothy turned his attention to the other man, who wore the white coat of Kawts' Medical Guild.

"You'll need to keep that cast on for a couple of weeks," the man instructed. "After that, you should be fine." The man turned to Ethos. "Not to worry, sir. It's not a terribly serious injury, although he should try to avoid putting pressure on it for a while. He'll be back on his feet in a few weeks." Then, turning, he saw Timothy for the first time.

"I'll leave you with your visitor," he said, gathering his instruments and leaving the room, shutting the door securely behind him.

"Hey, Tim," Aksell said with a weary smile as Timothy approached the side of the bed. "What do you think of this thing?" He gestured to the cast. "I've only had it on for a few minutes, and already I can't wait to get it off!"

Timothy laughed, his fears evaporating. "I take it you're okay, then?"

"Don't get me wrong, it still hurts. A lot. But I guess I'm fine. The doctor says it could easily have been much worse," he added, though Timothy noticed he winced when he moved. Aksell looked up at Ethos. "Would it be okay if we went back home until lunch?" He paused. "Actually, could we just get lunch at home? I'm not really in the mood for orange glop right now."

Timothy stifled laughter, nodding his head in agreement. If pink glop was the best food in Kawts, orange glop was the undisputed worst. So much so, in fact, that visits to the Kawts hospital for food poisoning nearly doubled during months when it was served frequently.

Ethos helped Aksell into a standing position, and Timothy handed him the pair of crutches that had been leaning against the wall. Ethos nodded in thanks before passing them off to Aksell. Between the two of them, they helped Aksell hobble home.

As they exited the hospital, Aksell stumbled, and Timothy and Ethos both reached out a hand to steady him.

"I've got it," Aksell said, giving them a bemused smile. "I'm perfectly capable of walking by myself."

Timothy abruptly dropped his hand. Ethos looked similarly sheepish, although he masked it well.

"You just broke your ankle, Aksell," Ethos scolded. "You'll have to understand why we're concerned."

"I suppose," Aksell said, dropping his gaze. "I just thought it was kind of funny, that's all."

Timothy frowned, glancing at Ethos. Part of him wanted to come to his friend's defense, but he stayed silent, a little scared of the head Councilman. They finished the rest of the journey in silence, although Timothy noticed that Ethos had backed off a little.

By the time they arrived at Ethos' house, Aksell had begun to get a feel for using the crutches. He limped over to the stairs, passing an old family portrait from when Aksell was little. His mother Edeline stared out from the picture, which had been taken only a few days before her death of the mysterious virus that had swept through the city.

"Timothy. Can you lend me a hand in the kitchen for a moment?" Ethos said.

Timothy nodded and followed him to the pantry. Ethos got out two plates of green glop and handed them to Timothy. Timothy turned to take them upstairs, but before he could leave, Ethos suddenly grabbed his shoulder. Timothy started guiltily as he turned around.

He's heard about the cart, Timothy thought. *Is he going to yell at me for breaking the rules?* To his surprise, however, the look on Ethos' face was almost sorrowful.

"Thank you," he said earnestly, his eyes softening. "Thank you for saving Aksell's life." There was a strange tone in his voice, one that Timothy had only heard him use once before - the day Edeline had died. Timothy shifted uncomfortably, and Ethos released him, quickly reverting to his normal demeanor.

"Now if you'll excuse me, I have some official Council business to attend to. I suspect Aksell will wonder where you are before long. I will see you both at job selections tomorrow morning." With that, he turned and strode quickly away. Timothy stood there in shock for a moment, watching as the stern-faced Councilman vanished deeper into the building. Then he shook off his surprise and climbed up the stairs to Aksell's room.

Aksell was sitting in his desk chair, and Timothy passed him one of the plates, taking a seat in an adjacent chair with his own plate. His gaze wandered to a large volume sitting on top of Aksell's desk, its bluish cover worn and faded with age.

"Is that a new book?" Timothy asked, choking down a forkful of the slimy, bitter glop.

Aksell looked behind him. "What? Oh, yeah. Samuel recommended it to me last night." He picked up the book and turned it over. "It's supposed to be a biography about the ruler of the Giants."

Timothy nodded. "Sounds interesting. Would you mind if I borrowed it once you're done?"

Aksell shrugged. "You could borrow it right now if you want. I still have quite a bit left to read of Samuel's last recommendation. You're a much faster reader than I am, anyway." Aksell handed him the book, and Timothy slipped it into his bag.

They spent the next hour in Aksell's room, talking and laughing and forcing themselves to choke down the rest of the green glop. They had just put their dishes away when Aksell grew serious.

"I want to thank you, Tim."

Timothy shifted uncomfortably. "About The Race? Anyone else would have done the same thing."

Aksell shook his head. "No, they wouldn't. They didn't. And no one else has ever even tried something like that before that I'm aware of!" He laughed in amazement. "You built a freaking cart in the middle of The Race! And you still won!" He paused for a moment, then added, "All I'm saying is that you were great back there. I owe you."

Timothy remained silent, at a loss for words. For a long moment, neither of them spoke.

"Well. I should probably get going pretty soon," Timothy said at last, glancing at his watch. "I was thinking of stopping by the library to say hello to Samuel on my way home. Do you want to come along?"

Aksell shook his head. "I probably shouldn't. Given the circumstances, I think my dad would freak out if he came back from work and I wasn't here."

Timothy nodded. "Good call. See you tomorrow, then."

Leaving Aksell's house behind him, Timothy made his way over to the Kawts library, an imposing, concrete building standing three stories tall. He pushed through the sturdy oakwood doors into a big, musty room lined with bookshelves. A large desk sat off to one side. Sitting behind the desk was Samuel, the city of Kawts' only librarian. He was an older man, in his mid-sixties, but his enthusiasm for good stories was infectious, and he always had a book set aside for Timothy and Aksell. And, at one time, for Quill.

"Timothy!" Samuel said, sliding the papers he had been studying into his desk as he stood to greet him. "What are you doing here at this time of day?"

"The Race," Timothy said.

Samuel paled. "Then, is Aksell…"

Timothy quickly shook his head. "No, he's fine. Well, not fine exactly. But we both made it." Samuel gave him a puzzled look, and Timothy explained what had happened.

"Amazing," Samuel murmured as Timothy finished. "In all my years in Kawts, nothing like that has ever happened." A sad smile crossed his face, and he fell silent for a moment. Then a new thought seemed to strike him. "That would make a really interesting story," he added, taking a scrap of paper from his pocket and jotting something down on it. He stared off into space for a moment, deep in thought. Finally, he shook his head and turned back to face Timothy.

"Truly remarkable," he murmured. The thoughtful look vanished from his face as he abruptly switched gears. "But I suppose you didn't come all the way down here just to tell me about The Race. I'd wager you're here for some new books."

He pulled out a book checkout form from his desk, a thick packet crafted by the Scribes Guild that seemed to have been designed to be as convoluted as possible.

Timothy shook his head. "I'm just stopping by for a visit," he said.

"Aksell lent me a new book earlier today. Which reminds me..." Timothy swung his backpack down onto the ground, rummaging through it for the last book Samuel had lent him.

"Finished already?" Samuel said, the sly smirk on his face testifying to the fact that he was not at all surprised. "What did you think?"

"It was good," Timothy said. "The ending seemed a little forced, though."

Samuel shook his head. "Exactly. I tried to tell the Council that their proposed changes would-"

He cut off abruptly as a siren began to blare outside. Timothy froze, his heart pounding.

"Go hide in the back room," Samuel said, his eyes growing wide. "I'll join you as soon as I can." Before Timothy could say anything, Samuel bounded over to the door, moving faster than Timothy would have given him credit for. Timothy hesitated for a moment, but the distant booming of an explosion somewhere in Kawts made up his mind for him, and he ran toward the back room.

He hunkered down beside a bulky machine, his heart racing as he strained to hear what was happening outside. After what felt like forever, Samuel appeared in the doorway.

"We'll be safe in here," he said, closing the door and locking it behind him.

"How do you know?" Timothy breathed. "One of the anarchists' bombs might still be able to-"

"Trust me," Samuel said, his voice level. "They won't get in here."

Timothy exhaled slowly, allowing some of the tension to drain from his body. He didn't allow himself to completely relax, however, keeping one watchful eye on the door.

For nearly fifteen minutes, the pair sat in silence, listening to the muted wail of the sirens outside.

"I wish they would get rid of those blasted sirens," Samuel muttered, grimacing.

"They have to have some way to warn people about the anarchists' attacks."

Samuel shook his head. "Kawts wasn't always like this, you know," he said. "The anarchists have only been here... well, about twenty years now, I suppose. They showed up around the time Ethos the 8th was assassinated."

"What do they have against Kawts?" Timothy asked. "What do they hope to accomplish by killing people at random?"

Samuel opened his mouth to reply, then he abruptly shut it again. "I don't know," he said at last. "Probably the same reason Milkop Quawz led his rebellion."

"And why did he do that?" Timothy pressed. "It doesn't make any sense."

Samuel didn't respond, his head cocked slightly to one side. His eyes narrowed, then he said, "I think the sirens have stopped."

Timothy paused, listening intently. "You're right," he said.

Samuel pulled himself to his feet and unlocked the door. "You should probably get home before they come back. Your parents are probably worried sick."

Timothy nodded. It had become a favorite tactic of the anarchists as of late to fake a retreat, only to strike again once the people had let their guard down. "Will you be okay here by yourself?"

"I'll be fine," Samuel said. "I should probably lock up soon, anyway."

He walked Timothy to the front door of the library, clearing away the improvised barricade he had erected against it.

"I'll see you at your job selection tomorrow," Samuel said as Timothy started back towards his house.

"Yeah. See you tomorrow," Timothy called back over his shoulder. He broke into a run, studiously avoiding looking in the direction that the sirens had come from. As he drew closer to his house, he slowed to a walk, satisfied that he was a safe distance from the center of the attack.

He took a couple of deep breaths, trying to slow his racing heartbeat. *I wonder if dad made it back from Aria before the sirens went off,* he thought, jogging up the stairs to his house and throwing open the door.

His parents were sitting at the dining room table when he entered, deep in discussion with Maurice. Maurice looked up as Timothy entered, a smile breaking out across his face.

"There he is!" he exclaimed, pulling Timothy into a hug. "We were starting to worry that... well, you know."

"I'm all right," Timothy said. "I was visiting Samuel at the library when the attack started. We holed up in the back room until it was over."

"I knew it!" Timothy's father shouted. "I told you he would be fine!"

"I got here as soon as I could," Timothy said with a glance at his mother. Her face looked strained, but relieved.

"I'm just glad you're alive," she said, unsuccessfully trying to hide the tremor in her voice.

"So... How was Aria?" Timothy asked, breaking the uncomfortable silence that followed.

His father smiled. "The mayor loved the chairs. He was so impressed that he even gave me a little extra."

"Did you see Ally while you were there?" Maurice asked. "She was supposed to be back a week ago."

His father nodded. "I saw her. She told me to give you this," he continued, pulling an envelope from his pocket and handing it to Maurice. Maurice snatched the envelope from his hand, looking at the back to make sure it hadn't been opened. The look of fear on his face quickly vanished, and he slipped the envelope into his pocket.

* * *

It was well past nine when Timothy got up to his room that night. He emptied his backpack, putting everything away. As he did, he saw Quill's box out of the corner of his eye. He took it down, overwhelmed by memories.

It's hard to believe that Quill's been gone for an entire year already, he thought, fighting back tears.

As he thought back on the last few days he had seen Quill, he wondered, not for the first time, if it was more than a coincidence that Quill had given him the box the day before he had lost The Race.

Did Quill know he was going to lose? But how would he have known?

Timothy shook his head, turning his attention back to the box.

What am I missing? he wondered, desperately wracking his brain for another possible combination to the lock. He puzzled over it for some time before finally nodding off to sleep, Quill's box still clutched in his hands.

Chapter 6

"Attention all students - your school day has begun. Today's lunch is blue glop. The eighth and ninth level students will be running The Race. Today, the twelfth level students will receive their jobs."

The students took their seats, Edwin's empty chair a sobering reminder of the events of the previous morning. The voice on the intercom droned on, but the babble of voices drowned it out. Despite the lingering memory of The Race, there was a general air of excitement in the room.

As the announcements came to an end, Mrs. Louise walked to the front of the room, flanked by the leaders of all of Kawts' career guilds that were looking for workers that year. Timothy spotted Quill's father and Ethos among the crowd, representing the Merchant Guild and the Council, respectively.

"Before you choose your jobs," Mrs. Louise announced, raising her voice to be heard over the babble of excited voices, "the leaders of each guild will introduce themselves and give us an overview of what their guild does." She nodded towards the line of guild leaders, and the nearest one stepped forward, the muscular leader of the Kawts Security Force.

"My name is Volker," he began, scanning the group of students with a practiced eye. "As a member of Kawts' Security Force, we are tasked with keeping the peace and managing the armies of Blanks and attack drones. It is our job to apprehend criminals and troublemakers, as well as assisting the Council in the defense of Kawts during raids."

There was polite applause, then Volker stepped back, replaced by the head of the Science Guild, the man who had taken over after the previous leader, Howard Kolt, had been convicted of treason and executed several years prior. One after another, each of the guild leaders repeated the process, although most of what they said was already common knowledge.

"It is now time for you to select your jobs," Mrs. Louise announced as the last person stepped back into the line. "Timothy, since you won The Race, you will get to pick first." She shuffled some papers around on her desk before finding what she was looking for. "You scored high enough on your exam to be employed by any of the guilds represented here today."

Timothy looked around at the guild leaders standing in front of him, his mouth suddenly dry.

This is it. This is the moment I've been waiting for. He opened his mouth to announce his decision, but then he hesitated, suddenly doubting his choice. He took a deep breath, quelling the butterflies in his stomach.

"I'd like to join the Library Guild."

Mrs. Louise glanced at her list with mild surprise. "Are you sure? You did well enough on your test to...."

"I'm sure," Timothy replied, any doubts that he had left rapidly disappearing.

"As you wish," Mrs. Louise said with a shrug, making a note on her clipboard. "Samuel will give you instructions for your first day on the job."

Samuel stepped out from the line, nodding to Mrs. Louise. "If it's alright with you, Timothy, I think we can head directly over to the library."

Timothy grinned and followed Samuel out of the school.

"How does it feel to join the ranks of Kawts' story-keepers?" Samuel asked with a smirk.

"I've been looking forward to this since I was a tenth-level student."

Samuel nodded. "I always knew either you or Quill would take my place one day." His words hung in the air for a moment. Then he cleared his throat, the thoughtful look vanishing from his face. "You never got a chance to work at the library during the Training Months, did you?"

Timothy shook his head. "I wanted to. But Quill beat me to it. He couldn't stop talking about how much he enjoyed it."

A strange look flickered across Samuel's face. "That's what I thought. I'll have a lot to teach you. This job is more than it seems."

"What-" Timothy started, but Samuel held up a hand to stop him.

"I'll explain everything in due time," he said, a twinkle in his eye. He withdrew a key from his pocket and unlocked the sturdy oak wood doors of the library. He pushed them open, leading the way into a large room, its walls lined with bookshelves.

Samuel walked over to another door in the back of the room and unlocked it, too. With a flourish, he flung the new door open.

"Are you ready to see what goes on behind the scenes?"

Timothy nodded, and Samuel rubbed his hands together, unable to conceal his excitement. "Alright! First lesson: sorting books for re-shelving! The books go in alphabetical order by author's last name. There are two crates of books in the back corner. You have two minutes to get them in the proper order. Ready... Go!"

Timothy didn't move, overwhelmed by Samuel's rapid-fire instructions. Samuel saw the startled look on his face and chuckled. "I'm just messing with you!" he exclaimed, shaking his head as he tried to calm his laughter. "To be honest, there are rarely that many books to put away in a month! Not many people find it worth their while to come here anymore."

"Then what do you do all day?" Timothy asked before he could help himself.

"Ah, that's the question, isn't it?" Samuel said, tapping the side of his nose. "A lot of my day is spent maintaining the catalog, submitting the checkout forms, and culling the collection for old books to sell. But that only takes up a small portion of our time."

Timothy waited for Samuel to elaborate, but Samuel only smiled wider. "But that can wait until tomorrow. For now, we'll just stick with the basics."

For the rest of the day, Timothy stayed in the library, learning to sort the books and how to submit the check-out forms to the Council via the bulky machine he had hidden behind during the previous day's attack. The machine vaguely resembled an old copy machine, attached to the wall by a mess of wires. Even with Samuel's patient teaching, it took Timothy quite some time to get a good grasp on how the bewilderingly complex machine worked.

The time seemed to fly by, and after several hours, Timothy left for home. He entered through the workshop, making his way to the back room. His dad looked up when Timothy entered, wiping one large, sawdust-covered hand off on his apron.

"Do you and Maurice need any help tonight?" Timothy asked.

His dad shook his head. "We were just about ready to pack it up for the night." His eyes flitted to the back of the room, and he added, "Although if you could help your brother tidy up, that would be great."

Timothy nodded and made his way over to where Maurice stood, idly sanding a lopsided chunk of wood while reading something from a piece of paper. Timothy cleared his throat, and Maurice looked up at him.

"Dad says it's time to pack up. He wanted me to lend you a hand."

Maurice nodded absently. "Yes. Right. Tell him that the chair will be done soon. I promise."

Timothy eyed the misshapen piece of wood skeptically. "If that is the chair in question, I really doubt it. What *are* you doing back here, Maurice?"

"Nothing," Maurice said quickly, folding the paper up and stuffing it into his pocket. He looked up at Timothy. "What were you saying?"

"Are you okay? You look kind of sick."

"I'm fine. It's just some news from Ally, that's all. Hard to digest."

"Did she break up with you?"

Maurice smiled, although Timothy noticed the smile didn't quite reach his eyes. "No, it's not that. It's about our... research project. Just like you said - nothing interesting they haven't already told us."

Despite the alarm bells ringing in his head, Timothy couldn't help but ask, "What did she say?"

Maurice said nothing for a long time. Finally, he leaned closer to Timothy. "You have to promise to keep this a secret."

Timothy nodded slowly, and Maurice continued. "It's about the first Race. Ally ran the numbers. The Race began around the time of Milkop Quawz' rebellion."

He let his words hang in the air, staring at Timothy expectantly. Timothy stared back, waiting for Maurice to elaborate.

"You don't get it, do you?" Maurice shook his head. "You know what? Just forget I said anything. You'd just think it's another one of my crazy theories." He turned back toward his workbench. "It won't take me long to clean up. You and Dad don't need to wait for me."

After a moment of hesitation, Timothy made his way into the kitchen, puzzled by his brother's odd behavior.

It's probably nothing, he decided at last. *He'll be back to his old self soon enough.*

* * *

43

The next morning, Timothy woke up earlier than usual, unable to sleep in his excitement for his first full day as Samuel's apprentice. He got ready as fast as he could and dashed off to the library. To his surprise, Samuel was already there when he arrived.

"Good morning, Timothy," he said cheerfully, seemingly unsurprised by Timothy's early arrival. "Today, I'm going to teach you one of the best-kept secrets of our guild." He paused dramatically, and Timothy couldn't help but wonder what the *other* best-kept secrets of the library were.

"As the keepers of Kawts' stories, we are tasked with a very important job - we are responsible for *writing* the stories."

Timothy looked up at him, puzzled. "You mean recording what happens? Doesn't the *Kawts Tribune* do that?"

"That certainly is a part of it," Samuel said. "And part of our job *is* to store and index every issue of the paper. But the members of the Library Guild are also tasked with writing all the books that grace these shelves."

Samuel saw the shocked expression on Timothy's face and continued with a laugh, "Many of the books I've recommended to you over the years I wrote myself. And my predecessor, Elijah, wrote quite a few as well."

Timothy looked around the room in disbelief. "The librarians wrote all these? How?"

Samuel's smile turned wistful. "The Guild used to be much larger than it is now. When Elijah was a boy, there were three librarians, and when his mentor was being trained, there were even more. The Council's restrictions on books have been whittling down our ranks since Milkop Quawz' rebellion."

An uncomfortable silence followed, then Samuel cleared his throat. "Anyway, that's not important right now." He reached into his desk drawer and pulled out a stack of blank papers, handing them to

Timothy. "I'll let you brainstorm for a bit, and then I can teach you some more of the logistical aspects of running the library. If you get stuck, I have a list of ideas on my desk that you could borrow."

"I think I'll be fine," Timothy said, sitting down at a reading table and beginning to jot down some ideas. He had only been working on it for a short while when he heard the front door creak open.

He looked up to see Jewel Macky. She waved in greeting, and Timothy nodded back. She walked over to Samuel, who was engrossed in a pile of papers at his desk. Jewel said something that Timothy couldn't quite make out, and Samuel looked up, his eyes wide. The two disappeared into his office, where they remained for quite some time, their muted voices barely audible through the closed door. After a while, Jewel emerged from the office, selecting a book seemingly at random from the shelves.

"Timothy, can you help Jewel at the checkout?" Samuel asked, following her out of his office and locking the door behind him. "The checkout forms are in a pile on my desk." Timothy nodded and rummaged through the papers scattered across Samuel's desk until he found the forms, pulling out one of the multi-page packets and handing it to Jewel.

His eyes wandered around the room, waiting for Jewel to fill out the form. She finally finished and handed the form back to Timothy, then left before he could say anything. Samuel emerged from the back room a few seconds later, wearing an old overcoat.

"Ah, that's fine. Just leave it there," Samuel said when Timothy tried to hand him the completed form. "I'll deal with it tomorrow."

"Where are you-" Timothy started, but Samuel cut him off.

"I'm sorry to do this on your second day, but I have some urgent business to attend to. I'm going to lock up for the night, if that's okay with you."

"I guess," Timothy said, "but what-"

"I'll explain later," Samuel said. He reached into his pocket and tossed Timothy a copy of the front door key. "Make sure you turn off the lights and lock the door on your way out." He started to leave, but then stopped and turned back toward Timothy. "Oh! And Timothy - don't come here tomorrow! Go to Franklin Plaza for the graduation ceremony!" Then he was gone, slipping out the door and leaving Timothy alone in the library.

Timothy stared at the place where Samuel had been, a puzzled frown on his face. "Now what on earth was that about?" he muttered to himself as he packed up his things. "Something's definitely bothering him. I don't think I've ever seen him in such a hurry."

He shook his head.

If Samuel wants me to know about it, he'll tell me, he decided at last.

Chapter 7

Timothy looked up from his book, seeing the first glimmers of sunlight creeping in through his window. He waited, watching, for several agonizing minutes as the sun crept higher and higher. Finally, he closed the book and slid out of bed, already dressed. A smile broke out over his face as he grabbed his empty backpack and dashed out onto the streets below.

I can't believe it's Graduation Day already! And this time, I'm the one who's graduating!

By the time Timothy arrived at Franklin Plaza, the square was already packed with people, eager to get an early start on the day's festivities. Brightly colored booths selling anything from pink glop to furniture had been set up along the outside edge of the plaza. Crisscrossing in the middle were strings of lights which supported multicolored banners, each one representing a different one of Kawts' outlying cities.

Timothy spotted his father and Maurice manning one of the stands, displaying some of their recent work. Maurice waved cheerfully at him as Timothy walked past, showing no signs of his distress from earlier in the week.

Across the plaza, Samuel was manning another stand, selling old books from the Kawts library. Ordinarily, the sale of books in Kawts was strictly forbidden, the Council deeming it too much of a security risk. But many years ago, Samuel had worked out a deal with the Council, enabling books to be legally bought and sold, though only by the Kawts library and only on Graduation Day. Timothy spotted Aksell in the crowd and headed in his direction, making a mental note to stop by Samuel's stand later in the day.

When Timothy caught up to his friend, Aksell was rather unsuccessfully attempting to win a ring toss game at one of the booths. He turned around when he heard Timothy behind him.

"Hey, Tim! Haven't seen you much these last few days."

Timothy smiled. "Samuel's been keeping me pretty busy," he said.

"How's it been?" Aksell asked, setting the remaining rings down on the counter. "Working at the library with Samuel?"

Smiling, Timothy told Aksell about what Samuel had taught him. Remembering Samuel's words, however, he left out the part about writing the books. As the son of the head Councilman, Aksell was probably entitled to know, but Timothy didn't want to be the one responsible for one of the best-kept secrets of the Library Guild becoming common knowledge.

"What about you?" he asked when he had finished. "How's your job going?"

Aksell scowled. "As expected, my dad's making me be his apprentice. So far, it's just been a bunch of legal jargon and politics. It's mind-numbingly boring." He brightened a little. "But at least I still get to see Larnell and Charles from time to time. Charles is on the Kawts Security Force now. And Larnell's in the Scribes Guild."

Timothy smirked. "That's hardly a surprise. I think he's been gunning for that since we were fourth level students."

Aksell smiled. "That's certainly true." He paused for a moment, looking around the town square. "But enough about the Council," he said suddenly. "We're supposed to be having fun!"

"What do you want to do first?"

"There's a new guessing game I've been meaning to try," Aksell said. "It's being run by the *Kawts Tribune*, I think."

"Sounds good to me," Timothy said. "Lead the way."

* * *

For the rest of the day, the pair went from booth to booth, enjoying the festivities. Almost before they knew it, the entire day had passed, and it was time for them to take their seats for the graduation ceremony. They made their way to the front of the plaza, where the Blanks had constructed a temporary stage for the occasion.

Two sets of chairs lined the platform, the ones on the left for the graduating class and the ones on the right for the Council and the mayors of the surrounding cities. The Council was already seated when Timothy and Aksell arrived, as were the mayors of most of the neighboring towns. Notably absent, however, was the mayor of Duncan's Ridge.

"Where's Mayor Finn?" Timothy muttered to Aksell as they took their seats.

"The anarchists attacked Duncan's Ridge last night," Aksell whispered back. "He had to stay back and supervise the clean-up."

Timothy opened his mouth to ask more, but at that moment, Ethos walked up to the front of the stage.

"Welcome, people of Kawts," he announced regally. "We are gathered here today to celebrate the future of our great city - and what better way to do that than by remembering our past? Nearly five hundred years ago, our ancestors were engaged in a desperate struggle for survival against an army of robots. The first Council, led by Ethos the First, saw that the world was in trouble and sought out a place where they could build a refuge for humanity. It was this vision that led to the founding of Kawts and the surrounding cities. It was this vision that guided generations of Councilmen in protecting them. And it is this vision that these students will now take an active part in making real."

Ethos stepped to the side, gesturing to the assembled students, which included several people from the other nearby cities. "These students have proven time and time again that they can measure up to this ideal, having successfully completed The Race twelve times, showing remarkable ingenuity in doing so," he added with a glance at Timothy. "It is my great honor to officially declare these students to be full citizens of Kawts."

The crowd cheered. Once they had quieted, Ethos called each of the students up one at a time, giving them their official Kawts ID cards and sending them back to their seats in the crowd. By the time Timothy's name was called, only Aksell remained sitting on the stage. As he walked across the stage to Ethos, he saw Quill's parents out of the corner of his eye. They were standing a few feet away from his own parents, and they looked like they were trying hard not to cry. As Timothy watched, his dad put his hand on Quill's father's shoulder. The look on his face was full of sympathy for his oldest friend.

They must've come out just for Aksell and I, he realized, trying to ignore the lump in his throat.

"This is Timothy Hawthorne, son of Rudolph and Martha. He is the new apprentice librarian," Ethos said. He handed Timothy his ID and Timothy left the stage. Behind him, he could hear Ethos graduating Aksell.

"And last, but not least, Aksell Deogol, my son and trainee for the Grand Council." Everybody cheered at Ethos' announcement. After Aksell took his seat, Ethos concluded the ceremony with another brief speech. As everyone packed up to go home, Timothy's thoughts wandered once more to Quill.

They had always joked about their graduation ceremony, never once considering the possibility that one of them would not complete The Race. They had seen friendships ended by The Race, but they'd never thought the same thing could happen to them. He sighed as he reached home.

There's nothing I can do to bring Quill back. I can't change the past.

* * *

The next morning Timothy woke up with a start, sunlight streaming in through his window.

I'm going to be late for work! he realized with a start. He threw on his clothes and dashed out the door, not even pausing to grab a breakfast cube.

He was a block away from the library when the sirens began to blare, undergirded by the sounds of battle in front of him. Timothy's heart sank, and he sprinted toward the library, hoping that he was wrong about where the sound was coming from. When he emerged onto the street, everything was in chaos. Blanks and members of the Kawts Security Force ran past him, apparently chasing someone through the foggy haze that had settled around the library. The smell of smoke permeated the air, making Timothy wonder if the anarchists had set something on fire. Attack drones zipped across the sky, trying to locate the person responsible.

With a growing feeling of dread, Timothy realized he had just run out into the middle of an attack by the anarchists. He increased his speed to a jog, trying to get out of the fog before something exploded. He glanced behind him, his heart pounding as he broke into a sprint.

Suddenly, Timothy came face-to-face with a strange man with a long grey beard and complex-looking robotic legs. Timothy recognized him instantly as the most infamous of the rebels, the one who the Council suspected was their leader. The man responsible for the explosions.

Time seemed to slow down as the man thrust a thick, leather-bound book into Timothy's hands.

"Keep this safe," he said gravely. Then he ran off, disappearing into the fog once more.

Timothy looked down at the book in his hands warily, half expecting it to explode. The text on the cover read "Holy Bible". Despite the fog and the noise and his own fear, the title of the book made Timothy pause.

I don't think I've ever seen this book before. He frowned, trying to figure out where the book might have come from. *I feel like I would have at least heard of it before if it came from the library.*

The library.

Timothy's blood ran cold as he remembered that Samuel always arrived early in the morning.

He must have been here when the anarchists attacked! he realized. *Was he able to get out in time? Or is he being held hostage right now - or worse?*

His fears mounting, Timothy weaved his way through the chaos to the library doors. One of the massive doors was lying on the ground, apparently smashed off its hinges. Timothy ran inside, afraid of what he might see. To his surprise, the inside of the library seemed to be mostly unscathed. Samuel was sitting behind his desk, working on some papers, apparently oblivious to the commotion above. He looked up when Timothy entered, the lighthearted smile fading from his face when he saw the book in Timothy's hands.

"Ah," he said quietly, biting his lower lip. "It appears you've met Gearwire."

Chapter 8

Timothy stared at Samuel in shock, unable to believe what he was hearing. "You?" he said, his mind frantically trying to come up with any other explanation for Samuel's words. "You're working with the anarchists?"

Timothy recoiled a pace, his head spinning. Dimly, he realized he was still talking, although he wasn't aware of exactly what he was saying.

"Timothy," Samuel said firmly, breaking through his panic. Timothy looked up at him, still clutching the book in his hands. "Timothy. I need to show you something."

For a moment, Timothy hesitated, glancing back toward the door. *The Security Force is right here. I could tell the Council that Samuel is an anarchist right now.* He looked back at Samuel.

No. I can't. They would kill him. I can't turn him in.

Besides, part of him insisted, desperate for any answer other than the obvious, *Maybe he was tricked - or maybe they blackmailed him.*

Timothy took a halting step toward Samuel, and Samuel smiled. "Come with me," he said, leading Timothy to the back room. He walked over to the device that they used to submit the book checkout forms and pressed a hidden button on the back. A heavy steel door on the other side of the room slid open with a loud grinding noise.

Samuel led the way into the room behind the door, which was

scarcely the size of a closet, and empty except for a door at the other end. Upon closer inspection, Timothy realized the door was locked with a mechanism similar to the one on Quill's box. Another book that Timothy had never seen before lay on the floor.

"Looks like they dropped one," Samuel muttered to himself as he bent over to pick it up. Book in hand, he walked over to the door and punched in a passcode on the keypad. A soft 'ding!' echoed through the tiny room, and Samuel swung open the door. Behind the door was a simple ladder, extending up into the ceiling above them. Samuel started up it, followed closely by Timothy.

They emerged into a vast room, completely illuminated by the morning sunlight that shone in through a massive skylight. The room was nearly as large as the main floor of the library, with thick red carpeting covering the floor. Timothy slowly turned in a circle, taking in the contents of the room. It was filled from floor to ceiling with shelves upon shelves of books.

"And now," Samuel said with a smile as Timothy took in the grandeur of the room, "I think it's time I told you the real secret of the library. To the best of my knowledge, there are less than ten living people in all of Kawts who know this place exists."

Timothy turned to face Samuel, shutting his mouth with an audible clop.

"This room here - this is the real library," Samuel said. "These books have come from all over the world, written at various times throughout history. Most of them were written long before the Robot War, collected by some wise bibliophile hundreds of years ago who didn't want humanity to lose the knowledge contained within their pages. And there's more than just nonfiction - this room also contains some of the greatest literary classics ever written! There's hundreds of years' worth of exceptional writing hidden away up here!"

As he spoke, Samuel grew more and more animated, gesturing wildly at the books around them. His eyes shone, and Timothy found that his doubts about Samuel's loyalties were lessened.

There's more going on here than I thought, he realized. *This is bigger than just Samuel.*

Samuel's face darkened as he continued, his voice becoming bitter. "But these books can only be read with specific permission from the Council, although not even all the Council members know they exist! In all my years of being Kawts' librarian, they've never sent anyone to see them," he added in disgust. "These books have all been restricted from the public. Including that one." Samuel pointed to the book Timothy was holding.

"One of the most important parts of the librarians' job is to guard this room," Samuel said. "To protect it from people who aren't supposed to know it exists. We alone are entrusted with the password that unlocks the door. The man who gave you that book, Captain Gearwire, is the leader of a group of rebels, fighting for the freedom of Kawts, just like Milkop Quawz did all those years ago."

"The freedom of Kawts? Samuel, listen to yourself! Maybe the Council should have released these books to the public, but how is working with a group of anarchists going to free Kawts? The Council is the only thing keeping us from total destruction!"

"Timothy, the City of Kawts is not what it seems," Samuel said sadly. He waved a hand at the rows of books. "These books tell quite a different story about the history of mankind than the Council. Crucial points that their history books have altered or ignored. There are old science books that describe devices with a level of technology that the Council has declared impossible. And of course, there are books filled with recipes for foods far more delicious than glop could ever be. The list goes on and on. These books are hidden away for one reason - they contradict what the Council has declared to be true. The Council is in the business of concealing the truth. They manipulate everything for their own gain. Anyone who seriously considers these things can see that. Gearwire and his crew see it. I see it. And so did Quill."

"Quill?" Timothy interrupted, Samuel's words hitting him like a sledgehammer. "Quill was involved in this, too?"

"Yes," Samuel replied, shaking his head. "He sought the truth about Kawts and the Council. And they killed him for it. The week before your eleventh Race, he told me he had made an amazing discovery - one that could change the fate of Kawts forever. But he said it was too dangerous for him to tell me until he was absolutely sure. He thought his discovery might be just enough to shake the people of Kawts out of their stupor to see what's really going on."

"You sound like Maurice right now, you know that?" Timothy said, feeling as though the floor had dropped out from under him.

"Your brother is a smart man," Samuel said. "Although I fear his confidence may be a little misplaced. If he isn't careful, the same fate might befall him that befell Quill."

Timothy shook his head. "No," he insisted. "Quill lost The Race. It had nothing to do with the Council."

"If only that were true," Samuel said. "In the days leading up to The Race, Quill grew increasingly paranoid, terrified that the Council would realize that he knew. Then, the day before The Race, he told me he had given you something which might help you unravel the mystery he was working on."

Timothy's protests died away, his heart pounding.

The box, he realized, the pieces falling into place. *He's talking about Quill's box.*

"He knew too much, and they had to silence him before he could share what he knew. The last time I saw him, he told me to give you this book if you ever entered this room." Samuel reached over and pulled a book from a nearby shelf, and handed it to Timothy. The title read: *A History of Codes and Ciphers.*

"I will admit, before Quill died, I knew little about the Council's lies beyond the existence of this room. But when he lost The Race, I knew it had to be connected to the secret that he had so desperately wanted to tell me. I did a bit of investigating, and I discovered that Quill had made several trips to visit Crystal and Jewel shortly before he met his untimely end. In time, I learned that they were working for Gearwire directly. Eventually, I met Captain Gearwire himself, and I became one of his informants in Kawts."

"The twins are working for him, too?"

"Not so loud!" Samuel said. "But yes. They know even more about the true state of things in Kawts than I do. There's a lot that you don't know about them." He hesitated, looking as if he wanted to say more.

"I'm sure you remember my unusual behavior the other day," he said at last. "Jewel brought me a message from Gearwire about the raid this morning. Crystal had built a special fog machine and left it in a drop-off location on the edge of town. They needed me to retrieve it and put it into place near the library, somewhere where no one would spot it. When I arrived here this morning, I switched it on to give Gearwire and his crew some cover while they... ah... *redistributed* some of these books. They're trying to help the rest of Kawts wake up to the Council's true nature."

"No," Timothy said. "The Council is the protector of Kawts. What did this Gearwire person threaten you with to make you go along with this?"

Samuel frowned. "You know me better than that, Timothy," he said. He let his words hang in the air for a few seconds before he continued, pointing to the books in Timothy's hands.

"You'll have to keep those books out of sight. Even the librarians of Kawts aren't technically supposed to actually enter this room, let alone read anything inside. Don't read them unless you're sure you're alone." Samuel allowed Timothy a few more moments to digest what he had said. Then he added, "We should probably get back downstairs before anyone gets suspicious."

Samuel quickly left the secret library, dragging Timothy along with him. Once the door was locked securely behind him, they re-entered the main floor of the library. Only a few minutes later, Volker and his security team arrived and whisked Samuel away to their headquarters for questioning.

Timothy didn't see Samuel again for the rest of the day, and he began to worry that Volker would discover the truth about Samuel's involvement in the attack. He tried to focus on his work, but he couldn't stop thinking about what Samuel had said. Again and again, Samuel's accusations came into his mind, leaving him in a dazed stupor. So much of what he'd thought he knew had been challenged in just a few minutes.

Hundreds of questions swirled in his mind.

Is the Council really lying about our history? What else are they lying about? How many other people do I know who are secretly working for Gearwire? Does Maurice know? And how did Quill get mixed up in all this?

His mind was still spinning as he walked home that evening. He could barely pay attention to the conversation at dinner, eating his glop without even realizing he had done so. Finally, he gave up and excused himself from the table, disappearing up to his room. He set the books on top of his dresser and sat down on the edge of his bed, staring at the wall.

After about half an hour, he heard a knock on his bedroom door.

"Yeah?"

"Are you okay, Tim?" Maurice called out, his voice muffled through the door.

Timothy didn't answer at first, hoping that Maurice would give up and go away.

Maurice might be the only person I know who could help me figure this out, he realized. He sighed, then said, "Come in."

Maurice eased open the door and stepped inside, shutting it again behind him. "Is this about the raid earlier today? I heard it was pretty close to the library."

"Kind of," Timothy said. "But that's not the problem. Samuel told me that-" He broke off, unable to bring himself to say it out loud. He swallowed hard, then added in a whisper, "Samuel told me that he helped arrange it."

For a moment, Maurice said nothing, his astonishment clear. Then a smile broke out across his face, and he laughed. "Ha! Good old Samuel is a rebel sympathizer! Who woulda' thought!"

"Not so loud!" Timothy said, panic surging within him. "If anyone else finds out about this, they'll turn him in to the Council!"

Maurice nodded. "Right. Sorry. So what exactly did he say?"

Timothy hesitated for a second, then he recounted everything that had happened, omitting only the names of his classmates who were involved. When he had finished, Maurice let out a low whistle. "Wow. Samuel's in pretty deep. Imagine working directly for the leader of the rebels!"

"What should I do?" Timothy asked.

"Do? There's nothing to do. Not unless you want to join him."

"But - shouldn't I tell the Council? Or try to talk him out of it? He's going to get people killed!"

Maurice shook his head, a bemused smile on his face. "I don't think the rebels are as dangerous as the Council makes them out to be," he said. "There's some pretty compelling evidence that most of the civilian fatalities were unintentional."

"This isn't helping, Maurice! My boss and a bunch of my closest friends are working for a group of anarchists!"

"Their methods might be a little more violent than I would prefer,"

Maurice agreed, "But I don't think they're anarchists. It's the Council's deception they seem to be fighting, not Kawts itself. They're revolutionaries."

"They're still evil! What do they think is going to happen once they take out the Council? Kawts will be destroyed by the nomads in just a few weeks!"

"But what if Samuel's right? What if *I'm* right? If the Council really is corrupt, shouldn't we all be trying to remove them from office? Besides, I'm not convinced that the nomads are any more evil than the rebels."

"So I'm just supposed to believe you and Samuel's crazy theories over the Council? They're the *Council,* Maurice!"

Maurice smiled sadly. "Timothy, did you ever stop to think that even if Samuel and I are wrong about the Council, they still murdered Quill? That alone should be enough to show you they've been corrupted."

"Leave Quill out of this."

Maurice raised his hands in surrender. "It's just something to think about. I get it if you don't believe me. Or Samuel either. But if there's one thing you and I have in common, it's that we both want to know the truth. So search for it. Then you can decide for yourself whether we're crazy after all."

Timothy said nothing, and Maurice stood up. "Just think about it. The worst that could happen is that it turns out that you know a disproportionate number of Kawts' crazy people." He turned and left the room, leaving Timothy alone with his thoughts.

Timothy laid back on his bed, staring up at the ceiling, Maurice's words mixing with Samuel's. Eventually, he drifted off, entering a troubled sleep.

Chapter 9

When Timothy arrived at the library the next morning, there was no sign of the previous day's chaos. Samuel sat at his desk, filling out some paperwork. He looked up when Timothy entered, a sympathetic smile on his face.

"Good morning, Timothy," he said. His smile faded slightly. "I know yesterday was a lot to take in. Especially during your first week on the job. You probably have a ton of questions right now, and I promise that I'll do my best to answer them in due time. I just wanted you to know that I don't expect you to agree with me or join the rebels simply because of my opinions. You need to make that decision for yourself. I only ask that you think about what's really going on."

"That's what Maurice said, too," Timothy said. He looked Samuel in the eye. "I don't know what to think about all this. But I'm willing to look at the evidence and see where it leads."

"That's all I ask," Samuel said with a smile.

"There's one thing I don't get," Timothy said. "Actually, there's a lot of things I still don't get. But how on earth did you convince Volker that you had nothing to do with what happened yesterday?"

Samuel laughed. "When you write stories for a living, it isn't too hard to come up with a believable excuse. Although I have to admit, this time, Gearwire and Jewel concocted most of it."

Timothy nodded, waiting for Samuel to continue.

"There's really not much to tell," Samuel said. "Volker asked me all the standard questions - how much did I know, was I working with the anarchists, what was taken - that sort of thing. The only question that really caught me off guard was when he asked me how the anarchists got inside the secret library without damaging the door. Until that point, I had believed that Volker was unaware the library existed."

"What did you tell him?"

"I stuck with the story Gearwire had given me," Samuel said with a small smile. "I told him I had just unlocked the door when the fog rolled in. A few moments later, a man with a long beard and robotic legs appeared and threatened me with a strange device if I didn't help him. I unlocked the door, and the next thing I knew, I was waking up in my office to find the library ransacked."

"And he bought it?" Timothy said. "That seems too simple to fool someone like Volker."

"He didn't have any real reason to suspect me," Samuel said. "I've covered my tracks well. But I think the thing that really convinced him was when I said that I had overheard the anarchists planning on regrouping at the old Kolt house after the raid."

"The Kolt house? As in, Howard Kolt? The old head of the Science Guild? The one who said he created a kind of motor cart?"

Samuel nodded. "That's the one."

"What does he have to do with anything?"

"You remember when he disappeared? *The Kawts Tribune* had an article on it. Something about how he was convicted of treason and executed in a secret location to prevent him from passing on any last messages to his compatriots."

Timothy nodded slowly.

"And I assume you are also aware that after his disappearance, his wife and several other close family members requested an investigation? And that they themselves disappeared a few days later? 'Exposed as his co-conspirators', I believe was how the paper put it."

Timothy nodded again, following the chain of events thus far.

"After that, his daughter Madison came to see me. Do you remember her? I believe she was in the level below you." Timothy shook his head. Samuel looked surprised. "No? Well, I suppose it was a few years ago. Anyway, she decided she would conduct her own investigation in secret. Eventually, the Council caught on, and she too disappeared. But the significance of the Kolt house is this: first, it is one of the only buildings in Kawts that nobody currently lives or works in, and second, it marks the first time since Milkop Quawz' rebellion where an entire family bucked the Council's authority. It represents the Council's failure.

"It may interest you to know that Howard Kolt escaped, and the Council believes he has joined up with Gearwire. Not that they'd admit it out loud, of course. That would be a further sign of weakness. But he really did escape. Quill saw him."

Timothy was silent, mulling over what Samuel had told him. "What happened next?" he asked at last. "With Volker, I mean."

"Well," Samuel said. "There's really not much more to say. He asked me a few more questions, then he released me, saying he was sorry for taking up my time and that I should go home and rest." Samuel looked over at Timothy. "Any more questions I could answer for you?"

Timothy shook his head. "Maybe later," he said. "I - I'm not sure I'm ready to hear the answers yet."

Samuel smiled. "Of course. Take your time. I'll be here whenever you're ready."

* * *

Many hours later, after the library had been closed up for the night, Timothy wandered aimlessly through the streets of Kawts, contemplating all that had happened over the past few days. He felt drained, still trying to wrap his mind around everything that had happened. He still didn't know what to think about Samuel working with the rebels, and he wasn't even sure who to believe anymore.

I guess I've already chosen a side as far as the Council's concerned, he realized. *By not turning Samuel in, I've already allied myself with the anarchists.* He frowned as he considered the implications of his lack of action.

I know there are some things about Kawts that I wish were different, he thought. *But the Council members are the defenders of Kawts. How could it even be possible that they're actually its oppressors?*

Timothy wandered through town, eventually finding himself across the street from his old school. It seemed like months had passed since he had last been there, although in reality it had only been a couple of days. He smiled as he recalled how simple everything had been just one week ago. Before he had known about Samuel and Quill and Gearwire and the twins.

As he reminisced, he tripped over something jutting out of the underbrush. He looked down to see one of the handles of his makeshift cart sticking out over the path. Timothy stared at it for a long while, deep in thought.

Things have been so crazy the last couple of days, I completely forgot I even hid this.

He stared at the cart a little longer, an idea beginning to take root in his mind. Before long, he was planning the best way to transform the hastily assembled contraption into a real cart.

He was so wrapped up in his plans that he almost didn't hear someone coming up behind him.

"Hey, Tim," came Aksell's voice. "Haven't seen you much the last few days."

Timothy turned to see his friend standing next to him, leaning on a pair of crutches. For one fleeting moment, he worried that Aksell would guess the secret that he was keeping from the Council.

Don't be ridiculous, he chided himself. *It's only Aksell. He wouldn't betray Samuel even if he knew.*

Timothy forced a smile. "Yeah, Samuel's been keeping me pretty busy."

Aksell gave a wry smile. "That makes two of us. I swear I haven't had a free second since Graduation Day." He paused, craning his neck to look at something behind Timothy. "What are you working on over here?"

"See for yourself," Timothy replied, stepping aside so Aksell could see the cart.

"Is that what I think it is?"

Timothy grinned. "I was thinking of making it into a more... usable cart. Do you want to help?"

"Sure," Aksell said with a laugh. "Sounds a lot better than more Council politics lessons!"

Timothy laughed too, his previous fears forgotten. "Let's meet here after work tomorrow," he suggested. "I'll bring the tools and supplies. I've got a few ideas already."

Aksell nodded, and the pair spent the next two hours catching up and swapping stories. Eventually, Aksell turned and hobbled away, not wanting to be late for dinner. After a few minutes, Timothy followed suit.

* * *

Timothy could barely concentrate on work the next morning, his thoughts constantly coming back to his plans for working on the cart with Aksell. Since they had gotten their new jobs, it seemed like they had hardly seen each other. According to Aksell, this was largely due to the fact that Ethos severely discouraged Council trainees from maintaining friendships outside of the Council.

Probably so there's less of a chance that they'll accidentally reveal some big government secret, Timothy reasoned, seeing the logic behind the rule even as he resented its existence. The day seemed to drag by, each minute seeming like an hour. Timothy glanced at his watch for the thousandth time that day, fidgeting with his pencil.

Only a few more minutes, he coached himself. *Just a little -*

"Oh, all right. You can go," Samuel said, interrupting Timothy's train of thought.

Timothy blinked. "What?"

"You heard me," Samuel said with a smile. "I said you can go. I'll take care of things here. Go take care of whatever it is that you've been so worked up about all day."

Timothy stared at him. "Are you sure?" he asked.

"I've been doing this by myself for nearly twenty years," Samuel replied dryly. "I can manage. Now go."

Timothy dashed to the track, taking only a slight detour to pick up some spare wood and tools from his father's workshop. His father wasn't home when he got there, so Timothy quickly jotted down a note for him on a stray sheet of paper before hurrying off to the track. To his surprise, Aksell was already waiting for him when he arrived.

"I snuck away a few minutes early," he admitted, shifting his weight to lean on his crutch. "I was too excited to focus on Council politics. You?"

"Samuel told me I should leave early," Timothy replied with a wry smile. "Apparently, he noticed I was a little distracted as well." He set the tools down on the ground and arranged the planks he had brought by size. Briefly, he outlined his plan, and they began to work, measuring and cutting the boards into the right shapes.

"This is a pretty fun idea," Aksell remarked as he passed Timothy a hammer. "I never would have even thought to make this thing into an actual cart. Of course, I never would have thought to make the cart in the first place." He paused, a thoughtful look on his face. "Hey, do you want me to try to find some real wheels for this? I'm sure I could find some spares lying around."

Timothy grinned. "I've got an idea for that. We won't need real wheels." He paused. "I hope."

Aksell gave him a quizzical look, but he didn't push the matter, sensing that his friend would explain when he was ready. Hours flew by as they worked on the cart, taking their time and enjoying each other's company. By the time night fell, they had barely finished nailing the floor of the cart in place over the original logs.

"See you tomorrow?" Aksell asked, using his crutch to pull himself to his feet.

"You bet," Timothy replied, gathering up their supplies and stashing them in a small hollow in the ground before heading home.

* * *

Soon, this became Timothy's routine. Each day at work, he worked on writing his book, and every evening he spent working on the cart with Aksell. The project was taking them a good deal longer than it should have, mostly because they worked slowly and incorporated a great deal of unnecessary details to their design.

After he got back to his room each night, there was only ever just enough time to skim through Samuel's latest "recommendation" before he fell asleep. The elderly librarian had begun loaning him some of his favorite books from the secret library, which he expected Timothy to discuss with him the next day. Effectively, this meant that they were less like book recommendations and more like reading homework, but Timothy didn't mind. The books were fascinating and exciting, even if they did keep him rather busy.

Chapter 10

"I don't know, Tim. It's just so... boring. There's so much paperwork and politics! I hate it."

Timothy looked up at his friend, who was sitting on a large rock beside his supply of tools.

"It can't be that bad," he said, examining the partially assembled cart in front of him. He frowned, trying to figure out the best method to attach the axles.

"I suppose it isn't the worst job in Kawts," Aksell conceded. "I would hate to be one of the food delivery workers. But it's just not something that interests me."

Timothy set down his ruler and focused his attention on Aksell. "You'll get to be a Councilman one day," he said. "A defender of Kawts." His mind flashed to what Samuel had said about the Council's corruption, and he couldn't help but wonder what Aksell would do if it turned out that he was correct.

Aksell would never be a part of something like that, he decided. *He wouldn't do the kinds of things Samuel says the Council does.*

"But I don't want to be a defender of Kawts," Aksell said. "That's the point. I'm glad there's someone around who can do it, and it would be cool to be able to fight like that, but I don't want to be a famous hero. I'd much rather work in the library with you and Samuel. Or even be part of the Science Guild."

Timothy was silent for a moment, thinking over what Aksell had said. "We both know that there's no way to convince your dad to let you choose a different job," he said at last. "But maybe you could convince him to let you do something else as a Councilman."

"Like what?"

"I don't know," Timothy said with a shrug. "Maybe you could be the person in charge of looking through the manuscripts people send to the Council for publication. Or you could be the overseer for the *Kawts Tribune*. The Council does both of those things too, right?"

"I suppose," Aksell said thoughtfully.

"And who knows?" Timothy added before he could stop himself. "Maybe you could even make things better."

Aksell gave him a funny look. "What do you mean by that?"

"We both know that things aren't perfect here," Timothy said, his mouth turning dry as he realized how dangerously close to treason his words were. "There were always things we dreamed about changing - like the book forms, remember? Maybe you could pull some strings and make them shorter or something."

Aksell nodded slowly, and Timothy kept talking.

"And maybe," he added quickly, "You could even convince them to stop doing The Race."

Aksell's face became somber as his thoughts drifted to Quill and all the other classmates they had lost to The Race over the years.

"Definitely," he agreed. "I'll bring it up to my dad tomorrow. I think I might be able to convince him to call a Council hearing on it."

* * *

The next day, Aksell didn't show up at the track to work on the cart. After waiting fruitlessly for his friend to arrive, Timothy noticed a small piece of paper fluttering in the wind from the middle of the pile of spare lumber he had brought over from his father's workshop.

Timothy - my dad's making me work late tonight. I have a lot of paperwork to do. I might not be able to work on the cart with you for a while.
  -Aksell

Just as the note said, Aksell did not show up to work on the cart that day. Nor the next day. Or the day after that. Had it been anyone else, Timothy might have suspected that Aksell was avoiding him. But from what he heard from Larnell, he truly was struggling just to complete his assigned work from the Council.

Despite Aksell's busyness, Timothy was not alone when he worked on the cart. One night a few days after he received Aksell's note, he ran into Ives, who had taken Maurice's place as a reporter for the *Kawts Tribune*.

When Timothy saw him, Ives had been walking along the outside edge of the track, apparently deep in thought. Timothy called out to him, and he started violently, looking around frantically to see where the sound had come from. When he saw Timothy, he relaxed, though he still seemed a little on edge.

"Hi, Tim!" he called back, walking over to where Timothy was working on the cart. "What's this?"

"It's a cart," Timothy replied. "At least, it will be soon. I used the cart I built during The Race as the framework."

Ives examined the cart thoughtfully. "I don't suppose you could use a hand on this, could you?"

"The more the merrier," Timothy replied, glad to have some company while he worked.

With Ives' help, the cart was finished only a few days later. Timothy sighed as he surveyed his handiwork.

If only Aksell could see it now.

Timothy remembered his surprise when he had revealed his idea for the wheels. He had, after nearly breaking several of his father's saws and chisels and wasting almost an entire box of sandpaper, smoothed out the stones that had been the cart's original wheels and bored a hole in the center of each. Using the original twigs as guidelines, he had then built special axles and attached them to the wheels with some rope (painted green for aesthetic purposes) and extra-strength glue.

"These wheels will last longer than wooden ones," he explained when Aksell had questioned his decision. "Plus," he added with a smile, "They were the cart's original parts."

Although Aksell had been present for most of the cart's construction, there were a few features even he hadn't seen. The first was a false bottom that Timothy had installed on a whim overtop of the floor he had built with Aksell. Actually, it had been Ives who suggested it, pointing out that you never knew when you might want to keep something hidden. Timothy had quickly agreed, thinking of the books from the secret library which were currently laying in plain sight on top of his dresser.

With the cart complete, Timothy had more time to select some books of his own from the secret library to read, in addition to the ones Samuel had assigned. To his amazement, the books talked about many impossible things - things that were apparently commonplace at the time the books were written.

In this way, he learned about plants that produced food, weapons wielded by ancient warriors, vehicles propelled by wind or large animals, and countless other possibilities that he'd never even considered before. The more he read, the more he realized that the Council's description of the limits of mankind and the outside world were woefully inadequate, although he still couldn't tell whether this was due to ignorance or something much darker.

After reading one particularly thrilling novel about a sea voyage,

Timothy returned to working on the cart, eager to try out a new idea. He fixed a wooden pole to the floor of the cart, tying a smaller branch horizontally across it near the top. To this, he attached an old bedsheet, hoping that it would mimic the behavior of a sail.

As the sun began to set, Timothy tied the last piece of rope into place. He took a step back, admiring his work. The wind was picking up, making tonight the perfect night for a test run. He pulled the cart out away from the trees, excitement surging through him as he saw the sheet flap in the wind. Grinning wildly, he jumped inside, prepared to sail across the street. To his disappointment, nothing happened. The cart sat there stubbornly, the sail flapping loosely.

Timothy frowned as climbed back out.

I must've missed something, he thought to himself, grabbing his book and re-reading the passage that described the ship. Realization dawned on him as he realized he had oversimplified the mast a great deal. After several more minutes of work, he had amended his mistake and was riding over the track, accustoming himself to the controls. As the city-wide curfew approached, he hid the cart back in the brush and headed home.

A few days later, as he returned to his bedroom after work, the book Gearwire had given him caught his eye. He had been avoiding the book for weeks, using his work on the cart and his readings from Samuel as an excuse not to read it. Now, though, he had no legitimate reason for continuing to ignore it aside from a vague sense of unease, which he strongly suspected stemmed from the fact that it had been given to him by Kawts' most wanted criminal.

But now, after reading the other books from the secret library, he found that his curiosity was overcoming his apprehension. He gingerly picked it up, wiping off the thick layer of dust that had settled on the front cover.

Why did Gearwire give me this book out of all the ones in the secret

73

library? he wondered. *From what Samuel said about him, the books he took weren't selected at random.*

He hesitated for a moment with his hand on the cover, then opened the book to the beginning of the first chapter.

In the beginning, God created the heavens and the earth.

Timothy paused, the sentence striking him as odd. Thinking about the origins of the universe was not something he did often - rarely ever, in fact. But in those brief musings, he had never once considered the possibility that something had *created* the world.

Could that be why Gearwire gave me this book? Timothy wondered as he pondered the statement. *Because it contains secrets about our history that the Council wants to keep hidden?*

He brushed the thought aside, electing to wait and see what else the book said before coming up with any theories. With curiosity and skepticism warring in his mind, he continued to read.

* * *

"Have you been reading that book from Gearwire?" Samuel asked out of the blue one afternoon a few days later.

"I started it earlier this week," Timothy said. "Why?"

"What do you think so far?" Samuel asked, wiping the dust off a shelf of books.

Timothy shrugged. "It's pretty interesting, I suppose. But there's some weird stuff in there. And it doesn't seem to stick to one genre. One minute it seems like a history book, and the next minute it seems like a fantasy novel." He paused. "What do you think? You've read it, right?"

Samuel nodded. "I have," he said slowly. "As far as I can tell, the book does claim to be nonfiction," he said evasively. He focused intently on the shelf he was dusting, debating whether he should say more.

Finally, he added, "And according to some of the other books upstairs, there's archeological evidence to support that claim. At least, there was before the Robot War. It's possible that it's all been destroyed by now."

Timothy nodded slowly, processing the information. But even with Samuel's input, there were still a few things that didn't quite make sense.

"You seem to know a lot about this book."

Samuel shrugged. "I've picked up a few things here and there," he said. "But I'm hardly an expert."

"Would you be able to explain a few things to me?" Timothy asked.

"I can try," Samuel said after a moment of hesitation. "Although I can't promise it will be helpful. What were you wondering?"

* * *

For the next several hours, Timothy and Samuel went back and forth, discussing the things Timothy had read so far. It would be the first of many such conversations, which Timothy soon came to enjoy, despite the fact that they often brought him into disagreement with his mentor.

In the months that followed, Crystal and Jewel often visited them, stopping by the library to talk to Samuel about various missions Gearwire had planned. Timothy always felt slightly guilty about witnessing these meetings, although whether it was because he felt like he was betraying the Council or because he envied their courage, he never could determine.

What is it that makes them so committed to fighting the Council? he wondered as he watched Jewel leave the library after one of these visits. *The Council's definitely done some questionable stuff, but it hardly seems like it warrants a full-on rebellion.*

He glanced over at Samuel, who was furiously scribbling Jewel's instructions down on a sheet of paper. He hesitated a moment, then said, "Samuel?"

Samuel looked up at him, eyebrows raised questioningly. "Yes?"

"What made you decide to join the anarchists?"

A shadow crossed Samuel's face. "I joined the *rebels* because of The Race," he said at last. He bit his tongue, seeming torn. Finally, he said, "There was a girl in my class - her name was Jane. She was a... a close friend of mine."

He hesitated again, and Timothy couldn't help but wonder if Jane had perhaps been more than that. Samuel continued, the strange tone in his voice confirming Timothy's suspicion.

"She and a few others decided that if they didn't run The Race at all, none of them could lose. They asked me to join them, but I was too afraid of what would happen." His voice caught. "None of them were ever seen again." He rambled on, talking to himself as much as to Timothy. "There hasn't been a day that's gone by since then where I haven't wondered what would have happened if I had joined her. Maybe she would still be here today."

Timothy sat in stunned silence. Like everyone else in Kawts, he had heard the story of the class that tried to cheat The Race, but he had never realized it was Samuel's classmates who had done it.

No wonder he's convinced that the Council is evil. It's hard enough to lose one person to The Race each year, let alone half the class.

He frowned as a thought struck him.

Maybe Samuel's on to something, he thought, realizing that wiping out nearly half the class directly contradicted the Council's official explanation for The Race. He shook his head, bringing his focus back to the present.

"Sorry. I didn't know," he said, feeling guilty about dredging up what were evidently painful memories.

Samuel sighed. "It's okay," he said. "It was a long time ago. Not many people still remember that was us. Of course, part of that was my doing. I've tried to keep out of the spotlight so the Council doesn't suspect me. They've gotten away with this sort of thing for far too long."

Chapter 11

"Hey, dad!" Timothy called out, ducking into the workshop. "Do you have a saw I could borrow for a few minutes? I promise you'll get it back in one piece this time."

"Dad's not here right now," Maurice's voice called back.

Timothy walked around the furniture in the store to try to catch a glimpse of his brother. He finally found him standing in the back room of the workshop with his fiancée, Ally, and Maverick, another friend of his. They were gathered around something on a half-finished table that Maurice was supposed to be working on.

"What are you doing back here, Maurice?"

"I'm keeping an eye on the shop," Maurice said, stepping between Timothy and the table.

"You know what I mean."

"It's just a little project we're working on," Maurice said evasively. "You'll find out about it as soon as it's finished."

Timothy looked at his brother, concern in his eyes. "Don't do anything stupid."

Maurice grinned. "You know me. I'll be fine." He pulled a saw from the shelf behind him and handed it to Timothy. "There. You've got a saw. Now we've got to get back to work."

Timothy hesitated a moment, then slowly turned and walked outside.

***

Timothy walked out of the library a few days later, ideas for his book swirling in his head. He was passing by the police station when he saw the crowd. He frowned, moving closer for a better look.

Plastered across the walls of the police station and a few of the other buildings were a cluster of haphazardly arranged flyers. Timothy's heart sank when he read the slogans printed on them.

The Race is murder!

What is the Council hiding?

Milkop was right!

Timothy tore his gaze away from the posters, his heart pounding. "No," he muttered. "No, Maurice. Please tell me this wasn't you..."

He turned away from the police station, breaking out into a run toward his house. He barged into the workshop, the door slamming against the wall.

"Where's Maurice?"

His father looked up at him, a puzzled frown on his face. "He left to pick up a lumber order a few minutes ago. Why? Is something wrong?"

Timothy ran back outside, making his way to the sawmill that supplied the planks for their shop. There was no sign of Maurice. His heart sank, and he ran back to his house. He explained the situation to his parents, and they set out at once to find him, recruiting a few of the neighbors to help. But by the time the sun set, they had found no sign of either Maurice or his friends.

Timothy slowly climbed the stairs to his bedroom that night, his feet feeling like lead.

Samuel was right, he thought. *Maurice finally went too far. And now he's gone.*

Fighting back tears, Timothy sat down on his bed. A scrap of paper fluttered to the ground, and he picked it up.

Timothy -

By the time you're reading this, I'll be long gone. We finally struck out against the Council. Now everyone will have to face the realities that they've ignored until now. If everything went well, me and Ally and Maverick will be hiding out with a group of nomads, trying to bolster support to help us come back and overthrow the Council. If something went wrong, then I'm probably dead. Either way, I'm sorry for putting you and mom and dad through this. It shouldn't be this way.

Search for the truth, and the truth will set you free.

-Maurice

Timothy stared at the note in his hands, tears trickling down his face.

* * *

Later that night, Timothy tossed and turned on his bed, unable to sleep. Eventually, he gave up and just sat there, letting his gaze wander around the room. He spotted something sticking out from behind his dresser and frowned, puzzled. Throwing off his sheets, he moved closer for a better look. He bent down and stared at it, trying to make out what it was. In the dim lighting, it took him several moments to realize that it was the corner of a book, wedged between his dresser and the wall. Slowly, he teased it out of the crevice it had fallen into and brushed the dust and lint off the cover.

The words 'A History of Codes and Ciphers, by Dr. Thomas Maddium' were scrawled across the front, the font resembling a handwritten note. Timothy hesitated, something about this book seeming familiar.

Then it struck him like a bolt of lightning - this was the book that Samuel had given him on the day of the library raid. The book that

Quill had asked him to pass along to Timothy.

Timothy's mind raced as he turned the book over.

I can't believe I forgot about this! he thought, skimming the text on the back cover. *I was so exhausted those first few days that I didn't even try to read it - and then I was so wrapped up with the cart and the books Samuel assigned me, I completely forgot this one even existed!*

Yet even with this revelation, something else still nagged at him. Quill had been the one to request that Samuel give him the book, but Timothy could see no reason why he would have done so. A book about codes was completely useless unless there was something to decode.

"Why this book, Quill?" he muttered, turning the question over in his mind. "You didn't give me any coded messages…." he trailed off as all the pieces fell into place. He hurried over to the shelf where Quill's box lay. The symbols on the cover of the box were almost identical to a set of symbols that decorated the book's front cover.

There was no doubt in Timothy's mind now. This book was definitely connected to the secret of Quill's box. He eagerly opened it up, suddenly full of hope once more that he could actually solve the riddle which had plagued him for the last year and a half. On the inside cover, there was a note in Quill's messy handwriting.

From the pages of this book,
see what none were meant to see.
The box conceals the secret
of the Council's treachery.

Timothy stared at the words, confused.

Is this the key to Quill's box? It's not terribly helpful.

He shook his head.

It can't be, he realized. *The symbols on the box have to mean something.*

And it looks like the only way to figure out what is to read this book.

Sitting down on his bed with the book, Timothy continued to read until he was too tired to go any further, finally drifting off to sleep around midnight.

Despite this monumental step towards discovering Quill's secret, life continued on like normal for the next week and a half. The book, though interesting, was long-winded, giving such in-depth explanations of each code and its implications that after ten days, he had only gotten as far as the start of the American Civil War.

He was beginning to think that he was on the wrong track when he noticed a chart printed in the book, underneath a heading that read, "The Pigpen Code in the American Civil War". Intrigued, Timothy skimmed through the paragraphs above it. According to the book, the chart was the key to an old code used hundreds of years ago, which substituted a set of symbols for letters. His heart skipped a beat as he realized it was the same code as the one on the lid of the box.

He quickly grabbed a piece of paper and a pencil and began jotting down the key. After a few moments, he had decoded the first letter. G. Timothy turned his attention to the second letter. An E. His excitement growing, Timothy hurriedly decoded the remaining symbols, jotting them down on the scrap of paper. Then, taking a deep breath, he entered them into the lock on the box.

G-E-A-R-W-I-R-E.

There was a faint click as the box unlocked. Timothy's pulse raced. He had wondered about the contents of the box for so long, but now that it was actually unlocked, he was almost afraid to open it. He took a couple of deep breaths to calm himself before cautiously lifting the lid and peering inside. All it contained were a pair of notebooks and a letter.

Timothy picked them up gingerly, as if he was handling delicate artifacts. A closer inspection of the notebooks revealed that only one had been written by Quill. Setting the notebooks aside for the moment, Timothy focused his attention on the letter. He picked it up and began to read.

Hello, Timothy. If you are reading this, it means that you know that all is not as it seems in Kawts. It also means that the Council has made me disappear, most likely by losing The Race. Tim, The Council is evil. Through my investigations, I've discovered things that the Council will go to any lengths to keep hidden. The contents of this box are all the evidence I have gathered. Tell Samuel as much or as little about this as you want, but tell no one else. Not even Aksell. Ethos is the most diabolical Council member of all. It is up to you to fight for the freedom of Kawts. Be careful.

-Quill

Timothy swallowed hard. This was it. He would finally hear in Quill's own words what exactly it was that he had discovered. Timothy picked up the first of the two notebooks, the one written by Quill, and began to read. The first entry was dated three years ago.

The most unusual thing happened today. I saw Howard Kolt, the inventor who disappeared. He was babbling about Blanks and The Council and other things that I couldn't make out and riding what could only have been his motor cart. He had a mad gleam in his eye and seemed insane. When he reached the spot where I was, he pulled me aside. That was when I recognized him. It had been a while since I had seen him at the guild meetings, but it was definitely him. For a moment, he seemed calm and perfectly sane. He must have recognized me, because he whispered, "Quill. Beware the Council" and rode off out of Kawts.

The next entry was dated a few days later.

I'm glad I didn't tell anyone about my encounter with Howard. There was another man who reported seeing Howard as well. Today, he disappeared from the hospital, where he was being kept under a diagnosis of insanity. This cannot be a coincidence. I need to figure out what's really going on.

* * *

I did it. Last night, I snuck into the Council Building to find answers. By pure luck, I found their records room. It took me a while, but eventually I found the information I wanted. Howard's file. According to what was inside, he had been head of the Science Guild for many years, which I already knew. It also listed all of his inventions, but it made no mention of his mysterious 'motor cart'. Obviously, he must have finished it at some point, which means that for some reason, the Council deliberately covered it up. It might even be the reason he disappeared in the first place.

The only other thing out of the ordinary about his file was a bright red 'B' stamped on the top. I also obtained the address where he had lived with Madison and Mrs. Kolt.

* * *

Today I stopped by the Kolt house. To my surprise, it was abandoned. A thick layer of dust coated everything. Evidently, they wouldn't be able to help me. I looked around for a while longer, but I couldn't find anything. Just as I was turning to leave, I tripped on an exposed floorboard. I scrambled over and examined it. One corner was sticking up, concealing a small cavity in the floor. Something was hidden underneath. I wrenched the board free and looked down into the small hollow I'd uncovered. Inside was a notebook and a slip of paper. On the paper was a hastily scrawled note:

In this book are dangerous secrets that will put your life in jeopardy. The truth about the Council. Do not read this unless you are prepared to bear the consequences.

Madison Kolt

As I finished reading this, I heard footsteps approaching. I scooped up the note and the book and ran.

* * *

The notebook I found in that old house has proved very useful. Apparently, once Howard disappeared, Madison did some investigating to find out why. The notebook was her record of everything she discovered. According to her, the upper floors of the library hold many books, all of them restricted in the city of Kawts. Among other things, there are entire books filled with instructions about how to make food. According to what the notebook said, they taste even better than pink glop! (Madison snuck into the food processing plant and tried out a few of the recipes.) The notebook also recounts a very significant recollection about Howard Kolt.

Apparently, when he was working on the water purifying system with Councilman Simms, he secretly took his own sample from the river. Upon testing it, he realized it was perfectly safe. Yet the samples given to him by Simms all contained lethal doses of poison, matching the toxins found in the blood of a man who rejected the Council's story about the river. According to Madison's notes, her father didn't really attach any importance to this discovery at first. But shortly before he vanished, it seemed to be all he could think about. The last entry of this notebook poses an interesting question: Where do the Blanks fit into all this?

* * *

The Training Months have arrived, and I've managed to become the librarian apprentice for this year. Now I can investigate the lead there!

* * *

Today Samuel showed me the secret library. So far, though, it hasn't given me any new information about Kawts.

* * *

Someone else attacked the Council Building today. The so-called 'anarchists.' I was heading back to try to find some new information when I heard the commotion. I ducked into a side street and watched the scene unfold. There was only a group of four attacking the building, but they fended off a small army of Blanks! They were using a variety of odd-looking gadgets to keep them at bay. I saw Ethos coming, along with a company of attack drones and two other Councilmen. Then, through the smoke that was rapidly filling the area, I caught a glimpse of their leader ordering a retreat.

At that moment, I knew I had to follow them. They kept up a rapid pace as they hurried through Kawts, but I managed to keep them in sight. Before long, they had left Kawts behind and had started up the trail to Mt. Elbrus. Somehow, I avoided their detection all the way up. At least, I thought I did. They went into a cave, and I followed them. But the second I stepped inside, I found myself lying on the floor with my arms pinned behind my back. They then subjected me to hours of questioning.

Finally, my captors decided I posed no threat, and they untied me. Their leader, a man with robotic legs who I would later learn was called Gearwire, entered the room and we began a conversation. We exchanged information about the state Kawts was in, and he revealed that he was in charge of the resistance effort to stop the Council. By the time I left that night, I was one of them. I was officially one of his undercover agents in Kawts.

* * *

I did some digging at Gearwire's request, and I discovered something shocking. Before today, I didn't realize just how evil the Council truly is. I was looking through their records again, and I found some scientific papers about the virus that swept through Kawts a few years ago. They were notes. Not on the antidote. They were detailed notes on the virus itself. They were accompanied by a record of a transaction between the Council and the scientist who manufactures the attack drones.

The Council purchased both the virus and the antidote from him a few months before the first case in Kawts. The Council was the source of the virus, all the while holding back the cure! Along with this, I found some old Council files about the resistance's attacks. These yielded a slew of other horrifying facts - the Council, not Gearwire, is behind the explosions. The Council must be stopped.

* * *

Like Madison, I can't help but feel that the Blanks are the key to this puzzle. You never hear of them being recruited, yet somehow there are always hundreds of them. And when I encountered Howard, he was talking about Blanks. It can't be a coincidence. But what does it mean?

* * *

It all makes sense now! I snuck into the Council Building again last night, and I uncovered some astonishing information. Information that will change Kawts forever if it gets out. I can't prove it for sure yet, but I think-

Timothy stopped reading. There was no more. The last page of the notebook had been ripped out.

His mind spun. What had Quill discovered? He picked up the other notebook and leafed through it, hoping to find another clue, but Quill had already summarized all the important details in his observations. As he recalled what Quill had said about the Council, he felt a sickening feeling in his gut. For the first time, he knew with absolute certainty that Samuel was right about the Council - they weren't the noble band of heroes that they portrayed themselves as. They were responsible for the deaths of many of their own citizens - all to strengthen their own control over Kawts. There was no doubt in Timothy's mind now. They had to be stopped.

Chapter 12

The next day, Timothy filled Samuel in about Quill's box and its contents.

"I'd like to find out what he discovered."

"I certainly would as well, Timothy," Samuel began carefully. "And I agree that the Council needs to be stopped. But I beg you not to dig any further into the matter. Too many of Kawts' brightest young minds have already met their deaths trying. First Madison, and then Quill, were killed following this same line of questioning. And after what happened to Maurice? Who knows how many others have died trying to unravel the mystery surrounding Kawts?"

Timothy nodded in agreement, but deep down, he knew he had to investigate further, despite Samuel's warnings. Quill had risked everything to find out what was going on. Timothy owed it to his friend to finish what he had started.

That night after work, Timothy jogged over to the Kawts Science Building. Crystal and Jewel were just leaving for the day when he arrived.

"I need to talk to you," he said in a whisper as they turned to look at him.

"About… what?" Crystal prompted, arching her eyebrow.

"About Quill," Timothy said. "I need to know what he discovered."

The twins exchanged glances. An entire conversation seemed to pass between them without either of them saying a word. "Meet us at the Kolt house at ten o'clock tonight," Jewel said at last. "Leave your watch at home."

"Why?" Timothy asked, his forehead furrowing.

"I'll explain later," Jewel replied, glancing quickly around to make sure there was no one within earshot. "Just don't forget."

She turned and hurried away, whispering urgently with her sister. Timothy watched them go, then returned home to retrieve Quill's box. He brought it out to the cart, packing it into the secret compartment below the false floor. If the Council grew suspicious of him, he could escape Kawts in a hurry with all the evidence he needed to expose them.

As he waited for ten o'clock to come, Timothy tried to calm his nerves. Until now, he hadn't actually done anything directly against the Council - nothing that could be proven, at least. But if they caught him sneaking around in the middle of the night, the Council wouldn't hesitate to brand him as a traitor and have him executed.

To take his mind off of what he was about to do, Timothy opened the Bible Gearwire had given him and continued to read. A few days ago, he had stumbled upon a section of poetry in the middle, which served as just the thing to calm his nerves. As he read further, he hardly noticed the passage of time until the alarm on his watch beeped softly.

Remembering Jewel's instructions, Timothy removed the watch from his wrist and left it sitting beside his bed. Then, shrugging on an old hooded cloak of his father's, he crept downstairs and out into the night. It took him several minutes to locate the Kolt house in the dark, a task made more difficult by the fact that he had never actually been there himself.

Jewel was already waiting for him when he arrived. "Crystal's keeping an eye out for the Council's patrols," she explained as she sat down on one of the dust-covered chairs in what had once been the dining room.

Swallowing his nervousness, Timothy said, "I want to join the rebellion."

Jewel frowned. "That's a huge commitment," she said. "And last time Samuel and I talked, you were still half-convinced that we were the bad guys. Why the sudden change of heart?"

"I found the notes Quill left me," Timothy explained. "He discovered something that the Council didn't want anyone to know, and they killed him for it. I want to know what he learned."

"I'll tell Gearwire," Jewel said hesitantly. "But I wouldn't expect to hear from him anytime soon. He's going to want to observe you for a while before he reveals any important information."

"You're afraid I'll tell Aksell. Or Ethos."

Jewel shook her head. "I don't. I know you well enough to know that you're not the type of person who would do something like that. But Gearwire has to keep the safety of the resistance and Kawts in mind, too. He can't risk letting a Council spy in on what we're doing."

Timothy sighed, reluctantly agreeing that she had a point. "I just wish I knew what Quill discovered."

Jewel shifted her gaze away from him, suddenly intent on inspecting a dead mosquito on the wall.

"You already know, don't you," Timothy realized suddenly. "The thing they killed Quill for?"

"I can't say. Not without Gearwire's approval," Jewel said, shaking her head.

"Tell me. Please," Timothy pleaded.

Jewel hesitated for a moment. The awkward silence that followed stretched out for what seemed like forever. Finally, she nodded. She was about to speak when Crystal rushed into the room.

"There's a squadron of Blanks on their way over here," she said quickly. "We've got to go."

Jewel stood up abruptly, her chair sliding across the floor. "Which way?"

"They're coming down MacGregor Street."

"Timothy, you leave out the back door. Get home as fast as possible. We'll keep the Blanks distracted," Jewel said.

"How-" Timothy started, but the twins were both already gone. He hesitated for a moment, torn between wanting to help and following Jewel's orders. Reluctantly, he slipped out the back door of the house. He glanced down at his arm to check the time, only to remember that he had left his watch at home.

I never got the chance to ask them about that, he realized as he ran back to his house, sneaking past his sleeping parents and into the safety of his own room.

* * *

The next morning, Timothy told Samuel all about his strange nocturnal meeting.

"...and then a group of Blanks came by and we had to leave," he finished. "Crystal and Jewel stayed behind to distract them. I'm not sure if they made it out."

Samuel smiled knowingly. "I'm sure they're fine. They've done this sort of thing before."

"That's a relief," Timothy said, feeling as though an immense burden had been lifted from his shoulders. "I was afraid I might have gotten them killed." He thought for a moment, then said, "I never got to ask them what was up with the watches, though."

"I think I can answer that one," Samuel said. "The Council has tracking devices installed in all the watches. They keep tabs on any unusually timed alarms, too."

Timothy's eyes widened. "I set my watch alarm last night to remind me of the meeting!"

"That's probably why there were so many Blanks out last night," Samuel said with a knowing nod. "But as long as you were back in your room before they reached your house, they'll probably dismiss it as an accident. And from what you've told me, it sounds like the twins made sure you had enough time to do that." He paused. "I would lie low for a couple of days, though. Just to be safe."

Timothy shook his head, still reeling. "I almost got all three of us killed."

"I wouldn't go quite so far as that," Samuel said gently. "As I said, the twins have done this sort of thing before. That being said, there's no sense in repeating your mistake."

"Did Quill know about the watches?"

Samuel nodded. "Gearwire sent word to both of us. Always remember to leave your watch where you're supposed to be when you're doing things that the Council doesn't want you to do."

"I'll keep that in mind," Timothy said uneasily, still half expecting a squadron of Blanks to charge into the library to arrest him at any moment.

* * *

By the end of the day, Timothy's fears had mostly dissipated, replaced by an eagerness to help to liberate Kawts. On his way home from work, he stopped by the Science Building again to talk to Jewel.

"Did Gearwire say anything yet?"

Jewel shook her head. "I told you it would probably take a while before he had any instructions for you. He'll take at least a few weeks to make up his mind. Probably even longer."

"Did you have to wait a few weeks when you joined?"

"No. But there were… other factors involved in our recruitment," Jewel said evasively. "Gearwire's going to be extra cautious because of your connection with Aksell."

"He didn't wait that long with Quill."

"He didn't have a whole lot of a choice with Quill," Jewel said, laughing. "Quill followed them back to their base! He either had to keep him there permanently or send him back as a spy before anyone noticed he was gone."

"So if I find their base…"

"He'll probably find it highly suspicious," Jewel finished. "Considering that he is already wary of you. Just be patient. He'll contact you when he's sure you're a safe choice."

Timothy sighed. "There's nothing I can do to make him decide sooner?"

Jewel shook her head. "Gearwire is an experienced general. If he thinks you're pushing things too fast, he'll probably delay longer. You just need to lie low for a while."

Timothy nodded reluctantly. "If that's what it takes to find the truth, I'll do it," he sighed.

Jewel smiled. "Good. I'll let you know if anything changes."

Chapter 13

"Samuel tells me you finished reading the book Gearwire gave you," Jewel said out of the blue one afternoon when Timothy stopped by to see if Gearwire had any messages for him.

"He mentioned that?" Timothy asked, suddenly wondering what else Samuel had told her.

Jewel nodded. "He said that you had a lot of questions."

"That would be an understatement."

Jewel said nothing for several seconds, seeming torn. "I know someone who might be able to answer a few of them," she said abruptly. "There's a group of us who all get together on Sunday nights to learn about the Bible."

"Like a book club or something?" Timothy said skeptically, recalling the term from one of the other books he had read from the secret library.

"Not quite," Jewel said. "It's... it's kind of hard to explain, I guess. But the guy who leads the meetings has spent years studying the Bible. Gearwire even lent him some books on it from before the Robot War. He could probably help clear up anything that you don't understand."

"I'll think about it," Timothy said disinterestedly, although his curiosity was piqued. "I should just drop by this guy's house sometime, then?"

"No," Jewel said quickly, shaking her head. "The Council might find it suspicious if you visited him during the day. The best way to get in touch with him is to attend one of the meetings. You can talk to him in private once it's over."

Timothy nodded slowly, seeing the logic behind Jewel's instructions. *No one in Kawts is even supposed to know this book exists, let alone be an expert on it.*

"When's the next meeting?"

"This Sunday at 11:00pm," Jewel replied. "273 Miller Avenue. Don't forget to take your watch off before you leave."

Timothy nodded. "I know, I know. And don't use the alarm either. I learned my lesson after last time."

"Good," Jewel said, smiling. "I'll see you on Sunday, then."

* * *

Several nights later, Timothy stood outside the man's house. He lifted his hand to push open the door, but he hesitated, hearing unusual sounds coming from inside the building.

It's singing, he realized suddenly, recalling what he had read about music. *That must be what singing sounds like.*

"Glad you could make it," someone said behind him, almost causing him to shout in surprise. He turned to see one of the blue-clad figures who often were involved in the attacks on Kawts. Timothy instinctively took a step back before realizing his fears were unfounded. If the two of them worked for Gearwire, they weren't a danger to him.

Besides, something about them seems familiar.

Timothy tried to catch a glimpse of the caped figure's face, but a jeweled mask covered the left half. The other side of the person's face was strangely blurred, as if seen through a foggy window.

"They just started," the figure explained. "You're just in time."

"Thanks," Timothy said, shaking off his concern and stepping inside.

The small crowd on the other side of the door didn't seem to register his arrival, their focus on the song they were singing. Timothy sat down in a chair near the exit, wondering what would happen next. As he waited for the song to be over, he looked around at the others in the room. Most were strangers to him, but there were one or two faces that he recognized. He didn't see any sign of Jewel, although he did spot the other blue-clad figure high in the rafters, watching the meeting from above.

They're here to protect the meeting, Timothy realized. *Gearwire must have sent them.*

As the song came to an end, a man got up in front of the crowd and began to read from the Bible, talking at great length about just a few verses.

He certainly seems like an expert, Timothy thought as he fingered the long list of questions in his pocket. When the man finished speaking and the crowd began to disperse, Timothy saw his chance.

"Excuse me," he said, stopping the speaker before he disappeared up the stairs. "I have some questions for you." The man stiffened, and Timothy realized that he should have phrased his statement differently. "Not like that," he said quickly. "I mean questions about the Bible."

The man relaxed as he realized he wasn't about to be arrested. "Come with me," he said, stepping into the next room over and taking a seat near the wall. He stared at Timothy. "You're Maurice's brother, aren't you?" he asked.

Timothy nodded. "Did you know him?"

"He was a member of our congregation before he disappeared," the man replied. "But tell me, what is it you wanted to know?"

* * *

For the next several hours, Timothy peppered the man with questions, asking about every single thing on the list he had written, and several more besides. The man did his best to answer them all, but even so, there were still a few things that weren't answered to Timothy's satisfaction.

"We should probably wrap this up for tonight," the man said at last. "You need to be home before morning. And a few hours of sleep wouldn't hurt, either."

Timothy nodded, suddenly realizing how tired he was.

"I'll try to do a little more digging into those questions you asked," the man promised. "And if you come up with any more, I'd be happy to talk them over with you next week. We're usually here at the same time every Sunday." He smiled. "I hope to see you again."

Timothy nodded again. "We'll see," he said as he stood up. He walked outside, hurrying back to his house to avoid any Council patrols. He had hardly crawled back into bed before he fell asleep, barely remembering to hide the evidence of his adventure.

* * *

In the weeks that followed, Timothy had several more conversations with the leader of the meetings, who called himself Pastor Shepherd. By the end, he felt like he understood everything better, although there were a few times that the man had admitted that he simply didn't know the answer.

Yet as satisfying as his conversations with Pastor Shepherd were, his pursuit of the truth about the Council was not. It had been nearly a month since he unlocked the secret of Quill's box, and he was growing tired of waiting for Gearwire to contact him. Finally, he resolved to find the answers for himself.

With Samuel's reluctant permission, Timothy soon found himself standing outside Larnell's office with a notepad and pencil in his hand.

Before he could change his mind, he knocked on the door.

"Come in!" Larnell called cheerfully. He looked up as Timothy approached. "Hello, Timothy!" he exclaimed. "How've you been?"

"I'm doing fine," Timothy said, keeping his tone light. "I need to ask you for a favor. I need to get into the records room for a project Samuel and I are working on."

"That's the second time today someone has asked me that," Larnell said, shaking his head with a smile. "Ives was over here a few hours ago looking for some documents for an article he was writing." He looked up at Timothy. "What sort of project are you working on?"

"We're trying to compile a record of when certain books were written. We figured the Council might have kept a copy of the publication forms."

"I see," Larnell said. "I'll tell you the same thing I told Ives. I'd love to help, but I can't just let people into the records room without permission. It would need to be approved by Aksell or Ethos or someone first."

"I've already talked to Ethos," Timothy lied. "He told me to come talk to you."

"Well, if Ethos already okayed it, I suppose it's fine," Larnell conceded. "But don't take too long. I have to be at a meeting in an hour, and I can't leave the door unlocked while I'm gone."

"That should be plenty of time," Timothy assured him. "I only need to find a few dates."

"You'd be surprised," Larnell said wryly as they walked down the hallway. "The records room is a mess. I don't think anyone's bothered to reorganize the place since Milkop Quawz' rebellion!"

Timothy laughed, but the mention of the rebellion had put him on edge.

I have to know what Quill discovered, he reminded himself, quelling his nervousness.

Larnell reached the door, punching in the passcode before Timothy could take note of it. The door swung open, revealing rows upon rows of cabinets surrounded by centuries of haphazardly placed stacks of papers.

"Happy searching!" Larnell said, gesturing to the messy room. "I'll be back in a little while to lock up again. If you need me, I'll be in my office!"

"Thanks!" Timothy said, stepping into the room.

Where do I even start? he wondered, looking around at the towering piles of loose papers.

Howard Kolt seems to be the key to this. I'll start there.

He walked up and down the rows of filing cabinets until he found a drawer marked with a K. He tugged at the handle, but it was locked.

It looks like they've increased the security in this place since Quill was here, Timothy thought, disheartened. His disappointment quickly faded, however, when he spotted something sitting atop a pile of papers a few feet away.

It was an old, stained notebook with Howard's name scrawled across the top. Carefully, Timothy picked it up and paged through it.

These are his research notes, Timothy realized. He paged through the notebook, passing several complex diagrams and mathematical equations before coming to a stop at Howard's notes about the water filtration system he had designed for Kawts.

A sound from the hallway brought Timothy's focus back to his mission.

"Did you find what you were looking for?" Larnell called.

"Yeah," Timothy called back, slipping Howard's notebook under his shirt and following Larnell out of the room. As soon as he was out of sight from the Council Building, he dashed over to where he had hidden the cart and stashed the notebook under the floorboard with Quill's box. Then he hurried back to the library. Samuel greeted him with a nod, confirming that no one had noticed he was gone.

When Timothy finally got a chance to go back and look at the book he'd found, it was after dark. He left his watch on his pillow and slipped out the window, dropping into the street below. Blanks and attack drones patrolled the otherwise deserted streets, but Timothy suspected they wouldn't bother to check the trees by the track.

Grabbing the notebook from the cart, he retreated into the trees, climbing up into the upper branches so he could read by the moonlight. To his dismay, he found that the notebook told him nothing that Quill hadn't already written in his own notes. The only thing of any interest at all was a scribbled note in the margins about the suspiciously high concentrations of poisons in the river water samples. Sighing, Timothy set the notebook down.

I'm not getting any closer to figuring out what Quill discovered.

* * *

Two nights later, Timothy stood outside the Council Building.

"Whatever discovery Quill made, he found after returning here," he muttered to himself. "It's the best lead I've got."

Silently, he crept closer to the building. There were no guards on the outside. Timothy eased open the door and started down the hallway, trying to ignore how his heart pounded in his chest. A squadron of Blanks marched by, and he ducked into the shadows.

This might be a little harder than I thought.

He took several deep breaths, settling his nerves. Once the Blanks had rounded the corner, he continued on his way. After evading three more squadrons of Blanks and two members of the Kawts Security Force, Timothy stood outside the records room.

This is it.

He cautiously approached the door and inspected the lock. It bore a striking similarity to the one on the door to the secret library, although it was evidently much newer.

Timothy hesitated for a second, then input the password from the library. The second he finished, an alarm began blaring throughout the building.

Timothy flinched, scrambling away from the door as fast as his feet would carry him. He could hear the sounds of footsteps as Blanks and Security Officers closed in on his location.

My only chance is to get out of the Council Building before they find me, he thought. *If I can manage that, maybe I can lose them in the darkness.*

Timothy ran, even faster than he had run during The Race. He was almost to the door when a pair of guards stepped out from the shadows and blocked his path.

He kept running.

The guards' eyes widened when they realized he wasn't going to stop, but they stood their ground. Seconds later, Timothy collided with them, and they all fell to the floor in a heap. Before the guards could react, Timothy scrambled to his feet and took off, empty-handed but alive.

Chapter 14

I t had been nearly a week since Timothy's failed attempt to raid the Council Building, and he had finally begun to relax. If the Council hadn't figured out it was him by now, they probably never would. At least, that was what Timothy thought. In truth, the Council already knew that whoever had broken in used the password for the library door. A password only two people in all of Kawts were supposed to know.

Timothy woke up and started off for the library, just like any other day. When he arrived, the door was ajar. Concerned, he hurried down the stairs and was greeted with an unpleasant surprise. The library had been ransacked. Books had been flung off their shelves and now littered the floor. Samuel was nowhere to be seen. Timothy sprinted into Samuel's office. It too was a mess. Samuel's papers had been flung everywhere, and his heavy desk had been tipped over, lying on its side by the wall. Timothy spotted a book lying amongst the rubble and picked it up. To his surprise, there was a note taped to the front. In Samuel's hurried handwriting, it read:

Timothy. The Blanks are breaking down my door even as I write this. Somehow, we've been discovered. They will come for you next. It's too late for me, but you still have a chance. The drawer in my desk has a false bottom. Inside is a resistance radio beacon. Take it with you. I've already activated it. Gearwire will see the signal and come get you. Be careful.

Timothy stood stock still for a moment, tears pooling in his eyes. His mourning was soon interrupted, however, by the sound of Blanks marching down the library stairs. His pulse raced as he realized the Council must have had someone watching the library. He quickly crossed over to the ruined desk and removed the radio beacon.

As the sounds of the Blanks' boots grew louder, Timothy realized he was cornered. The Blanks had completely surrounded the entrance to the library, and the single window in Samuel's office was too high for him to reach.

Maybe I can hide behind the bookshelves until Gearwire gets here, Timothy thought. His plan was shattered seconds later when he heard the Blanks approaching the office. He looked around desperately for somewhere to hide, but the ruined room offered no cover. Thinking fast, he shoved the desk up against the smashed door. It would buy him time, but not much.

Timothy wracked his brain for a solution, testing one idea after another in his mind. Finally, the solution dawned on him.

The window. If I stand on something, I just might be able to reach it. His heart pounding, he dragged Samuel's chair underneath the window. He scrambled up it, but the window was still just out of reach. The desk in front of the door lurched forward a couple more inches. The Blanks were forcing their way through.

Timothy glanced behind him, steeling himself for what he was about to do. He leapt for the window, barely managing to catch the edge of the windowsill and pull himself up. He shimmied through the opening just as the door swung open, then dropped to the ground and took off running, dashing through the streets of Kawts to the place where the cart lay hidden.

Timothy pulled the cart out of the brush and set the radio beacon inside it, piling branches on top of it. After Maurice's disappearance, he had devised an escape plan, something he was grateful for now. He shrugged on the old hooded cloak he had 'borrowed' from his father's closet. Then he hunched over and picked up the handles of the cart, dragging it toward the edge of town.

For a while, his disguise worked. He passed Blank after Blank, and none of them paid him any attention.

Once, he was nearly caught. As he crossed Franklin Plaza, he almost ran into Charles, his former classmate who now worked for the Kawts Security Force. It only took a single glance for Timothy to know that Charles had recognized him. Timothy saw him stiffen as he passed by. The conflict on his face was clear, torn between doing his job and sparing an old friend. Finally, he turned away, pretending not to have noticed.

Volker, however, was more suspicious.

"What are you doing here?"

"I'm delivering firewood to the stores near here, sir," Timothy answered gruffly, trying to disguise his voice. "I'm just an old firewood peddler."

"Then what's *this* for?" Volker asked, pointing at the sail and mast on the cart.

"It's an umbrella," Timothy replied, thinking fast. "It - um - protects the wood from the sun."

"That's the most ridiculous thing I've ever heard," Volker said, his eyes narrowing. "Wood grows outside. It doesn't need sun protection."

"But that's why my firewood is such high quality, sir," Timothy bluffed, desperately looking for a way out.

I need to get out of here before Volker asks any more questions. He turned to leave, but Volker grabbed his arm. Timothy spun around to face him, his hood falling from his head.

"It's him!" Volker shouted, his suspicions confirmed. Timothy twisted free of Volker's grip and ran, dragging the cart behind him. He had only made it a few blocks before he was yanked away onto a narrow side street. Timothy whirled around to face his new assailants, hands balled into fists.

They were a strange-looking bunch. One had a thick black beard and a hat and trench coat that completely concealed his face. Another one, a short, stocky man, had his arm encased in a battered green cylinder. Yet another one wore an orange mask over his eyes, a large red maple leaf emblazoned on his chest. Also present were the two blue-clad figures from the raids.

They're Gearwire's men! Timothy realized, lowering his hands.

Confusion quickly replaced his relief, however, when a sixth man ran out of the alley onto the main road where the Blanks were waiting. The leaf man and the bearded man ran after him, but Timothy hardly noticed, his attention fixated on the first person who had run out. A man who looked exactly like him.

"Who- who was that?" he stammered.

"For all intents and purposes right now, he is you," one of the blue-clad figures replied. They smiled. "It looks like you'll get to see the base after all. Now come on. They'll realize they've been duped before long."

Timothy stood stock still, the figure's voice sounding very familiar. Suddenly, it clicked.

"Jewel?"

The other blue figure held a finger up to her lips. "Not so loud. We're still undercover, you know."

"But yes," Jewel answered. "It's us. Now come on." With that, the twins walked swiftly away. Timothy jogged after them, his mind full of questions. Behind him, he could hear the sounds of a battle as Gearwire's men fought off the Blanks and attack drones. The trio ran through the streets of Kawts, keeping to the side streets as much as possible.

Timothy continued to pull the cart behind him, unwilling to leave Quill's box behind, and not having time to open the secret compartment to remove it. Finally, they abandoned the side streets for a large, open square near the edge of Kawts. They were halfway across when Blanks started pouring in from all sides.

"Run!" Jewel shouted. "We'll catch up with you later!" Before she had even finished speaking, she turned and began attacking their pursuers, working in tandem with her sister to encase the first wave of Blanks in blue crystal. The next group marched onwards, apparently oblivious to what had happened to the others. The twins fought back, freezing more Blanks in their tracks. Timothy watched them for a second, impressed by how quickly and efficiently they handled the Blanks.

Then he shook his head.

I have to go. Now.

Timothy took off, leaving the twins and the Blanks behind him. He rounded a corner and was met by a swarm of Blanks coming at him from the other side.

How do they know I'm here? His eyes flickered to his wrist, and he realized the answer.

Of course! he thought, quickly removing his watch and throwing it to the ground. *They've been tracking me this entire time!*

Timothy threw some chunks of wood from the cart at the Blanks as he ran, hoping to slow down his pursuers and make the cart lighter. He looked back to try to see the Blanks who were chasing him, but they were just out of sight. They were gaining fast.

Too fast.

Timothy kept running, trying to come up with something - anything - that could help him lose his pursuers. With a flash, he remembered the sail. If the wind was strong enough, he could leave the Blanks behind in a heartbeat.

But if it isn't, I won't have a chance to slip away again.

I'm running out of time as it is, he thought grimly. Without another moment's hesitation, Timothy leapt into the cart, untying the sail as he did. The wind filled the sail and propelled the cart forward. A grin broke out across Timothy's face.

"Yes!" he shouted, thrusting his fists into the air. His joyful celebration was cut short, however, when he returned his attention to the street. It was a dead end. On either side of him were buildings. Behind him was a squadron of Blanks. Ahead of him was a bluff overhanging the river. Before Timothy could react, the cart flew off the edge like a ramp and landed with a splash in the water below.

Timothy watched in horror as the beacon flew out of the cart, knocked loose by the impact. He grabbed for it, but he wasn't fast enough. The beacon sank beneath the water, taking his hope of being found by Gearwire with it.

Chapter 15

Timothy woke up with a start. He looked around at the trees, the events of the previous day flooding back to him. The river had carried him on for what he guessed to be several miles, until finally, the current had slowed enough for him to pull the cart to shore. After landing the cart, he had dragged it away from the bank into the nearby trees, hoping that if anyone from Kawts came looking for him, they wouldn't know he had been there. Once that had been accomplished, he had collapsed into the cart and fallen asleep.

Timothy stared at the vast expanse of water in front of him, deep in thought. By now, the radio beacon was probably miles away. And even if it could be found, the odds that it was still functioning were decidedly slim. Gearwire would have no way of finding him. He was on his own.

I could always wait by the bank of the river in case Gearwire comes looking for me. But that's exactly what the Council might do, too. I need to go deeper.

"At least I still have some firewood," Timothy muttered to himself, noticing the few chunks of wood still in the cart. Slowly, he got to his feet, groaning as his stiff muscles protested. He picked up the handles of the cart and started off into the maze of trees. He was almost to the tree line when a thought struck him.

If I'm going to survive this, I'm going to need a source of water. Timothy glanced back at the Kawts River. For a long moment, he stared at the water uneasily. The Council had claimed that the water had been poisoned. They had proven to be untrustworthy, but he still couldn't help but hesitate.

It's one thing to say that the Council is full of liars, but it's quite another to risk your life to test that theory.

Timothy looked around, hoping to see some other water source conveniently located nearby. There was none. He took a deep breath to calm himself and took a sip of the water. Then he waited, half-expecting to drop dead at any moment. When fifteen minutes passed with no sign of poisoning, he breathed a sigh of relief. The water was fine. But now a fresh problem revealed itself - if he was going to leave the river, he would need to bring water with him until he found another source.

Timothy stared at the cart, doing a mental inventory of all the supplies available to him. After a long moment, he removed the sail from the cart and dunked it in the river, allowing the water to soak into the material. Then he bundled the soaking piece of cloth into the cart.

It's not an ideal solution, but the sail should retain the water for a little while at least, he thought, inspecting his handiwork. *And it's my best option right now.*

The problem of water taken care of for the moment, Timothy headed off once more into the forest, shoving through the shin-high plants. The trees were clustered closely together, making it even more difficult to drag the cart behind him over the uneven terrain. He stopped to catch his breath, looking back at the cart. For a moment, he considered leaving it behind, but he quickly discarded the notion.

If I lose the cart, I lose my only source of water. And shelter.

He waited for a moment longer, then picked up the handles of the cart, dragging it through potholes and mud patches, even as his feet and legs were scratched by errant sticks and swarms of biting insects. He stopped only occasionally for a quick sip of water from the sodden sail. But by the end of the day, the water in the sheet was all but gone, and Timothy was again faced with the problem of how he was going to find food and water.

He slowed to a stop, shoving down the fear and panic that threatened to well up within him. He released the handles of the cart and wiped the sweat from his forehead.

It seems like I have two options, he thought, scanning the surrounding forest. *Do I keep going and hope I find food and water somewhere, or do I turn back into the waiting arms of the Council?*

He scanned the forest again, hoping to find something that would help him make up his mind. But the forest was devoid of any signs of food or water, unless he was willing to risk eating some of the shrub-like plants and weeds that made up the underbrush. His chances of survival were slim if he kept going.

Not that they're any less slim than if I go back, he thought grimly. *I'm pretty much doomed no matter what I do.*

As he pondered the direness of the situation, a glimmer of hope presented itself.

There is one other thing I could try, he realized. *If Samuel was right about the Bible, maybe God will help me.*

Not that it did Samuel any good.

Tears welled in his eyes as he remembered the last words of his deceased mentor. His grief overwhelmed him, and he felt numb, unable to move. Tears rolled down his cheeks, splattering onto the leaves below.

He stayed that way for a long time, mourning Samuel's death. After a while, his grief hardened into anger. Anger towards Kawts, anger towards the Council, anger at Gearwire for not arriving sooner, and even anger at himself.

The Council never would have come for us if I hadn't ignored Samuel's warning about exposing them.

It took Timothy several minutes to get his breathing under control, stifling his tears. He shoved aside all emotions except for his determination to survive. To make sure that Samuel and Quill and Maurice's legacies lived on. Leaving the cart a little ways behind him, Timothy moved into a gap in the trees where he could see the sky.

"Uhh... Hello," he said, craning his neck upwards. "I don't know if anyone's there, but if there is, could I maybe have some help?" he said, wincing at how awkward he sounded. "I'm not really sure what I'm supposed to do now. Is there a way you could tell me which way I should go so I won't die..." Timothy trailed off, watching the sky for some sort of sign. Nothing happened. He remained there for several minutes before finally giving up and going back to the cart.

"Yeah. That's what I thought," he muttered to himself. "Looks like I'm going to have to rely on my own devices to make it out of here alive." He glanced at the cart and the bone-dry sail, then up at the sky, judging how much daylight he had left. He squinted, wagering the distance he could travel at night against the chance of missing a potential food source in the darkness.

Finally, he sighed and picked up the handles, dragging the cart into the little clearing. He spent the night tossing and turning inside of the cart, only a thin barrier of leaves between him and the hard wooden planks.

* * *

By the time morning arrived, Timothy's body ached, but his mind was clear. He would continue on his current path for another day or so. If he didn't find anything by then, he would have no choice but to turn back. With luck, only Gearwire and his agents would still be searching.

With this goal in mind, he resumed his journey, his muscles screaming in protest. As the day dragged on with no signs of food or water, he grew more and more anxious, panic rising within him. More than once, he wondered whether he would die of thirst or hunger first. Each time, he pushed the thoughts aside, refusing to think about what might happen to him if he failed.

By the end of the day, however, he was no better off than he had been the previous morning. He spent another uncomfortable night sleeping in the cart, then resumed his journey once more. He continued on through the silent forest until midday, with no indication that his luck had changed. Hunger gnawed at him, and his mouth was dry. Finally, he gave up and sat down on the ground. A faint sound reached his ears, and he frowned, trying to place it. The realization struck him like a bolt of lightning, and he sprang to his feet.

It was the sound of running water.

Leaving the cart behind him, Timothy struggled through the densely packed plants for a couple more feet into a gap in the trees. There, laid out in front of him, was a narrow stream, likely a branch-off of the Kawts River. A smile broke out across his cracked lips and he ran to the edge of the stream, the crystal-clear water soothing his parched mouth and throat.

Timothy sighed contentedly, letting the water run down his face. Then, his thirst satisfied for the moment, he shoved his way back to the cart and hauled it over to the water. He took another grateful drink as he plotted his next move.

After examining the plants along the sides of the stream, Timothy elected to follow the river deeper into the forest in hopes of finding food. For a moment, he was tempted to stay right where he was, but the growling in his stomach forced him to dismiss the notion. The spot was good, but the lack of food meant that he couldn't survive there long-term. He allowed himself to rest for an hour, then he continued on his journey, discovering with relief that the vegetation was less dense on the banks of the river, making travel significantly easier.

* * *

Seventeen days later, Timothy was still doggedly following the little stream. He still hadn't found anything to eat, weakening him and slowing his pace to a crawl. If not for an old animal trail he had found several days earlier, he doubted whether he would even have been able to keep moving forwards. Hunger gnawed at him, even as his fear of starvation gnawed at his mind. He was no longer expecting that he would make it out alive, continuing only through sheer willpower. In his desperation, he called out to God several times, his doubts about his existence being overcome by the direness of his situation.

I guess I'll find out the truth soon enough, he thought morosely as he prayed one last time for deliverance. Finally, overcome by hunger, disappointment, and exhaustion, he stumbled into a large clearing and passed out beneath a tree.

* * *

Timothy woke up a few hours later, even hungrier than before. His situation wasn't any better than it was when he had gone to sleep, and he felt he could barely muster the energy to sit up. So he just closed his eyes, wondering how much longer it would take before he starved to death. Something bounced off of his foot, and Timothy glared at it, as if the small red sphere was the cause of his troubles.

In the midst of his hunger and self-pity, it took him a while to realize what had landed on his foot. When he did, he looked up at the leaves above him, realizing for the first time what kind of tree he was under.

Similar reddish spheres hung in the branches, and Timothy recognized it from one of the books he had read from the secret library.

This is an apple tree, he realized, his hope returning. According to the book he had read, its wood was good for carving, but what Timothy was most concerned about was its fruit, which was supposed to be edible. With the last remnants of his strength, Timothy pulled himself up into the tree and dropped some apples down into the cart. Then he half slid, half fell to the ground, landing hard on his side. Picking himself up, he bit into one of the apples.

The sweetness took him by surprise. The flavor was unlike any he had ever experienced, putting even pink glop to shame. The bitter aftertaste only heightened the impression.

I'm not going to starve after all, he thought, a smile breaking out across his face. It took every ounce of his willpower not to immediately devour the remaining apples, but he forced himself to go slowly, recalling from a different book the effects of an excess of food after a long time of near-starvation.

Once he had eaten his fill of apples, Timothy fell asleep once more. For the next several days, he repeated this process, slowly regaining his strength. By the fourth day, Timothy felt he had recovered sufficiently to explore the clearing. There were apples on a couple of other trees as well, interspersed with the tall oaks, bushy maples, and spreading hornbeams that dotted the nearby forest. Sunlight shone into the clearing through the gap in the leaf cover, illuminating the grassy carpet that covered the forest floor.

The more Timothy looked at the space, the more convinced he became that this was the perfect place for him to set up a permanent camp. It had food, water, plenty of shelter, and it was quite a distance away from the Kawts River. For the first time in nearly a month, Timothy was hopeful that he would survive.

Chapter 16

Once he had recovered from his near starvation, Timothy set to work building a shelter. Ever since he left Kawts, he'd had to make do by sleeping in or under the cart, but this form of shelter would be inadequate if it rained or snowed, offering him no protection against the weather. After inspecting several of the trees in the clearing, he finally selected one of the largest oak trees to be the foundation of his new residence.

Timothy searched the nearby trees for dead branches and fallen boughs, which he dragged into the clearing and sorted by size. He selected the four largest and arranged them in a square at the base of the tree before binding them together with some of the rope-like plants common to the area. He tied one corner to the tree trunk to act as a support beam for the structure.

Now comes the tricky part, Timothy thought as he took a step back. *How do I build the walls?* He scanned the clearing for anything he could use, his eyes finally landing on the cart. A flash of inspiration struck him, and he quickly found three other long branches, securing them to the other three corners, perpendicular to the ground.

After this, he removed his former sail from the cart and draped it over the upright branches. Using more of the rope-like plants, he tied down the corners of the sail to the branches. After bracing the upright branches with some smaller bits of wood, Timothy stepped back and surveyed his handiwork.

It isn't the most durable structure, he thought, staring at the flimsy wood-framed tent he had created. *But it isn't bad for a start.*

His shelter complete for the moment, he explored the area around the clearing, hoping to find some additional source of food or some useful plant. For the next several hours, he wandered through the forest, making sure to keep the river in sight at all times. After searching for a while without finding anything of interest, Timothy finally turned back. He had almost reached his camp when he heard a great crash in front of him. He ran the rest of the way back, arriving just in time to see a bearlike creature disappear into the brush.

The house Timothy had only just finished building was in shambles, the jagged ends of broken sticks poking out through the sagging fabric, many of them bearing teeth marks. Timothy felt his blood run cold.

Whatever that thing is, it's dangerous. He examined the wreckage of his shelter. *It seemed pretty big. And strong. And it must have some pretty sharp teeth and claws.* He shuddered.

And it's still out there.

With this fear gnawing at him, Timothy slowly began to rebuild his shelter.

"I'm going to need something more durable than cloth this time," he muttered to himself. "I need wood. But where would I get the boards?"

He paced the clearing, searching for anything he could use. As he passed the pile of sticks and branches he had gathered earlier that day, an idea struck him. He grabbed a handful of the smaller, more flexible sticks and intertwined them, weaving them together to create a small piece of wooden mesh. By the time night fell, Timothy had created a chunk big enough to cover the top of the cart. He laid down inside it and dragged the section of his new wall into place over top of him. Protected for the night, he soon settled into a worried slumber.

* * *

Timothy woke up the next morning to the sunlight streaming through the gaps in the piece of wall above him. He pushed the wall off of the cart, and sat up, groaning as he stretched his cramped legs.

I've got to get this house built soon, he thought. *I'm not sure how much longer I can stand sleeping in the cart.* He cracked his neck, wincing a little at the sound. Then he slowly turned to look out over the clearing, relieved to find no signs of the creature's return.

As he munched on an apple for breakfast, Timothy resumed the task of rebuilding his house. By noon, he had finished two of the four walls and had started on the third. He took a break to take a drink from the river and to rest his aching fingers.

As he stared at the gently flowing water, his mind began to wander. He thought about Samuel and the Council and the books from the secret library. There had been several novels among them about resourceful castaways, and Timothy tried his hardest to remember everything he could about what they had done in order to survive. His thoughts drifted, and before long, he was thinking about beavers. He shook his head, annoyed with himself for getting sidetracked. Then he stopped, a new idea striking him.

When building their dams, beavers use mud to hold the sticks together, Timothy recalled, scooping some mud out of the bottom of the river and spreading it over the surface of the walls he had already completed. *The mud helps to cement the sticks together.* He went back to the river, returning with another handful of mud.

It took him nearly half an hour to get enough mud to cover all the walls he had finished. He left the mud-covered walls out in the sun to harden as he continued his work on the other two. By the time night fell, his fingers ached, and he had yet to connect the walls into a solid structure.

Looks like it'll be another night in the cart, he thought with a sigh as the sun dipped below the horizon. He climbed into the cart and pulled one of the newly completed walls over him. Despite his discomfort, he fell asleep within minutes.

* * *

When morning came, Timothy resumed his task once more. He laid out all four walls next to each other, puzzling over how to attach them.

"The creature could probably still get in if it was determined enough," he muttered to himself, inspecting his work.

He glanced up at the tree that had been the support for his original shelter.

"I wonder..." He trailed off, leaving the walls behind and climbing up the tree. A few meters off the ground, he found what he was looking for.

There's only one problem, Timothy thought, chewing on his lower lip as he inspected the branches. *To build a house in a tree, you need a floor. Twigs and branches might be okay for the walls, but I wouldn't trust them to hold up as a floor.*

As Timothy pondered the question, his eyes came to rest on the cart. His eyes widened as the solution occurred to him. He ran over to the cart, collecting several wedge-shaped pieces of wood on his way. After several minutes of struggle, Timothy pried up the boards that made up the cart's false bottom. The false floor was still mostly intact, but as an added precaution, Timothy bound the boards together with the rope that had once held the sail to the cart.

Then he began the trip up the tree, lugging the floor behind him. Under normal circumstances, he could have made the climb in under a minute, but it was impossible for him to even approach that speed while dragging a sizeable chunk of wood behind him. In the end, it took him several hours to get his entire shelter up the tree. Once that was complete, though, it only took a few minutes longer to anchor the pieces into place.

Now that his shelter was complete and hopefully beast-proof, Timothy could finally relax. Tomorrow he could worry about what to do about his exile from Kawts, but for now, he was content to simply admire his new dwelling and give his aching muscles a rest.

I won't be sleeping in that cramped old cart tonight, Timothy thought with a smile as he gazed up at the sky.

Chapter 17

The next morning, Timothy awoke to see that the creature had returned while he had been asleep. Claw marks were gouged into the trees and the walls of his house.

"Apparently, it can climb," he said to the trees around him, feeling more than a little concerned. "Good to know."

The cart lay on its side a few yards away from the base of the tree where Timothy had placed it, as if it had been batted aside by a large paw. A feeling of dread came over him as he saw once again what the creature was capable of. While a part of him was pleased that his shelter had held up, Timothy suspected that this would not be the last he saw of the beast.

I need some way to defend myself against that thing if it ever comes after me.

After checking to make sure the beast was no longer lurking nearby, Timothy climbed down from his house and set about righting his campsite. Once that task was complete, he searched the pile of leftover sticks for a fairly large, smooth branch. Several of the books in the secret library featured warriors who fought using a wooden staff, and it seemed to be the best way for him to defend himself if the beast should try to attack him. After finding a suitable branch, Timothy built another small section of wall and propped it up against a tree, using it as a target to teach himself how to use his new weapon.

* * *

For several weeks, Timothy's life continued in this manner. Every morning, he woke up, gathered some food, and then practiced with the staff, until using the weapon became almost instinctual. Some mornings, he would see evidence that the beast had returned, but for the most part, the creature left the campsite alone.

After a couple of weeks, however, Timothy realized that he would soon have to start making preparations for winter, when the apples would all be gone. It didn't take him long to see that his best option would be to teach himself to hunt.

His first several attempts were unsuccessful, his prey bolting before he got close enough to use his staff. So Timothy forced himself to move slower. Quieter. He analyzed each failed attempt to see exactly what he had done wrong. After nearly a month, he found with pleasure that the animals hardly noticed his approaches now. Not long afterward, he made his first kill, clubbing an unsuspecting bird with a rock before it could realize he was there.

He brought it back to his campsite and did his best to pluck and cook it. His first attempt ended poorly, the outside a burnt husk, while the inside remained mostly raw. It took him another few weeks to master cooking, at least to a level where he wasn't in danger of giving himself food poisoning every time he had a meal. He started cooking apples too, and was pleasantly surprised to find that it made them even sweeter.

He began storing extra dried meat beneath his house, hoping to create a stockpile should anything prevent him from going out and looking for food during the winter. But even as he began these preparations, his thoughts wandered more and more frequently to the situation in Kawts.

I made it out alive, but how many others are still trapped by their own ignorance? Or by the Blanks? There's no way that the Council is still looking for me. They've probably forgotten I even exist by now.

As time wore on, Timothy resolved to find his way back to Kawts. *I have Quill's notes. And that book Gearwire gave me. I can show them that the Council is not what they seem to be. If everyone joins forces, the Council wouldn't be able to stop us.*

With this goal in mind, he set off, following the river in what he hoped was the direction of Kawts. He had been walking for several hours when he saw them.

Footprints. Footprints that exactly matched the ones sometimes left behind at his campsite.

The beast has been here, Timothy realized.

Recently, he added, examining the tracks closer. Silently, he crept onwards, completely invisible unless you knew exactly where to look.

He hadn't gone far before he saw the beast and got his first good look at the creature that had terrorized his campsite since he'd first arrived. It was a greyish color, and had a large, black-and-white striped tail. There were patches of black fur around its eyes. It was huge, nearly the size of a bear.

Timothy crept closer, not making even the slightest noise as he approached the creature. So far, it hadn't noticed him. Before long, he was within arm's reach of its tail. He readied his staff and leapt onto the beast's back, intending to knock it unconscious with a blow to the back of its head.

The beast immediately began thrashing about, trying to throw Timothy off. Timothy only barely managed to hold on as he climbed up the creature's back. He released his grip on the creature's fur and was about to strike when the creature bucked again, sending him tumbling over its head. He landed hard on the ground, a piece of dried meat falling from his pocket.

As he lay there, trying desperately to catch his breath, the creature slowly approached him. Timothy reached for his staff, but it had flown into the brush when he fell.

This is it, he thought, tensing up as he waited to be torn to shreds by the creature. Several seconds passed, and still nothing happened. Timothy opened his eyes to see that the creature had stopped only a few feet away. Instead of attacking, it was sniffing at the food he had dropped. Suddenly, it snatched up the little strip of meat and devoured it.

Timothy stared at it in shock. Then he slowly reached into his pocket and pulled out an apple, holding it out to the creature. The creature sniffed at it suspiciously, then gobbled it up.

Timothy sighed with relief, doing everything in his power to avoid breaking out into laughter.

I wonder, he mused as he watched the creature snuffling around for more food. *Would it be possible to tame it? Having a giant, sharp-clawed creature on my side might come in handy when I go back to Kawts.*

Making up his mind to try, Timothy started back to his campsite, occasionally dropping bits of food behind him to get the creature to follow.

Once he arrived back at his camp, he quickly gathered a large pile of apples in the center of the clearing. The beast wandered over to it and began to eat. Knowing he didn't have much time, Timothy retrieved the leftover rope from the rigging of the cart and tied it to a couple of nearby trees. Then, holding the other end, he carefully approached the creature.

The creature, oblivious to everything but its meal, took no notice of him. Before it realized what was happening, Timothy tied the rope around it, tethering it to the trees. The creature thrashed about wildly, but the ropes held firm. Eventually, it gave up and fell asleep. Timothy breathed a sigh of relief.

"Step one, complete," he said to himself. "Now I just have to tame it."

* * *

The next morning, Timothy walked over to the trees to check on the creature. It growled as he approached, an apple in his outstretched hand. Suddenly, the creature reached out and batted him aside with one of its paws. Taken by surprise, Timothy flew through the air, slamming into a nearby tree. He groaned and got to his feet, gasping for air. He glared at the creature, which had returned to its previous position, munching happily on the apple. Timothy shook his head at the beast.

"This is going to be harder than I thought," he muttered as he gingerly rubbed his bruised side.

For many days afterward, this scene repeated itself. Every morning, Timothy brought the creature an apple. And every morning, the creature would send him flying across the clearing before enjoying its breakfast. Finally, Timothy decided that the creature couldn't be tamed, and that he might as well just release it back into the forest.

With great disappointment, he started to untie the knot that bound the creature to the tree. It had grown tight through the creature's wild thrashing, and it was proving to be a much more difficult task than he'd imagined. The knot was only halfway undone when a pack of wolves slunk into the clearing, creeping towards Timothy's food reserves. Leaving the creature tied, Timothy grabbed his staff and ran after them, trying to shoo them away.

The wolves, however, paid no attention to him, fully focused on the food. Hoping to scare them off, Timothy swung his staff at the head of their leader. The staff collided with the wolf with a sickening thud. The wolf staggered backwards, dazed. The rest of the pack, however, did not. They turned on Timothy, flying at him from all directions. Timothy shouted with pain and surprise as the wolves' claws dug into him. He swung his staff desperately, but for each wolf he batted away, two more seemed to take its place.

Fear filled him as he realized that his odds of survival were minimal. He resigned himself to death by the wolves, determined to go down fighting. Suddenly, he felt himself knocked to the ground as something ran past him. The wolves all scattered, giving him a much-needed reprieve. He quickly got back up, only to see the grey creature attacking the wolves, batting them aside like it had done to Timothy many times before. It only took a few minutes of this before the wolves decided they didn't want Timothy's food so badly after all. They retreated into the forest, vanishing as quickly as they came.

Timothy stared after them in shock. Slowly, he turned toward the creature, half expecting it to turn on him next. To his surprise, the creature limped over to him and nuzzled him with its snout. Then its leg buckled, and for the first time, Timothy noticed the massive gash that ran along the creature's side. Quickly, he removed his shirt and pressed it against the creature's wound, sealing it off. Long minutes passed as Timothy held the makeshift bandage to the creature's side. The creature did not object, seeming to understand that Timothy was acting in its best interest. A few hours passed, and the wound seemed to be closed. Only then did Timothy feel confident that the creature was going to be okay.

"Now that we're friends, you need a name," he said to the creature, stroking its snout. "How about Snipps?" he suggested.

The creature stared at him inquisitively, as if questioning his judgement.

"It'll be fine," Timothy assured it. "You'll get used to it."

The creature made a chuffing noise that sounded suspiciously like it was laughing.

Timothy narrowed his eyes. "This conversation is over," he told it. "Your name is Snipps."

* * *

In the days and weeks that followed, Snipps slowly recovered from her wounds from the fight with the wolves. The grey creature seemed to be grateful for Timothy's help and seemed to constantly be trying to return the favor. Timothy soon discovered that Snipps excelled at collecting apples, although he quickly learned that he had to keep a close eye on her to make sure she didn't eat them all before he arrived to carry them back to the house.

After a few trials, he had given Snipps the freedom to roam about, satisfied that she would return. Where exactly she went, he never knew, but she often brought back useful things. Sometimes she brought back fish, which Timothy did his best to cook over a fire. Other times, she would only bring back oddly shaped sticks, something the creature seemed to have a strange obsession with.

It was during this time that Timothy began trying to construct a saddle for the creature. He spent several days weaving together twigs to form a rudimentary seat to go on the creature's back. After his first attempt to ride it, however, he was left sitting on a tree stump with nothing more to show for his efforts than a tangled mass of broken sticks and a few fresh bruises. With an exasperated sigh, he threw the decimated saddle into the underbrush. Snipps approached him slowly, nudging his hand with her snout.

"Would you mind explaining why you did that?"

Snipps looked at him innocently.

"You know what I mean," Timothy said, pointing to where he had thrown the saddle. "You intentionally went and broke it. I watched you. You can't deny it."

Snipps chuffed happily, and Timothy laughed. "All right. I guess it probably wasn't the most comfortable thing in the world. But what else do you want me to do?"

Snipps chuffed again, sticking her head underneath Timothy's arm. Timothy scratched behind her ears absently.

"There's not much I can use for a saddle aside from sticks," he said. "Not that I know how to construct a proper saddle, anyway." He was silent for a moment, thinking through the situation. "I guess I could try bareback riding," he said at last.

Slowly, he stood up on the stump and jumped onto Snipps' back. Four seconds later, he was lying on his own back in a patch of grass.

"We'll have to work on that," he wheezed, struggling to catch his breath.

In the end, it took Snipps several weeks to get accustomed to the feeling of having a rider. But nothing could match Timothy's exhilaration when he found he could steer the huge creature whichever way he wanted. Before long, his life settled into a pattern as he and Snipps explored the area around the camp. For a while, everything seemed perfect. But unbeknownst to Timothy, something would soon happen that would throw him once more into the fight against the Council.

Chapter 18

Timothy was patrolling the nearby woods with Snipps one afternoon when he first heard the voices. Intrigued, he slid off of Snipps' back.

"Stay here," he whispered as he set off alone towards the sound. He hadn't gone far before he came across their tracks - a group of three had recently passed through the area.

Silently, he crept through the forest until he reached a secluded area further up the path. He climbed up a nearby tree and waited. The voices grew louder as the travelers drew closer. Two of them were doing most of the talking, speaking in a foreign dialect. The voices came to rest underneath him, and Timothy knew that if he looked between the leaves, he would see them.

He shifted around to get a better angle when the third person spoke. In his shock, Timothy almost fell out of the tree. It was a voice he had heard only once, but it was one that he would never forget.

Gearwire.

The question is, are the other two his companions or his captors? he thought, cautiously peeking through the leaves at the small group below.

Gearwire stood in the middle of the group, his face unreadable. The two people flanking him were definitely not from Kawts.

I'm not sure where *they're from,* Timothy thought, squinting at the pair. Both appeared to be humans, but they were both covered from head to toe in dust-yellow scales. One had porcupine-like quills growing from his back. The other had a shell that resembled a beetle's. Both were armed.

Are they working for the Council? Maybe they're Blanks without their masks. Or are they allies of Gearwire from beyond Kawts?

"Only one way to find out," he muttered. He jumped down from the tree and landed softly in front of the group, readying his staff as he did so. All three of the travelers looked up, startled. The man who resembled a beetle drew his sword. The one with the quills drew his bow, one of his own quills serving as the arrow. Timothy gulped.

Perhaps that wasn't the best idea.

"Timothy?" Gearwire said, the first to get over his shock. "Idalbo. Adalbo. Put your weapons away. He's a friend." The man with the quills complied at once, but his companion hesitated.

"Are you sure? If his motives really are innocent, why was he following us?"

"The Captain knows what he's doing, Adalbo," the man with the quills said. A flicker of concern flashed across his face, and he added, "Although I'd be lying if I said I'm not wondering the same thing."

"Idalbo, Adalbo, this is Timothy. We tried to extract him and Samuel Deacon from Kawts a few months ago." Gearwire looked up at Timothy. "Timothy, this is Idalbo," he said, gesturing to the quilled man. "and this is his brother, Adalbo," he continued, pointing to the man with the beetle shell. "They're mutants from a place called Alpen. One of our allies."

Timothy nodded, filing the information away for future reference.

"Pleased to meet you," Adalbo said, giving a goofy bow. As he straightened up once more, he locked eyes with Timothy. "Although that doesn't answer my question."

Gearwire looked at Timothy expectantly.

"It's a bit of a long story," he said. "The important part is, Snipps and I were patrolling this part of the forest, and I saw you guys go by. I thought maybe you'd kidnapped Gearwire."

Adalbo laughed. It was a light, cheerful sound, and Timothy couldn't help but smile.

It's been far too long since I've heard someone laugh, he realized.

"You thought we'd kidnapped Gearwire? It's far more likely to be the other way around!"

Idalbo frowned at his brother's outburst. "You said you were with Snipps," he said, eyeing Timothy with suspicion. "Who's that? And where are they?"

Timothy's smile grew wider. "Snipps! Come here!" he called. Snipps bounded out of the trees, and Timothy swung himself up onto the creature's back. Gearwire and his companions stared at him, frozen in place.

Gearwire was the first to find his tongue. "Fascinating," he breathed. "I knew Lars did some of his early experiments on raccoons, but I've never seen one in person before." He shook his head. "This must be the Great Forest Beast the tree people always warned us about. I never guessed it was one of Dr. Lars' experiments!"

"Is it dangerous?" Idalbo asked, his bow already in his hand in case Snipps attacked.

"Don't worry," Timothy said. "Snipps isn't a threat to you."

Slowly, the brothers put their weapons away once more, although Timothy noticed that they still watched the raccoon warily.

The ensuing silence lasted several uncomfortable seconds before Gearwire cleared his throat. "It appears you've been rather busy since we lost track of you. I'm glad to see you're still alive." He checked a dial on his robotic legs. "We're in the middle of an important mission right now, so we're in a bit of a hurry. But if you're willing to tag along, we can bring you back to the base with us once we're finished."

"That would be great," Timothy said, lowering his staff. "Where are you guys going?"

"We're headed to the village of the tree people. They sent us an urgent message that they said was of great importance."

"Speaking of which, Prime Minister Deeproot will be getting worried if we don't show up soon," Idalbo said. "We'd better keep moving."

They walked on through the forest, Timothy telling Gearwire everything that had happened to him since the day he had left Kawts. They hadn't gone far before they began to see large, one-room houses perched in the trees, connected to each other by a network of rope bridges. Only a handful of them had staircases, which spiraled around the trunks of the trees and reached all the way up to the buildings themselves. The remaining buildings had only rope ladders, most of which abruptly disappeared as the travelers drew closer.

If not for this, the houses would have seemed abandoned, although Timothy caught occasional glimpses of people watching them from the doorways. He noted with surprise that their skin was green and leaf-like. Following Timothy's gaze, Gearwire quickly deduced what he was wondering.

"It's genetic manipulation," he explained. "After the Robot War, food was scarce, so a scientist named Lars Becker used genes from a plant to allow a group of humans to photosynthesize. The tree people are their descendants."

Timothy nodded hesitantly, pretending that he had understood Gearwire's explanation. The group continued on through the forest, the few tree people they encountered fleeing at the sight of Snipps. Eventually, they reached the center of the treetop village, where a magnificent palace intertwined with a massive, gnarled, old tree.

The palace had been constructed primarily of lightly colored logs, creating clusters of octagonal towers that peeked out through gaps in the leaves. In several places, the branches of the tree seemed to have been built directly into the towers, making it difficult to determine where nature left off and where man had begun. Strips of pinkish alder wood ran along the edges of the building, accenting the contours of the palace walls. From the lofty arched entrance, a grand staircase gradually twisted toward the ground, connecting the uppermost reaches of the sprawling tree to the forest floor.

In front of this staircase stood the prime minister of the tree people, awaiting their arrival. He was about average height and wore a plain brown tunic, a light grey cape the only outward marker of his lofty position. His hair was short and forest green, matching his goatee. A crooked, long-bladed dagger hung at his side. His green, leaf-like skin paled when he saw Snipps, but he stood his ground.

"Good afternoon, Cedar," Gearwire said with a nod. "We received your message. What happened?"

At Gearwire's casual greeting, Prime Minister Deeproot appeared to find his tongue. "How does your companion ride the Great Forest Beast? How has it not torn him apart?"

"It sounds like he's tamed it," Gearwire said. "He calls it Snipps."

Cedar Deeproot turned to Timothy. "On behalf of all the tree people, I extend our thanks to you, sir. This creature has menaced our lands for many years."

Timothy glanced over toward Gearwire, not knowing how to respond. Gearwire's face remained expressionless, so Timothy simply nodded. Cedar turned back to Gearwire.

"But that's not why I called you here," he continued. He glanced around, his emerald eyes wide. "We should discuss this inside. There are too many prying ears out here." With one last look around the area, he turned and led them into the palace.

Timothy hesitated outside the doorway, reluctant to leave Snipps unattended outside. As Gearwire and Deeproot got further and further away, he made up his mind.

"Stay here until I get back, okay?" he said, looking sternly at Snipps. The giant raccoon cocked her head to one side. "Stay," Timothy repeated, and she sat down, tail twitching. Timothy turned back towards the palace, jogging to catch up with the others.

The inside of the palace was even more impressive than the outside, the walls decorated with intricate carvings depicting the history and legends of the tree people. Despite the prime minister's urgency, Timothy fell further and further behind.

Samuel would have loved this, he thought, the experience made bittersweet by the memory of his deceased mentor. He traced the lines of one of the carvings, wondering about the history behind it.

If only I had some paper and a pen, he thought wistfully, imagining himself as the self-appointed historian of the tree people. A low creaking sound drew his attention away from the carvings, and he turned to see Gearwire and Deeproot disappear behind an open door at the end of the hallway. Tearing himself away from the carvings, he hurried to catch up with them, ducking inside the room just before the door swung shut. As he looked around the room he found himself in, he was once again impressed by its beauty.

Though the walls were made of the same wood as the rest of the palace, there was no solid roof, the top of the room being covered only by a layer of overlapping leaves. The sunlight shone in through them, giving the entire room a cheerful greenish glow. Several large, open windows faced outside toward the village, offering a clear view of the entire street. In the center of the room, there was a table and chairs that appeared to be carved from the tree itself.

Deeproot gestured to the chairs. "Have a seat," he said, beginning to pace back and forth in the front of the room. Once everyone had settled in, he began his story.

"Captain," he said, addressing Gearwire. "We need your help. Our people are disappearing. Fourteen of our people have gone into the forest and vanished in the past week alone. At first, we assumed it was the work of the Forest Beast, but no longer. One of our finest warriors, Elmer Evergreen, was out in the forest on patrol when he heard cries for help. He rushed over to see one of our people being tied up and dragged out of a pit by Blanks and attack drones. Elmer fought them off and rescued the unfortunate man. What he told us revealed the answer to the mystery - the Council has been laying traps for our people and carrying them off to who knows where. I have asked you here to see if you, being our allies, can help us."

"Don't worry, Deeproot," Gearwire said. "We'll try our best to-" He cut off suddenly, listening with narrowed eyes. Then he leapt up and ran to the window. "The city is under attack!" he shouted as he turned back, unholstering his glue gun.

"There's hundreds of them - Blanks, attack drones, even Councilmen," Idalbo reported, looking out the window himself. "We need to get out of here."

Deeproot remained rooted in place. "I will not abandon my people," he said levelly.

Gearwire turned to face him. "Deeproot, believe me, I understand your problem. But you need to understand that the odds are against us here. The five of us could put up a fight for a while, but we would be overcome before long. Then there would be no hope for your people or for Kawts. The best thing we can do is to escape with as many of your citizens as we can."

"We can't just abandon our city to the Council!" Deeproot protested.

"We're not abandoning the city," Gearwire began. Then he stopped. "Alright. Technically, we are abandoning the city. But the Council is going to take the city whether you stay and fight for it or not. If you and your people are to have any chance of surviving, they need to leave now."

Deeproot sighed, knowing that Gearwire was right. "Okay," he said, his shoulders sagging. "But how are we going to get out? They have to have reached the main door of the palace by now."

"I think I can help with that," Timothy said, moving to the window and sticking his head out. "Snipps!" he called out. "Come here!" A few seconds later, the huge raccoon appeared under the window, a gap of just a few feet separating them. "Get on," he instructed, extending a hand to help the others out the window and onto Snipps' back. Once they were all safely out, Timothy jumped down himself, sitting at the front of the group. As he directed Snipps out of the city, Deeproot shouted a warning to what remained of the tree people.

"Run! Escape into the woods! Make your way to Grimshaw!" he ordered as they raced by. Upon hearing him, many of the tree people fled into the trees and quickly lost their pursuers in the dense forest. Others weren't fast enough, being captured by the Council's forces before they could escape. Only a few continued to fight, a number which was rapidly diminishing.

"Which way?" Timothy asked Gearwire, shouting to be heard over the noise.

"Straight ahead," Gearwire replied, his voice calm despite the circumstances. "The quickest way to our base is through Kawts."

Snipps broke into a run, carrying them at a rapid pace towards the rebel base. After just half an hour, they reached the bank of the Kawts River. Timothy stared at the city in surprise, realizing for the first time how close his little clearing had been to Kawts. As they reached the water, Snipps stopped short.

"Which way now?" Timothy asked, hearing the buzz of attack drones in the distance, a sound that grew louder with every passing second.

"We'll have to swim," Gearwire said. "You and your raccoon can swim, right?"

Timothy nodded slowly. He had gone swimming once or twice

before the river had been declared poisoned. He had not, however, been exceptionally good at it even then.

"What about the current?" he asked, remembering how quickly the cart had been swept away from Kawts.

"Idalbo will shoot us a guideline," Gearwire said, handing Idalbo a length of rope that he withdrew from a compartment in his robotic legs.

Idalbo quickly tied one end of the rope to one of his quills and shot it across the river, sending it slamming into the wall of a building on the other side. He tugged on the rope experimentally, making sure it held firm. Satisfied with his work, he nodded to Gearwire.

"Alright!" Gearwire barked. "Let's move! Everybody, make sure you keep one hand on the rope at all times. If you get swept down the river, we might not find you again," he added with a look at Timothy. Then, without any further delay, he splashed into the water, pulling himself along by the rope. The others followed his example, holding on tightly to avoid being dragged downriver. As it turned out, Snipps managed the crossing the easiest, apparently a strong enough swimmer to fight the current without the use of the rope.

By the time Timothy hauled himself out of the water, tired and soaking wet, Gearwire was already on the move, quickly scouting the area while the others emerged from the river. Once everyone had reached the shore, they set off again, jogging through the center of Kawts. They had just reached Franklin Plaza, in front of the Council Building, when Blanks poured in from every direction, blocking their path.

Gearwire charged towards them, removing a cartridge of something from his belt and loading it into his gun. He fired his weapon at half a dozen Blanks in rapid succession, spraying them with great globs of sticky glue. As attack drones flew in to reinforce, he barked, "Idalbo! Adalbo! Drones at three o'clock!"

Idalbo strung his bow and fired several of his quills into the nearest attack drones. The dome-shaped drones crashed to the ground, sending up showers of sparks. The drones returned fire with the guns mounted on their undersides, but he was already gone, ducking into a side alley before reappearing somewhere else seconds later.

Adalbo unsheathed his sword and joined the fray, knocking Blanks unconscious using the hilt and the flat of the blade. The attack drones he showed no such mercy towards, cleaving through any drone that got too close.

They seem to be trying to avoid killing the Blanks, Timothy noticed, a puzzled frown crossing his face.

But why not? he thought at last. *For all I know, the Blanks still think that the Councilmen are heroes.*

Or, he added darkly, *they're being blackmailed.*

Timothy shrugged his staff free of his cloak and ran forward to help Gearwire, who was slowly being surrounded by Blanks. Snipps followed him, bowling over several Blanks in her path.

Timothy pressed onward, leaving stunned and unconscious Blanks in his wake until he reached Gearwire. Carried away by the excitement of the battle, he kept going, all the way to the top of the stairs of the Council Building. Part of him hoped to make it all the way to the Council chamber, daydreams of defeating the remaining Councilmen dancing in his head.

When he reached the top of the stairs, a Blank slowly approached him. Timothy swung his staff at it, but missed. The Blank continued on, unphased. Before Timothy could attack again, the Blank had closed the distance between them too much for him to use his staff effectively. Timothy retreated a couple of steps, hoping to gain some distance. He reached the edge of the stairs and stopped, sensing the drop behind him.

Suddenly, the Blank lunged at him, sending them both rolling down the marble stairs. Timothy's staff clattered to the pavement, along with the Blank's mask, knocked loose during the fall. Timothy reached out to find his staff and resume his attack when he stopped cold. Without his mask, the Blank's face was clearly visible.

It was Quill.

It can't be him! Timothy thought, his mind racing. *Quill is dead!*

Yet even as he had the thought, he knew that his first impulse had been correct. The Blank's messy brown hair and blue eyes were unmistakable. Quill stood up, his face devoid of any emotion. He lifted his club above his head, about to deal a finishing blow.

Timothy felt a hand on his collar, dragging him clear of the attack. He turned to see Idalbo, the quilled mutant. As Idalbo helped him to his feet, he spoke.

"We need to get out of here. We've cleared a path through the Blanks." Seeing the pain and confusion on Timothy's face, he added, "We'll explain later!"

He dragged Timothy along through a gap in the hordes of Blanks, Timothy being in too much shock to notice. Seeing her master abandoning the battle, Snipps followed, knocking over several more Blanks on her way.

The Blanks and attack drones followed them as they fled, but soon, a dense fog rolled into the area.

Gearwire smiled softly to himself. "Perfect timing," he murmured as he and the others escaped from Kawts, slipping out over the wall before the guards realized that anything was amiss. They arrived at the rebels' base without encountering any further resistance.

Timothy was still in shock from his fight with Quill. Dimly, he was aware of the fact that he was being led into a spare bedroom in the cave that served as the rebels' base. That was the last thing he remembered before he fell asleep, physically and emotionally exhausted by the day's events.

Chapter 19

Gearwire was sitting beside his bed when he awoke. Timothy started violently when he saw him, the events of the previous day flooding back.

"I know that what happened yesterday was a lot to take in. I'm here to straighten things out," Gearwire said.

"What happened back there? How was Quill-"

Gearwire held up a hand to silence Timothy's outburst. He took a moment to collect his thoughts before he answered.

"This all started when we found Howard Kolt. He was babbling gibberish about Blanks and the Council. We tried to get him to explain what was going on, but his brain was fairly scrambled from his escape from Kawts. But I'll get to that part later," Gearwire said, looking at Timothy to make sure that he was following what he said so far.

"That was our first indication that maybe there were things about Kawts we still didn't know. By all accounts, Howard had been executed months ago. Something didn't add up. But it was Quill who finally figured out what was really going on.

"At the time, we only noticed that he was acting strangely. He grew exceedingly paranoid and refused to speak either to myself or the other agents I sent to Kawts. A few days later, after he lost The Race, we found a page that he had ripped out of his notebook in one of our information drop-off spots. That page explained his discovery."

Gearwire removed a torn piece of paper from a compartment in his robotic legs and began to read. "'...the people who have disappeared in Kawts, including the ones that lost The Race, have been turned into Blanks somehow. The 'B' on Howard's file - what else could it stand for other than Blank? When I was in the Council Building, I stumbled upon the blueprints of a machine, which I have sketched below. I also found a dispatch from Ethos to Taranis, ordering him to take the losers of The Race to the hospital. On the back of the page was a map of the hospital, an 'x' overtop of a secret room.'"

Gearwire paused. "Underneath this entry, Quill had drawn a machine I knew all too well," he said, a melancholy note in his voice. "In fact, I was part of the team who built it. The notes on the drawing, though, showed that someone had altered it from its original purpose. When it was first built, it allowed humans to wirelessly control computers with their minds. Now, it allowed a computer to wirelessly control the minds of humans.

"Beneath the sketch of this device was the final entry in Quill's notes. It reads, 'My suspicions have been confirmed. I snuck into the basement of the hospital and uncovered the truth. There is no boiler down there. The noises people have heard didn't come from a machine. Instead, there is a wall of cells and a strange device that looks like a match for the blueprints I found. Hanging up on the wall were empty Blank suits. Since my arrival seemed to be unnoticed, I risked a glance inside the empty armor. The masks and helmets were filled with crisscrossing wires. I wanted to do some further investigating, but I heard footsteps coming to the secret room and I got out of there.'"

Gearwire lowered the page slowly. "After we found this message, I had a fairly good idea of what happened to Howard. Using Quill's sketch and what I remembered about the machine, I was able to rig up a device to undo most of the damage the device had done to his brain. Eventually, he was able to explain what had happened. He had indeed been turned into a Blank, as Quill had suspected. But then one day, for reasons I did not understand at the time, something caused the device's grip on him to weaken.

"In his semi-conscious state, Howard realized that he was more aware of his surroundings and fought the Blankness, refusing to let it take control of him again. Finally, with one last effort, he wrenched his mind free of its control. It was this effort that caused his mind to become scrambled. The human brain is a very fragile thing. It doesn't take much to knock it all out of whack."

Timothy opened his mouth to speak, but Gearwire cut him off. "He's doing much better now," he said. "Although he still has occasional relapses."

Timothy sat in silence, trying to make sense of it all. Hundreds of questions filled his mind, but only one of them rose to the top as the most important.

"So, Samuel…" he began hesitantly, afraid that he was wrong.

"Is probably still alive," Gearwire confirmed. "Although not everyone who goes missing gets turned into a Blank. There are a few people, among them myself and the Council members, who are immune to the device's control. Whenever the Council finds someone with this trait, they are quickly executed."

"How do you know you're immune?" Timothy asked. "You just said that you didn't know what was going on until after Quill disappeared."

"We don't know much about the traits that allow a person to resist the device's control," Gearwire said after a moment's hesitation. "But a prominent co-trait often expresses itself in an inability to distinguish between the flavor of pink glop and the others."

"I'm immune, too," Timothy realized aloud. A shudder ran through him as he suddenly remembered how he and Aksell had often discussed pink glop.

If Ethos had overheard us, they would have executed me without a second thought.

Gearwire looked slightly surprised at this, but he said nothing.

"Isn't there any way to free the Blanks?" Timothy asked, his thoughts returning to Samuel and Quill. "Howard escaped, right?"

"There is a way," Gearwire said. "Although the method is far from safe. Over the entire history of Kawts, only two people have ever escaped the Blankness. One was Howard Kolt. The other was his daughter. Our method has been tested only once, and it caused great confusion and delirium in the patient for a while. The way things stand now, the only way to free them is to shut off the machine."

"Then why doesn't someone sneak into Kawts and do it? Take out all the Blanks, and then lead your army to destroy the drones and the Council!"

"Sneaking into the secret room from the outside is much easier said than done," Gearwire said. "Three of our agents have already met their deaths trying. And even if they could get in, they would need to have a very complete knowledge of the machine in order to de-activate it without causing permanent memory loss. I'm not sure that even I remember how the machine works well enough to do that. For the time being, they're stuck."

Gearwire's words hung in the air for several moments before he abruptly stood. "Come. I'll show you around the base. It looks like you'll be living here with us for a while."

Gearwire led Timothy out of the room and into the main corridor. It was crowded and noisy, full of people going about their daily lives. Timothy was surprised by how many of them there were, his previous experiences with the rebels being limited to a small pool of a few individuals.

There's no way all these people came from Kawts, he thought, taking in the teeming mass of humanity.

"Where did they all come from?"

"Many of them are from the nomadic tribes in the area," Gearwire explained. "Or what remained of those tribes after the Council finished massacring them. Some of them are soldiers, people who served under me once in battle - a long time ago. Some are their children, people who have spent their entire lives in this cave. But quite a few of them are, in fact, from Kawts." Timothy waited for him to elaborate, but Gearwire's thoughts had already moved on.

He gestured to the crowd around them. "Some of us came here to fight the Council," he said, his blue eyes shining with determination and pride. "To avenge our fallen friends and relatives. Others came here simply to escape Kawts and to enjoy the things that are banned there, like music and science. Either way, this cave is a safe haven from the Council."

Gearwire's words triggered something in Timothy's mind, and his thoughts suddenly flew to his missing brother. If Maurice had made it out of Kawts, he might very well have come here.

"Gearwire?"

Gearwire looked over at him expectantly.

"Is my brother in this base?"

Gearwire frowned. "This cave complex is home to over 2,000 people. You're going to need to give me a little more information."

"His name's Maurice. He tried to leave Kawts several months ago with two of his friends. It was right after they put up those anti-Council posters around town."

At the mention of the posters, Timothy saw a flicker of recognition in Gearwire's eyes. "I remember getting a report from the twins about that," he said, shaking his head. "I don't think your brother ended up here." Timothy's face fell, and Gearwire added, "But I'll look into it. If he's still alive, we'll find him."

As he finished speaking, he came to a stop in front of a thick steel door reinforced with iron bars. "In the meantime, we'd better continue with the tour. This is our technology wing," he said, pulling the door open and revealing a massive dent on the inner side. Timothy eyed it warily, wondering what sort of deadly weapon could cause that kind of damage.

A man with sandy-blonde hair and a large mustache looked up from his workbench as they entered.

"Howard, this is Timothy," Gearwire said, nodding in the man's direction. "Timothy, this is Howard Kolt, our resident scientist."

"Pleased to meet you," Howard said, extending his hand. Timothy didn't notice the gesture, still fixated on the large dent in the door. Howard followed his gaze and deduced what was troubling him. "Ah. That," he said, "is from a minor mishap with my rocket propelled toaster. That's when they added the bars to the door."

Timothy turned his scrutiny to Howard. "Rocket propelled toaster?"

Howard shrugged. "It was during one of my... relapses," he said, choosing his words carefully. "I seem to invent the strangest things when my mind gets scrambled up." He grabbed an orange domino mask from the table next to him. "Like this. It's a mask that lets me telepathically control things." He allowed his words to hang in the air for a few seconds before adding, "as long as they're no bigger than a leaf. I really need to fix that bug," he muttered, staring off into space.

"You were one of the people who helped me escape from Kawts," Timothy said, recognizing the mask.

Howard nodded, his focus back on the present. "Glad to finally be properly introduced. The twins told us a lot about you."

Looks like they were trying to persuade Gearwire to trust me after all, Timothy realized, remembering how impatient he had been waiting for Gearwire's decision. It all seemed so long ago now.

"Why don't you show Timothy around the lab?" Gearwire suggested, standing near a messenger who had arrived while they were talking. "I need to take care of something quickly. I'll be back in a few minutes," he promised before hurrying out the door.

In deference to Gearwire, Howard took Timothy all over the lab, his brown eyes shining as he showed him the various gadgets lining the tables, all in varying stages of completion. Aside from the two of them, there was no one else in the room.

"Are you the only scientist here?" Timothy asked, wondering how one man could have invented so many things.

"Most of these are mine, if that's what you mean," Howard replied. "Although quite a few of them are Dr. Maddium's. There's even a few of Gearwire's creations here and there. He's pretty handy with tools himself, you know. He and Dr. Maddium built his robotic legs themselves."

He looked as though he wanted to say more, but at that moment, Gearwire re-entered the room.

"Are you ready to go?" he asked. Timothy nodded, his reluctance to leave without hearing the rest of the story overshadowed by his excitement to see the rest of the base. He was not disappointed. Gearwire led him into a massive cavern, filled with shelves upon shelves of books.

"This is our grand library," Gearwire explained. "This room contains copies of all the books we could find from before the Robot War. It could very well be the largest library left on the planet. We've managed to get our hands on quite a few books from Kawts over the years too, but not nearly as many as I would have liked."

Gearwire introduced him to the librarians and the others in the room before moving on.

I'm coming back here as soon as the tour's over, Timothy promised himself as he left the library behind.

As they approached the next room, Timothy heard a sound that he recognized from when he had visited the house church in Kawts. "Is that - music?" he asked, listening intently.

"It is," Gearwire said with a slight smile. "Yet another thing the Council has tried to destroy. Many decades ago, they tried to confiscate all musical instruments - probably after seeing the effect that the music had on Blanks. It has a way of loosening the device's control over them. We suspect it played a role in allowing Howard to escape."

Gearwire introduced him to several of the base's musicians, who were more than happy to tell Timothy all about their instruments. After a few minutes, they moved on, Gearwire being eager to finish the tour.

"Here's the chapel," Gearwire explained as they arrived outside another door. "We gather here for worship every Sunday morning at nine." He stared at Timothy, his brow furrowed in concentration. "You were one of the people I gave one of those Bibles to, right?"

Timothy nodded, and Gearwire examined him thoughtfully. "What did you think?"

"It was very… interesting," Timothy said carefully, not sure how Gearwire would react if he admitted that he had dismissed the whole thing as wishful thinking after Samuel's arrest. A flicker of sadness flashed across Gearwire's face, but he quickly concealed it.

"Well, if you have any questions, Pastor Noah or I would be happy to try to answer them," Gearwire said, peeking through the doorway to see if the chaplain was inside. Timothy felt a small stab of guilt, knowing that he had no intention of taking Gearwire up on his offer.

"It looks like Noah isn't here right now," Gearwire said. "We'll have to check back later. We'd better keep moving in the meantime."

"This here is the kitchen," Gearwire said as he led Timothy into another room. "This is where the food is made for our entire base." Timothy's lip curled in disgust, and Gearwire turned to face him. "Don't worry. It tastes much better than glop," he said with a wry smile. "We use actual ingredients to make actual food. Not that vile ooze they serve in Kawts."

Timothy smiled, looking around the room. Dozens of people hurried about, fetching ingredients and chopping up strange objects, which they promptly deposited into pots full of boiling water.

Vegetables, Timothy realized, remembering reading about them in the secret library. Slowly, he looked around again, overwhelmed by the commotion of the kitchen. Yet even through the chaos, the smell held his attention. The closest thing to it he had ever smelled had been his own attempts to cook meat. As Timothy tried to pinpoint the source of the smell, Gearwire walked up to a person in the center of the kitchen and whispered something into her ear. She left what she was doing and came over and greeted Timothy.

"Timothy, this is Madison Kolt," Gearwire said.

Timothy nodded slowly, recognizing the name.

"She is the second person to escape the Blankness," Gearwire continued. "She works here in the kitchen."

"Nice to meet you," Madison said, shaking Timothy's hand.

"Madison is also part of my crew," Gearwire said.

"Your crew?"

"We're Gearwire's top warriors and advisors," Madison explained. Timothy looked at her with a new respect. "If you don't need anything else, I should probably get back to the soup," she said.

"Don't let me keep you," Gearwire said. "We need to get going, anyway."

"We're almost done," he assured Timothy as they headed towards the next area of the base. "We only have two more stops before I let you go."

Timothy followed Gearwire through the twisting corridors of the base, finally emerging into a vast cavern. A large group of people was spread out throughout the room, practicing with their weapons on wooden dummies. Gearwire led Timothy over to the center of the room, where two men were engaged in a sword duel. Timothy recognized one of them as the man in the trench coat from his escape. On closer inspection, he realized that he also recognized the other from some of the raids on Kawts.

On seeing Gearwire's approach, the pair stepped apart and sheathed their weapons, dripping with sweat.

"Where's Henry?" Gearwire asked as they approached.

"Target practice," the trench-coated man said. "You!" he shouted to one of the rebel soldiers standing nearby. "Run and get Henry!" The man nodded and darted off, disappearing into a side cavern.

"So what do you need, boss?" the other man asked, beaming as he wiped the sweat from his forehead. His black hair was slick with perspiration.

"We've got a new recruit," Gearwire said. He turned to Timothy. "This here is the training hall. This is where all the resistance's soldiers and warriors hone their skills." He gestured to the bearded man with the trench coat. "The Mysterious Man is in charge here. He'll be your trainer if you decide you want to fight with us." He pointed to the other man. "This is the Golden Knight. Both of them are part of my crew."

As Gearwire finished speaking, a burly man approached them from the direction that the messenger had gone, the battered green cylinder on his arm still smoking. "What's going on?" he asked. His eyes settled on Timothy. "New recruit, eh?"

Gearwire nodded. "Timothy, meet Henry. He's one of my oldest crewmembers."

"I'm no older than you," Henry said with a grin, running his free hand through his ginger hair, which was streaked liberally with white.

Gearwire shook his head. "He's also our resident smart alec."

Timothy couldn't help but smile at the exchange, their banter reminding him of him and Aksell.

As Gearwire continued a conversation with the trio, Timothy contented himself by looking around the room, studying the different weapons he saw.

It looks like no one's using a staff, he noted with mild disappointment. Then he shrugged.

Not that it matters much, anyway. I have no intention of going into battle. I'm done with that sort of thing.

Chapter 20

Timothy had been living at the base for only a few days when he was awakened early in the morning by a commotion outside. He ran to the solitary window in his room and looked out onto the street.

A young man sitting atop a large animal was riding rapidly toward Gearwire's quarters. Curious, Timothy left his room, emerging onto the street below a few minutes later. He watched as the rider knocked on Gearwire's door. Gearwire opened it, looking tired, but alert. The rider dismounted and he and Gearwire disappeared into the building. Timothy waited, sensing that something big was about to happen.

A few minutes later, Gearwire emerged, apparently in a hurry. He stopped suddenly when he saw Timothy.

"Thank goodness you're here," he said. "We have a dangerous situation on our hands. I need you to bring this message to Madison Kolt," he continued, handing Timothy a scrap of paper.

"What-" Timothy started, but Gearwire cut him off.

"You have to hurry," Gearwire said. "This is a matter of life and death." Then he was gone, running off down the streets to wake the rest of his crew.

Message in hand, Timothy ran in the opposite direction. Madison would already be in the kitchen by now, he knew, helping to prepare breakfast for the base.

By the time Timothy arrived, they had already begun, the smell of freshly baked bread hanging in the air. He quickly located Madison among the other chefs and handed her the note. She brushed a strand of strawberry-blonde hair out of her eyes as she accepted the message.

"Amani tribe attacked. Meet at the edge of the cave," she murmured, a hint of fear creeping into her voice. Then, without saying a word, she crossed the room and flung open a cupboard near the floor. Timothy followed, curious. From the cupboard, she removed a folded jumpsuit. Coiled neatly on top were a pair of energy whips surrounding a small pile of ravioli-shaped grenades.

Timothy stared at the weapons, his forehead furrowed. Madison, guessing the reason for his confusion, attempted to clear it up.

"It started out as a bit of a joke," she said with a laugh. "I really enjoyed cooking, so when I joined Gearwire's crew, I modeled my weapons off of foods. Particularly pasta."

Timothy nodded slowly. Madison gave a strained smile and ran out the door. Timothy wandered back to his room, having completed his mission.

Gearwire and his crew left less than an hour later, following the horseman back to where he had left the rest of his tribe. They were gone for nearly three days, with no news making it back to the base on how they were. Timothy was beginning to feel that they should send out some sort of search party when finally, at about sunset on the third day, they returned, battered and weary. With them came about a dozen others, presumably all that remained of the Amani tribe.

* * *

The next morning, Timothy was awakened by a knock at his door. Yawning, he rolled out of bed and cracked open the door. Standing in front of him was one of Gearwire's messengers, clearly marked by his deep blue uniform. The messenger nodded sharply when he saw Timothy.

"The commander wants to see you," he said. "He said it was important."

Timothy nodded, all thoughts of sleep driven from his mind. He threw on his clothes and hurried outside, making his way to Gearwire's house, which also served as a command center for the rebellion. He was quickly shown up into the war room, a large, open space with a massive table in the center. Timothy's eyes roamed around the room, hoping he wasn't in trouble.

"Please, sit down, Timothy," Gearwire said, emerging from his office with two other men. Timothy recognized the one on his right as being one of the tribesmen who had arrived with the rest of the refugees. The man on Gearwire's left was unfamiliar, dressed in a white lab coat and sporting a tangled mass of curly grey hair.

Gearwire took a seat across the table from Timothy, the other two joining him. "I don't believe you've met Dr. Maddium," he said, gesturing to the mystery man. "He procures most of the supplies we need to sustain the rebellion. He's a good friend of mine."

Dr. Maddium reached forward to shake Timothy's hand, his eyes sharp and probing. "It's a pleasure to meet you, Timothy," he said. "I've been hearing a fair bit about your adventures recently."

Timothy nodded slowly, still not entirely sure what all this was about. "Thanks," he said, hesitantly shaking the scientist's hand.

"We have news about your brother," Gearwire said as Dr. Maddium resumed his seat.

Timothy felt his heart sink, looking at the grim-faced trio opposite him. "He's dead, isn't he?"

Gearwire shook his head. "I'm afraid it's not that simple. After we spoke last week, I looked through some of our old reports. The day those posters went up, Crystal and Jewel reported helping your brother and two others escape from Kawts. During the ensuing skirmish, they got separated from the twins, but Crystal is positive that they made it out. Until a few days ago, that's all the information we had."

He nodded to the tribesman sitting beside him, and the man nodded nervously in return.

"Right. That's where I come in, I guess. Several days ago, three travelers arrived at our camp by the names of Maurice, Ally, and Maverick. They asked for our help in fighting against the Council. Our chief-" His voice broke, and he fell silent for a moment. He took a few seconds to regain his composure, then continued. "Our chief agreed. We were preparing for the battle when the Council attacked us."

Timothy glanced between the faces of the three men opposite to him. "What happened? Where are they now?"

"We don't know," the tribesman said. "Their tent was the closest to the Council's forces. We assumed they'd been killed. But there weren't any bodies."

"You think the Council took them?"

Gearwire nodded. "It would appear so. Although it is possible that they escaped during the battle."

"Or they were killed by one of the Council's bombs," Timothy said.

Gearwire smiled sympathetically. "It is a possibility."

Timothy pushed his chair back, taking a step away from the table. "I think I need to be alone right now."

"We understand," Gearwire said. "It's a lot to take in. We'll let you know if we find anything else."

"And Timothy," Dr. Maddium called after him. "If you need someone to talk to, don't hesitate to reach out. It can be difficult dealing with things like this alone."

∗ ∗ ∗

A few days after his meeting with Gearwire, Timothy found himself in the base's library, a stack of books on a cart beside him. He looked at the label on the book in his hand, then back up at the bookshelf. Smiling to himself, he slid the book into place. He had been working at the base's library for a little over a week, quickly realizing he would go crazy sitting in his room with nothing to do all day. Fortunately, Gearwire had been more than willing to help him secure the job.

"Of course, they probably would have taken anyone at this point," Timothy muttered to himself, looking at the stack of books on the cart beside him. "The downside to having a library that people actually use is that there are a lot more books to reshelve."

He grabbed another book and started up the ladder when he heard a voice from behind him.

"Gearwire told me I could find you here."

Timothy glanced over his shoulder to see Jewel standing behind him. "Jewel! What are you doing here?" he asked, dismounting the ladder.

"Gearwire has either Crystal or I bring him an in-person report every so often. I think it makes him nervous not to be able to check in on his crewmembers face-to-face." Jewel sat down at a nearby study table, and Timothy joined her, setting the book in his hand back on the cart.

"I'm glad to see you made it out of Kawts alive."

A wry grin crossed Timothy's face. "Me too." He fell silent for a moment, then said, "How are things in Kawts? It feels like such a long time ago since I was there."

Jewel shook her head. "More of the same, mostly. The Council still sucks, and most people are still unaware of it. Although come to think of it, Ives might be starting to figure things out. He's been doing some

155

digging that the Council isn't the biggest fan of."

Timothy nodded. Ives had been one of his classmates before he had taken Maurice's place on the *Kawts Tribune*. Now that Jewel mentioned it, he suddenly realized how strange Ives' behavior had been when Timothy had invited him to help him finish up the cart. He said as much, and Jewel nodded sagely.

"Exactly. It's stuff like that. I'll have to see if Drusi knows anything about it. They're dating now, by the way."

Timothy forced a smile. "That's fun news."

His smiled faded, and he said, "How are my parents doing? Have you seen them lately?"

Jewel's face grew serious. "They're doing as well as can be expected. It was quite a shock to them when Maurice escaped, but losing you so soon afterward really hit them hard."

Timothy swallowed down the lump in his throat. "What about Maurice? Have you heard anything about him?"

Jewel shook her head. "Sorry. I don't know anything more than you do. I haven't seen him since we helped him and his friends get out of Kawts."

Timothy forced a smile. "Well, thanks for trying, anyway."

"If he's still out there, we'll find him," Jewel said, reaching across the table and putting her hand on Timothy's arm.

"It's the 'if' that I'm worried about."

"I know."

They sat in silence for a few moments longer, then Jewel stood. "Well, I just stopped in to say hello. I need to be getting back to Kawts before anyone notices I've been gone."

Timothy nodded, smiling feebly. "Right. You'd better get going." He shook his head. "It would have been nice to have longer to catch up, though."

Jewel nodded. "You know what... If you talk to Howard, he can get you a radio beacon that will communicate directly with the one Crystal and I have. Then we can talk some more once I get back to Kawts."

Timothy blinked. "Really? Gearwire's okay with that?"

Jewel's face scrunched up. "To be honest, I'm not entirely sure that Gearwire *knows*. But we do already have a direct line to Madison. We were friends before she got turned into a Blank," she explained before Timothy could ask.

"I'll have to talk to him," Timothy said. "Thanks. For everything."

Jewel smiled back at him, already halfway gone. "Don't mention it."

* * *

Timothy had been at the base for a little less than two weeks when he received a message from Gearwire, summoning him for a meeting at Gearwire's quarters. Gearwire and Cedar Deeproot were seated at a large table when he arrived, along with the rest of Gearwire's crew. Their heated discussion died away as Timothy entered. Gearwire gestured to an empty chair.

"Sit down please, Timothy," he said. "We need your help."

Chapter 21

"We're assembling a team to make contact with Cedar's people, who are currently in their hidden fortress, known as Grimshaw," Gearwire said. "We'd like you to be part of that team as your first mission. You are under no obligation to accept," he said. "You may remain here if you wish, but we hope you will consider joining us. You have skills that the rest of us lack. Your impressive fighting skills and ability to get into places undetected may be of great use in this mission. But the choice is yours."

Timothy was silent for a moment, thinking over Gearwire's offer.

I never thought I'd be fighting the Council again.

But how can I turn down a direct request from Gearwire?

"I accept the mission."

"Wonderful," Gearwire said. "We'll be leaving the base from the mouth of the cave in fifteen minutes. If you have any gear you need to bring with you, go get it now."

Timothy shook his head. "I lost my staff in Kawts," he said. "And I don't have any other gear."

"We'll have to fix that once we get back," Howard said. "Just tell me what sort of thing you're looking for, and either Dr. Maddium or myself will make something up for you."

"Thanks," Timothy said with a nod.

"In that case, I think we can head out right now," Gearwire said, looking around at the rest of his crew, all of whom were already fully prepared for the mission. "Henry, you stay here and keep an eye on the base. We won't be long."

"Aye, aye, Captain," Henry said with an exaggerated salute. Timothy glanced at Gearwire, but if Henry's comment had offended him, he offered no indication of it.

Without any further delay, the team left the cave, taking only a slight detour for Timothy to pick up Snipps from the rebellion stables. Cedar Deeproot led them toward the hidden fortress, and Timothy followed close behind, keeping an eye out for any signs of the Council's presence.

The group traveled without speaking, the silence broken only by the sound of their footsteps. As the minutes stretched into hours, Timothy couldn't take the silence anymore. He rode up beside Cedar, hopping lightly to the ground. Cedar barely glanced at him, his attention focused on the path in front of him.

"So... how long have you been Prime Minister?"

Cedar answered without turning his head. "Nearly twenty-seven years."

Timothy waited for him to elaborate, but Cedar showed no indication that he intended to do so.

"Is that a hereditary position, or..."

"Elected."

The silence returned.

"There's one thing I don't get," Timothy said at last. "How come I never saw any of you guys while I was in the forest? I mean, I was living out here for months!"

Cedar turned to face him, an irritated light in his eyes. "Because we have a policy of avoiding your kind." He jerked his head in the direction of the old village. "And for good reason." He faced back toward the path in front of them, scanning the trees ahead.

"We're here."

Timothy looked up to see a circular clearing in the trees in front of them, the fortress of Grimshaw sitting neatly in the center. The ancient stone castle had been reduced to a vine-covered mound some centuries previously, lending it a sort of natural camouflage with the surrounding forest. According to what Cedar had said, most of the castle had actually been constructed underground, which explained how the apparently derelict structure could house the entire remnant of the tree people.

Eager to make sure his people were okay, Cedar started towards it, but Timothy abruptly jerked him back. The prime minister turned on him, fear and anger in his eyes.

"Attack drones!" Timothy hissed, pointing up at the trees where the drones were hovering. Cedar nodded, his eyes widening as he realized how narrowly he had avoided death.

"We have to get over there," Cedar whispered as the others arrived on the scene.

"Leave that to me," Timothy replied, gauging the space between their current location and the castle. "Is there any message you want me to deliver?"

Cedar hesitated for a moment, then whispered something in Timothy's ear. Timothy nodded, then crept slowly away from the group. He spent the next several hours slowly approaching the fortress, slithering through the shadows at a snail's pace.

The sun was high in the sky when Timothy reached the mossy stone walls of Grimshaw.

Only thing to do now is find a way in, he thought, carefully examining the wall. He slunk around the outside of the fortress, but all the entrances were blocked up or barricaded.

Finally, after several tense minutes of searching, he discovered a narrow shaft partially hidden behind some vines. It was covered by a wire screen, but Timothy pried it loose with little effort. Then he shimmied down into the hole, pulling the screen back into place behind him.

He lowered himself down the shaft, reaching the bottom after only a couple of minutes. An angled mirror blocked a good portion of the connecting tunnel, directing the incoming sunlight deeper into the castle.

Timothy shimmied through the small gap between the mirror and the wall of the tunnel, crawling to the other end as quickly as he could. Five minutes later, he emerged into a large, open room, split down the middle by a subterranean river.

He crept through the twisting corridors of the fortress, making no more sound than a shadow. He passed room after room of the dark, dusty castle until he saw a light in the distance. He stumbled out into a brightly lit room, right into the middle of the tree people's council of war.

"Greetings, people of Grimshaw," Timothy said as the tree people spun around to face him, startled. "I have a message from Cedar Deeproot for Elmer Evergreen," he continued, realizing for the first time how precarious his position was.

No one spoke. Finally, one of the tree people stepped forward.

"The forest is vast," he said.

"But the trees will lead you home," Timothy replied, repeating the counter-sign that Cedar had given him.

The tree person nodded, satisfied with Timothy's response. "I am Elmer Evergreen, Captain of the Guard of the Tree People," he said. "What is your message?"

"Cedar escaped the raid at the castle and has been living with Gearwire and the rebellion for the last several weeks," Timothy said. Elmer nodded, relieved to hear that Cedar had escaped. "We've found a few other tree people since the battle, but not many."

"There are quite a few of us here as well," Elmer said. "But it's only a fraction of the population of our village. What happened to the others?"

"Gearwire believes the Council turned them into Blanks," Timothy said. "Although he doesn't think we can rule out the possibility that they were executed."

Elmer nodded stiffly. "I was afraid that might be the case. We're in a bit of a rough spot ourselves. Many of us sustained minor injuries in the battle. Most of them aren't serious, but there are a few cases that desperately need medical attention. We have plenty of food and water, but if the Council attacks, we won't be able to hold out for long."

Timothy nodded. "I'll let Cedar and Gearwire know," he said, committing the information to memory. He handed Elmer a resistance radio beacon, much like the one he had dropped in the Kawts River months earlier. "If anything goes wrong before you hear from us again, activate this. It'll let Gearwire know you're in trouble."

Elmer nodded, slipping the beacon into his pocket. "Will do."

Timothy exhaled heavily, then went back the way he came, sneaking out of the castle and starting across the clearing. As he made his way back to the others, his mind began to wander.

It's kind of fun to get a chance to strike back against the Council every once in a while. Maybe I should try to do this kind of thing a little more often.

As Timothy debated whether he should officially join the rebellion, he began to move faster than usual, the excitement accompanying his visions of grandeur overcoming his disciplined training. As a result, an attack drone spotted him, immediately opening fire. Instinctively, Timothy dove behind a tree, his heart pounding. All fantasies were chased from his mind as he reviewed the situation in his head, trying to remember exactly where the drone had been.

Not that it matters much, I suppose, he thought morosely. *It'll be right on top of me before long. My only chance is if it thinks I'm already dead.*

As the drone fired another round of bullets into the tree behind him, Timothy dropped to the ground, lying still. The attack drone advanced slowly, no longer firing, yet still wary.

As the drone drew closer, Timothy wished fleetingly that he still had his staff.

If only I hadn't lost it back in Kawts! I might still have had a chance at destroying this drone.

As it stands, it seems much more likely that it's going to destroy me!

He closed his eyes, bracing himself for the moment when the drone would realize that he was only pretending.

A sharp rock dug into his back, and it took all of Timothy's willpower not to move into a more comfortable position. Something clicked in his mind, and he remembered another weapon that he had read about in the secret library, one that was often used in situations where stealth was important. A shuriken. Timothy closed his hand around the rock. The drone hesitated, sensing the movement.

In one smooth motion, Timothy leapt up and whipped the rock at the drone. The projectile whizzed through the air, embedding itself in the drone's primary optical sensor and severing the wires that connected it to the rest of the drone. Before it could recover, Timothy darted off between the trees, hurrying back to where the others waited.

"Are you okay, Timothy?" Gearwire asked as soon as they were outside the range of the drone's sensors. His concern was evident in his voice.

Timothy nodded mutely, still winded from his desperate sprint into the trees. "I'm fine," he said at last. "I got a little distracted. But I'm good now." Without wasting another moment, he recounted everything Elmer had told him about the state of affairs inside of Grimshaw.

Gearwire frowned as he processed what Timothy said. "The situation doesn't look good. I can't see any way to send reinforcements to Grimshaw without sustaining heavy casualties. The number of drones stationed here will only increase after what happened today."

"We cannot abandon my people to their fates," Cedar said. "If what your assistant says is true, some of them will die if they don't get medical treatment soon!"

"We don't have the personnel to spare for a rescue mission," Gearwire said. "We need every man we've got right now."

Silence fell over the group, Gearwire's words hanging in the air.

There's got to be some solution, Timothy thought. *Some way to get everyone out without risking a frontal assault.*

A persistent scratching noise started up behind him, making concentration all but impossible. Annoyed, he turned to see Snipps a few yards away, burying some unidentifiable object under a tree. Timothy opened his mouth to tell her to stop when an idea struck him.

"What if we dig a tunnel?" he said, turning back toward the group. "from the base to Grimshaw? Then we could have a secure supply line to and from Grimshaw. We could bring them all the supplies and reinforcements they need, and we could evacuate the wounded to the base."

Gearwire stroked his beard thoughtfully, considering Timothy's proposal. "That might work," he said slowly. "But only if we can find some way of digging it quickly. It sounds like the situation is rather urgent."

"What about Henry?" Idalbo said. "He could use his arm cannon to tunnel through the rock much quicker than we could by hand."

"And Snipps could help too," Timothy said. "She seems to be quite good at digging."

Gearwire considered the idea for a moment. "That might do the trick," he said at last. "Timothy, you'll have to go back to Grimshaw to tell Elmer the plan. We'll send you with as many medical supplies as we can scrape together."

Timothy nodded, and the group quickly packed a first aid kit with all the supplies that they could fit inside. They forced the bulging kit closed and handed it to Timothy. He set off once more towards Grimshaw, the gathering darkness ensuring his safe return. When he finally made it back to Gearwire, they set off back toward the base, taking a slight detour so Timothy could retrieve Quill's box from his old campsite.

The next day, construction on the tunnel began, with Henry acting as both the foreman and the primary laborer. Aiming his arm cannon at the end of the tunnel, he blasted the rocks to pieces. Whenever he lowered his weapon, Timothy and Snipps jumped in, removing the loose soil from the tunnel so that the resistance engineers could put in the supports for the ceiling.

Between the three of them, they made great time on the tunnel, finishing it in just a few weeks. Before the month was over, supplies for Grimshaw were being dragged through the tunnel on sledges, and the injured tree people were brought back to the base for treatment, replaced by some of Gearwire's men.

Inspired by the effectiveness of the tunnel to Grimshaw, Gearwire also ordered the construction of a tunnel dug to the middle of Kawts - to the basement of the Kawts library, to be exact. Crystal and Jewel had confirmed that the Council hadn't found a replacement librarian yet, so the abandoned building became the perfect place for the tunnel, both practically and symbolically.

Chapter 22

"I'd like to start battle training," Timothy announced, walking up to the Mysterious Man, who was supervising a group of rebellion soldiers at the firing range. The Mysterious Man turned to look at him, his face unreadable.

"I'm glad to hear you're rejoining the fight. Which weapons do you prefer?"

Timothy told him about his staff and his idea with the shurikens, and the Mysterious Man nodded. "You'll need to talk to Howard about that," he said. "We don't have any of those lying around the cave." Timothy's face fell, and he added, "We can practice your stealth later today, I suppose. Once you actually have a weapon, come back and we can discuss your training further."

With that, he hurried away, barking orders at a group of swordsmen that he deemed to be lax in their technique.

Realizing that the Mysterious Man had moved on to something else, Timothy sought out Howard, finding him in his lab.

"Ah! Timothy!" the scientist exclaimed as he entered. "You're here about getting some weapons, aren't you?"

Timothy nodded. "I was thinking I'd like to use a few shurikens and a staff," he said. "Could you make them for me?"

"Yes to the staff," Howard replied thoughtfully. "And maybe to the other thing. You're going to have to explain to me what a shurrythingummy is." Briefly, Timothy explained what he was looking for, and Howard nodded. "That I can do," he said. "I'm a bit busy at the moment, but if you check back in a day or two, I should have something for you."

"Thanks!" Timothy said, returning to the training area, where he spent the rest of the afternoon trying to sneak up on the Mysterious Man.

It took him nearly two hours to get close to the Mysterious Man without arousing his suspicion. He crouched behind a rack of shields, watching as the Mysterious Man corrected the sword technique of a middle-aged soldier. He glanced behind him, and Timothy quickly ducked out of sight. Several seconds passed, and he slowly peeked out again, only to see the Mysterious Man standing over him.

"Here's a tip-" he said, moving the rack out of the way. "If you want to sneak up on someone, it helps to stay still when they're looking at you. Even when you think they've seen you already." Then he walked off, leaving Timothy to stand alone in the training hall.

* * *

A few days later, Timothy stood in the doorway of the kitchen, looking around for Madison. Madison looked up from the pot of stew she was stirring, noticing Timothy for the first time. She called to one of the other cooks to take over for her and jogged over to where he stood.

"I knew I'd see you back here eventually," Madison said. "Let me guess - Gearwire sent you over here as part of your training?"

Timothy nodded slowly. "But he didn't say why."

Madison smiled. "Gearwire has a policy that all of his soldiers have at least a rudimentary understanding of cooking. You never know when you might need to make your own food on a mission."

"I already know how to do that," Timothy protested. "I figured it out while I was in the forest, remember?"

Madison frowned. "In that case, this will be a short lesson. But let's see what you already know." She tossed him an apron from a nearby rack. "Put this on and wash your hands. Then meet me back by the cooler."

Timothy hesitated, then did as Madison requested.

"Since you already know a little about cooking, I'll just watch you to start," she said. She handed him an armful of vegetables and led him over to the counter.

Timothy dumped the vegetables onto the counter, and Madison handed him a knife. "Cut these into bite-sized chunks."

Timothy lifted the knife, keenly aware of Madison's eyes on him. He picked up one of the vegetables and began to chop.

Madison watched him closely, giving no indication of how Timothy was doing. When Timothy had finished, he looked up at her.

"How'd I do?"

"Not bad," Madison said, taking the knife back from him. "You cut evenly, but your technique still needs a little work. Watch."

She picked up a carrot from the pile and chopped it into tiny pieces, the knife seeming to fly in her hands. When she was done, she handed the knife back to Timothy. "Now you try."

For the next several hours, they went back and forth, Madison frequently stopping to correct Timothy's technique. After a while, Timothy begrudgingly acknowledged that he had needed Madison's training.

"Don't mention it," Madison said. "You'd be surprised how often people come down here thinking that they already know how to do this."

Timothy nodded, his face flushing. "So how did you start cooking, anyway?" he asked. "I mean, I know Quill's notes said that you found a cookbook in the secret library, but what made you decide to try that, of all things?"

Madison smiled. "It was an experiment. I wanted to test whether the Council was lying. I never did much science stuff, so I couldn't test it that way. And the theology was interesting, but it's not exactly empirically testable. At least not in a foolproof way. But the cooking? I could do that. Especially since my mom used to work at the food production plant."

Her voice caught a little on her last sentence, and Timothy instantly regretted his question.

"I'm sorry - I didn't mean to bring up bad memories."

"It's okay," Madison said. "I know she's not gone forever." She looked over at Timothy. "And neither is Quill."

"Gearwire told you about him?" Timothy asked.

"He did," Madison said. "But we were actually pretty good friends even before that. His dad was the head of the Merchant Guild, and my dad was the head of the Science Guild, so we saw each other quite a lot."

Timothy glanced over at Madison, wondering at the warmth that crept into her voice as she spoke about Quill. Madison noticed Timothy's expression and abruptly turned away.

"I think that should be good enough for today," she said. "I'll let Gearwire know you've completed the cooking part of your training."

* * *

"I ran into Madison the other day," Timothy said to Jewel, leaning back in his chair. "Gearwire had her give me a cooking lesson."

"From what I've heard, that's a pretty standard part of the training," Jewel's voice said from the radio beacon on Timothy's desk.

"It seems so." He hesitated a moment, then added, "You know, it's kind of odd - it almost seemed like she had a crush on Quill."

169

For a moment, Jewel did not reply. "I can neither confirm nor deny that conjecture," she said at last.

Timothy couldn't help but smile. "I wonder if Quill knew."

"You'll have to ask him someday."

"I'm not so sure that will be anytime soon," Timothy said, shaking his head. "I'm sure Gearwire is a fine general, but..."

"You're wondering why the rebellion hasn't made much progress."

"Yeah. I mean, from what Samuel told me, Gearwire's been in the area for almost twenty years now. And nothing's changed. Except now the Council has someone to blame their crimes on."

"Timothy, do you remember how the mayor of Duncan's Ridge never showed up at our graduation?"

Timothy nodded slowly. "Yeah... Aksell said something about an anarchist-" He stopped himself, then started again. "Sorry - *resistance* attack he had to deal with."

"I suppose that is true - in a manner of speaking," Jewel said. "The real reason he wasn't there was because Gearwire and his crew had retaken the city."

For a moment, Timothy was stunned. "Gearwire took over Duncan's Ridge? That was months ago! How has no one noticed?"

Jewel laughed bitterly. "The Council is pretty good at covering up things they don't want people to know."

"I guess we really are making progress," Timothy said, still trying to process this information. "Still, Kawts is a lot bigger than Duncan's Ridge."

"You sound awfully pessimistic about this whole thing for someone who just officially joined our ranks."

"Getting stranded in the forest for a few months will do that to you," Timothy said, a trace of bitterness in his voice. "I don't know. I am committed to taking the Council down. And I certainly hope we can do it. I just wish we were doing it a little faster."

Jewel laughed. "That makes two of us. Being a double agent twenty-four seven is exhausting. And it would be nice to see Samuel and Quill again. And everyone else."

"Speaking of Quill and Samuel, there's one thing I still don't get. We have a way to cure the Blanks, right? Everyone keeps saying that's how Madison escaped. So why aren't we using it?"

"It's not quite that simple. There are some pretty severe side effects."

"Gearwire said something about that when I first got here. But Madison seems perfectly fine to me."

"You weren't with us yet when Howard actually cured her," Jewel said, her voice suddenly becoming serious. "She was a wreck for months. She could barely even remember her own name. If Howard hadn't been there to anchor her memories, I honestly don't think she would have recovered."

"No one ever mentioned that part." Timothy sighed. "It's just really hard to know exactly where they are, but not be able to do anything about it. Sometimes I think I'd rather Samuel and Quill actually be dead instead of being the Council's puppets."

"I know what you mean. But some of the resistance's best scientists have been working on a cure for a while now. They're bound to have a breakthrough soon."

"I hope so," Timothy said. A pleasant silence followed. Timothy was about to ask Jewel another question when Crystal's voice came through the radio.

"Jewel? We have to go. Pastor Shepherd is expecting us in five minutes."

"One second!" Jewel called back. Then, to Timothy, she said, "Sorry. I have to run. Talk to you again next week?"

"Of course," Timothy said.

"Great," Jewel said. "I'll see you then."

* * *

Two days later, Timothy was back in the training hall, his new weapons in tow. He presented them to the Mysterious Man, who nodded approvingly. "You'll be working with Gearwire on your staff," he said. "He's the only one of us with any experience fighting with a quarterstaff. You'll mostly have to practice with your shurikens independently. You can use the target range over there," he added, gesturing to the place where Henry had been when they had first met. "I'll handle your stealth training," he added with a malicious smile.

Despite the warning bells in his head telling him it was a bad idea, Timothy couldn't help but ask, "What do you know about stealth? Gearwire said none of his crew members had that skill set."

The Mysterious Man stared at him for an unnaturally long time before responding. "I know a few tricks you don't," he said. "Besides," he added coolly, "I don't have to know how to sneak up on you. All I have to do is know when someone's sneaking up on *me*."

Thus began Timothy's training as a resistance soldier. The Mysterious Man pushed him hard, showing him no mercy in their training sessions, which soon grew to include sparring as well. Timothy quickly came to realize, however, that it was for his own good that the Mysterious Man was being so harsh. If he ever hoped to hold his own against a Council member, he had to become an expert in his field, and training with the Mysterious Man left little room for error. The work was worth it, and Timothy's skills grew better by the day.

About three weeks after the tunnel to Grimshaw was completed, Timothy received another summons from Gearwire.

Chapter 23

"We've just received some concerning news," Dr. Maddium said as he entered the room from Gearwire's study. Several of Gearwire's other crew members were already there, including the Mysterious Man and Madison. Gearwire himself, Timothy noted, was not present.

"Gearwire's in a meeting with the twins as we speak," Dr. Maddium continued, as if reading Timothy's mind. "It appears that the Council plans to destroy the Kawts library."

Destroy the library? They'll destroy centuries worth of knowledge and art! Timothy swallowed. *Not to mention some of what might be my last memories of Samuel and Quill.*

But I suppose it makes sense from the Council's perspective, he realized. *How many people have rebelled against the Council because of that library? And now that Samuel is a Blank and I'm here, there isn't anyone left in Kawts who's trained to run it. They're killing two birds with one stone.*

"Obviously, we cannot allow this to happen," Dr. Maddium said. "That library contains some of the last known copies of some of the world's greatest stories and discoveries from before the Robot War, not to mention the work of hundreds of Kawts' own authors and biographers. The information contained within those books could prove to be the key to restoring Kawts after we defeat the Council. That's why we called you here."

"You impressed us with your skills at Grimshaw," he continued. "And you used to work at the library in question. Gearwire has stated that he wants you to lead this mission."

Timothy was stunned. "Me? Lead Gearwire's crew on a mission?"

"He's waiting for you in his study," Dr. Maddium told him with a slight smile, pushing open the door.

Gearwire sat alone in the room, although the speaker sitting on the table testified to the fact that Crystal and Jewel were listening in as well. Timothy stepped inside, and Dr. Maddium shut the door behind him.

For the next several minutes, Gearwire and the twins brought Timothy up to date on the situation in Kawts. When they finished, Timothy was silent, thinking over what they had said.

"We need you to remove all the books from the library if you can," Gearwire said. "Dr. Maddium will give you a device that will allow you to carry all of them at once. Ideally, you'll be in and out before the Council even knows you've been there." He paused for a moment. "You'll be leading this mission, so the planning will be left entirely up to you."

Timothy nodded, mulling over everything he knew of that might affect the mission.

You are in way over your head, a voice whispered in the back of his mind. *Gearwire's making a huge mistake.*

He shook his head, banishing the thought. He hesitated for a moment, then laid out his plan.

* * *

Twenty-four hours later, Timothy arrived at the edge of Kawts. Only two people accompanied him: the Mysterious Man and Madison Kolt. After much discussion, he had decided to go with only these two, knowing that each additional person they brought with them drastically increased the likelihood that they would be detected. Ideally, he would have liked to go by himself, but he knew that there was no way he could complete the mission alone.

As the sun began to set behind them, Timothy kept one eye on the old watchtower. Gearwire's last instructions to him were still ringing in his ears as he waited for the signal from Crystal and Jewel.

"Avoid confronting the Council directly," Gearwire had told him sternly. "They're much stronger than you think. If at any point, the situation becomes too dangerous, retreat. The books are important for us and for Kawts, but they're not worth dying over."

A flash of blue flew up from the balcony of the old tower, bringing Timothy back to the present. Without saying a word, he motioned for the others to follow him as he started off through the darkened streets of Kawts.

As Timothy had expected, the Mysterious Man proved to be quite adept at sneaking through the shadows, although he still made a good deal more noise than Timothy would have liked. Madison had a more difficult time, but eventually, they reached the library without being spotted.

When they finally arrived, Timothy removed a coil of rope from a satchel he had slung over his shoulder. He passed the rope to Madison, who whirled it over her head like a lasso several times before finally releasing one end, sending it sailing through the air. The end of the rope, which had been outfitted with a grappling hook, caught on the corner of a nearby building. After making sure that the rope was secure, Timothy scrambled up it, followed closely by the Mysterious Man. He glanced over at the library roof, only a few feet away from where they now stood.

"This way," he whispered, starting towards it.

The Mysterious Man cleared his throat, and Timothy turned back to look at him.

"Aren't you forgetting someone?"

Timothy narrowed his eyes, realizing for the first time that Madison had not joined them on the roof. His confusion rapidly giving way to concern, he rushed to the edge of the building. To his relief, Madison appeared to be fine, standing in the street with the rope gripped tightly in her hand. Yet she made no effort to climb up, instead staring intently at the wall in front of her.

Timothy glanced over at the Mysterious Man. "What's going on? What is she doing?"

The Mysterious Man merely raised an eyebrow, as if to say, "How should I know?"

Timothy turned his attention back to Madison, standing at the bottom of the wall. "Madison!" he hissed. "What's going on?"

"Just give me a second," Madison replied, her voice sounding strained.

Timothy looked over at the Mysterious Man again. This time, the grim figure decided to take pity on him.

"Madison isn't a huge fan of heights."

Timothy stared at him. "And you knew this the whole time? You knew we would be climbing up here. Why didn't you say something?"

"You didn't ask. Besides, you were rather vague with the exact details of your plan."

Timothy sighed, pinching the bridge of his nose. He had chosen Madison and the Mysterious Man primarily because they were the two members of Gearwire's crew that he knew the best. Now, it was beginning to seem he had made a mistake.

He shook his head.

There's no use regretting it now, he thought. *We'll just have to make the best of it.*

Leaning over the edge once more, he whispered, "Madison. I know this isn't exactly what you'd prefer to be doing. But you've got to climb up here. The longer we're standing out on this rooftop, the more likely it is for some attack drone to spot us."

"I'm working on it," Madison said. She hesitated for a moment longer, then began her climb up the rope. She moved slowly, her movements jerky. Timothy glanced around the silent city, scanning the skies for drones. Satisfied they hadn't been discovered, he looked back down at Madison. She had almost reached the top, and the Mysterious Man reached down to help her up the rest of the way.

As Madison quickly moved toward the center of the rooftop, Timothy could feel the Mysterious Man's gaze on him, as if he was silently rating his performance.

"Alright," Timothy said. "Let's move." He ran across the rooftop and jumped across to the library, making hardly any sound as he landed. Madison and the Mysterious Man followed closely behind him.

At Timothy's instruction, the Mysterious Man withdrew a crowbar from the sheath on his back, a temporary replacement for one of his twin swords. He knelt down at the edge of the skylight and pried up one of the panels. Utilizing the rope once again, they slowly and cautiously rappelled down into the darkened library.

The Mysterious Man opened the Infini-case, a device created by Dr. Maddium several years prior. It appeared to be an ordinary black briefcase, but it had been modified to allow it to hold a near-infinite number of things.

The Mysterious Man set the case on the floor, and the three of them ran up and down the aisles, systematically gathering all the books and throwing them inside. Once the secret library had been emptied, they crept down the ladder to the main floor. Timothy removed a screwdriver from his satchel and set to work on the door between them and the main library, removing it from its hinges. Then they snuck inside and repeated the process on the bottom floor.

They were just putting the last books into the case when the doorknob began to turn. They froze, not daring to make a sound. The door swung open, and Volker stepped into the room. He slowly scanned the area, a suspicious frown on his face. At one point, he looked directly at Timothy.

It took all his willpower not to move, remembering his training sessions with the Mysterious Man. His heart was pounding, and part of him worried Volker would hear it. For one long, agonizing moment, Volker didn't move, his eyes narrowed as he listened for any signs of life. Finally, he seemed satisfied that the room was empty and turned to leave.

Timothy sagged against the bookshelf, the tension draining from his body. He was about to whisper something to the others when Volker suddenly turned around, staring at the door to the back room, which had been left ajar. The head of the Kawts Security Force took a cautious step forward. Then his eyes widened.

As Volker dashed back outside to grab a lantern, Timothy was already moving.

"We need to get out of here!" he said. "Get back to the roof!" He turned and sprinted toward the back room, following right behind Madison and the Mysterious Man. As he reached the door, he heard Volker burst into the library, flanked by a squadron of Blanks.

"Traitors!" Volker roared as he ran after Timothy, the Blanks right behind him.

Timothy slammed the door shut, frantically scanning the room for something to barricade the door with. His eyes finally landed on the bulky machine used for submitting paperwork to the Council. He dashed over to it and tried to pull it towards the door, but it was attached to the wall by a plethora of tubes and wires.

Seeing what Timothy was trying to do, the Mysterious Man ran over to him, slicing through the wires with a single stroke of his sword.

Together, the three of them dragged the machine into place, only barely managing to block the door before Volker reached it.

Volker collided with the door with a sickening crunch, the resistance catching him by surprise. Shaking off his pain, he shouted orders to a squadron of Blanks, who began shoving at the door. Slowly but surely, the heavy machine began to move.

But Timothy and the others were already gone, escaping up the ladder to the secret library. While the Mysterious Man helped Madison up onto the roof, Timothy toppled a bookshelf over the trapdoor he had just emerged from, sealing off the entrance.

That should keep him busy for a few minutes, he thought. *At least long enough for us to get away.* He turned and scrambled up the rope, joining the others on the roof.

They had just gotten to the roof of the next building over when a squadron of attack drones arrived, responding to the disturbance. The flying robots dive-bombed them, spraying a hail of bullets in their direction.

So much for secrecy, Timothy thought, throwing one of his new shurikens at the nearest drone. The specially designed alloy collided with the drone's propeller, severing it and sending the drone plummeting to the streets below. To Timothy's right, a pair of drones burst into flames, blown up by one of Madison's grenades. He risked a glance behind him and saw The Mysterious Man and Madison standing back-to-back with their weapons drawn.

A faint glimmer of sunlight was visible in the east, and Timothy realized with surprise that it would soon be light. His heart sank as he saw what was going to happen.

Unless I do something right now, none of us are going to make it out of this alive, he realized. *The Mysterious Man is an expert fighter, but his swords aren't going to be very effective against these attack drones. And neither will Madison's electro-whips. They'll be able to hold out for a while, but sooner or later, there'll be more drones than they can handle.*

He glanced back at the horizon.

And once the sun comes up, there'll be nowhere for them to hide.

"You have to go!" Timothy shouted. "Make your way back to the edge of town. I'll meet you there!"

He turned his attention back to the drones, throwing another shuriken as he did. Another drone crashed to the ground. Behind him, he could sense the others hesitating.

"Go!" Timothy shouted. "I said I'll meet you there!"

Galvanized into action, the pair turned and ran, jumping to the next rooftop. A couple drones turned off from the pack to follow them, but Timothy quickly dissuaded them, dropping another half-dozen drones in the space of just a few seconds.

He looked up at the rapidly growing swarm of attack drones, swallowing hard.

Unless something changes soon, I don't stand much of a chance, either. The Council has to be on their way by now. Once they get here, I'm done for.

The memory of Samuel's sacrifice flitted through his mind, and Timothy found his resolve strengthening. He exhaled slowly, withdrawing another shuriken from his satchel.

If I'm going to die, I'm going to take as many of these drones with me as I can.

Timothy launched another volley of shurikens at the advancing drones. He reached into his satchel for another throwing star, but his hand found nothing but air. The satchel was empty.

Great. Just what I needed.

As if sensing that Timothy was out of ammunition, the attack drones closed in, firing more rapidly than before. Timothy dove out of the way, rolling behind a large metal structure on the roof. The attack drones followed, spewing bullets in his direction. Timothy cursed under his breath. It was only a matter of time before the Council would arrive, and he was pinned down by the attack drones' fire.

Taking a deep breath, he dashed out of his hiding spot, sliding behind a large box on the roof of a nearby building. The drones opened fire, but then they hesitated, losing his location for a moment. Still, Timothy knew they would find him soon, and once they did, it would be all over. There was nowhere else to run.

From the street below, he heard Ethos' voice, shouting orders to Volker and his accomplices, who had just emerged onto the roof of the library.

Then, to his surprise, he heard another sound - the sound of an attack drone falling to the ground. The sound was followed closely by another of the same nature. Timothy peeked out of his hiding spot to see Jewel fighting the attack drones. Several drones already lay in a sparking heap on the rooftop, impaled by shards of crystal.

"We figured you could use some help," Jewel said with a smile, taking her eyes off the battle for a second to check on Timothy.

"Thanks," Timothy replied shakily, getting to his feet.

Suddenly, Crystal appeared behind him. "When I give the word, run," she said, holding up a small metallic sphere. She pressed a button on the top and rolled it across the rooftop.

"Now!" she shouted as a dense smoke filled the air.

Timothy took off running, sliding down a drainage pipe to the street below. He hit the ground hard, but he quickly got back up, dashing off toward the edge of town. Out of the corner of his eye, he saw Crystal and Jewel running in opposite directions, splitting up to avoid detection.

Once he had put some distance between himself and the library, Timothy slowed down, realizing that he would attract less attention in the waking city by simply walking. Unlike Gearwire's crew, he hadn't gotten around to making a disguise or armor yet, and if he used his staff as a walking stick, he just might pass for a citizen of Kawts.

I just hope no one recognizes me, he thought as he wandered through the growing crowd, slowly making his way to where Madison and the Mysterious Man waited. Then, as day broke on the city of Kawts, the trio slipped out of town and returned to the cave.

Gearwire was waiting for them in the mouth of the cave when they returned, turning the Infini-case over to one of the base's librarians.

"Mission accomplished, I see," he said with a nod, and Timothy realized that Jewel must have already filled him in on what had happened. Gearwire stared at him for a long moment, but he said nothing more, turning and disappearing back into the cave.

Chapter 24

A few days after returning from the mission, Timothy paid a visit to Howard Kolt to replace the shurikens he had lost on the rooftop. As he resumed his training with the newly minted weapons, an idea began to take shape in his mind, inspired by his recent mission.

But even as his plans solidified, he found his thoughts coming back more and more frequently to Maurice. Even after all this time, his brother's ultimate fate remained a mystery. The more he thought about his brother's disappearance, the more determined he became to find the truth. Finally, unable to wait any longer, he made his way down to the lab, hoping that Howard would be willing to help both with upgrading his gear and finding his brother.

"Timothy!" Howard said with a smile as Timothy entered the room. "What can I do for you?"

"There's a few upgrades I'd like to make to my gear," Timothy said, forcing himself to wait for the right moment to ask about Maurice. "But I'm going to need a suit of my own in order to make them work."

Howard idly twisted the ends of his mustache. "What kind of suit are you thinking of?"

"Nothing fancy. A lightweight suit of armor would be ideal."

"Building a proper suit from scratch could take a while. But if you're not opposed to the idea, we could probably cobble something together out of leftover bits of other suits in the next week or two."

Timothy nodded. "That would be great. At least as a temporary thing."

"Happy to be of assistance," Howard said. He glanced down at the tools strewn across the table in front of him. "I can help you get started in just a minute. I just need to find that..."

His hand suddenly darted forward, and he snatched a tool from the table, depositing it in one of the workbench drawers. He brushed the remainder of the items on the table into a rough pile, then stood and led Timothy to the back corner of the lab, where several other prototype pieces of armor already sat.

"You were saying something about wanting to upgrade your weapons too, right?" Howard said, clearing off a space from a cluttered workbench.

Timothy licked his lips. "Yeah. But there's actually something else I wanted to ask you about first."

Howard paused and looked up at him, one eyebrow raised. "Go on."

Timothy hesitated a moment, then sighed. "I've heard some of the stories people have told about you and Madison, and I was wondering..." He trailed off, hoping that Howard would catch on. The scientist's face showed nothing but puzzlement, and Timothy took a deep breath and continued. "I was wondering if you could locate a specific Blank in the Council's system for me."

Howard frowned, but Timothy could see he was considering it.

"You've heard about how I rescued my daughter from her fate as a Blank, and now you want me to do the same thing for someone you know?" Howard said. He shook his head. "I'm afraid I can't do that. Gearwire gave me strict instructions not to pull a stunt like that again. Trying to rescue individual Blanks by request is too dangerous. And the cure itself is far from safe."

"I know," Timothy said. "Which is why I'm not asking you to help me rescue him." He sighed. "It's my brother. He's been missing for a while - either dead or a Blank. I just want to know which one."

Howard's eyes narrowed. "All you want is to see if we can find your brother in the Council's mainframe?" He drummed his fingers on the desk. Then he sighed. "Alright. I'll fire up that old program of Maddium's. As long as we're just checking, I don't see the harm in it. But I don't want a word about this to leave this room. Understand?"

Timothy nodded. "I won't tell a soul."

"Then let's see what we can find," Howard said, booting up an old computer that sat in the corner of the lab. His fingers seemed to move agonizingly slowly across the keys.

"Computer programs aren't really my area of expertise," he said apologetically with a brief backward glance at Timothy. "Dr. Maddium actually wrote most of the code. All I did was tweak it a bit." He glanced back at Timothy again. "What's your brother's name?"

"Maurice."

Slowly, Howard input the name into the system, one key at a time. When he finished, he leaned back in his chair. "It might take a few minutes for the program to do its thing. From what I can tell, this computer's seen better days."

The computer let out a soft 'bing!' and Timothy looked at the screen with a mixture of hope and fear.

NO RESULTS FOUND

Timothy felt the excitement drain out of him. "So that's it, then. He's dead."

"He isn't a Blank," Howard said. "That's all we can know based on the information we have."

Timothy shook his head. "No. Even if he were still alive, he could be anywhere by now. He's gone. But thanks for checking."

* * *

Timothy was putting the finishing touches on the gauntlets of his suit when Henry showed up at the lab with a summons from Gearwire. Leaving his suit where it was, he followed Henry back to Gearwire's house. When they arrived, Gearwire motioned for them to have a seat before he spoke.

"Several days ago, three Councilmen left Kawts for an unknown destination," he began, unrolling a tattered world map on the table. "Crystal and Jewel did some investigating, and they've discovered that they're picking up a shipment of new attack drones from their supplier, who lives somewhere in Ellada," he continued, stabbing at the country in question with his finger. "I want you and Henry to intercept the shipment and destroy it."

"How do you recommend we do that?" Timothy asked, sensing that Gearwire had a specific plan in mind.

"You're going to track which way they went. Once you know where they're going, you can either catch up to them or stage an ambush further along the path - whichever one is safer. Henry will be the one to actually destroy the drones. Your job is to get him as close to the shipment as you can."

Timothy nodded slowly, thinking over the situation. Finally, he asked, "Do you have any idea which direction they're going?"

"The twins were unable to determine exactly which way they went, but if they were picking up a drone shipment, they would have to be traveling southwest."

Timothy frowned. "That's still a pretty big area to cover," he said. "They might be back in Kawts before I even pick up the trail."

"It is possible," Gearwire said. "Although I think that's unlikely. Previous trips to get more attack drones have taken them around four months."

"I guess I have some time, then," Timothy said with a smile. "But their tracks will be easiest to find when they're fresh."

Gearwire nodded. "Of course. I can arrange transportation to the southwest side of the city if you like."

Timothy shook his head. "I'll ride Snipps. That way, I can make sure we don't mess up the tracks."

"As you wish," Gearwire said, inclining his head toward Timothy. "You're the expert." Then, addressing both of them at once, he said, "I don't imagine this will be a problem with you two, but I need to clarify that Timothy will be in charge in all matters relating to tracking and stealth, and Henry is to take charge when it comes time to actually destroy the shipment."

Timothy nodded.

"The quartermaster will get you some tents and survival gear. I've already sent him a message to have it ready for you when you arrive."

"I'll go pick up the supplies," Henry said.

"Thanks," Timothy said. "Once you've got everything, meet me at the stables."

"Whatever you say, boss," Henry said, grinning. He winked at Gearwire, then followed Timothy out of the room.

Several hours later, Timothy, Snipps, and Henry arrived near the southwest border of Kawts. Timothy dropped lightly into a crouch, searching the ground for signs that the Council had passed through. When he didn't find anything, he moved further out, scouring the ground in a wide arc for any indications of human presence.

Henry stood back beside Snipps, watching Timothy work.

"I think I found something," Timothy called out after a while. Henry ambled over to where he stood. Timothy pointed to a broken branch at the edge of the forest. "Someone or something came through here."

Henry frowned thoughtfully, inspecting the branch even though he didn't know what he was looking for. "Recently?" he asked, and Timothy hesitated.

"I'm not sure. It would have to have happened at least a day or two ago."

"So it could be something completely unrelated to our mission."

Timothy nodded. "But it's the best lead we have right now."

"Fair enough," Henry said with a grin. "Lead on, tracker-man."

Timothy followed the tracks for several days more, Henry his silent shadow. As he stooped down to examine part of a footprint in the snow, he shot a sidelong glance at Henry. The rebel general was seated atop Snipps, scanning the woods for dangers. For a moment, he almost looked like a giant meerkat. As Henry's gaze moved back towards the space directly in front of them, Timothy quickly brought his attention back to the tracks.

This track was different from all the others they had seen so far. The footprint was a different size and seemed to have been made much more recently.

"Either we're getting really close to catching up to the Council, or someone else has been here since they passed through."

"I think I'm going to go with someone else being here," Henry said evenly, pointing his arm cannon at something in the treetops. "And they know we're here."

A blast of energy shot from his weapon and disappeared into the canopy of leaves. There was a muffled grunt, and then a rough-looking man toppled out of the tree, landing on his face in the dirt.

For a second, nothing happened. Then dozens of other bandits suddenly jumped out of the trees. Henry was already in motion by the time the first wave reached him, dropping several of them before they even reached the ground. Some of the men, seeing him busy with their companions, tried to sneak up on him from behind.

Timothy opened his mouth to shout a warning, but Henry was already moving, whirling Snipps around and swinging his arm cannon into the faces of his would-be attackers. Timothy winced at the sound of bones crunching. The remaining bandits took a hesitant step back, suddenly unsure of their course. Henry raised his weapon again, and their minds were made up. They fled back into the forest, not even pausing to retrieve their unconscious comrades.

Henry smiled in satisfaction as he watched them leave, then dropped his arm to his side once more. Timothy stood there, dumbfounded.

"How did you do that?"

Henry shrugged, an impish grin appearing on his face. "You pick up a thing or two when you work for Gearwire." His smile widened. "Namely, some really cool weapons."

Timothy nodded slowly, still stunned by the speed with which Henry had dispatched their attackers. Instead of commenting, he turned his attention to the remaining bandits, who still lay on the ground, unmoving.

"Do you think they're... Are they dead?"

Henry shook his head. "I doubt it. Even my cannon has a nonlethal setting. Gearwire's orders. But I imagine that some of these fellows will have pretty awful headaches when they wake up."

"Are we just going to leave them here?"

It took Henry several seconds to respond to this. "I suppose not," he said at last, begrudgingly sliding off of Snipps' back. He moved to the nearest bandit and dragged him to the center of the clearing. "We'll treat any severe injuries as best as we can and leave them a few days' worth of food and water. There's not much else we can do past that."

They spent the rest of the morning doing exactly what Henry had suggested, with the addition of tying the bandits' hands together behind their backs.

"It's just a safety precaution," Henry told Timothy in a low voice. "We don't want them following us and trying to ambush us for the next few weeks. I'd give them an hour or two after we leave to be on the loose again."

The rest of the day passed without incident, and before Timothy knew it, they were sitting beside a roaring fire, preparing dinner from their dwindling supply of food. As they ate, Timothy found himself once more wondering about his mysterious companion's past. Despite Henry's friendly cheerfulness, he realized he actually knew next to nothing about the man himself.

"Why did you join?"

Henry blinked at him, confused.

"The rebellion," Timothy explained. "What made you decide to join up with Gearwire?"

A fond smile appeared on Henry's face as he was transported back to his past. "I joined Gearwire before there was even a need for a rebellion. Before Gearwire was even Gearwire." He hesitated for a moment, unsure of how much to say. After a long pause, he began again. "We're going to be spending a lot of time together over the next few months," he said at last. "I suppose we'd better get to know each other's stories a little better."

He leaned back, staring up at the sky. "It was Gearwire who brought us all together. Although like I said, he didn't go by Gearwire back then. There was a great war, and people from all over the world were forced to band together to defend the planet."

Timothy nodded, enthralled by the story even as a part of him tried to pinpoint exactly which war Henry was talking about.

"Gearwire was a low-ranking officer, but after the death of his commander, he became an extremely important person practically overnight. He got promoted to the leader of our division. I was not impressed, to put it mildly. The first time we met, we got into a bit of a fistfight." Henry chuckled as the memories came back to him.

"Gearwire won. Put me in the medical ward and everything. But when I woke up, he came to check on me. Wanted to make sure that there were no hard feelings. That's when I knew he was by far the best replacement for our late commander." Henry paused, deep in thought.

"It was a few days after that - or maybe it was a few weeks. I really can't remember. Anyway, a while after that, he came down to the training grounds, absolutely livid. He was looking for volunteers to go on an unsanctioned rescue mission. A denied mission, as a matter of fact. Me and the Professor - that's what we used to call Dr. Maddium - and a few others joined him. We became his first crew. We would have followed him anywhere. So when he said he was coming over here, I came with him."

Timothy sat in silence, stunned by Henry's story. It was a side of the gregarious soldier he had never noticed before. The deep loyalty he had for Gearwire reminded him of Quill and Aksell. Before Quill had disappeared, each of them would have done the same had the situation arose.

And look where we are now - Quill's a Blank, Aksell is being trained by a man who's secretly an evil psychopath, and I'm hanging out in the middle of the forest with an alleged dangerous anarchist.

"And what about you?" Henry said, staring directly at Timothy. "What made you decide to join Gearwire?"

Slowly at first, Timothy began to tell his story. Before long, he was telling Henry about everything that had happened to him over the last two years. The Race, Samuel, Quill's box - the entire story tumbled out. Tears formed in his eyes as he recalled his parents and his friends who were still in Kawts, completely unaware that the very people who claimed to be the city's protectors were actually its oppressors.

Henry looked at him with concern in his eyes. "You're worried about them, aren't you?" The tenderness in his voice caught Timothy by surprise. He looked up to see similar tears standing in Henry's eyes.

"Would you mind if I prayed for them?"

Timothy hesitated, half of him wanting to tell Henry that it wouldn't do any good, and the other half of him hoping that he was wrong. "I guess," he said at last.

Henry nodded solemnly, then bowed his head. "Dear Lord, I ask today that you would be with Timothy's family and friends back in Kawts. I ask that you would open their eyes to the Truth and that you would keep them safe from the Council. You are the defender of the defenseless, Lord. It's in your name I pray, amen."

Henry lifted his head and opened his eyes. For a long moment, neither of them spoke.

"I've seen a lot of terrible things in my life," Henry said at last. After a moment of silence, he added awkwardly, "But when I look back, I can see how God used even those things for good."

Why did Samuel and Quill get turned into Blanks, then? Timothy thought bitterly. *Where's the good in that?*

But even as he had the thought, he couldn't help but wonder what would have happened if Quill and Samuel hadn't gotten captured.

Would I have found out the truth about the Council? Would I have ever encountered Snipps? Or met Gearwire and his crew?

Timothy shook his head, clearing his thoughts. *None of that really matters now.*

Or does it?

* * *

By the end of the week, their supplies were running dangerously low, and Henry decided that they would have to take a break for a hunting expedition.

"This should be fun, eh?" he said as he slid his cannon over his arm.

"If you say so," Timothy said, donning his own suit. "What exactly are we trying to hunt?"

"Anything we happen across!" Henry exclaimed with a laugh. "Although hopefully, it's bigger than a rabbit. A deer or a bear or something would last a lot longer." A huge grin broke over his face as he continued, wiping some dirt off of his weapon with an old rag.

"There was this one time, back before we came here, when Gearwire and I were doing a bit of hunting ourselves. We heard this rustling noise in the bushes, and we snuck over there real quietly, thinking it was a squirrel or something. Turns out, it was actually a scout robot trying to find a path into our base! Gearwire had the thing glued to the ground before I could even aim my cannon!"

Henry chuckled to himself and turned to Timothy, temporarily pausing his polishing. "You're a pretty good hunter yourself, aren't you?"

"You get pretty good at a lot of things when your survival depends on it," Timothy said.

"Fair enough," Henry replied. "How about a friendly competition, then?" he said suddenly. "Whoever brings back the most meat in an hour wins."

Timothy thought for a moment. Slowly, a smile spread across his face. "You're on."

"Alright! Meet back here in an hour. May the best hunter win!"

Timothy and Henry headed into the woods, leaving Snipps behind to guard their campsite. Timothy trudged through the undergrowth, moving silently despite his excitement. He had little doubt that he could beat Henry by virtue of stealth alone.

Yet despite his confidence, Timothy spent most of the hour without seeing any signs of animal life. He had almost made it back to the campsite when he suddenly heard a twig snap. He whirled around, watching as the vegetation moved.

Is that Henry, or some sort of animal? he wondered, slowly opening his satchel to retrieve a shuriken just in case.

A wild boar suddenly burst into the open. It snorted at Timothy, then barreled towards him. Timothy leapt out of the way at the last second, only barely avoiding being skewered on the boar's tusks. Adrenaline surged through his veins as he launched the shuriken at the back of the boar's neck. The shuriken hit the boar and stuck fast, quivering. The boar turned, enraged.

That could be a problem, Timothy thought, fear welling up inside him. The boar charged again, and Timothy slid to the side, this time earning a shallow cut on the side of his leg. Frantically, he glanced around the forest. His only chance of survival lay in making it back to the camp.

Flinging another shuriken towards the boar, Timothy took off running.

"Henry!" he shouted, waving his arms over his head. "I could really use your help right now!"

Timothy burst out into the clearing, coming to a stop in front of a grim-faced Henry.

"What is it?" he asked, scanning the forest from which Timothy had emerged.

"Wild... boar," Timothy gasped, trying desperately to catch his breath. "Tried to... kill it... didn't work."

Henry nodded and stepped in front of Timothy, lowering his arm cannon at the rustling underbrush. Seconds later, the boar charged into view. Henry fired his weapon at the boar, dropping it to the ground. Before the boar could recover, he was on it, killing it with a few swift strokes from a long hunting knife.

"Well," Henry said as he slowly got to his feet again. "I think you won." He wiped the blade of his knife off on the grass, then removed his arm cannon. "Why don't you get a fire ready? I'll take care of this fellow here."

Chapter 25

For two months, Henry and Timothy trailed the Council across the continent, living off of what they could forage after their supplies ran out. Several times, Timothy lost the trail completely, and they had to rely on guesswork and intuition until they found it once more. Finally, they stumbled upon the location of the Council's current camp, emerging from the tree line to see a tent pitched on the bank of a massive body of water.

Quickly, Timothy scrambled back into the forest before whoever was inside could see him. As he did, he nearly collided with Henry, who was standing right behind him.

"What is it?" Henry asked, keeping his voice low.

"A tent," Timothy whispered back. "Probably the Council, but I'm not sure."

As if summoned by his words, Councilman Payat emerged from the tent. He squinted in the late afternoon sunlight, looking around as if he had heard something.

"Don't move," Timothy muttered to Henry, freezing as Payat turned his attention to the forest. He stared intently at the tree line, and for a moment, Timothy was afraid that he had seen them.

Then Payat shrugged and returned to his tent, satisfied that he was alone.

"That's the Council, all right," Henry whispered. "Or one of them, anyway. Where do you suppose the other two are?"

"Once night falls, I can slip over there and check it out," Timothy suggested.

Henry nodded. "Good idea. In the meantime, though, we should probably move our camp to somewhere else. If the other Councilmen are in this forest, they might stumble upon our camp on their way back to theirs."

"We still need to keep an eye on them," Timothy pointed out, although secretly, he was impressed by Henry's foresight. If he had been alone, he knew, he never would have thought of that.

"After we set up camp, we'll take turns keeping watch until sunset," Henry said.

"Try to stay still as much as possible while you're watching," Timothy said. "It makes it harder for people to see you."

Henry grinned. "This isn't my first time on sentry duty," he said. "But thanks for the tip," he added before Timothy could feel embarrassed. Then, leading the way back through the forest, he selected a secluded spot for their campsite. Timothy took the first watch, keeping an eye on Payat for a couple of hours before turning the job over to Henry.

By sunset, there was still no sign of the other Councilmen, and Timothy was beginning to worry that they were up to something. Finally, after several agonizing hours of waiting, the sun sank below the horizon, providing the darkness Timothy needed to fully investigate the camp.

Even then, he had to wait a few hours longer. At Henry's suggestion, he agreed to postpone his investigation until he was sure the Councilman was asleep. After several more hours, the sound of gentle snoring carried to Timothy's ears, and he emerged from the trees, the pitch blackness of night more than making up for the lack of suitable cover on the sandy beach.

He approached the camp with caution, not ruling out the possibility that Payat was only pretending to be asleep. As it turned out, the Councilman had no such plan, and Timothy was soon satisfied that no one knew he was here. He inspected the Council's supplies first, checking to see if they had already picked up the drones. A quick search through the scattered crates of food and survival gear turned up no sign of the deadly robots. Or, more concerningly, any sign of the other two Councilmen.

Did Payat kill the other two? Timothy wondered. Then he dismissed the idea. It was certainly possible, but it was hardly the most plausible explanation. *Did they leave Payat here and go somewhere else?*

That was more likely, Timothy decided, but it was a much scarier prospect. If they had parted ways, there was no way to know where the other two were, or even if Payat was actually the one retrieving the drones.

His fears were soon assuaged, however, when he noticed two other patches of dead grass beside Payat's tent.

They were here just a few days ago, he realized. *But where are they now?* Against his better judgement, he hazarded a glance inside the Councilman's tent. To his relief, the man didn't stir, although there was still no sign of the others.

Sure now that the other two Council members were not in the camp, Timothy inspected the ground nearby, searching in the dark for any signs of what had happened to them. After nearly an hour of searching, he found footsteps in the sand leading up to the water. Several days of tides had nearly wiped out the tracks, but Timothy was sure he saw another, larger indentation as well.

A boat. They took a boat.

Quickly, he retreated to the camp to inform Henry of what he had discovered. "They don't have the drones yet," he reported. "I think the other Councilmen took a boat somewhere."

"Probably to Ellada," Henry said thoughtfully. "It'd be easier to sail there than to traverse the mountains."

"So what do we do?" Timothy asked. "Do we take the camp now before he wakes up?"

Henry rubbed his stubble. "It's not a bad idea," he conceded. "We have a unique opportunity to take one of the Council members out of the picture." He considered it for a few seconds more before discarding the idea. "No," he said at last. "We might get Payat, but the others will probably suspect something and escape with the attack drones. And above all, we can't let them get back to Kawts with the drones."

"Then what *is* the plan?"

"The way I see it, we've got two options," Henry said after a moment's thought. "Either we ambush them and steal the drones, or we destroy them from a distance as the Council passes by." He thought for a minute longer, then said, "The obvious advantage to the first plan, of course, is that we can make sure we get all the drones. If I blow them up from a distance, we can't guarantee I'll get them all." He paused. "On the other hand, confronting the Council directly is exceedingly risky, especially seeing as how there's only two of us and three of them."

"We can take them, though, right?"

Henry shook his head, suddenly serious. "The Council is not to be taken lightly. They're all experts with their weapon of choice. They're formidable foes even for Gearwire." He stared at Timothy until he was sure he understood his words. "Whichever plan we end up with, we'll have to strike unexpectedly and escape before the Council can retaliate." He leaned back, deep in thought.

"I think it'll work best if we wait to see this shipment," he said at last. "Once we know what kind of packaging and security we're dealing with, we can formulate a better plan of attack."

"So we just wait for the Council to come back?" Timothy asked, his excitement draining away.

Henry nodded. "'Fraid so," he said with a wry smile. "But with luck, it'll be a boring couple of days."

* * *

They stayed in their camp for nearly a week, spending their days silently watching Payat as he lounged about on the beach. Timothy was composing a sonnet in his head when he saw a dark speck appear on the horizon. He watched it for a few minutes and realized that it was getting closer.

Forgetting all about his poem, he nudged Henry, who was idly paging through a worn pocket New Testament. When Henry looked up, Timothy silently pointed to the rapidly growing thing in the distance. Slipping the book back into his shirt pocket, Henry was at Timothy's side in an instant, watching intently. He whipped out an antique pair of field binoculars and peered through them, studying the speck on the horizon.

"It's them," he confirmed in a low voice. "Two Councilmen, a bunch of large crates, and an unidentified man at the helm. If I had to guess, I'd say he was their supplier." He studied the situation for a few more seconds before adding, "We'd better get back to the camp. I suspect they'll want to set out as soon as they get everything unloaded."

As if proving his point, Payat began to take down his tent, noticing the ship for the first time.

Timothy and Henry hurried back to their camp, packing it up in record time. They returned to their hiding spot in the woods just in time to see the Council disembark from the boat, followed by several wooden crates, each of which was propelled by a pair of heavily armored robots. As they watched, the fourth man handed Payat a small remote control.

"This certainly complicates things," Henry observed, keeping his voice so low that Timothy could only barely hear it. "I'm not sure we'll be able to sneak off with fifty large crates that are being guarded by two drones each, in addition to three Council members."

"Not unless we come up with a really incredible diversion," Timothy agreed. He heard Henry's sharp intake of breath and looked over at him, only to find with surprise that Henry was avoiding his gaze.

"What is it?" he asked, dreading the response.

"I... I just had an idea," Henry replied slowly, making Timothy's unease grow. "But it's extremely risky. Borderline suicidal, in fact."

"Just tell me," Timothy said quickly, not sure he liked where the conversation was heading.

"If you lead the Council away from their campsite, I could sneak in and destroy the drones."

"So far, that doesn't sound too bad," Timothy said slowly, sensing that Henry wasn't finished.

"The only way I can do that is if you draw *all* the Councilmen away from the camp. And that will only happen if they recognize you *and* think you're alone." He took a deep breath and looked Timothy in the eyes. "I'm asking you to step out in front of the Council without any sort of armor or weapons to draw them away from their campsite for an extended period of time."

Timothy licked his lips nervously. He wasn't opposed to the idea of facing off against the Council. What he wasn't particularly excited about was the idea of him leading the Council on a prolonged wild goose chase without any of his gear. But he could see that Henry was right about that part of the plan. If he showed up wearing body armor and wielding throwing stars, they would know for sure that he had joined the resistance, and they might suspect a trap. The only way he could get them all to follow him was if they thought he was alone. An easy target.

"If you don't want to, I'm sure we can come up with another plan,"

Henry said quickly. "I wouldn't blame you. As I said, it's practically a suicide mission."

"How long do you think you'd need?" Timothy asked, slowly processing the suggestion.

Henry squinted as he did the math. "There's about fifty crates, with roughly eight drones per box. Counting the transportation drones, that's approximately 500 drones. Unless those transport drones are a lot tougher than they look, it shouldn't take me more than five minutes to destroy all the drones, but first you'd have to lead the Council far enough away so that they couldn't hear the explosions and get back before I'm done. All total, you'd probably need to keep them busy for about fifteen minutes."

Timothy said nothing, weighing his options. It would be dangerous - easily the most dangerous thing he had ever done. Yet the thought of Quill and Samuel living the rest of their lives as Blanks made his mind up for him.

"I'll do it," he said at last. "Whatever it takes to stop the Council."

"Are you sure?" Henry asked. "The odds of you making it out alive are pretty slim."

Timothy took a deep breath before responding. "I'm sure," he said. "Just don't take too long."

"I'll do my best," Henry said. "We'll have to wait a few days to make sure that their supplier doesn't interfere. And that way, we can also choose when and where we strike."

Timothy nodded, grateful to have some delay before he faced off against the Council.

"In the meantime," Henry continued, "We'll continue to keep an eye on them. And see if we can't come up with a less dangerous plan."

Their efforts to avoid Timothy's mission proved to be in vain, however, and several days later, Timothy found himself crouched behind a tree just outside the Council's camp. His heart was pounding, but he didn't move, trying to work up the courage to follow through with the plan.

If you don't do this now, you're never going to, he realized. *It's now or never.* Springing to his feet, he dashed out into the camp.

"Help!" he shouted, running up to one of the tents. "There's a bear or something in the-" he skidded to a halt as Payat emerged from the tent.

"Payat," Timothy whispered, pretending to be shocked. Recognition flashed in the Councilman's eyes.

"You," he muttered darkly. "Jilt! Karr! Timothy's here!" he shouted into the tent.

Timothy took off at a sprint, trying to put as much distance between himself and the Council as possible. Already, he could hear them crashing clumsily through the forest behind him, unaccustomed to running through the dense vegetation.

As he ran, he tried to recall which weapons were favored by the three Councilmen behind him. Suddenly, he tripped on a rock and went sprawling onto the ground. He heard the report of a gun and saw a bullet whiz through the air where he had been standing a second before.

Payat's an expert marksman, he remembered with a sickening sense of dread. Quickly, he rolled to his feet and continued to run, keeping as low to the ground as possible without disappearing completely. The plan depended on the Council being able to keep him in sight for a minimum of seven minutes. Another bullet whizzed through the air, smacking into a tree just inches from Timothy's head, showering him with splinters of wood and scratching up his face as he ran past.

His heart was pounding as he ducked behind another tree. He was beginning to tire, but he knew that to slow down, even for a moment, would get him killed. He glanced behind him briefly to make sure that the Council was still following him.

Another bullet from Payat answered that question for him, grazing the side of Timothy's cheek.

There's no way I can keep this up for a full fifteen minutes, he realized, beginning to panic. Then he shook his head.

I'll just have to alter the plan a bit, he thought, veering suddenly to the left.

He ran through the trees, this time trying his best to stay concealed. He had no doubt that the Council would see him anyway, but it was probably for the best. If he had disappeared without a trace, they might become suspicious. His only goal for the moment was to make their job more difficult. Already, a new plan was taking shape in his mind. He suddenly changed direction again, heading to the right this time. Behind him, he could hear the Council shouting as they tried to catch up.

Suddenly, something heavy hit him from behind. He stumbled, but then he righted himself. He felt another impact, and everything went black.

* * *

When Timothy woke up, he was back in the camp, his shoulder throbbing painfully. He tried to sit up, but the wave of pain that washed over him made him reconsider the idea. He gasped, stifling a scream of pain. Henry, who had been boiling a pot of water a few yards away, turned when he heard the sound.

"Lie back down," he said, removing a cloth from the water and walking over to Timothy. "You were shot," he explained as he gently cleaned the wounds. "Twice." Timothy winced and tried to sit up again. "Lay back down," Henry repeated, more firmly this time. "You need to rest right now. You've lost a lot of blood."

Giving up on sitting for the time being, Timothy lay back down.

"What happened?" he asked, trying to remember.

"The Council heard me destroying the drones and came running. I managed to get all the drones, but the Council put a few dents into my arm cannon," he said, patting the battered green cylinder affectionately. "After I got away, I went back to the camp, but you didn't show up. So Snipps and I went looking for you. We found you in a shallow gully with two bullets in you."

"How bad is it?"

"The actual wounds aren't too serious, but like I said, you lost a lot of blood. But if you can just hold in there for a few more days, I think we're in the clear. It'll still be a week or two before you're well enough to travel, but that shouldn't be a problem. The Council made a beeline back to Kawts once they saw the drones were destroyed."

"Mission accomplished, then," Timothy said with a weak smile. Then he drifted off, settling back into a deep sleep.

* * *

For the next several weeks, they stayed where they were while Timothy recovered, Henry tending to his wounds as best he could. Finally, after inspecting Timothy's progress for the hundredth time, Henry declared him fully recovered. He was still a little weak, and he still felt a small twinge of pain if he moved wrong, but he was glad to be leaving, eager to get back to the base.

The return trip took them longer than the way out due to Timothy's injury, but finally, about five months after they had left, they emerged from the forest to see the cave in front of them.

Timothy slid down off Snipps' back, exhausted from the journey. Noticing this, Henry said, "Why don't you go home and get some sleep? I'll let Gearwire know we're back."

Timothy nodded gratefully, returning to his room and falling asleep in just a few minutes. When he woke up, he made his way to Gearwire's office to take part in the debriefing.

"Henry told me what happened back there," Gearwire said as he entered. "He told me how you risked your life to buy him enough time to destroy those drones." He paused, looking Timothy in the eye as he continued.

"Loyalty, courage, and fighting ability. These are qualities we value very highly here. You've impressed all of us with your performance on your missions. In fact, I'd like you to join my crew."

Timothy was silent, surprised by Gearwire's proposition. "I - I'll have to think about it," he stammered at last.

Gearwire nodded, smiling faintly. "Of course. It's not a decision to be taken lightly. But we could really use someone like you on the crew."

Excusing himself from the command center, Timothy wandered through the tunnels of the base, mulling over Gearwire's offer.

If only Samuel was here. He'd know exactly what to do. But even as he had the thought, he knew what Samuel would have done in his position. He had risked everything to stop the Council's reign of terror.

With sudden clarity, Timothy knew what he had to do. Walking quickly back to Gearwire's house, he burst into Gearwire's study.

"I'm in."

Chapter 26

A few weeks after his decision to join Gearwire's crew, Timothy was hard at work in the training hall, practicing with his staff against a training dummy. As he paused for a drink of water, Henry came up to him, a small cluster of Gearwire's crewmembers trailing behind him.

"Timothy!" Henry called. "Just who we were hoping to see!"

"What's this all about?" Timothy asked, staring at the small crowd that was beginning to gather.

"Come here," Henry said, grabbing Timothy's wrist and pulling him along. "Down to the shooting range."

"Why?" Timothy said, breaking into a jog to match Henry's pace.

"Idalbo and I have a wager about which one of us is the better marksman."

"No, we don't!" Idalbo protested. "There is no wager! I never agreed to any wager!"

Henry waved a dismissive hand in his direction. "You're only saying that because you know I'll win!"

Turning back to Timothy, he said, "I've seen you in action with those shurikens of yours. I reckon you could make a pretty good showing."

"That's what this is about? You want me to join your marksmanship contest?"

"Why not?" Henry said. "You're a member of the crew now, too.

What harm could a little friendly competition do?" They had reached the shooting range now, and Henry released Timothy's hand. "So what do you say? Are you in?"

Timothy looked around at the rapidly gathering crowd. "Sure. Like you said, what harm could it do?"

"Great!" Henry said, grinning like a madman. He clipped his battered cannon into place around his arm. "GK! You wouldn't mind watching the line for us, would you?"

The Golden Knight nodded, moving into position along the borderline between the shooters and the targets. He gave Henry a thumbs-up, his brown eyes shining with something akin to amusement.

"Since you've already got a line judge and a bunch of competitors, I guess I'll be the announcer," Adalbo said as he landed beside Henry, his wings folding back up into his shell.

Idalbo groaned. "We don't need an announcer," he said. "We're just having a friendly contest."

"That is precisely why you need an announcer, my dear brother," Adalbo said, unable to hide his glee.

"You're welcome to commentate if you want," Henry said. "Just make sure you're not giving preferential coverage to your brother."

Adalbo grinned, his eyes sparkling. "I wouldn't dream of it. Good luck, Idalbo," he added before shooting up into the air to watch the contest from above.

"I'll go first," Henry said, stepping up to the line. He squinted at the row of slightly singed targets in front of him, the fingers of his free hand drumming against his leg. Then, in a sudden flurry of movement, he fired his arm cannon at five of the targets in rapid succession. The blasts dissipated when they hit the targets, leaving behind new scorch marks.

"Nearly perfect!" Adalbo called out from the air. "Three bullseyes and two just shy."

Henry grunted. "I knew I should have aimed a tad higher on that last one."

"Idalbo, you're up," the Golden Knight said.

Idalbo took a deep breath and stepped up to the line, drawing his bow and loading it with one of his quills. He lined up the shot and then fired, moving on to the next target before he had a chance to see the results of his first shot.

Once the fifth quill had been fired, Adalbo flew down to the targets to collect his brother's arrows. "Only two bullseyes. But the other three are about as close as they can be without being in the middle."

"Alright, Tim. You're up," Henry said, giving him a light push toward the line.

Timothy stared at the targets, turning his shuriken over in his hand. He exhaled slowly, whipping the projectile into the target, striking it directly in the center. Taking his time, he moved on to the next target, doing the same thing. He moved to the third target and let the third shuriken fly. To his great surprise, the shuriken never reached the target, suddenly jerking out of sight. Puzzled, he turned around to see Gearwire standing behind him, his glue gun still raised.

"I think it's safe to say I've won," he said drily, giving Henry a meaningful look. "Sorry to break up the party, but we have important business to discuss." He looked up to face the rest of his crew members. "Meet me at the command center in five minutes. We have work to do."

With that, he turned and disappeared back into the crowd.

* * *

Five minutes later, Timothy arrived at Gearwire's house. As he entered the room, he was immediately struck by the subdued atmosphere of the meeting, a stark contrast to the excited energy of the training room just a few minutes prior. The impression was only strengthened by the presence of Gearwire's entire crew, with the exception of Crystal and Jewel. Yet even as he had the thought, he noticed Gearwire's radio transmitter lying on the table and realized that they, too, were present.

Gearwire was silent as he entered, waiting until he took his seat at the table before he began. "Many of you have been with us for years," he said. "You've waited patiently as we built this base and gathered our resources. It's only been in the last couple of years that we've had the tools and manpower necessary to actually begin the liberation of Kawts."

"Now it's time to liberate another city," Gearwire continued. "I've called this meeting to begin planning for an invasion of Garrington."

"Garrington?" Henry objected. "You picked that spot for a city because it was virtually inaccessible from the outside. How could we possibly take Garrington?"

"We'll use a tunnel," Gearwire said, looking at Timothy. "We've already dug tunnels to Grimshaw, Kawts, and Duncan's Ridge. With a tunnel, we could take the city from behind before they even realize we're there."

"You'll have to trust that the Council won't be able to react in time," the Mysterious Man said, his eyes narrowing. "If they mobilize before we get clear of the tunnel, we'll be sitting ducks."

"Not to mention the fact that they could follow the tunnel back to find the location of our base," Idalbo added.

"Very good points," Gearwire conceded. "Jewel? How long do you think it would take the Council to get to Garrington if there was trouble?"

"Without any sort of advance warning, they can be ready for battle in just a few minutes. I can't say how long it would take them to actually reach Garrington, though."

"How long would it take for them to mobilize the Blanks and attack drones?" Dr. Maddium asked.

"If Garrington's chief of security is anything like Volker, it's safe to say that they could mobilize the Blanks within the city in minutes. Logically speaking, though, he's probably not quite as fast as Volker, considering he's never had to deal with a raid before."

"And as for the attack drones," Crystal said. "Their maximum speed is around one hundred miles per hour. Factoring in the time it would take the Council to learn about the attack, I would say to expect attack drones between ten and twenty minutes after we break through the tunnel."

"That's a pretty narrow window," Adalbo said. "And don't forget, we know nothing about the layout of this town. It's the one place we've never managed to gain a foothold."

Gearwire nodded solemnly. "It's ambitious, I know," he admitted. "But if the town was built according to my blueprints, we do actually know quite a lot about its layout."

"We can't count on that," Henry said, shaking his head. "After all, there was supposed to be a wall and several turrets around Duncan's Ridge. And we all know that there weren't."

"And even if it was originally built to your designs, towns change over time," Dr. Maddium agreed.

"I could go there to scout it out in advance," Timothy suggested.

"The only entrance we know of is heavily guarded," the Mysterious Man said. "You'd practically have to be a ghost in order to get through unnoticed!"

Gearwire inhaled sharply.

"What is it?" Dr. Maddium said, recognizing the reaction.

"I might have something that could help with that," Gearwire said, looking meaningfully at Henry and Dr. Maddium.

Dr. Maddium's eyes grew wide as he realized what Gearwire was talking about. "You don't mean..."

"Gwen's belt?" Henry asked, equally surprised. "I didn't know it still existed!"

Gearwire nodded slowly. "I still have it," he said, his voice heavy with sadness. "We can use it to sneak into the city."

Timothy looked around at the rest of Gearwire's crew, wondering if they were as confused as he was. The Mysterious Man and the Golden Knight were as stoic and unreadable as ever. And if Idalbo and Adalbo were confused, they showed no sign of it. Only the Kolts seemed to share his bewilderment.

Fortunately, Dr. Maddium came to the rescue. "Gwen Aria was a former crew member of ours before the resistance. She had a device that allowed the wearer to walk through solid objects and turn invisible."

Timothy was on the verge of asking what had happened to her, but a look at Gearwire and Henry's faces was enough to tell him that she was dead.

"That might do the trick," the Mysterious Man said after a long pause. "But regardless, we'll only have a few minutes to gain control of the city before hordes of attack drones arrive."

"Bah! We can take them!" Henry exclaimed suddenly, his eyes shining with excitement. "We'll make short work of those stupid robots! It'll be just like the old days! We'll blast our way through!"

"I doubt very much if that's a wise idea," Dr. Maddium said, a hint of a smile on his face.

"Regardless, I do think there's something we can do to delay them a bit," Howard said. "If we have a few people create a diversion off to the south of Kawts, we can draw the Council in the opposite direction and increase the time it will take for them to hear about the attack and send drones to help."

Gearwire nodded. "Good. That might be just enough to give us the extra time we need." He turned to Henry. "Start working on a tunnel toward Garrington. I'll go up there tonight to find the best entrance point."

"Whatever you say, captain," Henry said with a salute.

"The rest of you, start preparing for battle. Make sure your weapons are all in order and re-stocked." He hesitated for a moment, looking around at the faces of his crew members. "And pray that this will work."

* * *

The next several weeks passed slowly. With the help of Snipps and under Henry's direction, the tunnel to Garrington grew longer and longer. Gearwire returned from his expedition with a rough map of the interior of the cave, copies of which had been distributed to everyone who was to play a role in the coming attack. Timothy spent nearly all his time at the training center, honing his skills in anticipation of the battle.

Eventually, the Mysterious Man felt compelled to intervene.

"I think that's enough training for one day," he said, coming up behind Timothy as silently as a ghost.

"For that matter, it's probably enough training for the entire week," Henry added, appearing beside the Mysterious Man.

Timothy threw another shuriken into the target, ignoring them. "I have to be ready."

He drew his hand back to throw another shuriken, but the Mysterious Man grabbed his wrist. "Let me rephrase," he said sternly. "You are done training for today. And tomorrow."

Timothy opened his mouth to protest, but the Mysterious Man cut him off. "Need I remind you that Gearwire put me in charge of this training facility? If I say you're done, you are done." He looked directly at Timothy, his face unwavering.

"Fine," Timothy sighed at last. The Mysterious Man released his wrist, and Timothy recalled his shurikens, putting them back into his bag. He walked out of the cave, and Henry followed him.

"Mind if I walk with you for a bit?" he asked. Timothy didn't respond, and they walked a short distance in silence. "Man was meant to labor for six days and rest on the seventh," Henry said at last, breaking the silence. "You've been going nonstop for nearly ten days now. It's not healthy. You'll burn yourself out."

"What else do you want me to do?" Timothy asked, hoping that his fear didn't show in his voice. "We're going to go into battle any day now, and you want me to just sit and relax?" He shook his head. "I'm not ready yet. I need more practice."

"You're a fine fighter," Henry said. "But that won't do you any good if you are too exhausted to actually function during the battle. And only a fool would ever think they are completely prepared for a battle. Your fear is perfectly natural."

"For everyone who isn't a member of Gearwire's crew," Timothy said. "You can't honestly tell me that Gearwire and the Mysterious Man are scared."

Henry bit his lip. "Well, I wouldn't say scared exactly. But have you seen Gearwire recently? He's been holed up in his office all week, trying to think of anything that might possibly go wrong. And I can't speak on behalf of the Mysterious Man, but I suspect that he's concerned as well. He went through a lot before he came here."

"You seem perfectly calm."

Henry cracked a smile at this. "One might say I've had a lot of experience. And one thing I've learned is that it makes people feel safer if their leader doesn't show their fear. So I put on a bit of an act. I'm every bit as nervous as the next guy. But I've been through battles before, and I've come out in one piece. I figure that if the Lord wants me to stay here awhile longer, that's fine by me. And if it's time for me to go, I'm okay with that too."

The silence that followed seemed to stretch on forever as Timothy took in what Henry had said.

"Thanks for the words of encouragement," he said at last. He took a few steps toward the tunnel that led to the residential area. "I guess I should go get some rest," he said, realizing for the first time how tired he was.

Henry smiled knowingly. "You have plenty of time to prepare between then and now. You'll be ready when the time comes."

* * *

It had been nearly a month since the initial meeting of Gearwire's crew by the time the tunnel was completed, only a thin wall of dirt separating it from the city itself. The very afternoon the tunnel was finished, Gearwire again called his crew together for a strategy meeting, this one even more somber than the first.

"It's time we plan our attack," Gearwire said, unrolling a map of the city onto the table. "You've all seen this map. The tunnel we've dug lets out right about here," he said, tapping a spot against the back wall of the cave.

"Before the Council arrives or sends reinforcements, we need to gain control of this gate," he said, pointing to a spot on the other side. "Crystal has estimated that we'll have no more than twenty minutes, and possibly as little as fifteen. I'd like Henry and Timothy to lead a small platoon directly to the gate to fend off any attack drones that show up."

He looked at each of them in turn. "I don't need to tell you that the outcome of the battle may very well depend on holding that gate. If we can't keep them bottlenecked at the entrance, we won't have another chance to stop them until they reach the tunnel." He turned to face the rest of the group. "We'll also need someone to lead the diversion raid in Johnson's Clearing."

"Madison," Howard said immediately, his face set in determination.

Madison looked at her father with surprise.

"Me?" she said in disbelief. "I've never led an attack this big before..."

"You'll be fine," Howard said. "You just need to create some sort of disturbance - enough to draw the Council away from Kawts. Destroy some attack drones, immobilize a few Blanks - just long enough to get the Council's attention."

"Once the Council arrives, get back to the base," Gearwire said. "They're too dangerous for one person to face alone. Don't do anything reckless. Remember, it's just a diversion."

Just a diversion, Timothy thought, watching Howard's face as he listened to Gearwire's instructions. *Which is probably why he volunteered Madison,* he realized. *He's trying to keep her out of the battle.*

"The only question now is when," Henry said. "When would they be the least likely to be in the area?"

"As far as we can tell, they're all in Kawts right now," Jewel reported through the radio.

"But they're planning on taking a tour of the other cities sometime in the next few weeks," Crystal said. "The sooner we pull this off, the better."

"We'll attack at dawn tomorrow," Gearwire said. "With luck, they won't even notice we're there until we've taken the city."

* * *

Yet despite Gearwire's sound plan, unforeseeable circumstances decreed that the battle would not be so easily won. Over the course of that night, one of the citizens of Garrington had run through the streets with an improvised spear, threatening the Council and the

215

Blanks. As a result, the local Security Force was already on high alert, and Councilmen Ethos, Wade, and LeSalle had left Kawts in the dead of night to escort the would-be revolutionary back for questioning. As such, they were nearly to the city gate by the time Henry broke through the thin barrier blocking the end of the tunnel.

Chapter 27

Timothy, Henry, and the men under their command ran out of the tunnel, making for the gate as quickly as they could. The attack drones in the city suddenly opened fire, killing several of the rebels before they could react. Without even slowing down, Henry turned and blasted them out of the sky with his arm cannon, leaving behind only smoldering wreckage. The sound of gunfire echoed through the cave, testifying to the shocked rebels that they had somehow lost the element of surprise.

"Keep going!" Henry bellowed, shouting to be heard above the commotion. "Attack drones or no, we need to secure the gate!" Urged on by their commander, the platoon increased their speed, breaking into a jog. But as they drew nearer to their destination, Henry suddenly broke away from the group.

"What is it?" Timothy asked, slightly panicked.

"Ethos," Henry answered, barely pausing to answer Timothy's question. "I saw Ethos. He's heading towards the tunnel!" In a flash, he was off, in hot pursuit of the head councilman.

Timothy hesitated. If Henry couldn't stop Ethos from reaching the tunnel, he would discover the location of the rebel's base. And, as Henry himself had told him, the Council members were all skilled warriors and formidable foes. Whether Henry could defeat him by himself might come down to who attacked first.

Follow him, a voice said in his head, breaking through Timothy's panic. Realizing he didn't have much time, he came to a decision.

"Hold the gate at all costs," Timothy told the lieutenant in charge of the platoon.

"Aren't you-" the lieutenant began, but Timothy was already gone, running off after Henry.

By the time he caught up with him, he was already confronting Ethos, standing between the Councilman and the entrance to the tunnel.

"You won't win this battle, Ethos," Henry said grimly. "Your reign is over."

He leveled his arm cannon at Ethos and prepared to fire. Ethos smirked and gave an almost imperceptible nod. Instantly, there was a loud bang, and Henry staggered and fell to his knees, a patch of red spreading across the front of his shirt.

Timothy looked up to see LeSalle standing in the alleyway behind Ethos, his sniper rifle planted up against his shoulder. Before the Councilman could realize that Timothy was there, he threw a weighted shuriken at him, striking him in the head. He crumpled to the ground, unconscious.

Timothy brought his attention to Ethos, who was slowly approaching Henry. Henry staggered to his feet, swaying as he tried to aim his cannon at the Councilman.

"Goodbye," Ethos said with a smile, impaling Henry with his sword.

As Henry fell to the ground again, Ethos started for the tunnel. Just as he reached it, however, Henry managed to prop himself up on one elbow and fire one last shot, burying the Councilman in a shower of dirt and gravel as he collapsed the top of the tunnel. Then, exhausted by the effort, he fell back to the ground.

Timothy ran over to him, desperately hoping that his wounds weren't as bad as they appeared. But one look at his blood-soaked shirt was enough to dispel this idea. Henry's breathing was shallow, and Timothy could tell that he wouldn't survive much longer.

"Timothy? Is that you?" Henry gasped as Timothy knelt beside him.

"It's me," Timothy said, his voice quavering.

Henry coughed up blood and said, "You've got to hold the gate. Don't let them get reinforcements in here."

"I can't leave you here!" Timothy protested. "There's got to be something I can do. I'll go get a doctor - or Gearwire, or-"

"I'd be dead before you got back," Henry said with a pained smile. "But it's okay. I know where I'm going. I'll be fine." He coughed again, and his breathing became more labored. "Tell Gearwire-" he began. "Tell Gearwire thanks for everything. I wouldn't have missed fighting alongside him for anything." He closed his eyes, and for a moment, Timothy thought he was dead.

"Go," he gasped with one last effort. "Don't let the Council win." He took in one last, shuddering breath, and then lay still.

Henry was dead.

Timothy staggered to his feet, numb. He and Henry had grown close over the last few months, and part of him refused to acknowledge that he was gone. Of all the members of Gearwire's crew, he had always been the most gregarious and friendly. Even in the final minutes leading up to the battle, he had remained cheerful and encouraging, cracking jokes with the men to settle their nerves.

And now he was dead.

Timothy lurched away, his stomach churning. He fell to the ground and vomited into the alleyway. Part of him just wanted to stop, to give up and surrender to the Council. But Henry's last words came back to him. He had used his dying breath to remind him of his role in the battle. Shoving his sorrow and nausea aside, Timothy forced himself to his feet and ran back to the gate.

He returned to find that his platoon had been nearly wiped out. The lieutenant he had left in charge limped up to him as he approached, a bullet wound in his leg.

"A force of attack drones came at us from the city," he said. "We weren't ready for them. Before we could take control of the situation, another attachment of drones arrived from Kawts."

Timothy's heart sank. "So the Council's reinforcements have already arrived."

The lieutenant nodded.

"Is there anyone left who's in good enough shape to run?"

"Only two," the lieutenant replied. "Three, if you need me to."

"Send them to alert Gearwire," Timothy said, impressed by the man's courage. "You and I will hold the entrance."

The lieutenant shouted Timothy's order to the two remaining uninjured men. Then he took his place with Timothy at the mouth of the cave, shooting down any drone that dared to show itself. They fought side by side for several hours until the lieutenant passed out from loss of blood.

Timothy fought on alone, the only man of a force of thirty still standing.

* * *

Fortunately for the rebels, the Council made no effort to call in additional reinforcements, partially due to Madison's diversion and partially because they believed the attack to be of only minor importance. In the end, the rebels pushed the Council's forces out of the city, though nearly a third of their men now lay dead and hardly any were without injuries. No trace of LeSalle or Ethos was found, but only time would tell if they had escaped the town alive.

Henry's funeral, along with hundreds of others, was held the next day. Leaving a small group of soldiers behind to guard the two captured cities, the rest of the inhabitants of the base gathered in an enormous cavern at the back of the complex to say their final farewells to their friends and relatives. As the crowd gathered together at the mouth of the cavern, Pastor Noah climbed up onto a large boulder and began to speak.

"We have all lost people we love at the hands of the Council," he said somberly. "Yesterday, we all united to free another city from their control. The brave men and women who lie behind me paid for our victory with their lives." His voice caught a little as he said this, remembering his own brother who had been killed by the Council several years prior.

"But despite all that, we know," he continued with a renewed sense of hope. "We know that, though our loved ones are dead, we will one day see them again. We look forward to that day when we will all stand before the Lord in a place where death, mourning, and pain will cease."

He let his words hang in the air for a moment, and Timothy couldn't help but remember Henry's last words. It was clear he had shared Pastor Noah's views, although Timothy couldn't quite bring himself to believe it himself.

The chaplain spoke for a few minutes longer before closing with a prayer. Then he stepped off the boulder, clearing the stage for people to share their memories of the deceased.

Timothy glanced over at Gearwire, wondering if he would offer a eulogy for Henry. As soon as he did, however, he immediately regretted it. Gearwire was sobbing quietly on the other side of the cave, looking a far cry from the confident, determined leader of the rebels he had been the morning before.

As the rest of Gearwire's crew gathered around Henry's coffin, Timothy slipped out the back of the room. He wandered aimlessly through the nearly empty halls of the cave before finally stepping out into the open area that overlooked Kawts.

He was still sitting there, lost in thought, when Dr. Maddium found him.

"How are you holding up?" he asked gently, sitting down beside him. Timothy turned to face him, noting the scientist's tear-streaked face.

"It's all my fault," he said, turning away once more. "Henry, the gate - all of it."

"You're not to blame for the Council's actions," Dr. Maddium said with a surprising fierceness. "Not even Gearwire is to blame for that." There was a long pause, then he continued in a softer tone, "You can't blame yourself for his death. This is a war. People will die no matter how hard we try."

"I didn't stay with my men to hold the gate," Timothy said. "I left to help Henry guard the tunnel. And I couldn't do that right, either."

Dr. Maddium said nothing for a long time. "You had a choice to make," he said at last. "No battle plan could have anticipated it. And if you hadn't gone after Henry, you'd probably be dead and the Council would have made it to the tunnel."

Timothy stared down at Kawts. From here, it looked so peaceful. It was hard to believe that it was ruled by murderers and tyrants.

"But if I had been where I was supposed to be, maybe I could have prevented the Council from getting in. We could have fought off the drones and captured Ethos."

"Perhaps," Dr. Maddium admitted. "There's no way to know for sure what would have happened if you had made a different choice. But you can't blame yourself. I've seen firsthand what happens when people blame themselves for choices they made while under fire. It destroys them."

Timothy said nothing. For a long time, both of them just sat in the mouth of the cave, each lost in his own thoughts. Finally, Dr. Maddium stood.

"I should probably get back inside," he said. "Don't be afraid to reach out. Most of us here have experienced what you're going through at one point or another." With that, he turned and walked slowly back into the base.

* * *

Timothy threw a shuriken into the target, rapidly followed by two others. Henry's death flashed before his eyes, and he increased his pace, throwing shuriken after shuriken as fast as he could. After a moment, he recalled the shurikens to his hand and began the process over again.

"You're going to miss your call if you don't pack this up soon," the Mysterious Man said, coming up beside him.

Timothy stared at him. "What call?"

"You know what call I mean. You and Jewel have a call around this time every week. It's not exactly a secret."

Timothy shook his head. "I don't have time."

"It might help to talk to someone about it."

"I'd rather not." Timothy threw another shuriken at the target. "And besides, I need to train."

The Mysterious Man grabbed him by his shoulders and turned him around. "Look around, Timothy. No one else is here. You're allowed to take time to grieve. Take a few days off. Talk to Jewel - or anyone, really."

Timothy shook his head. "You told me the same thing last week - that I needed to take a break, that I would be ready when the times came. Well, the time came. And I wasn't ready. And because of that, Henry is dead." He took a deep, shuddering breath. "I can't let anyone else die because of me."

He turned back toward the row of targets, hoping that the Mysterious Man would give up and go away.

"Timothy. Timothy - listen to me," the Mysterious Man said. "What happened with Henry was not your fault. Trust me - I know what it's like to have friends die because of something you did. This is not that."

"Is that supposed to make me feel better?"

"No. But you can't live your life like this, blaming yourself whenever someone dies under your command. It's possible that if you had trained more, Henry would still be alive. It's even more possible that if you had trained more, he still would have died, and you along with him. You can't get stuck lamenting what might have been. All you can do is to find a way to move forward."

The Mysterious Man's words hung in the air for a long moment. "Look," he said at last. "I know you're not exactly sold on the whole Bible thing. But I think it would do you good to join us at the service tomorrow."

"I'll think about it," Timothy said, turning away again. He picked up a shuriken.

"Just make sure you give yourself time to grieve," the Mysterious Man said. "And don't train too hard."

Timothy heard the sound of the Mysterious Man's footsteps retreating back to the main cave. Only when the footsteps had faded behind him did he turn around again, tears streaming down his face.

* * *

On Sunday morning, Timothy stood outside the door to the chapel, the Mysterious Man's words replaying in his head. As he hesitated outside the door, he could hear the sounds of singing, the stirring echoes of a centuries-old song. Overcoming his reluctance to enter, Timothy slipped inside, taking a seat at the end of the last row.

"Our text today is from the book of John," Pastor Noah began once the singing had stopped. "John chapter eleven says this: 'Martha said to Jesus, 'Lord, if you had been here, my brother would not have died. But even now I know that whatever you ask from God, God will give you.' Jesus said to her, 'Your brother will rise again.' Martha said to him, 'I know that he will rise again in the resurrection on the last day.' Jesus said to her, 'I am the resurrection and the life. Whoever believes in me, though he die, yet shall he live, and everyone who lives and believes in me shall never die.'"

Pastor Noah looked out at the faces of his listeners. "We've been through a lot in the past couple of days," he said. "In times like these, we sometimes feel like Mary and Martha. We cry out, 'Lord, if only you had been here...' If you had been here, my brother would not have died. If you had been here, my friend wouldn't have been turned into a Blank. Our families would not have been separated." He smiled bitterly. "And yet, as Christians, we know that this is not the end of the story. The same Jesus who saves us from our sins is even now preparing a place for us in Heaven. But let's take a look at these verses in more detail..."

Timothy listened intently as Pastor Noah continued on, retelling fully the story of Lazarus and expounding at length on the concept of Heaven. The more the chaplain added to his description, the more Timothy came to understand why Henry had been so calm about his imminent death.

If I could be sure that a place like that was waiting for me, it wouldn't matter what Ethos tried to do to me.

Timothy walked out of the service strangely comforted, knowing that, at the very least, Henry had died with the hope that he was going somewhere better.

Chapter 28

"The Council is attacking Duncan's Ridge!" a voice shouted, waking Timothy from his slumber. Timothy sat up to see one of the resistance officers standing over him. "Gearwire sent me to tell you to get there right away."

Timothy groaned and stood up, quickly putting on his armor. He mounted Snipps and rode off down the tunnel as fast as he could. Gearwire and several of his other crew members were already engaged in a desperate battle with the Council's forces by the time he emerged from the tunnel.

Timothy scanned the chaos for Gearwire, but found that the rebel general was nowhere in sight. A flash of light caught his eye, and he turned to see Madison a short distance away, her energy whips darting among the incoming Blanks like snakes. Timothy jogged over to her just as she backflipped into the middle of a group of Blanks, whirling the whips around her. The Blanks twitched and dropped to the ground as the whips touched them, unconscious. As Timothy approached her, she turned on him, only barely avoiding zapping him as well.

"Have you seen Gearwire?" Timothy asked, dancing out of the way.

Madison nodded, unhooking one of her grenades from her belt and tossing it at a cluster of attack drones. "He's over by the ridge."

Timothy nodded and ran off, spotting Gearwire at the bottom of the steep ridge that surrounded the town. As he approached, Gearwire quickly blasted a pair of attack drones from the sky.

"Where do you want me?" Timothy asked, trying to conceal his fear as he casually took down an attack drone with one of his shurikens.

Gearwire ducked as a group of attack drones dive-bombed him, rolling behind a boulder. He turned and fired his glue gun at the robots, destroying them all before they could turn around.

"Hold the ridge!" he shouted. "It's our best chance of pushing them back!" He blasted a Blank with his glue gun, this time spraying out a sticky glue that pinned the Blank to the ground.

Timothy nodded and jogged towards the ridge. He scrambled up it, sliding backwards as his feet found patches of loose gravel on the steep incline. He forced himself to advance slowly, crawling on his hands and knees on multiple occasions. Finally, he reached the top, his armor scuffed and dusty.

From where he stood now, he could see the entire battlefield laid out before him, the steadily advancing hordes of Blanks and attack drones on one side of the ridge and the rebels' hastily arranged defenses on the other.

A makeshift barricade had been erected along the outside edge of the town, running along the outer walls of the outlying buildings. Behind that, Timothy could see the tiny forms of some of the rebellion's less able fighters, evacuating the remaining citizens of the ancient town. On the outside of the barricade, the rebel's forces were in disarray, overwhelmed and disoriented by the unexpected attack.

Yet even as Timothy watched, he could see Gearwire shouting something to the soldiers nearest to him, organizing them into a rough defensive line. For the time being, they were holding their own against the handful of the Council's forces that managed to break through, but Timothy could see that if the Council managed to punch a big enough hole in their lines, they were done for.

Looking around, he spotted Idalbo standing atop a boulder a few yards away, doing his best to take down any drone that tried to cross over into the town below. Timothy scrambled up beside him, using his throwing stars to take down any attack drones that got too close. From his new vantage point, he could see Dr. Maddium facing off against a squadron of Blanks, the palms of his leather gloves crackling with balls of raw electricity. The Mysterious Man stood nearby, engaged in a sword duel with Councilman Alexis.

Alexis, Timothy thought with a start, recalling what he knew about the Councilman. *Which means Wade is probably -*

As if warned by some sixth sense, Timothy wheeled around just in time to see Councilman Wade crest the ridge, bearing down on Idalbo with his sword. Idalbo, focused on the battle below, didn't see him.

"Look out!" Timothy shouted, sweeping Idalbo's legs out from under him and stepping between the startled mutant and Wade. He quickly grabbed one of his shurikens and thrust it at Wade's incoming sword, knocking it aside. As Wade reeled back, Timothy threw the shuriken at him. At the last second, he ducked, grinning evilly. Timothy raised his hand, and the weapon flew back to his glove, scoring a shallow cut across Wade's forearm as he twisted to avoid it.

Wade snarled and lashed out with his sword. Timothy leapt back, the sword swishing through the place where he had been standing seconds before. He slashed at Wade with the throwing star, but Wade blocked the attack easily. He struck at Timothy again, and Timothy again jumped out of the way. This time, his foot caught on a crack in the boulder, and he fell. He hit the ground hard, momentarily winded. As he struggled to regain his breath, Wade raised his sword high into the air for a killing strike.

Suddenly, the Golden Knight barreled into the Councilman's side, sending him sprawling.

"You looked like you needed some help," he said brightly, his brown eyes shining with excitement as he watched Wade get to his feet. As Wade began to recover, the Golden Knight quickly slid his visor back into place, concealing his face once more. Wade charged at him, but the Golden Knight blocked the stroke casually, almost as an afterthought. Wade's eyes narrowed as he realized he was now dealing with an experienced swordsman. He circled the Golden Knight like a wolf on a hunt, assessing his level of skill. He was about to launch an attack when Adalbo flew onto the scene, his own sword drawn. Wade hesitated, then fled, unwilling to face two expert swordsmen at once.

"That takes care of that problem," the Golden Knight said. "Thanks for the help," he said with a nod to Adalbo.

"Are you both okay?" Adalbo asked, landing on the ridge beside them, his beetle-like wings folding back up into their shell.

"I'm fine," Timothy said, standing and helping Idalbo to his feet. "Sorry about tripping you like that."

"I'd much rather be a little bruised than dead," Idalbo said, rubbing his elbow.

"If you all are quite finished with this little party, I suggest you get back to the battle," Dr. Maddium said, hovering behind them in his battle suit.

"Aye, aye, captain," the Golden Knight said, giving Dr. Maddium a goofy salute and jumping into the fray once more. Adalbo flew after him, darting among the approaching drones like a deadly hummingbird.

"That was... interesting," Timothy said as Dr. Maddium flew off in search of a new opponent.

"What was interesting?" Idalbo asked. "Almost getting killed?"

"No, the Golden Knight. I think that might be the most I've ever heard him say at one time."

"The Golden Knight?" Idalbo said absently as he shot one of his quills into the optical sensor of a nearby attack drone. "He's usually like that during battles."

"Why?"

Idalbo shrugged. "How would I know? Maybe it's because being the Golden Knight is his only hobby."

Timothy paused for a second, turning to look at him. "Really?"

"Yes," Idalbo said, fitting another of his quills into his bow. "Now please stop talking. I need to focus." He squinted, gauging the distance between himself and the nearest attack drone before releasing the quill.

Timothy shut his mouth, turning his attention to not being killed by the Council and their drones. Finally, after several hours of intense fighting, the Council withdrew to a hill about a mile away. Wearily, Timothy climbed down from the ridge to where the rest of Gearwire's crew had gathered.

"They'll be back," Gearwire said as Timothy approached. The rebel commander's normally neat uniform was torn, and there was a bloodstained rag wrapped around his lower arm. "The only question is when?"

"I can sneak over to their camp," Timothy said, even though at the moment, he wanted nothing better than to go back to bed. "Maybe I can pick up some useful information."

"You're no match for the Council," the Mysterious Man said bluntly. "Your throwing stars are useful in battle, but they aren't very effective against expert swordsmen and sharpshooters."

"That won't be a problem if they don't see me," Timothy said, turning to Gearwire. "I have to at least try to find out what they're planning."

Gearwire was silent, weighing the potential value of the information Timothy could bring against the risk of him being caught.

"Do it," he said at last. "Dr. Maddium and Idalbo will wait for you at the top of the ridge. The rest of you, help get the wounded back to the base," he said, turning to address the remaining rebels. "And send someone to bring the other two battalions up here. We're going to need every man we've got."

* * *

Staying under the cover of the boulders that dotted the outer edge of the ridge, Timothy made his way to the place where the Council's forces were camped. Their sheer numbers made it difficult to get close, but after several hours, he had wormed his way to a spot only a stone's throw away from the Council's tent. He rifled through his satchel until he found a special throwing star that he and Dr. Maddium had designed for reconnaissance missions several weeks prior.

Taking it in his hand, he activated it and tossed it into the grass near the edge of the tent. Then he slipped back out of the camp, stopping a safe distance away to remove the other part of the device from his satchel. He pressed the button on the side, and the Council's voices came through.

"-ack now. We can take them," Wade snarled.

"They're too strong. They pushed us back earlier today," Ray said.

"We utilized something known as a 'strategic retreat,'" Wade mocked. "I'm sure a coward like you would be familiar with the concept."

"Gentlemen," Ethos said firmly, interrupting the argument. There was a surprising harshness in his voice that Timothy could hardly reconcile with the calm, regal tone he normally employed. "We will not be run off by a bunch of rabble," he said, spitting out the last word as if it disgusted him. "But we won't fare well if we counterattack now. Rabble or not, their commander is an excellent strategist. By now, he'll have reinforced the ridge with fresh troops."

"What do you suggest we do, then?" Simms asked in his high, nervous voice. "Do we try to poison the man?"

"Don't be such an idiot," Sargent snapped. "You'd never get close enough to poison him without being seen. Besides, if he dies, one of his gang will just assume command. Now, if we could get his entire gang at once, that would be a different story. As it is, killing him would only momentarily check their momentum."

"We'll wait to attack until tomorrow," Ethos said. "His new troops can only stay on duty for so long. If we play our cards right, we can strike at the moment when his men are the weariest."

Timothy switched off the device. He had heard enough. He lifted his hand to call his throwing star back to his hand, but then he stopped.

If I let the shuriken just fly through the camp, it could very well kill someone, he realized. *Not to mention the risk of revealing that I was here. But if I leave it there, they might come to the same conclusion.*

It'll probably be fine, he decided after a moment's thought. *It was hidden pretty well. And even if they do find it, they won't know what exactly it is. Or how long it's been there.*

There's not much I can do about it, anyhow, he realized at last. *The best thing I can do right now is to let Gearwire know what I heard.*

Timothy hurried back to Duncan's Ridge to find that preparations had already begun for the Council's second attack. A small crew was working to remove the dead and wounded from the battlefield as the rebellion's second battalion stood guard.

"Where's Gearwire?" Timothy asked Dr. Maddium as he re-entered the city.

"He's over there," Dr. Maddium replied, pointing. "In the watch-tower."

"Thanks," Timothy said as he jogged off. He found Gearwire marching back and forth, issuing orders in preparation for the coming battle. His injured arm was now in an improvised sling.

"Timothy." Gearwire looked towards him as he entered the room. "What did you find out?"

"The Council's planning to attack tomorrow," Timothy reported.

"Whenever they think the men will be the most tired. He knows that we'll be on high alert all day and wants to wait until we're worn down."

Gearwire frowned, not knowing for sure if their dwindling army could survive another frontal assault. "Go get Dr. Maddium," he said at last, his face clouded over.

By the time Timothy returned with Dr. Maddium, Gearwire's mood had improved slightly.

"I have an idea," he said slowly. "Our only chance at surviving their attack is to bluff them out. We have to make the Council think that there are more of us here than there are." He looked at Timothy. "And it wouldn't hurt if they thought that some of our men were invisible."

Timothy smiled, knowing what Gearwire was hinting at. The book he had read about the shurikens had mentioned that they were often used to make nervous sentries believe they were being attacked by invisible swordsmen.

"Focus your attention on Ray and Simms," Gearwire said. "They'll be the easiest to spook. But if you see the opportunity to go after one of the others, take it." He turned to Dr. Maddium. "How quickly can you make some more of those spy devices you made for Timothy?"

"Howard and I could have a few extras built in an hour or two. What do you have in mind?"

"We'll scatter the speakers among the rocks along the ridge," Gearwire said, tracing a line on a hastily drawn map that covered the table. "When the Council reaches a certain point, we'll have everyone yell into the microphones. Then we'll charge over the ridge."

"It's risky," Dr. Maddium said. "If they realize how few of us there are, I'm not sure if we'll be able to stop them."

"I know," Gearwire replied. "But it's our only chance of pushing them back." He turned to Timothy. "I'm going to give you temporary command of two platoons. I'd like you all to wait in the rocks at the bottom of the ridge and start harassing the Council and their drones when they arrive."

Timothy nodded. "Can you try to make me a few more shurikens before the battle?" he asked Dr. Maddium.

"I can try," Dr. Maddium said. "If I have enough time after making the speakers. I can't make any promises, though."

"Whatever you can get done is fine," Timothy said. "I've still got quite a few left. I just don't want to run out in the middle of the battle."

"I'll see what I can do," Dr. Maddium said. Then, turning to Gearwire, he started, "Would you like me to-"

"I'm fine," Gearwire said, a little abruptly. "We've lost men before."

Dr. Maddium looked as though he were about to say something, but instead, he nodded and left the room. Timothy followed slowly, the details of Henry's death flying back into his mind once more.

Henry and Dr. Maddium have been with Gearwire since even before he started the resistance, he recalled. This was the first major conflict with the Council where Henry had not been present, and Timothy could tell that his absence weighed heavily on Gearwire's mind.

The rest of the day passed slowly. At Gearwire's orders, most of the troops were sent home to rest and prepare for the battle.

Timothy was just finishing his breakfast when a messenger ran in to tell him that the Council appeared to be preparing for an attack. Timothy quickly donned his armor and gathered his shurikens into his satchel. He took his place in the rocks and waited, instructing his men to do the same. From where he sat, he could see only half of them as they crouched behind the boulders.

Timothy took a deep breath, trying to calm his nerves. This was his second direct battle with the Council, and he dreaded the moment when they would come into view. Henry's death at their hands only a few weeks before only made this worse.

What would happen if the Council killed me *today?* he wondered darkly. He shook his head, banishing the thought from his mind.

I can't think about that right now, he chided himself, gripping his shuriken tighter in his hand. As he stared off in the direction of the Council's camp, he had to wonder if Samuel and Quill were among the Blanks who would soon be attacking them.

Before he could contemplate the matter further, the Council's army came into view. Timothy crouched, motionless, scanning the army for his target. After several minutes of searching, he finally spotted Ray standing near the other Council members a short distance away. Timothy took aim and threw his shuriken at him before quickly ducking back behind the boulder.

As the others fired their weapons at their targets, Timothy heard Ray's cry of shock as the throwing star dug a shallow furrow across his chest.

"What are you screaming about?" Wade demanded irritably.

"Something attacked me!" Ray cried. "We need to get out of here. Right now!"

"Nonsense!" Simms said. "There's no one-" his words cut off suddenly as Timothy's throwing star slashed across his arm. "Might I suggest a retreat, sir?" he asked, suddenly changing his tune. "It appears that we're being targeted."

"We'll keep going," Ethos said disdainfully. "They're just trying to scare us off."

I hope Gearwire's strategy works, Timothy thought, realizing that if it failed, it was quite possible that the resistance would be wiped out by the end of the day. Timothy took a deep breath and threw another shuriken, eliciting another startled yelp from Ray.

"Quit whining," Wade snapped just before a throwing star glanced off his hand. He cursed and yanked his hand back, dropping his sword. He flexed his injured hand gingerly, wincing. "Ethos, we may have a problem," he said. "I'm not sure I can really hold a sword right now."

"Deal with it," Ethos said harshly. "We are in a position to end this war right now."

"What good will that do me if I'm dead?" Wade demanded.

"If they were really trying to kill you, you'd already *be* dead," Ethos snapped.

Before Wade could reply, a loud shout rang out from the other side of the ridge, magnified several times over by the recording devices. The rebel army surged over the ridge, led by none other than Henry.

"Impossible," Ethos said, his face turning as white as a sheet. "I killed him myself."

"He's a ghost!" Ray wailed. "He's come back from the dead to get his revenge!"

Henry raised his arm cannon and fired it at the Council, missing them by a few feet and setting a nearby tree ablaze.

"Retreat!" Ray shouted, turning and running back towards Kawts. Several of the nearby Blanks followed him.

"No! Stay and fight!" Ethos ordered, but his voice faltered as Henry raised his weapon again. He hesitated, then screamed, "Fall back!"

The rebel troops let out a cheer as they watched him flee, the rest of his army trailing behind him.

Chapter 29

Once Timothy was sure that the Council could no longer see them, he and his men emerged from their hiding places. He walked directly up to Henry, his mind reeling.

"How-" he began, but Henry shimmered and morphed back into Gearwire.

"Just a little extra trick," he said quietly, removing Henry's battered green cannon from his arm.

Timothy stood in silence, at a loss for words. "Well, it worked," he said at last. "I think that seeing Henry was the last straw. It seemed to be the only thing that had any effect on Ethos."

"I'm afraid it's only a matter of time before they figure out what happened," Gearwire said, shaking his head. "We need to get word to our allies in Alpen if we want any chance of fending them off again."

"The fastest way to do that would be to take your ship," Dr. Maddium said, coming up to the pair. "I could fly over there tonight."

"No," Gearwire said. "No - I need you here in case the Council returns."

"The journey will take weeks by foot!" Dr. Maddium protested. "And you know that you and I are the only two who know how to fly your ship!"

"The ship isn't big enough to bring back reinforcements anyway," Gearwire said. "It would still take at least a couple months before they arrive here."

"The journey would only take a few hours if we took the ship! Do you really think that the Council will attack in the next five hours?"

"No," Gearwire said at last. "But I need your help to prepare for the next attack, which may be tomorrow, for all we know. It won't take Ethos too long to realize he's been tricked."

"I could go," Timothy said. "If I ride Snipps, I could probably get there quicker than by foot."

"You'd need a guide," Gearwire said, pondering Timothy's suggestion.

"Idalbo and Adalbo could accompany him," Dr. Maddium said. "But they'd need their own mounts."

Gearwire shook his head. "Neither of them are riders. And besides, I can't afford to lose three of my crewmen right now."

"What if you just sent Timothy and Adalbo?" Dr. Maddium said. "Adalbo could probably keep up if he flies."

"Even then, I'm still missing two of my crewmembers on the eve of a major battle."

"I could go in the ship *myself* and only be gone a few hours!" Dr. Maddium repeated, his voice rising.

Gearwire was silent for a long time, weighing his options.

"If we can convince Draagetsew to give us some reinforcements, they'll need someone to guide them to the base once they get close," he said finally. "And make sure that the Council doesn't pick up their trail."

"I could do that," Timothy said. "You don't really need me at the moment, anyway."

"I'll need you once the battle starts. And I might need you to gather intel on the Council's movements even before that."

"If we don't get those reinforcements, it won't matter much if I'm there or not," Timothy said. "You know I'm probably the only person in the entire resistance who could get them here without detection."

"All right," Gearwire said wearily. "You're right. Both of you." He turned to Dr. Maddium. "When you fly to Blancstadt, take Timothy and Snipps with you. He can guide their army to the base once they get close. In the meantime, send someone through the tunnels to Grimshaw to tell Prime Minister Deeproot the situation and request backup. We're going to need the tree people's help."

"Right away," Dr. Maddium said, nodding. "I'll send Howard over to lend a hand until I get back."

"Thanks."

"Let's be off, then," Dr. Maddium said, addressing Timothy. "With luck, we can be in Blancstadt by noon."

After packing some supplies for the return journey, Timothy and Snipps arrived at the launch bay. Timothy stared in amazement at the massive flying machine.

"That's Gearwire's ship?" he asked, craning his neck back to see it in its entirety.

"Yes," Dr. Maddium said, opening the cockpit door. "It was a - well, a present of sorts from our old commander."

"*Your* old commander?"

Dr. Maddium smiled faintly. "This isn't our first war. Henry and I were part of Gearwire's crew during the Robot War."

"You fought in the Robot War?"

"It's a bit of a long story," Dr. Maddium replied evasively. "But let's just say that Gearwire's crew was the most renowned squadron in the entire army."

"What happened to the others?"

"Technically, I suppose they're all dead by now," Dr. Maddium said after a moment. "Henry and I were the only ones who came with Gearwire to this time."

"What do you mean 'to this time?' Did you guys come from the past?"

Dr. Maddium nodded, a knowing smile on his face.

"Why did you come here, then?" Timothy asked. "Why would you risk so much to free Kawts?"

"I'm afraid I'm not at liberty to discuss that at the moment," Dr. Maddium said as he pressed a series of buttons on a control panel in the corner of the hangar. The hangar door slid open, and the bright morning sunlight streamed in, making Timothy blink. "You'd better get on board the ship. We'll be taking off in a few minutes."

Timothy hesitated, unsure of where to go.

"Ah! I forgot that you've never been on a ship before," Dr. Maddium said. "Bring Snipps up that ramp in the back and take a seat in the room just beyond that one."

Timothy quickly complied, securing Snipps before sitting down on one of the benches that lined the outer walls of the ship. A few minutes later, Dr. Maddium emerged from a different door and stepped into a third room.

"Ready for takeoff?" his voice asked over a loudspeaker. "Liftoff in five… four… three… two… one!"

As Dr. Maddium shouted this last number, the ship rose into the air. Under Dr. Maddium's skillful piloting, the ship flew quickly out of the cave before turning and flying off toward Alpen.

"It'll be a couple hours before we arrive," Dr. Maddium announced over the speakers. "You might want to check on Snipps. Animals generally don't handle takeoffs very well."

Timothy stood and went into the cargo hold. To his relief, Snipps seemed unphased by their flight. He returned to his seat, glancing out the window as he did.

The ground was far below them, the city of Kawts looking like a tiny anthill. Timothy felt a brief surge of panic at the sight before reassuring himself that they weren't about to plummet to the ground.

He stared out the window in amazement for a few minutes more before finally falling asleep, exhausted from the battle and the tense, watchful night before it.

* * *

By the time Timothy woke up, they were landing, touching down in a cluster of rocks a short distance outside the capital city of Blancstadt. Dr. Maddium emerged from the cockpit.

"We're here," he said simply. "Now we've just got to meet up with Draagetsew."

"Who is this Draagetsew guy, anyway?" Timothy asked as he followed Dr. Maddium into the city.

"He's the president of Alpen," Dr. Maddium said. "And our ally. Gearwire and I came here to ask for help not long after he took office."

"And he sent Idalbo and Adalbo?" Timothy guessed.

"Exactly. Alpen's government promised to send us more men as soon as they could spare them. The only problem is, until recently, they were involved in a war of their own." He stopped and looked at Timothy. "I'm not going to sugarcoat the situation. Barring a miracle, if the Council attacks again before we get reinforcements, they'll wipe us out. There's simply not enough of us left to fight them off. It's by God's grace alone that we survived that last battle."

"It was that close?" Timothy asked with a growing sense of dread, realizing for the first time how close they had come to losing.

Dr. Maddium nodded. "That's why it's so essential that Draagetsew sends us more men. Not that there'll be any trouble about that," he added quickly, seeing the unease on Timothy's face. "Draagetsew's always been very... enthusiastic about helping us. And now that the war's over, he'll actually be able to."

"But what if he won't?" Timothy asked. "Or can't? Then what?"

241

"Then we'll have to withdraw from Garrington, Duncan's Ridge, and Grimshaw and find a new base," Dr. Maddium said gravely. "But one thing's for certain - we won't stop fighting until the Council is defeated or we've all died by their hands."

"Hopefully, it'll be the first one," Timothy said with a shudder.

Dr. Maddium frowned sympathetically. "We'll be fine," he repeated.

They walked on in silence down the bustling street. Several mutants gave them strange looks as they passed by, but Dr. Maddium took no notice of their attention.

"There's the castle, up ahead," he said presently. "Draagetsew's probably inside as we speak."

Timothy glanced upwards, gazing at the castle over the heads of the mutants in front of him. Even from his vantage point, he could see the majestic keep stretching up to the sky, its blue-tipped towers glinting in the sunlight. Surrounding the castle was a thick stone wall, unbreached since the ancestors of the mutants built it centuries ago. Every so often, Timothy caught a glimpse of movement inside the castle as people passed in front of windows and guards patrolled the top of the wall. As they approached the castle's front gate, Dr. Maddium came to a stop, motioning for Timothy to do the same.

The beaked mutant who served as the gate's external guard adjusted his grip on his spear. He stared at them sternly, as if hoping to intimidate them into leaving. When he received no reaction, he asked, "Who are you? And what is your business here?"

"I am Dr. Maddium of Kawts," Dr. Maddium said firmly. "I need to speak to Draagetsew immediately."

The guard frowned. "You'll have to make an appointment. President Draagetsew is very busy."

"Let him in, Deyeneek," a tall mutant with a monkey tail called out from the wall. "Don't you remember Gearwire and Dr. Maddium? They were here five or ten years ago to officiate a treaty. They're friends."

The first mutant sighed, then begrudgingly opened the gate. "He should be in the dining hall. Second corridor on the right."

Dr. Maddium frowned as he and Timothy walked into the castle. Timothy looked up at him quizzically, noticing the expression. Dr. Maddium leaned closer and muttered, "I must admit, I have my doubts about that man's loyalties. Even on our first visit, he seemed to want Draagetsew to ally with the Council. If he's one of the men who's sent to help us, make sure to keep a close eye on him."

Timothy nodded, stealing a sidelong glance at the gatekeeper as they entered the castle. They rounded the corner into the dining hall to find Draagetsew and Alpen's Prime Minister enjoying their lunch.

The burly four-armed mutant looked surprised at Dr. Maddium's arrival. "Dr. Maddium!" he boomed jovially, standing. "How've you been? Where's Gearwire? Why don't you and your friend sit down and join us?"

"I doubt they're here for a friendly visit," the prime minister observed in a raspy tone, his batlike wings twitching.

"I'm afraid Suorotiart's right," Dr. Maddium said. "The resistance is in dire straits. We've had two large battles recently that have decimated our troops. We've come to call in some reinforcements."

The smile disappeared abruptly from Draagetsew's face. "How bad is it?"

"If the Council attacks before the reinforcements arrive, it'll be the end of the resistance," Timothy said.

"That does sound rather serious," Suorotiart agreed.

"We'll gather as many men as we can spare and set out at daybreak tomorrow," Draagetsew promised.

"Good," Dr. Maddium said. "Once you get closer to Kawts, Timothy here will lead you to where you need to be. It's absolutely vital that everyone knows Timothy is in charge once you cross into Council territory."

"Will do," Draagetsew said, nodding.

"What will you be doing?" Suorotiart asked in his snakelike voice.

"I need to return to Gearwire to help him prepare for the battle," Dr. Maddium said.

"You'd best be off, then," Draagetsew said, using two of his massive arms to shoo Dr. Maddium away. "We'll handle things here."

Dr. Maddium nodded gratefully. "I'll leave Snipps over by where we landed," he said to Timothy as he left the room.

"Suorotiart!" Draagetsew boomed. "Gather all our soldiers who are stationed here in Blancstadt. And send someone to round up the Kriegerhelden!"

Chapter 30

"So you're the famous Timothy, eh?" Draagetsew said as Suorotiart flew out of the room. "Idalbo and Adalbo mentioned you in their most recent report. They said you proved to be a valuable companion in the battle of Garrington."

Timothy's stomach churned as Draagetsew's words reminded him of what he'd spent the last several hours trying to forget. "A lot of people died under my command," he said, images of the bodies of the rebels flashing through his mind.

Draagetsew, however, did not catch on to Timothy's uneasiness. "From what Idalbo and Adalbo said, a lot more people would've died without you," he said. "I am sorry to hear about Henry, though," he said, shaking his head angrily. "Why, if I weren't president, I'd-"

"STOP!" Timothy said, grimacing. "Just - stop. Please."

Draagetsew opened his mouth to reply when he noticed for the first time that Timothy seemed miserable.

"I see," he said, his expression softening. "War's a horrible business," he said softly. "Especially when your opponent has no sense of fair play. That's why we allied ourselves with Gearwire. The Council needs to be stopped before they start looking to expand further."

"I know," Timothy said, breathing heavily. "But let's not talk about it, okay?"

The mutant leader nodded solemnly, his eyes filled with compassion. "We'll be fine," he said reassuringly, unknowingly echoing Dr. Maddium's words from earlier that afternoon. He took a breath as if he was going to say more, but at that moment, the mutant who had verified their entry to the castle appeared in the doorway.

"Draagetsew!"

"Ah, finally! You're here!" Draagetsew exclaimed as the guard and several other mutants filed into the room. "It's been far too long since we've had all the Kriegerhelden in one room again!"

"Well, almost all the Kriegerhelden, sir," a tentacled mutant in a kilt corrected. "Revenant and Legov refused to come barring a direct order from you."

"And Ederba's out of town," the guard added. "And, of course, Idalbo and Adalbo are in Kawts. But aside from that, all the Kriegerhelden are here."

"Very good point!" Draagetsew boomed, his natural cheerfulness quickly returning. "Actually, that's why I've called you all here."

"Suorotiart told us about the situation in Kawts," a tall, gilled mutant put in.

"Exactly. We'll be sending all the men we can spare to help them," Draagetsew said. "And I was hoping I'd be able to send some of you as well."

"I'll go," the mutant in the kilt said at once. "It's been far too long since I've been a part of the action."

"Tapfer and I are at your service," the tailed mutant said, bowing.

"Speak for yourself," the mutant Timothy assumed to be Tapfer replied jokingly, lightly shoving the mutant who had spoken.

"I'd hate for you to have to close your café, Inn," Draagetsew said.

Inn waved a tentacle dismissively. "Seililyad can run it alright without me."

"Speaking of Seililyad, shouldn't she be here too?" one of the mutants asked.

"You know full well why she's not," Inn said, a warning tone in his voice. He took a step toward the other mutant, one of his tentacles balling into a fist.

"Inn and Loyola will accompany the troops," Draagetsew said, cutting short the argument before it could escalate further. "You'll lead them over to the general vicinity of Kawts and then hand over the reins to Timothy here." He slapped Timothy on the back, causing him to stumble. Timothy eyed Draagetsew warily, but the burly mutant didn't seem to notice.

"He'll lead you to the base so the Council won't see you," Draagetsew continued. "Whatever he says goes."

"Sure thing, captain," Inn said with a salute before leaving to prepare for the journey.

"They're some of our finest warriors," Draagetsew whispered to Timothy as the Kriegerhelden left the room. "Just like Idalbo and Adalbo."

"They don't seem like they like each other very much," Timothy said, eyeing them skeptically.

"They're a great team," Draagetsew insisted. "At least, they were. When Idalbo and Adalbo left, there were arguments about what they should do next. They couldn't agree, and things were said that shouldn't have been. The group dissolved. They haven't really talked much since then," he said sadly, shaking his head.

"I should probably go check on Snipps," Timothy said, breaking the awkward silence that followed. "Do you know when and where your army will be gathered?"

"We probably won't be able to leave until tomorrow at the earliest," Draagetsew said. "So just come back to the castle with Snipps and someone will update you once we have a more accurate idea of how long it will take."

"Okay," Timothy said, turning to leave. "Thanks for lending us a hand."

"We should have done this months ago," Draagetsew said, shaking his head. "But we're here now. The Council is going down."

Timothy left the room and headed back to where they had landed the ship. Snipps chirruped joyfully as he approached, straining forwards against her tether to reach him. Timothy laughed as he untied the massive raccoon, who nearly knocked him over in her excitement.

"Hey!" Timothy exclaimed, smiling. "Calm down! We've got to go to the castle now!"

Snipps sat back on her haunches, looking at him, her head cocked to one side. Timothy shook his head, amused by the sight of the five-foot tall raccoon behaving like an excited puppy. He vaguely recalled Gearwire mentioning that Snipps had DNA from a horse, a bear, and a dog, although he wasn't entirely sure what that meant. Evidently, though, it had some impact on the raccoon's behavior.

"Let's get back to the castle," he told Snipps, gently tugging her tether. Snipps stood up and followed him placidly. They remained at the castle for the rest of the day, receiving regular updates from Suorotiart on what was happening. By sunrise the next morning, everything was ready for their departure.

Draagetsew stood with Timothy on a small hill overlooking the assembled army. "This is all the men we could gather on such short notice," Draagetsew said. "I'll send a more substantial army after you as soon as we can get it organized."

"Thanks," Timothy said again. Draagetsew merely nodded and returned to the castle.

Timothy climbed down from the hill to where the army waited. Now that he was at ground level, he could see that they all stood on some sort of large, wheeled platforms.

"What's this?" he asked, his forehead furrowing.

"Revenant designed them during the war. We use them to transport troops quickly," Inn explained.

"They don't look very stealthy," Timothy said, trying to imagine how he could conceal the massive machines from the Council.

"They're not," Inn agreed. "But that's why Revenant designed them so that we can disassemble them once we reach our destination."

Timothy nodded as understanding dawned on him. "How fast can they go?"

"They top out at around forty-eight kilometers per hour. Little less if the terrain is bad."

Timothy's eyebrows shot up. The only vehicle he had ever seen move faster than that was Gearwire's ship. Nothing else even came close.

"Wow," he said, impressed. "That'll do the trick, I suppose."

Inn extended a tentacle to help Timothy up onto the platform.

"Alright," he bellowed, making Timothy jump. "Let's move out!" He reached down and flicked a switch on the control panel in front of him. The motors of the devices roared to life, sending vibrations all throughout the platforms. They set off at a rapid pace, rolling steadily towards the cave.

Seven days passed before Timothy began to recognize the surrounding terrain. He waited until about noon, then made his way to the front of the platform.

"Stop the column here," he told Inn and Loyola. "I'll go scout ahead." Then, before either had the time to respond, Timothy hopped off of the platform and rode off into the brush.

He had a general idea of how to get the mutants to the base, but his plan hinged on whether the Council was still in the area. He rode along his intended path for a short distance, listening intently for any signs of the Council. Finally, satisfied that there weren't any Blanks in the immediate vicinity, Timothy rode back to the army.

"The Council isn't nearby," he reported. He fell silent for a moment, gathering his thoughts. "Split the men into groups of ten or twenty," he said at last. "I'll take them to the base one group at a time."

Inn called a young lieutenant over to them and relayed Timothy's instructions. The man nodded and hurried off to set the plan into motion.

"I'll go with the first batch," Loyola said. "I can let Gearwire know our exact situation."

"Good," Inn said. "I'll hold down the fort here."

A short time later, the army had been fully separated into smaller groups, as Timothy had requested. He surveyed the groups, trying to determine which one would be the most adept at sneakery. Coming to a decision, he led the first group into the forest, instructing them to stay in a single-file line behind him. Briefly, he considered having them spread out to leave a less obvious trail, but then he decided against it, realizing that would only make it more likely that the Council would pick up their tracks.

Finally, after a good deal of turning and backtracking, they arrived at the mouth of the cave. Motioning for the others to stay hidden, Timothy stepped out into the clearing.

"Identify yourself!" a voice called, and Timothy realized with relief that it was one of the resistance sentries. The rebel base, at least, was still under Gearwire's command.

"Agent Shadow," Timothy replied, using the codename Gearwire had given him. "I've brought the first part of the mutant army with me."

"Bring them in," the sentry said, relief evident in his voice.

Timothy nodded to the others, who emerged from the bushes and followed him into the cave. "By the way," Timothy asked the sentry. "Do you know where Gearwire is right now?"

"I think he's over at Duncan's Ridge," the man replied after a moment's thought. "Or maybe Garrington. But if he's not there,

Dr. Maddium will be."

"Thanks!" Timothy said, jogging down the tunnel that led to Duncan's Ridge. After searching for a few minutes, he spotted Dr. Maddium standing up on the ridge, along which some impressive fortifications had already been constructed. A high wall now ran along the crest of the ridge, although as he got closer, Timothy could see that it was far from complete. In the center of the wall was a tower, at the top of which was mounted Henry's arm cannon.

As he took in the changes to the town, Dr. Maddium noticed his arrival. Or rather, he noticed the commotion caused by a squadron of fifteen mutants suddenly appearing in the middle of a town who had previously only seen Idalbo and Adalbo.

"Please tell me that's not the entire army," Dr. Maddium said half-jokingly as he climbed down the ridge.

"The others are waiting for me to bring them in," Timothy said. "Is the Council around?"

Dr. Maddium shook his head. "They went back to Kawts and have been behaving themselves a lot better than usual. I think Gearwire's trick with the arm cannon really rattled them. They're still not sure what to do about it. But they'll be back before too long."

"Thanks for the update," Timothy said. "Loyola here can tell you the specifics of this army we've got. I've got to go get the others."

Leaving Dr. Maddium to take care of the mutants, Timothy retraced his path back to the waiting army, trying his best to conceal the traces of their passing as he went. He repeated this process several more times, taking each group on a different route to one of the three cities controlled by Gearwire's forces.

By nightfall, however, there were still nearly one hundred mutants left, so Gearwire took advantage of the growing darkness to ferry them back to the base in his ship. By the end of the night, the rebel's forces had been strengthened by 2,000 more men, all seasoned fighters.

It was all the reinforcements from Alpen they were destined to get, however. Desperately wanting to avoid another war while they were still recovering from their first, the Congress of Alpen had ruled that no additional men were to be sent to the rebels' aid. As it was, it had been all that Draagetsew could do just to convince them to allow the battalions currently stationed there to remain.

Chapter 31

Timothy walked into the training complex, scanning the room for the Mysterious Man. After a few minutes of fruitless searching, he walked over to the Golden Knight, who was practicing with a wooden replica of his sword. Timothy stood off to the side, watching him attack the dummy with a dizzying flurry of strikes.

The Golden Knight stepped back from the dummy, resting his weapon on the ground as he took a long drink from a water bottle. Now that he was out of the way, Timothy could see that the dummy was badly dented.

"Looking for the Mysterious Man?" the Golden Knight asked, noticing Timothy for the first time. Timothy nodded, and the Golden Knight said, "He's on a mission. You're training with me today."

Timothy eyed the training dummy warily. "I'm not sure I've trained enough for that."

"I'll go easy on you," the Golden Knight said, picking up his stick. "But if you can hold your own against me, you can hold your own against the likes of Wade or Alexis."

Timothy hesitated a moment, then drew his staff, holding it in front of him while he watched the Golden Knight. Suddenly, something struck his staff, almost knocking it out of his hands. He tightened his grip and lashed out with his weapon, narrowly missing the Golden

Knight's midsection. The Golden Knight staggered back, a slow grin spreading across his face. Then he charged at Timothy, his weapon a blur of movement.

It was all Timothy could do to continue to block the blows, any hope he had of beating the Golden Knight vanishing in an instant. From time to time, he managed to swing his weapon at the Golden Knight, but each time, his attacks were quickly deflected.

Finally, the Golden Knight thrust his sword at Timothy's stomach. Timothy moved his staff to block it, but at the last second, the Golden Knight pulled back, flicking his weapon toward the staff itself. The staff flew out of Timothy's hands, clattering onto the ground. The Golden Knight touched the tip of his weapon to Timothy's chest.

"Care to go again?"

Timothy nodded mutely, trying to catch his breath. "Just… give me a minute," he gasped. He took several deep breaths, trying to slow his racing pulse. He reached over and picked up his staff, searching for any damage to the weapon. Then, without warning, he threw himself at the Golden Knight.

They continued sparring for several hours, until Timothy was drenched in sweat, too tired to continue.

"I yield," he gasped, stretching his aching muscles. "I can't fight anymore."

"You did well today," the Golden Knight said. "The Mysterious Man has been training you well."

"Thanks…" Timothy started, fumbling for the name. "Isn't there something else I can call you? Other than 'the Golden Knight?'"

The Golden Knight shook his head. "Henry used to call me GK, but that's about it. It's just the Golden Knight."

"What do you mean, 'it's just the Golden Knight?' You have a name, don't you?"

"I suppose I must," the Golden Knight said with a frown. "But if I do,

I have no recollection of it. The earliest thing I remember is waking up in a cave outside of Kawts with no memory of my past life. It was my old partner in crime who gave me the moniker of the Golden Knight."

Before Timothy could say anything more, the Golden Knight turned away. "I'll see you tomorrow," he said. He vanished back into the training room, leaving Timothy alone in the hallway.

* * *

Once he had recovered from his training session with the Golden Knight, Timothy made his way down to the rebellion stables to check on Snipps. He had made it a point to visit the massive raccoon every few days at least, though he rarely waited until this late in the afternoon.

When he arrived, the stables were nearly empty, most of the workers having already gone home for the day. Timothy passed by several horses belonging to members of the nearby tribes before he reached Snipps' stall. The raccoon chuffed happily when she saw him, nudging him with her snout.

Timothy smiled and stroked her head for a moment, unlatching the gate. "How does a little ride around the arena sound?" he said, leading Snipps out of the stables through the back door.

Behind the stables, a wide area had been carved out of the mountain, meticulously designed to be as much like a grassy plain as possible, complete with a skylight overhead and a thick bed of grass underfoot. The horses at the stable had more or less free rein of the space during the day, only being sealed in their pens for the day after the stables closed.

As Timothy led Snipps out toward the middle of the space, he was surprised to see that someone else was already there, dressed in a red and yellow jumpsuit and standing atop the back of a horse as it trotted along the outside of the circle.

As the figure drew closer, Timothy realized suddenly that the rider was Madison Kolt, one of Gearwire's crewmembers. As Timothy watched, she jumped into the air, a length of rope trailing from either hand as she twisted into a somersault. For a moment, she seemed to almost fall off the horse, but she swung herself back onto the horse's back before she touched the ground. Lowering into a crouch, she flipped off the back of the horse, landing deftly on her feet. Clipping the two lengths of rope to her belt, she grabbed onto the reins and walked the horse back towards the stables.

"Hey, Timothy! Come to take Snipps out for a ride?" she asked, noticing Timothy for the first time.

Timothy nodded. "I didn't expect to see you here!" he called back. "That was pretty impressive."

Madison smiled. "It's something of a hobby of mine. Gives me a chance to practice my fighting style. If you can pull off a flip on the back of a horse, you can do it on solid ground."

Timothy's mind went to the ropes that Madison had been holding while on the back of the horse. "That's what the ropes were for," he said.

Madison nodded. "Yep. Even when they're just set to stun, it would be a little too risky to use my actual whips on the back of the horse. Too many ways that could go wrong. The ropes made a good substitute." Before Timothy could say anything more, Madison glanced down at her watch. "I'd better get going if I want to be on time for my shift in the kitchen. I'll see you around." With that, she turned and disappeared into the stables, leaving Timothy and Snipps alone in the field.

* * *

Timothy was awakened in the middle of the night by someone violently shaking his shoulder. He opened his eyes to see Gearwire standing over him.

"What's going on?" he asked, yawning.

"Get your gear and Snipps and meet us at the mouth of the cave as soon as possible," Gearwire whispered urgently before dashing back out of the room.

Now thoroughly awake, Timothy threw on his suit and made his way over to the mouth of the cave. The Mysterious Man, the Golden Knight, and Gearwire were already there.

"What's-" Timothy began, but the Mysterious Man shushed him.

"We're still waiting for Idalbo and Adalbo," he said. "There's no sense in explaining the same thing four different times."

Timothy stayed silent, waiting for the mutants' arrival. Idalbo and Adalbo appeared only a few minutes later.

"Let's go," Gearwire said, motioning toward Kawts. "I'll explain on the way." He set off down the mountain at a brisk pace, making it difficult for the others to keep up.

"What happened?" Idalbo asked, breaking into a stiff jog.

"The Council found the location of the Kawts underground church," Gearwire said. "They attempted a raid a few minutes ago. The twins are holding them off as we speak."

But they won't last long, Timothy finished in his head, remembering how just two Council members had been the death of Henry. He had little hope that Crystal and Jewel could hold their own against all twelve of them for more than a short time.

"We'll never get there in time by foot," he said, subconsciously quickening his pace.

"They've barricaded themselves inside the building," Gearwire replied. "They'll be relatively safe until the Council either forces their way in or tries to burn-"

Gearwire's eyes grew wide as he saw a column of smoke rising from the middle of Kawts. "They already are," he breathed. "Come on!" He took off at a run towards the city, Timothy and the others close behind.

As they neared the wall, Timothy threw two shurikens at the nearest Blanks, knocking them unconscious even as Idalbo fired a grappling line into the wall. Without wasting a second, they scrambled up it and charged down into Kawts.

The street that the church was on was in chaos, people fleeing the burning building only to encounter the force of several hundred Blanks waiting for them outside. From inside the building's upper windows, Timothy could see flashes of blue, showing that one of the twins, at least, was still alive.

"Timothy!" Gearwire barked. "Go into the building and try to get everyone out! Idalbo, keep the drones at bay. The rest of us will try to clear a path for Timothy to lead the people to safety!"

Timothy nodded and ran up to the house, moving as quickly as he could without being spotted. In his hand, he held a specially crafted shuriken, designed to spray water as it flew. He threw it through the flames that had flared up in the doorway, temporarily extinguishing them.

Pausing to remember the layout of the building from his last visit, Timothy soon found the staircase. Making use of another of his water stars, he doused it in water, hoping to delay its burning. Then he ran up the stairs himself, heading for the room where the flash had come from.

Crystal, Jewel, Pastor Shepherd, and several others were in the room when Timothy entered. The twins were doing their best to fight the fire with their powers, but their efforts proved ineffective, the fire spreading faster than they could contain it.

"Someone's here!" Shepherd called out, noticing Timothy.

"Timothy!" Jewel exclaimed with relief, looking up from the burning baseboard. "Are the others here, too?"

Shepherd stared at Timothy in surprise as he answered.

"Idalbo, Adalbo, Gearwire, the Golden Knight, and the Mysterious Man are all here," Timothy said. "They're trying to clear a way out right now."

"Wait - you're Timothy Hawthorne?" Shepherd said.

Timothy nodded quickly.

"We thought you were dead!" Shepherd exclaimed. "How did you escape?"

"I'll tell you later," Timothy said. "Is anyone hurt?"

"My nephew, Archer, was hit when those drones shot out the windows," the pastor replied, shaking off his momentary surprise.

Timothy looked to Jewel to elaborate, but it was Crystal who answered.

"There's a bullet lodged somewhere in his shoulder," she reported. "We've managed to slow the bleeding, but he'll probably be dead within the hour unless we can get him back to the base."

"Is he still awake?" Timothy asked, and Crystal nodded in confirmation.

"For now."

"Let's get everyone to the ground floor," Timothy said, a sense of urgency rising within him. If Archer was to have any chance of survival, they would have to be ready to act fast. Even if they left now, it was still possible that he would die before they reached the base.

Unless, he realized, *I carry him back on Snipps. If I can get him to the edge of town, he might have a chance.*

He turned to Shepherd. "Where's your nephew?"

Shepherd pointed to the corner of the room where a young man sat propped up against the wall. He was clutching his left shoulder, the makeshift bandage around it turning an ominous shade of red. He was maybe five or ten years older than Timothy, and he seemed to be in shock over his injury.

Timothy ran over to the man and helped him to his feet. "We're going to get you to a doctor," he said, and the man nodded in understanding. He followed Timothy down the stairs and onto the main floor, where several of the church's other members were already waiting.

Timothy noticed with dread that the stairs were now stained with blood. He glanced outside and saw that Gearwire and the rest of the crew were still trying to clear a path through the Council's army. He hesitated, looking from the injured man beside him to the battle outside, calculating. There would be a path soon, he realized, seeing how the Blanks were slowly giving ground before Gearwire's attack. Even so, their progress was painfully slow. Far too slow if they wanted to have any chance of saving Archer.

Coming to a decision, Timothy turned to Jewel. "As soon as there's a safe path, take everyone out to safety." Jewel opened her mouth to ask a question, but Timothy forestalled her. "I'm going to take Archer back to the base."

Jewel frowned, but she nodded. "Be careful," she said before turning back to the group and relaying Timothy's instructions.

Timothy turned to the injured man. "We're going to sneak out past the Council," he said, keeping his voice calm and level. "It's very important that you do exactly what I say. Stay in the shadows and out of plain sight. With luck, no one will notice we're there. But if they do, and I have to fight them, make your way to the foothills of Mount Elbrus. I'll meet you there." The man nodded in acknowledgement, grimacing as the movement sent a fresh wave of pain through his shoulder.

Timothy stared out the window, waiting until he was sure that none of the Councilmen were facing his direction. Then he slipped out the door, beckoning for Archer to follow him. Keeping to the shadowed side alleys, Timothy set a rapid pace through Kawts in the direction of the base.

As he neared the place where he had left Snipps, he slowed, rethinking his plan. It was crucial for this man's survival that he reached the base. Yet it might be equally crucial for the survival of all the others that he went back to help. He eyed the man critically, trying to judge his remaining strength.

"Do you think you could keep yourself on this raccoon for a few miles by yourself?"

Archer hesitated. "I'll manage," he said at last with a pained smile, although Timothy suspected he was putting on a brave face for his benefit. He said nothing, pretending not to notice. He helped the slightly older man up onto Snipps' back, and then he whispered into the giant raccoon's ear.

"Bring him home." Immediately, Snipps broke out into a trot toward the base, the injured man struggling to remain on her back. Timothy frowned as he watched them disappear from sight. He wasn't terribly optimistic about Archer's chances, but he had done his best. Now, it was just up to Snipps and the man himself.

And God, I suppose, Timothy added, glancing at the sky for a brief moment. *Assuming he exists.*

Timothy shook his head, bringing his focus back to the mission. When he had left, the twins and several citizens had still been trapped inside the burning house.

Please let them be fine, he thought frantically as he dashed back to the fire. As he rounded the final corner, he almost ran into Jewel, skidding to a stop at the last second. He opened his mouth to apologize, but stopped when he saw the panicked look in her eyes. He glanced upwards with a growing feeling of dread.

Gearwire and the rest of his crew stood surrounded by Blanks, their hands raised in surrender. Several Councilmen moved among them, picking up their fallen weapons. Realizing that they hadn't seen him yet, he quickly ducked back around the corner.

"What happened?" he hissed.

"The Council sent a company of Blanks and drones to attack us from behind," Jewel whispered back. "We couldn't fight them and the Blanks at the same time."

"Are Payat and LeSalle here?" Timothy asked.

There was a pause, then Jewel said, "Yes. LeSalle's on top of the building across the street."

That's pretty far away, Timothy thought, turning the problem over in his mind.

"What's he doing?"

There was another pause as Jewel watched the Council's resident sharpshooter. "He's just standing there. He's got his rifle in his hand, though."

"What side of the roof is he on?"

"Pretty close to the middle."

"How many others have guns?" Timothy asked.

"Councilmen? Just two or three."

Timothy was silent for a moment, visualizing the situation in his head. "I'm going to step out and hit LeSalle with a shuriken. When I do, you and Crystal need to blast everyone else who has a gun."

"Okay," Jewel said, relaying Timothy's instructions to her sister.

Timothy took a deep breath and stepped back around the corner, whipping a shuriken at LeSalle with all of his might. The man staggered back, dropping his weapon off the side of the roof. At the same moment, Jewel quickly encased the weapon of the nearest Councilman in a chunk of crystal.

As the Council tried to pinpoint the origin of the unexpected attack, Gearwire stomped on the blade of his sword, sending it spinning up into the air. He snatched it in midair, driving his shoulder into the stomach of the nearest Councilman as he did. The Councilman grunted in surprise and doubled over, dropping Gearwire's glue gun. Idalbo reached behind his back and tossed one of his quills to his brother, who shot up into the air and quickly dismantled several attack drones, using the quill as a rapier.

Knowing that the Council would recover in a matter of seconds, Gearwire barked an order for them to retreat. His crew quickly regathered their weapons and fell back, keeping themselves between the Council and the survivors of the church attack. Suddenly, the square filled with smoke, and Timothy caught a brief glimpse of Crystal grinning as their surroundings faded from sight. Under the cover of the fog, the little band slipped away through the darkened streets.

"We're gonna head out," Jewel's voice announced through the fog. "Unless you still need us."

"That's fine," Gearwire's voice replied. "Get back home before the Council realizes you're missing."

They soon arrived back at the base, the refugees in tow. Gearwire dispatched Idalbo and Adalbo to get them settled in, then turned to talk to Timothy. Timothy saw the movement and cut him off.

"I need to make sure Archer's okay first," he said. Gearwire frowned, not understanding. Briefly, Timothy explained what had happened, and Gearwire nodded in approval. He called to the sentry standing nearby.

"Did a man come through here recently on a giant raccoon?" he asked.

The sentry nodded. "He was barely conscious and had a bullet wound in his shoulder. The doctors took him to the medical ward."

"Is he alright?" Timothy asked.

The sentry shrugged. "I don't know. I've been standing here all night."

"Go check for us, please," Gearwire said. "We'll guard the door until you get back." The sentry hesitated, but then realized that Gearwire and Timothy would probably do a far better job of guarding the entrance than he ever could. He disappeared into the base, leaving Timothy and Gearwire alone in the mouth of the cave.

They stood in silence for a moment, then Gearwire said, "Good work today. We'd all be dead right now if it hadn't been for you."

"Jewel helped a lot," Timothy said, although secretly, he relished the compliment.

"That may be," Gearwire said. "But Jewel was in the same boat as the rest of us until you showed up." He let his words hang in the air for a few moments. Then he added, "If something should happen to me, I want you to assume command of the rebellion."

"Me?" Timothy exclaimed, unable to contain his surprise.

Gearwire nodded. "After myself, you're the best man for the job."

"But what about the Golden Knight? Or Dr. Maddium? Or Idalbo?" Timothy protested.

"The Golden Knight is an excellent fighter, but he's not a strategist. Idalbo has the leadership experience, but his first loyalty is to Alpen, not Kawts. And Dr. Maddium can't be here all the time. He'll help you whenever he can, but he needs to spend most of his time in the past to gather the supplies that are keeping us afloat."

Timothy said nothing. Gearwire's words had left him speechless. Gearwire smiled softly as he noted Timothy's reaction. He looked as if he was going to say something further, but at that moment, the sentry returned.

"He's stable," he reported, either not noticing or else ignoring Timothy's stunned expression. "The doc thinks he'll recover." He looked at Timothy. "He's sleeping right now, but it sounds like he was asking to see you earlier."

Seeing that Timothy was only half paying attention, Gearwire thanked the man on his behalf. "Try to get a few hours of sleep before tomorrow," he suggested gently. "We'll debrief in the morning."

Timothy nodded gratefully, suddenly realizing how tired he was. He returned to his quarters, leaving his armor scattered about on the floor as he climbed into his bed and fell asleep.

* * *

When Timothy woke up the next morning, he made his way over to Gearwire's quarters. When he arrived, only Gearwire and Pastor Shepherd were in the room, consulting the twins about how to move forward.

"What's going on?" Timothy asked. Gearwire and Shepherd looked up, startled.

"We're trying to figure out what to do about the Kawts church," Gearwire told him. "Almost all of them were either killed or are here now. There's only a few believers left in Kawts."

"I'm telling you, I need to go back," Shepherd said. "I have to help them rebuild."

"That's ridiculous!" Timothy said before he could stop himself. "You'll be killed before you even get in!"

Shepherd looked at him defiantly. "I knew that was a risk when I accepted the role of pastor. I'm not afraid of becoming a martyr."

"Timothy has a point," Gearwire said gently. "If I could see how that would have any meaningful impact, I'd agree with you. But as soon as you're spotted by just a single attack drone, you'll probably be killed on the spot. They know exactly who you are and they're waiting for you. You probably won't even get *into* Kawts without dying, let alone actually rebuilding the church. You'll be giving up your life for nothing."

"What if I just went into Kawts for services?" Shepherd suggested, backing down a little. "At least until we find someone to take my place."

Gearwire stroked his beard thoughtfully. "That might work," he said at last. "If you use the tunnel, and Timothy gives you a few stealth tips…" He trailed off, assessing the plan's chances of success. He remained lost in thought for several minutes. Finally, he turned to Shepherd. "Let's pray about it," he suggested, and the pastor nodded. "Good idea."

"In the meantime, we could really use a pastor in Garrington," Gearwire said. "We started planning an outreach mission there a while ago, but we still haven't found someone to lead it."

"I'll think about it," Shepherd replied.

"I'll have Crystal and Jewel contact the remaining members of the church and help them pick up the pieces," Gearwire said. Shepherd nodded, then ducked out of the room.

"I assume you're here for your debriefing?" Gearwire asked once they were alone.

Timothy nodded. "How did the Council flank you?"

Gearwire's smile faded as he answered. "Two Council members and Volker took a force of Blanks and drones through the back alleys. We were too busy trying to clear a path to notice that they'd left." He shook his head. "I should've brought the entire crew. But we were short on time, and I thought the six of us would be enough. If you hadn't done what you did, we'd all be in serious trouble right now."

"It really wasn't a tactical decision," Timothy admitted. "I was just trying to get Archer back to the base."

"I know," Gearwire said. "But you still orchestrated a plan to take the Council by surprise. I saw the way you three took out the sharpshooters first. That was a good move." There was silence for a moment. "You've impressed all of us with your leadership skills -

266

the way you solved the Grimshaw issue, the way you led the library raid, the way you took charge of the gate after…" Gearwire trailed off. He cleared his throat. "You've got a lot of potential. And you have a knack for spur-of-the-moment problem solving."

Timothy looked away, feeling like an imposter.

If I was really that good at improvising, Henry would still be alive.

"I'll be making the announcement tonight," Gearwire continued. "We've already gone far too long without having a clear chain of command."

"I can't do it," Timothy said. "I've only been on your crew for less than a year! You need someone with more experience!"

Gearwire shook his head. "This isn't a decision I've taken lightly. I've been thinking and praying about this for a long time. Believe it or not, you *are* the best person for the job."

"If you say so," Timothy said, backing down a little. "But I'd rather you just not die."

Gearwire smiled. "I'll try not to." There was silence for a moment, then he added, "Archer's still in the infirmary if you wanted to see him."

"Thanks," Timothy replied, making a mental note to stop by after his weapons practice. "The Council can't be allowed to get away with stuff like this anymore," he added under his breath as he left Gearwire's office.

Chapter 32

"Congratulations on your promotion," Jewel said.

Timothy grimaced, shrinking down in his chair even though Jewel was not actually in the room. "You heard about that?" He shook his head. "That's a stupid question. Gearwire told everyone in the rebellion. Of course you heard about that."

"You don't sound excited," Jewel said. "I would have thought that this was exactly the kind of thing you would be thrilled about. This is your chance to help coordinate the fight against the Council."

Timothy shook his head. "I'm not qualified for this, Jewel. I'm barely qualified to be a member of Gearwire's crew, let alone his second in command! I have the least experience out of anyone here!"

"That may be true. But you do have more battlefield experience than most of us. Particularly when it comes to leading in battle."

"I don't think anyone would want to serve under someone whose entire platoon got wiped out under his command."

Jewel's voice softened. "You really can't see it, can you? Yes, you lost most of your platoon - but you still held that gate. You incapacitated a Councilman and lived to tell the tale. Not many people would have survived that encounter. You're a lot better at this stuff than you realize."

Timothy shifted uncomfortably, and the silence stretched on. Finally, he said, "I heard you and Crystal have been helping out Pastor

Shepherd."

"I suppose you could say that," Jewel said. "Right now, we're mostly just trying to account for everybody. A lot of the church members made it out with you and Gearwire, but there are quite a few that haven't been seen since. And of course, some of them are still here in Kawts. For obvious reasons, we never kept an official directory, so we're just going off of memory here. Interviewing whoever's left, seeing who they remember being there."

"That sounds like a headache."

"It's not so bad, really. It's giving us a chance to talk to some pretty interesting people. You should hear some of the stories they told us about being part of the church while Ethos the 8th was in charge. It almost makes our Ethos look like a nice guy."

Timothy shook his head. "Are you guys really planning on starting those meetings again? If I were you, I would lie low for a while - probably cancel the meetings altogether. There's too much of a risk the group could be infiltrated."

"It's pretty near impossible to follow Christ effectively by yourself," Jewel said. "And there's a witnessing aspect, too. By continuing to meet, we're showing that we're not afraid of the Council or what they can do to us."

"I get that, but it just seems too dangerous to be worth it."

"It's not about being safe. It's about having a relationship with God."

Timothy scrunched up his face. "If you say so."

"I do," Jewel said. "But it's not just me. There's a really long history of people continuing to gather to worship God, even at the cost of their lives. I bet the cave's library has some of their stories - you might find them interesting."

"I'll have to check. I can't promise I'll get around to reading them anytime soon, though. Turns out, being a part of Gearwire's crew is a huge time commitment."

Jewel laughed. "I get what you mean. Speaking of, there is some stuff I still have to get done before tomorrow. Would you mind if we cut this a little short?"

"Do what you need to do."

"Thanks. I'll talk to you next week."

"Talk to you then," Timothy agreed, reaching over to turn off the radio beacon.

* * *

Timothy stood outside the mouth of the cave, staring down at the city of Kawts and the surrounding land. It was a beautiful day, and he was happy just to be outdoors. The cloudless sky was a brilliant shade of blue, contrasting wonderfully with the rich green of the trees below.

It's hard to believe something so small could cause so much pain, Timothy thought, staring down at the town below, which seemed tiny from this height.

"Timothy!" a voice called, interrupting his reflections. He turned to see one of Gearwire's couriers, distinguished as such by his deep blue jacket.

"Gearwire wants you to report to the command center at once! He says it's a matter of life and death!"

Timothy nodded and jogged off, making his way to Gearwire's quarters as fast as he could. When he arrived, the room was in chaos. Gearwire and the rest of his crew were dashing about, grabbing supplies from the shelves on the walls. Under different circumstances, it would almost have been comical.

"One of our agents in Kawts has activated his radio beacon," Gearwire told Timothy as he ran by. "We have to extract him!"

Five frantic minutes later, the team was on their way to Kawts - Timothy, Gearwire, and Madison riding ahead on Snipps, and everyone else following on foot.

"Where are we supposed to meet this guy?" Timothy asked as they galloped toward Kawts. "What's the situation?"

Gearwire shook his head, only half listening. "I should have known he was about to do something foolish! He was always urging me to do something about The Race!"

"What did he do?"

"He's trying to smuggle the loser of The Race out of Kawts. They're hiding out at his house for the time being, but it's only a matter of time before Taranis figures out what's going on." He shook his head again. "We don't have any time to waste."

Timothy nodded, silently urging Snipps to run a little faster. After what seemed like an eternity, they arrived at the edge of town, where they met up with Crystal and Jewel before riding onwards to the place where the beacon was.

Within minutes, the entire team was assembled outside the man's house, with the exception of Dr. Maddium. The door was ajar, and Timothy had a sinking feeling that they were too late. Gearwire kicked the door open and stepped inside, his glue gun at the ready. He lowered his weapon slowly as he took in the trashed room. There was no sign of their agent anywhere.

"They've already brought him to the Blanking room," Gearwire said grimly. "We're too late." He and the others turned to leave, but Timothy lingered.

"We know where the Blanking room is," he said. "Why don't we go there and rescue him?"

Gearwire turned back to face him. "We've tried that a few times," he said. "But it always ends in the same way. They call out hordes of Blanks and attack drones to fight us. And if we get too close, they just kill our agent. There's no way to get close enough for a rescue. The best thing we can do to help him is to find a way to cure the Blanks."

271

He turned to leave again, but Timothy wasn't ready to accept failure yet.

"You didn't have me before," Timothy said, an idea forming in his head. "Attack the hospital. I'll slip in and get our agent out."

"Are you sure you can do it?" Gearwire asked. "The place will be crawling with Blanks."

Timothy nodded. "Trust me. I can handle it."

"You all heard him," Gearwire said as Timothy slipped off down the street. "We're storming the hospital!"

Timothy jogged through the familiar streets of Kawts, doing his best to stay in the shadows. He reached the hospital and crouched down in one of the bushes near the doors, waiting. After a short time, he heard the sounds of battle and saw Blanks pouring out of the building. He waited only a minute after the last Blank left before entering the hospital, sprinting past the startled receptionist and into the main hallway. He abandoned stealth in favor of speed as he ran through the hallways, trying to remember what Quill had written about the location of the Blanking Chamber.

As he neared the spot, Timothy slowed down, aware that the Council might have left a few Blanks behind. He cautiously glanced around the corner to see a pair of Blanks and a handful of drones guarding the door. He reached into his satchel and pulled out five shurikens, which he threw in rapid succession - three razor sharp ones for the drones, and two blunted ones for the Blanks.

Seconds later, the hallway was clear. Timothy extended his hand, and his shurikens flew back through the air towards him, landing harmlessly in his gauntlet. Without any further delay, he eased the Blanking room door open, ready for a battle.

A cursory glance proved that there were no Council guards inside the room, and Timothy relaxed. He took a longer look around the room, doing his best to analyze its contents. It was just as Quill had described it. Up against the wall was a trio of cells, the first two of which were currently occupied. The first of the cells housed the resistance agent, which Timothy was surprised to discover was Edward, the record-keeper for The Race. The other cell contained a ninth level student, evidently the loser of a recent Race.

"It's alright," Edward said, trying to calm the frightened student. "He's a friend. He's here to get us out of here." He looked over at Timothy. "Isn't that right?"

Timothy nodded. "Gearwire sent me to rescue you." He turned to Edward. "Do you know where they keep the key?"

"Councilman Marciano took it with him when he left," Edward replied. "But it's possible that the Blanks would have one too."

Timothy nodded and ducked outside, searching the bodies of the unconscious Blanks for a key. His efforts proved fruitless, however, and he returned to the Blanking chamber empty-handed. Fortunately, he had an idea.

If my shurikens can shear through an attack drone, surely they can cut through the bars of a jail cell.

He slipped a pair of shurikens from his satchel and passed one to Edward, instructing him to cut his way out as he set about doing the same on the other cell.

As Edward finally cut through the bars, Timothy turned his attention to the rest of the room, trying to cause as much damage to the chamber as he could. He stopped short only of destroying the Blanking machine, unwilling to risk whatever side effects might occur if the device was destroyed while people were still under its control. He did, however, cut the bars on all the cells, doing his best to make it as hard as possible for the Council to Blank anyone else in the near future.

He was about to leave when he heard footsteps in the hallway outside. Silently urging the prisoners to stay out of sight, Timothy stood against the wall by the door, shuriken in hand. Seconds later, someone ran into the room.

It was Darren, one of the lesser Councilmen. He stopped suddenly when he saw the damage that had been done to the room. Timothy seized his chance and threw a shuriken at him. But even taken by surprise, the Councilman was still a force to be reckoned with. Tipped off by some slight sound that Timothy had made, Darren ducked, drawing his sword as he did. He lunged at Timothy, but Timothy sidestepped, shoving Darren forwards.

He staggered into the room, and before he could recover, Timothy drew another shuriken from his satchel and threw it at the Councilman's sword. Unprepared for Timothy's quick reaction, Darren lost his grip on the sword. Before he could retrieve it, Timothy launched another throwing star at him. It collided with the back of his head, knocking him unconscious. He crumpled to the floor, and Timothy dragged him into one of the damaged cells.

"Let's go," he told the captives. "Before the Council realizes Darren was unsuccessful." He didn't elaborate further, but he could see by the look on Edward's face that he understood exactly why Darren had come. Timothy turned to lead the former prisoners to safety when he remembered the Blank suits on the wall. He ran back inside the room and grabbed as many of the suits as he could, stuffing them into his satchel before leading the former prisoners through the hospital.

They had almost left the secret corridor when they rounded the corner and found themselves standing face-to-face with Ives, one of Timothy's old classmates who now worked for the *Kawts Tribune*.

Timothy froze, not sure what to do. Ives froze as well, squinting at him as if trying to make out Timothy's identity. Finally, he gave an almost imperceptible nod and walked away.

Well, that was weird. What's Ives doing down here? Is he writing a story about the Kawts hospital? Timothy shook his head. Whatever Ives' reasons were, it was clear that he was intentionally allowing them to escape.

"Stay close," he told the prisoners, leading them out the hospital's back door and out of Kawts. A few minutes later, they were joined by Gearwire and the rest of his crew, and the whole group slipped over the wall and back to the rebel base.

As the others began to disperse, Timothy walked up to Gearwire and handed him the Blank suits he had taken. Gearwire's eyes went wide as he realized what Timothy had just given him.

"Are these *unused* Blank suits?" he asked. Timothy nodded. "Do you know how significant this is?" A rare expression of excitement crossed Gearwire's face. "If we compare these to the Kolts' old suits, we might be able to pinpoint exactly how they work!" He looked Timothy in the eyes. "I'll send these to the lab right away," he said, quickly recomposing his features. Timothy turned to go, but Gearwire added, "Good work today. Edward would be a Blank right now if not for you."

Timothy smiled to himself and continued walking, leaving Gearwire alone with his thoughts.

* * *

The next night, Gearwire hosted a celebration in honor of Edward's rescue. Timothy was finishing up some adjustments to his suit, and by the time he made it to the great hall, the party had already begun. Some tables had been dragged together to create a makeshift stage, where several of the cave's musicians were playing. To Timothy's surprise, Adalbo was among them, strumming on a lute.

Timothy spotted some of the Gearwire's crewmembers sitting around a table a short distance away and wandered over to them. Idalbo was regaling the others with stories from his time in Alpen, Inn standing beside him.

"So there we were, surrounded by the Baron's army," Idalbo said. "Our reinforcements were still a few hours behind. We were prepared to fight our way out, but we knew we didn't have a chance. Barring a miracle, we were doomed."

"And then Seililyad hit the Baron in the head with a brick!" Inn roared, slamming his palm on the table. "We escaped in the confusion and led our troops to victory!"

Idalbo arched an eyebrow at his friend. "Yes. I was getting to that part."

"You were taking too long! I couldn't help myself!"

"Sure you couldn't," Idalbo said, laughing. He was silent for a moment, then he asked, "Did I ever tell you guys about the time we fought Dr. Dram?"

The Golden Knight shook his head. "Not that I can recall."

"It's quite the story," Idalbo said. He glanced back at Inn. "No interruptions this time, please."

Idalbo began his tale, but Timothy was only half listening. He took a slow look around the room, watching the rest of the rebels enjoying themselves. A group of them around Timothy's age huddled near the stage, deep in a discussion of their own. Every once in a while, one of them said something that sent the others into fits of laughter.

Timothy felt a slight pang of jealousy as he watched them. For a moment, he considered going over to join them, but then he decided against it.

No. I've seen and done too many things they wouldn't understand. And I wouldn't understand them anymore, either.

I wish Jewel were here, he thought with a sigh. *I can just be myself with her. Instead of having to be Mr. Future-leader-of-the-resistance.*

"You look like you're having fun," the Mysterious Man said, coming up behind Timothy.

Timothy started. "Huh? Me? No, I'm just-"

"It's okay. I get it. They're a good bunch of people, but it's not quite the same as having close friends."

Timothy looked up at him. "How did you-" he started, but the Mysterious Man cut him off.

"If you'd rather not hang around here, Gearwire has a mission he'd like to speak with you about." He pointed over toward the entrance to the hall, where Gearwire was shaking hands with a couple who had just arrived at the party.

"I'll keep that in mind," Timothy said. "Thanks."

"My pleasure," the Mysterious Man said, vanishing back into the crowd.

Timothy turned back toward the festivities, but his mind kept coming back to what the Mysterious Man had said. After a few minutes, he excused himself and walked over to Gearwire.

"I heard you had a mission for me," he said, keeping his voice low.

Gearwire nodded, stepping away from the door. "Howard and Thomas haven't had long to examine those Blank suits you found, but they both agree that something is still missing. In order to complete their cure, they need to get their hands on the blueprints for the Blanking machine itself. I need someone to sneak into the Council's records room and steal the blueprints. Without letting the Council know there was a break-in."

"I can leave tonight," Timothy said.

"That's not necessary," Gearwire said. "This mission is important. Take a few days to plan. The fate of Kawts might depend on the outcome."

Timothy nodded. "In that case, I'll start *planning* tonight." He slipped out the door, making his way back to his quarters.

* * *

Timothy spent nearly a week planning for the mission, trying to cover every eventuality. On such an important mission, there would be little room for mistakes. Finally, at sundown one evening, he set off on Snipps, a few new gadgets stashed in his satchel.

Timothy reached Kawts shortly before nightfall. He left Snipps on the edge of town and moved into the city, climbing up over the wall while the Blanks' backs were turned. He darted from shadow to shadow, staying out of sight of the attack drones and Blank patrols. Slowly, he made his way towards the Council Building, reaching it a little before midnight.

As he stood outside the door, he remembered the last time he had stood in the same spot. Despite all he'd learned and all the new weapons he had, he still hesitated, recalling clearly how his previous unsuccessful escapade had gotten Samuel Blanked and himself chased out of Kawts.

If I turn back now, I'm surrendering to the Council, he reminded himself. *And dooming Samuel and Quill to be Blanks forever.*

His resolve strengthened, he slipped inside, keeping to the shadows as he crept noiselessly across the floor. A few minutes later, he stood in front of the door to the records room. He stared at the lock on the door, quelling the sudden surge of anxiety that flooded him.

You'll be fine, he chided himself. *You've been planning this for days.*

Taking a deep breath, he removed a new type of shuriken from his satchel and placed it on the lock. There was a soft whirring sound as the device went to work, followed by a click as the door unlocked. Timothy felt a grin break across his face. He was in.

As he stepped inside, he could see that the records room was just as much of a mess as it had been when he was last there. Documents were piled in haphazard stacks all across the room, swaying alarmingly as he walked by.

Timothy scanned the labels on the filing cabinets, searching for the

B section. When he finally found it, he noticed with relief that the lock had been smashed, leaving the cabinet door ajar. There was no doubt in his mind that this was where Quill had found the blueprints.

Timothy pulled the drawer out further and rifled through the files inside, many of which were fragile and yellowed with age. After several minutes, he found the files relating to the creation of the Blanks, all tucked together in a bulging beige folder. Timothy checked to make sure that the blueprints were among them before slipping the folder into his satchel.

No sooner had he done this, however, than he heard footsteps and voices in the corridor. Heart pounding, he quickly pulled the door closed and retired to the far corner of the room, crouching down in the middle of a circle of filing cabinets. Several agonizing seconds passed.

Then the door clicked open.

* * *

When Ethos and Aksell entered the records room, they saw no signs of anything amiss. As they walked between the winding rows of documents, Timothy slipped out the door, not knowing that he had just missed seeing his friend. He took his time getting out, not wanting to risk capture now that he had in his possession what were arguably the most important documents in all of Kawts. After several hours of creeping through the shadows, he finally reached the city walls. He quickly climbed back over and made his way to where he had left Snipps, then rode back to the base.

Chapter 33

"We need you to capture a Blank," Gearwire announced as he approached Timothy during one of his daily training sessions.

Timothy picked up one of his shurikens, waiting for Gearwire to explain.

"Howard and Dr. Maddium have created a prototype de-Blanking device. They need you to capture a Blank so that they can test it."

"Is there anyone in particular you want me to bring here?" Timothy asked as he sent one of his throwing stars whizzing into the wooden target.

Gearwire shook his head. "Just capture whichever Blank is easiest to smuggle out of Kawts. If this works, we'll be able to free everyone before long."

"Got it," Timothy said, stretching out his hand. The throwing star flew into his glove, and he slipped it into his satchel.

"One more thing," Gearwire said. "We've discovered that there's a tracking chip in each of the Blank suits - in the heel of their left boot. Use this to deactivate it before you bring the Blank to the base," he added, handing Timothy a slender metal wand.

"I didn't deactivate the tracking chips in those suits I brought here! The Council might know where we are!" Timothy said, his eyes wide.

"Don't worry about that," Gearwire said. "The chips in those suits hadn't been activated yet. The Council apparently doesn't bother turning them on until there's someone inside."

Timothy nodded, relieved. "I'll go tonight," he promised, heading off to his quarters to prepare. As the sun began to set, he made his way over to the corral to pick up Snipps. He climbed up onto the giant raccoon's back and rode out of the cave in the direction of Kawts.

As he neared the wall, he came to a stop, watching from a distance as the two Blanks on the top marched back and forth. He knew from past experience that their replacements wouldn't come for several more hours. But by then, he would be long gone.

Dismounting, he jammed several of his shurikens into the wall, embedding them into the crevices between the thick stones. After testing to make sure that they were secure, Timothy scrambled up the wall, using the shurikens as a ladder.

As he neared the top, he removed two blunted shurikens from his satchel. He waited until both Blanks had turned away from him before vaulting over the edge of the wall, throwing both shurikens in rapid succession. The first found its mark, knocking the Blank unconscious. The other missed, the Blank having sidestepped it at the last moment.

Timothy frowned.

That's odd, he thought. *Blanks don't usually have the reflexes for tricks like that.*

Quickly, he reached for another throwing star, but the Blank raised its arms in surrender.

And that's really *odd,* Timothy thought, alarm bells ringing in his head. *There's no way a Blank could willingly surrender. Unless...*

Slowly, the Blank reached up toward their face and removed their mask. A silver-haired woman stared at him from inside the Blank suit. Timothy held his shurikens at the ready, wary.

She doesn't look like she's brainwashed, he thought, noting that she didn't seem as emotionless as Quill had been.

"I would really appreciate it if you didn't throw that at me," the woman said drily, her voice cracking as if she hadn't used it in a long time.

"How- how..." Timothy stammered, shocked at hearing the Blank speak.

The Blank smiled in amusement. "When everyone takes it for granted that you're completely brainwashed, they don't pay much attention to what you do. I've been playing their game for the last forty years. I'm done pretending."

Timothy blinked, still trying to wrap his head around what was happening. "You're done pretending what?" he asked at last. "What exactly are you saying?"

"I want you to bring me back with you. I know you work for the rebels."

"Why didn't you ask the twins, then?" Timothy said. "They've been here for years."

"Twins?" the Blank asked, puzzled. Realization dawned on her. "You mean those two with the crystal powers?"

She doesn't know the twins' identities, Timothy realized, suddenly aware of his near blunder.

"I'll talk to Gearwire," he said, ignoring her question. "He'll send someone to contact you."

"That won't do me any good. This is my only chance to sneak off unnoticed."

"How do I know this isn't a trick by the Council?"

"I suppose you don't," the Blank said after a while. "But I know better than most that the Council is evil. And they don't like it when people try to beat them at their own game. When we refused to cooperate, they turned all of us into Blanks," she added bitterly.

Timothy frowned, her words tugging at something in his memory. Suddenly, it clicked. "You're one of the people who refused to run The

Race!"

She nodded. "It was my idea. A friend of mine had been injured a few days before, and I knew she didn't stand a chance of finishing. I got nearly half the class to boycott The Race. The others were all brainwashed. But for some reason, I wasn't."

"Samuel thought you were dead," Timothy said.

"You know Samuel, then?"

Timothy nodded. "Do you know if - is he still alive?"

"Technically speaking, yes," the Blank replied sourly. "Although I'd hardly qualify being a Blank as living. But do you know him?" she repeated.

"I was his apprentice."

Recognition flashed in the Blank's eyes. "Timothy," she said simply, connecting the dots. "Samuel fought as hard as he could to delay us long enough for you to escape," she added, a touch of sadness in her voice. "He was trying to help you up to the very moment they took over his mind."

"He'll be free soon enough," Timothy said firmly, echoing Gearwire's words. "The resistance is working on a cure for the Blankness. That's why I was sent here tonight. To capture a Blank so that they could test it."

The Blank brightened. "Then there's still hope for him? For them?"

"That's what we're trying to find out," Timothy replied with a sigh. "But I know it is possible. Two of the rebels' highest-ranking officers are former Blanks."

"The brainwashing isn't permanent," the Blank repeated with relief, more to herself than to Timothy. "I was worried they were gone forever."

"Speaking of that," Timothy said, glancing at the unconscious Blank behind him. "I should get him back to the base before he wakes up." He removed the wand from his satchel and deactivated the Blank's tracking chip. He hesitated, then tossed the device to the other Blank. "Here. Wave that over the back of your left boot. It'll deactivate the Council's tracking chip."

"You're letting me come with you."

"I think I can trust you," Timothy said at last. "And anyway, when the Council comes to investigate, they might discover that you've been faking. If they do, they'll kill you for sure. Too many people have already died at their hands."

As the Blank deactivated her tracking chip, Timothy recalled his shurikens to his hand, returning them to his satchel. He tied the unconscious Blank up with a length of rope and slowly lowered him to the ground below. Then he shimmied down himself, lifting the man onto Snipps' back.

"Climb down the throwing stars," Timothy told the other Blank from his place on the ground, pausing in his task.

Hesitantly, the Blank began her descent down the side of the wall. Once she reached the ground, Timothy retrieved his throwing stars, leaving hardly any indication that he had even been there at all.

"I'm Jane," the Blank said, extending her hand.

Timothy nodded, remembering the name from Samuel's story. "Nice to meet you," he said, shaking her hand. "We should probably get out of here," he added, hopping up onto Snipps' back and extending a hand to help Jane up after him.

He rode back to the base in a roundabout fashion, occasionally taking lengthy breaks for no discernable reason.

"Why are we stopping again?" Jane asked after the second such stop.

Timothy avoided looking at her as he answered. "Just in case that wasn't the only tracking device you had on you."

"You still don't fully trust me, do you?" she asked, amused. "I suppose I don't blame you," she said after a pause. "I wouldn't put it past the Council to try a trick like that."

"We'll wait here awhile to see if anyone comes," Timothy said, ignoring her last statement. "Snipps, stay here," he ordered the raccoon as he dismounted. "I'll go scout out the area," he said, slipping off between the trees. As soon as he was satisfied that he was out of sight, he turned and headed directly for the rebel base.

"Identify yourself!" a sentry demanded as he approached the mouth of the cave.

"Shadow," Timothy said. "I have a message for Gearwire," he said, passing a folded-up scrap of paper to the sentry. "Tell him that we'll be waiting at Riss' Gulch."

Then, before the weary sentry could reply, Timothy melted back into the shadows, waiting nearby just long enough to confirm that his message had been passed along before dashing back to where he had left Jane and Snipps.

"The coast is clear," he said, stepping into the open. He walked over to the still-unconscious Blank. "Since we'll be here awhile, we'd better make sure he doesn't wake up and call for reinforcements." He removed the Blanks' mask and double checked to make sure his knots were secure.

Satisfied that the Blank couldn't escape, he leaned up against a nearby tree, watching the darkened sky for any sign of attack drones. The night passed slowly, without any word from Gearwire. Then, as morning broke, Timothy became aware of a rustling in the brush behind him. Slowly, he stood and crept off in the direction of the sound.

To his relief, he found only Dr. Maddium and Howard Kolt, both dressed in their battle gear. Timothy stepped out onto the path in front of them, making them both jump in surprise.

"What's the verdict?" he asked, smiling to himself under his helmet.

"We're going to try the treatment on the Blank right here," Dr. Maddium said.

"If it works, we'll try it on Jane as well, just to make sure she's not still under the Council's control," Howard finished, adjusting his backpack.

"And once we're sure she's not?"

"She can come with us to the base. If she's telling the truth about her identity, she has no reason to help the Council."

"They're in a clearing over here," Timothy said, satisfied with the scientist's answer.

The two scientists followed him back to the camp and opened their bags, setting up a makeshift laboratory.

Jane watched with interest as Timothy untied the now-conscious Blank. "Who are they?"

"The scientists who are working on the de-Blanking device," Timothy said. "I removed his mask already," he said to Dr. Maddium. "I didn't want to take the chance of him calling in backup when he woke up."

"The mask shouldn't affect the device," Dr. Maddium said, adjusting a dial on a strange-looking contraption. "But I'll make a note of it, anyway. On second thought-" he said, frowning in concentration. "It is conceivable that the glass of the lenses might block some of the wavelengths we're using. We'd better test it with him wearing the mask."

"Won't he just call for backup, then?" Jane asked.

"The microphone is on the bottom half of the mask," Howard suggested. "We could break that part off and just use the top half."

This idea was quickly carried out, and soon the Blank sat propped up against a tree with his mask over his eyes. Dr. Maddium opened his Infini-case and removed a small, rectangular device. He jotted down a note on a pad of paper, then aimed the device at the Blank. The Blank immediately began thrashing about, convulsing wildly. Dr. Maddium frowned deeply and adjusted a knob on the side of the device. The man stopped thrashing suddenly, his mask falling to the ground. He blinked in the sunlight and looked around in confusion.

"Where am I?" he asked, bewildered.

"Do you know who you are?" Howard asked gravely. Timothy held his breath, painfully aware of how much depended on the man's answer.

The man squinted. "Uh… Crofton. Crofton Butler," he said. He looked around the clearing in confusion. "What happened? I remember being taken under the hospital," he said, thinking hard. "Ethos was there - what did they do to me?" he demanded suddenly, lurching to his feet.

"You've just spent the last several years as a Blank," Howard replied, a look of pure joy breaking out across his face.

He's thinking about his wife, Timothy realized. *Now he finally has a way to free her.*

"I've been a Blank?" Crofton asked in disbelief. "But how - who are you people?"

"We can explain everything," Dr. Maddium said, beaming.

"Could you start by explaining how I got this massive headache?" Crofton asked, grimacing.

Dr. Maddium's smile faded a little. "It could be a side effect of the cure…" he said slowly.

"I think that one might be my fault," Timothy interjected. "The only way I could get you over here was to knock you unconscious."

"Well, thanks for that," Crofton said somewhat sarcastically.

"It's your turn now, ma'am," Dr. Maddium said, turning to Jane. "It's a necessary precaution, I'm afraid."

"Fire away," Jane replied, staring directly at the box.

Dr. Maddium activated the device. Nothing happened.

"Welcome to the resistance," Dr. Maddium said, a smile breaking across his face.

"If we're finished here, we really need to get back to the base,"

Howard said, his eyes shining. "We need to build a lot more of these."

Chapter 34

For the next several weeks, the rebellion worked at a fevered pitch, trying to stockpile as many de-Blanking devices as they could in the shortest time possible. But even as their hopes grew higher, the situation in Kawts grew steadily worse. The reports from Crystal and Jewel became more and more concerning, with more and more people disappearing from Kawts each day. Some days, as many as ten people were turned into Blanks - and for no discernable reason. It seemed that the Council had given up all pretense of being noble heroes, although what had tipped their hand, no one could guess.

Then one day, the messages abruptly stopped coming. Three days came and went, and there was still no word from the twins. Gearwire was in the middle of assembling a team to search for them when they stumbled into the command center, looking battered and weary.

"Crystal! Jewel!" Gearwire exclaimed, alarmed.

"Are you injured?" Dr. Maddium asked, rising from his seat.

"Nothing serious," Jewel said with a glance at her sister. "We're mostly just tired."

"Then you need to rest," Gearwire said. "I'll have a space cleared out in the barracks."

"We need to give our report first," Jewel insisted. "It's important."

Gearwire nodded. "Okay," he said at last. "Give your report, and then I'll take you to the barracks."

Jewel nodded. "Once the disappearances became more common, we knew we had to discover the reason," she said. "We did some investigating and uncovered something alarming. Somehow, the Council had stumbled upon an ancient text from the Great Heroes' War. A few days ago, they received a package from the man who supplies the attack drones. We weren't able to figure out exactly what was in this package, but as best as we can tell, it's some sort of communicator."

"A communicator?" Gearwire interrupted, frowning. "Why would they go through all this trouble for that?"

"We don't know for sure," Jewel said. "But based on what we were able to piece together, it seems that they're planning to make contact with the aliens who invaded earth during the Heroes' War. But regardless of who they're contacting, the Council has started building an army that they plan on using to conquer the rest of the world. They're no longer satisfied with just Kawts."

Crystal picked up the story now. "As soon as we discovered this, we tried to come back to tell you, but we were met with an unpleasant surprise. The Council corralled the entire population of Kawts into Franklin Plaza, forcing them to build weapons and gear for their new army. Security was strict, and no one was allowed to leave for any reason. People disappeared three times as fast as before. For those three days, we prepared for our escape. In doing so, we discovered an unexpected ally. Volker helped us to get out of the city, staging a diversion on the other side of Kawts."

"It was just as you suspected, Gearwire," Jewel said. "Volker's primary concern has always been the good of Kawts. He was just as deceived about the Council and the Blanks as anyone else until they ordered him to forcibly gather everyone in the city center. He was merely a pawn in the Council's game. Once he realized what the Council was truly like, he was appalled. He's willing to do whatever it takes to free Kawts."

Gearwire exhaled deeply and ran his fingers through his hair, clearly understanding the dire straits that the city was in. If they didn't save Kawts now, there wouldn't be a city left to save. "Do we have any other allies in the city?" he asked.

"No one that could help us," Crystal answered. "Although Ives, Charles, and a few others have managed to evade the Council and are hiding out somewhere in Kawts."

Gearwire was silent for a long time. Finally, he stood up. "We'll attack tonight," he said grimly. "You two should get some rest before then."

The news spread through the base like a wildfire. Everyone gathered their weapons, tools, and musical instruments in preparation for the battle. Gearwire sent a messenger to Grimshaw to warn them about the coming attack.

At the end of the evening meal, Gearwire climbed up onto the table and addressed the crowd.

"Friends! We are gathered here in preparation for the attack on Kawts. All the years of the resistance have led up to this battle. Each one of us has been affected in one way or another by the Council's treachery. Tonight, we will strike back against them. We will end the Council's tyranny once and for all, or perish in the attempt."

The crowd cheered. Gearwire glanced at Dr. Maddium before he continued. "As many of you already know, we have been working for some time on stockpiling a supply of de-Blanking devices. We will distribute them to as many of you as possible. But remember this - do not use lethal force on the Blanks if it can be avoided. They are the very people we are trying to save. The attack drones will receive no such mercy. They are to be completely destroyed. But now, prepare yourselves. Tonight, the Battle of Kawts will begin."

There was a resounding cheer from the assembled rebels, the volume of which was nearly deafening. In the midst of the cheers and the war cries, Timothy saw Gearwire step down from the table and duck out of the room. Noticing a strange sadness in their leader, Timothy followed.

When he finally caught up with him, Gearwire was standing in the entrance of the cave, praying and looking down at Kawts, stars twinkling in the sky overhead. He stood and turned to face Timothy as he approached. There were tears in his eyes.

"None of this was supposed to happen, Timothy," he said, his voice heavy with sadness. There was silence for a while, and Gearwire was once more looking at Kawts. After what seemed like an eternity, he continued.

"I founded Kawts, Timothy. Did you know that? I was the one who gave the Council their power. I created the monster that ruined so many lives."

"But now you're working to stop it, right?" Timothy stammered, caught off guard by Gearwire's confession.

Gearwire smiled sadly. "My actions are coming several hundred years too late, I'm afraid. I believed my system to be perfect. I was too much of a fool to see its flaws until it was too late."

There was silence for a while as Timothy tried to wrap his head around Gearwire's words. Hundreds of questions swirled in his head, but he knew that now was not the time to ask them.

"Is-is there anything you need me to do?" he asked at last, not sure what else to say.

Gearwire turned once more to face him. "Prepare for the battle. And pray that the Lord will grant us victory."

* * *

Timothy scooped his entire supply of shurikens into his satchel as he donned his suit. He was almost ready to leave when the Mysterious Man approached him, an unusual staff in his hands. The end of the staff had a wind chime dangling from the end, producing a faint music as the Mysterious Man drew closer. When he was just a few feet away, he stopped, handing the staff to Timothy.

"Take this," he said quietly, his voice catching. "It belonged to a good friend of mine. He would have wanted you to use it tonight."

Timothy examined the staff with a critical eye, impressed by the care that had been taken in its construction. He looked up to thank the Mysterious Man, but he had vanished again into the shadows. After a moment's hesitation, Timothy slung the staff onto his back, leaving his old staff leaning against his door.

* * *

It didn't take long before the rebels were ready to get underway. Howard stood in the mouth of the cave, passing out the de-Blanking devices to each of the rebels as they passed by. For the first time since the founding of the resistance, the cave lay completely empty, with every man, woman, and child taking part in this final charge. The fate of Kawts had all come down to this.

The wind picked up and dark clouds filled the sky as the rebel's primary attack force neared the edge of the city. The distant roll of thunder could be heard as Gearwire turned and addressed his troops.

"Tonight, The Council will fall and a new era will begin," he said, his voice rising in intensity. "An era of freedom!" The rebels cheered. Gearwire gave a loud shout and led the charge towards the sleeping city.

As they neared the wall, Gearwire slowed to a halt. "Grappling hooks!" he shouted. A small group of rebels emerged from the crowd behind him, twirling their grappling hooks over their heads.

"Release!" Gearwire shouted, and the rebels complied, sending the hooks sailing over the edge of the wall and embedding themselves in the catwalk. "My crew up first," Gearwire called. "Melee weapons next, archers and sharpshooters last!"

Timothy grabbed onto one of the ropes and scrambled up, vaulting over the edge of the wall at the same time as Gearwire and the Mysterious Man. Timothy quickly threw two weighted shurikens at the Blank sentries, knocking both of them unconscious in seconds. While Gearwire and the Mysterious Man cleared the rest of the area, Timothy knelt down beside the fallen Blanks, ripping off their masks and flashing the de-Blanking device in their eyes. The Blanks blinked, bewildered, but Timothy was already gone, keeping watch for the Council's forces while the rest of the rebels scaled the wall.

The last squadron was just climbing over onto the wall when the first attack drones appeared on the horizon.

"Drones, dead ahead!" Crystal called, pointing.

"And the Blanks aren't far behind," Jewel added.

"Archers and sharpshooters - stay up here on the wall!" Gearwire ordered. "Musicians too! Start playing as soon as the Blanks arrive. Everyone else, follow me down to the ground!"

The rebels poured down from the wall and into the city, hastily forming a defensive line just in time to meet the oncoming Blanks. Slowly, the musicians began to play - hesitantly at first, but growing in volume as they gained more confidence. The Blanks faltered as the sound reached them, the music awakening something in their brainwashed minds.

One of the less affected Blanks raised his club, aiming to bash Timothy over the head. At the last moment, Timothy saw it and pivoted to avoid the blow, striking out with his staff. The staff caught the Blank in the knees, and it fell to the ground. Someone reached out from behind Timothy and pulled the writhing Blank past the rebel's lines, both to keep him out of the way of the fighters and to give the rebels a chance to de-Blank him.

Timothy returned his focus to the battle to see a drone swooping down at him. It spewed bullets into the crowd at random, hitting several of the Blanks in the process. Timothy dispatched the drone easily with one of his shurikens, motioning for the rebels behind him to take care of the wounded Blanks.

Out of the corner of his eye, Timothy could see Gearwire standing where the fighting was the fiercest, taking down drone after drone with globs of molten glue from his glue gun. A strange light shone in his eyes as he jumped into the fray with a reckless abandon, an ever-growing pile of smoldering drone parts littering the ground at his feet.

The drones regrouped for a concerted charge, but before they could, a whirlwind of leaves blocked their view. Howard Kolt was behind them somewhere, using his mask to temporarily conceal them from the drones' sight. Taking advantage of their momentary blindness, Idalbo and the other archers unleashed a volley of arrows into the clustered mass of drones, sending several plummeting to the ground. The drones returned fire blindly through the leaves, hitting several of the archers.

As he fended off another wave of Blanks, Timothy could hear Idalbo giving orders to his troops, telling them to scatter along the top of the wall. A short distance away, the Golden Knight and the Mysterious Man darted among the rebels, plugging a gap in their front lines. Bullets pinged off of the Golden Knight's indestructible armor as he used his broadsword to cleave through a batch of drones that tried to exploit a gap in the lines. Howard redirected most of the leaves to fly among the Blanks, further disorienting them.

On the roof, Idalbo's archers unleashed another volley of arrows at the drones. Their line of sight no longer concealed by the leaves, the drones swooped down at them, trying to take out both the archers and the musicians. Before they could get close enough, several of them fell to the ground, impaled by razor-sharp shards of familiar blue crystal. Crystal and Jewel stood back-to-back a short distance away, working in tandem to eliminate or immobilize the Council's army. By the time the drone's attack force reached the wall, it had been depleted to well under half its original strength, their damaged formation easy prey for the rebels' archers.

The Blanks, however, kept coming, their superior numbers beginning to push the rebels back. The bullets of the remaining drones began to strike home, taking out several of Gearwire's men. Timothy saw the Mysterious Man go down under a hail of bullets, but whether he was dead or merely wounded, he was too far away to tell.

"We need to push these Blanks back!" Gearwire shouted. "Crystal! Do you have any of those smoke canisters left?"

Crystal nodded and tossed a small silver sphere into the middle of the crowd of Blanks, filling the air with dense smoke.

"Idalbo!" Gearwire ordered. "Take some of the archers and musicians up into those buildings over there!" he added, pointing his sword at the row of houses in front of them. "No more than two people per window. Take down any drone that gets within range."

Idalbo nodded and turned to his men. "Second Archer Battalion! Come with me!" He turned and climbed down from the wall, disappearing into the fog along with his men.

Meanwhile, Gearwire was taking advantage of the momentary lull in the fighting to reorganize the rebels' ranks into a stronger defensive formation, distributing his crew members along the front lines.

"Where is Elmer?" Timothy heard him mutter as they waited for the disoriented Blanks to emerge from the fog. "The Council will be here soon."

* * *

Dr. Maddium stood on the edge of the raft, looking out over his brigade. The night was silent except for the quiet splashes of their paddles in the water. If all went according to plan, his forces would be in control of the Council Building within the hour.

"We'll reach Kawts in a few minutes," he said quietly to Adalbo. "Have everyone wait on the banks until all the rafts have arrived." Adalbo nodded and flew off to pass Dr. Maddium's instructions on to the rest of the brigade.

"Do you think we have a chance?" Madison asked.

Dr. Maddium considered the question for a moment before replying. "Between Gearwire and Elmer's brigades, I doubt the Council will be paying much attention to the river. They never have." He paused. "But even if we can't get through, there's a good chance that Timothy will."

There was silence again as Dr. Maddium's thoughts wandered to what would happen if they were unsuccessful tonight. The Council's army outnumbered them by more than two to one. Their best chance to take them down would be a quick, decisive strike at the heart of their control - to take the Council members and the Council Building in one deft movement. From there, it would only be a few short steps to deactivating all the drones and Blanks simultaneously.

"The first raft has reached the shore," Adalbo said softly, snapping Dr. Maddium from his ruminations.

"Good," he replied. "Have them organize into a wedge formation."

Adalbo flew off once more, and Dr. Maddium fell back into the past, remembering what had happened the last time they had tried to overthrow the Council. This time, the stakes were much higher, and he couldn't help but feel a twinge of regret for his own role in the Council's rise to power.

The raft came to a gentle stop on the riverbank, and Dr. Maddium returned his focus to the present.

Father, keep us safe tonight, he prayed silently as the brigade looked to him for their next instructions. *And don't let the Council win this battle.* Then he cleared his throat and addressed his troops.

"It's our job to take the Council Building," he said. "There will be no talking or unnecessary noise until we reach our destination. Stealth is our primary goal." He let his words hang in the air for a moment longer before adding, "If we run into any Blanks, keep going unless I say otherwise. We've got to take that hill."

As he finished speaking, he gave a nod to Adalbo, who started out with the first of the companies. While he waited for the rest of the brigade to get underway, Dr. Maddium yanked a cord on his lab coat. The coat began to shift and change, transforming into his battle suit. The suit was a particular pride of his, having built it himself many years earlier, during the Robot War.

The brigade crept through the empty streets of the town, getting all the way to the track without encountering any opposition. But as they turned toward the hospital, the air suddenly erupted with gunfire. The rebels' ranks disintegrated into chaos as dozens of their comrades suddenly fell, dead before they even hit the ground. Dr. Maddium looked towards the source of the attack to see a company of attack drones, reinforced by Councilmen LeSalle and Payat. As the drones continued firing into the rebel's tightly grouped formation, Dr. Maddium came to a decision.

"Into the trees!" he ordered, shouting to be heard over the sounds of the battle. As the rebels fled towards the shelter of the track, the drones moved to intercept them. Dr. Maddium raised his hands and fired a blast of raw electricity from his gauntlets, taking down the nearest group of drones. More drones swarmed in to fill the gap, but this time, the rebels fought back, clearing a path big enough for them to get through.

As the last of the rebels escaped into the trees, the drones backed off a few yards, waiting for any targets to present themselves. They fired a few warning shots into the brush, trying to hit some of the rebels hidden there. But the rebels had already retreated deeper into the trees, hunkering down to wait out the attack.

Dr. Maddium surveyed what remained of his brigade. Nearly a third of his men were dead, wounded, or missing. And, judging by the sound of gunfire outside, the survivors were trapped for the time being.

It's all up to Timothy now.

Chapter 35

Gearwire drummed his fingers on the side of his robotic leg, watching the fog for any signs of the Council's army. As he did, he realized the musicians had trailed off.

"Keep playing!" he shouted, turning back towards his own troops for a fraction of a second. Startled by Gearwire's abrupt order, the musicians hastily resumed their song, playing even louder than before.

All at once, the fog cleared, revealing the hordes of Blanks barely a yard away. A massive swarm of attack drones hovered over the battlefield. The second the fog lifted, they dive-bombed the rebels, only to be taken out by Idalbo and his men. The remaining drones scattered, trying to pinpoint the source of the shots.

Capitalizing upon the momentary confusion in the Council's forces, Gearwire barked an order to the rebel army. "Onwards!" he shouted, brandishing his sword over his head. "Charge!"

The rebels surged forwards, crashing into the ranks of the Blanks. Slowly, the Council's forces gave ground, retreating to the point where the rebels had passed even the buildings where the archers were hiding out. The Blanks withdrew further, but Gearwire slowed his pace, not wanting to risk the chance that it was a ploy.

"Mysterious Man! Golden Knight!" he called. The Mysterious Man materialized next to him, his left arm dangling limply at his side. If Gearwire noticed his crew member's injury, however, he gave no sign of it. "Take your companies up Miller Avenue. Make sure the Council doesn't circle back behind our right flank." The Mysterious Man nodded and jogged off down the street, his company following close behind him.

"Timothy, you and the twins take your companies up Pathos Lane," he continued, seeing Timothy standing a few feet away. "If the coast is clear after a few minutes, you and your stealth platoon are free to complete your mission." Timothy nodded, remembering the special instructions Gearwire had given him before they had left the cave.

"Be prepared for a fight, though," Gearwire added. "If I were in the Council's position, I'd launch an attack through one of those streets. I'd be willing to bet that one or both of you will encounter resistance." Timothy exhaled slowly, taking Gearwire's warning to heart as he started off down the street that he had named.

* * *

Timothy cautiously peeked around the corner of the building at the end of the street, inspecting the plaza in front of him for any sign of the Council. Several agonizing seconds passed as another roll of thunder echoed across the city. Overhead, the clouds finally burst, and rain pounded the ground, turning the pavement dark and blurring Timothy's vision. Suddenly, a loud bang echoed through the air, and something struck Timothy's helmet, knocking him off his feet.

As he lay sprawled out on the sodden ground, stunned, Crystal and Jewel quickly organized the three companies into formation across the narrow street. The street was only wide enough for three people to enter at a time, so the majority of the rebels hung back, ready to take their place in the fighting if the current fighters were to tire or be wounded.

Timothy scrambled to his feet just in time to see a large force of

Blanks gathering in the plaza. Though the blinding rain concealed their exact numbers, Timothy was sure he spotted three or four of the Councilmen among them. The Council hesitated for a moment, not expecting to encounter resistance so soon.

But once they realized how few the defenders were, they quickly regained their confidence. They charged forwards, hacking and slashing at the rebels with frightening ferocity. The rebels fell back before the Council's onslaught, several of them already lying dead on the cobblestones.

Quelling the panic that always gripped him whenever he faced the prospect of going head-to-head with the Council, Timothy stepped to the front of the rebel's ranks, joining Crystal and Jewel in fending off the Council's attacks. No sooner had Timothy taken his place on the front lines than a bullet ricocheted off his chest plate, leaving behind a large dent. He looked in the direction of the attack to see Councilman Marciano standing a few feet away, reloading his pistol for another shot.

Timothy whipped a shuriken at the gun, knocking it from its owner's hands. As Marciano scurried off to retrieve his weapon, Timothy pivoted to face the next closest Councilman, who happened to be Karr. He swung his staff at the man's head, but the Councilman deflected the attack easily, sweeping Timothy's feet out from under him with his leg. Timothy was back up in an instant, slashing at Karr's head with a shuriken.

The move caught Karr by surprise, and he faltered, his hands flying to the cut that Timothy's counterattack had opened across his face. Seizing his opportunity, Timothy kicked the Councilman in the stomach, causing him to double over on the ground. A Blank immediately took his place in the battle, giving the Councilman time to recover.

But Timothy took no notice of his new opponent, because at that moment, Jewel crumpled to the ground, impaled by Alexis' sword. Alexis raised his sword again, and Timothy stepped between the Councilman and his wounded friend, raising his staff to block the strike.

The sword hit the staff with a jarring thud, biting deep into the wood and staying there. Alexis yanked on the sword, nearly pulling Timothy's staff from his hands in his efforts to recover his weapon. The sword remained firmly stuck, and Timothy suddenly jerked his staff to one side, catching the Councilman in the jaw and sending him crumpling to the ground in a heap.

As the wind began to pick up once more, Timothy turned his attention to Jewel. She was still breathing, although she appeared to be unconscious. Crystal was already by her sister's side, a medical kit open on the ground next to her.

"How bad is it?" Timothy asked, barely keeping the fear from his voice.

"I think - I think she'll make it," Crystal replied, her tone contradicting her words. The wind blew harder, whipping her hair into her face.

"We need to get her to a medic right now," Timothy said, images of Henry's death springing to his mind.

"If we leave now, the Council will take Gearwire's forces from behind. The resistance will be wiped out," Crystal said, tears streaming down her face.

"We can't just leave her here to die!" Timothy shouted back. "Not again!"

Crystal blinked back the tears, an idea occurring to her. "There-there might be another way," she said softly, only barely audible over the howling of the wind. "I-I could freeze her in crystal. It'll keep her from dying until we can actually get her to a medic. It's just..." She trailed off, and Timothy could see the indecision on her face.

"It's just what?" he prompted.

"Some of the people we've encased in crystal - they've had some pretty severe amnesia afterwards."

"It's the only way," Timothy said firmly.

After a brief hesitation, Crystal nodded and encased her sister in crystal before she could change her mind.

Timothy turned his attention back to the battle, trying to take his mind off of his gravely injured friend. Through the blinding rain, he caught a glimpse of the Council's forces fleeing, the Council finding the resistance there a little too strong for their liking. They waited several minutes longer to ensure that the Council wasn't coming back, then Timothy headed off with his stealth platoon under the cover of the driving rain, leaving Crystal in command of the remaining rebel forces.

* * *

Elmer Evergreen jogged through the tunnel to Kawts, the mutants and tree people following close behind him. Gearwire's battle plan depended heavily on him being in position in time, and he was determined to be ready. He rounded the final corner and skidded to a halt, his heart sinking. A huge mound of debris blocked the tunnel, sealing off any hope of passing through.

"Inn!" he shouted. "Bring your platoon up here!"

"What's the problem?" the tentacled mutant asked as he ambled over to the tree people's captain of the guard.

"There seems to have been a cave-in," Elmer said. "We'll have to dig it out."

Inn nodded. "Worrub! Lennut!" he called. "We need your help!" Two mutants emerged from the brigade, swishing their mole-like claws excitedly. They eyed the soil eagerly, squinting. One of them rapped his claws against the dirt, listening intently.

"Half an hour," he said at last. The other mutant nodded in agreement.

"More or less," he confirmed, nodding like a bobble-head. "Less if we have help movin' the dirt outta the way."

"You heard the man!" Inn bellowed. "Everyone helps move dirt!" Before he had even finished speaking, the two mole-like mutants burrowed into the mound, sending dirt flying at an astonishing rate. The others frantically started moving the dirt out of the path, barely managing to keep it from piling up.

As predicted, nearly half an hour passed before the tunnel was clear again. Elmer sprinted the remaining distance to the exit in the library's basement, eager to make up the time they had lost to the cave-in.

Elmer charged out of the tunnel with his spear at the ready, flanked by half a dozen of the tree people's finest warriors. He ran up the stairs to the main entrance, hoping against hope that he wouldn't be too late. He collided with the door with a sickening thud and staggered back, the wind knocked out of him.

One of the warriors peered out through the window. "The door's boarded up, sir," he reported.

Elmer rubbed his aching head. "Thanks. Already figured that out," he gasped. "Break it down."

As more of the soldiers emerged from the basement, Inn organized several of the more muscular mutants into teams, using the empty bookshelves as battering rams. They charged the door, swinging the bookshelf with all of their might. The door buckled under the impact, but it held firm.

"Again!" Inn ordered. The mutants charged the door a second time, resulting in a satisfying crack.

"Again!"

As the bookshelf hit the door a third time, it gave way, sending the mutants stumbling out into the street.

"Thanks," Elmer said, getting to his feet, and trying to ignore the throbbing in his head.

"No problem," Inn replied easily. "Now let's go help Gearwire."

Chapter 36

Gearwire looked over the battlefield, his frown deepening. Things had not been going well for the rebels' forces since his crew members had left to secure the side streets. The Council had held back at first, but they soon returned with a vengeance, pushing the rebels back. The archers in the buildings ahead of them had largely fallen silent, and Gearwire knew with grim certainty that there was little chance that any of them were still alive.

And still, the attack drones continued to hammer the rebels' lines, forcing them to slowly give ground.

As the drones swooped down for another attack, Gearwire caught a glimpse of Idalbo standing atop the roof of a nearby building. Even from a distance, Gearwire could see the look of grim determination on his face. His heart sank as he realized what the mutant was about to do.

Don't do it, Idalbo, he thought with horror as Idalbo reached for one of his quills. Then, with a defiant yell, the mutant charged the drones, dropping half a dozen of them before they could determine where the attack was coming from. The surprise wore off quickly, however, and the remaining drones opened fire on him. Idalbo got off a couple more shots before he stumbled and fell face down on the roof.

Gearwire felt a familiar rage well up inside him. By now, he was sure that something had gone horribly wrong with his plan. Whether the other two brigades had been wiped out or merely delayed, he couldn't say, but it was plain that Gearwire's brigade was Kawts' last hope.

"Alright!" he shouted to the exhausted rebels. "On my signal, we're going to charge the Council's army!" The rebels exchanged glances, understanding fully how desperate the situation had become. "If we strike now, we can push them back," Gearwire continued, reassuring himself as much as his troops. A frontal assault was certainly a gamble. But what other choice did they have?

Gearwire faced the sea of Blanks and drones, his sword in one hand and his glue gun in the other. Though he knew he was about to die, he felt strangely at peace.

I never thought this would be how I went out, he reflected as a grim determination filled him. He was just about to issue the order to charge when he heard a roar coming up from behind the Council's army.

Elmer.

"Charge!" he shouted as hope flooded back to the rebel forces. He leapt into the fray, catching the Council's troops between the two halves of the rebel army. Together, they pushed the defenders back towards the center of the city.

"Sorry about the delay," Elmer called to Gearwire as he jabbed at an attack drone with his spear. "Part of the tunnel collapsed - we had to dig it out before we could get through."

Gearwire nodded in understanding, blasting a pair of drones out of the sky. "I'm just relieved that you're here now. We were in serious trouble for a moment there."

"The mutant on the roof - Idalbo?" Elmer began hesitantly. "He saw us coming. Drew the drones away from our position until we were close enough to strike."

"He was a brave man," Gearwire agreed somberly. "We can't let his sacrifice be for nothing."

Their ranks bolstered by a second brigade, the rebels surged forwards once more, pushing the fleeing Councilmen towards the center of Kawts.

* * *

Timothy slipped silently through the streets of Kawts, his platoon right behind him. The Council was preoccupied in fighting the rebels' other three brigades, so his journey to the center of Kawts was completely unhindered. When he arrived at the edge of the plaza, he motioned for his platoon to wait in the alleyway while he approached the Council's forces who had stayed behind to guard what remained of the citizens of Kawts. Scanning the crowd of security officers, he quickly located Volker and crept up behind him, making no sound in his movements.

"Hello," Timothy said, interrupting his broodings. Volker jumped and spun around, his eyes wide with fear. Relief flickered across his face as he realized it wasn't the Council.

"Oh, good. You're here. They said they'd send someone," he said. "I was getting worried."

Timothy handed him a de-Blanking device. "Use this on the Blanks," he instructed. "It'll free them from the Council's control."

Volker nodded sharply, then led him down to the people, unlocking their chains as he went. Timothy waved his platoon over to where he stood, instructing them to stand guard until he returned. Then he slipped off to the Kawts hospital to liberate the people there who had not yet been turned into Blanks. As he passed the track, he saw the ongoing firefight between the Council and Dr. Maddium's brigade, but he slipped by them unnoticed, the rain masking his movements.

When he finally made it to the Blanking chamber, he wasted no time in releasing the prisoners before turning his attention to the Blanking machine itself.

Their original plan had been for Dr. Maddium to be the one to deactivate the device, but Gearwire had given Timothy a crash course in how to do it himself, prepared for the possibility that one of them would be waylaid or killed. Timothy consulted the instructions Gearwire had given him as he deactivated the machine, taking his time to ensure he didn't make a mistake. Finally, the machine's gentle whirring died away as it shut down. Hoping he had done everything correctly, Timothy returned to the central square.

He wasn't a moment too soon. As he arrived at the plaza, a horde of attack drones flew in and blocked the exits, trapping the people inside. The drones leveled their guns at the citizens of Kawts, poised to wipe them out.

Luckily, Gearwire had anticipated this move from the very beginning. It was the reason he had sent Timothy to the plaza in the first place. Timothy reached into his satchel and pulled out several shurikens. He threw them at the drones, the tempered material shearing through the enemy robots. His platoon opened fire, dropping several more.

More drones gathered, turning their focus to Timothy and his men. As more and more drones poured into the square, Timothy worried for the first time that they wouldn't be able to take them all down, even with his platoon and Volker lending a hand.

Suddenly, from a side street, he heard a roar of anger. Into the square charged Ives and Charles, followed by the few other citizens who had escaped the Council's imprisonment. All of them were armed with improvised weapons. The drones wavered, torn between attacking the small group of skilled fighters in front of them and the poorly equipped mob behind them.

The distraction was just what Timothy needed to gain the upper hand, quickly downing dozens of the drones with his shurikens. The arrival of Dr. Maddium and his brigade a few minutes later sealed the robots' fate. In a matter of minutes, nearly all the drones had been reduced to piles of scrap metal.

Seeing that Dr. Maddium and his men had things under control, Timothy stepped back from the fighting, resting his throwing arm. Then, out of the corner of his eye, he saw Ethos slink off into the Council Building. Quickly scanning the skies to make sure he wasn't needed outside, Timothy ran up the stairs and into the Council Building, close behind the head Councilman. But by the time he arrived, Ethos was nowhere to be seen.

Instead, he found himself face-to-face with Aksell. Timothy sighed with relief at the sight of his friend.

Aksell will know where Ethos went, he thought, walking up to him. To his surprise, Aksell backed up against the wall, wary and tense. Timothy took a step closer, puzzled. Suddenly, realization dawned on him.

My suit completely covers up my face! Aksell doesn't know it's me!

Timothy hastily removed his mask and smiled at his friend. Aksell stopped moving, recognizing him.

"Aksell," Timothy said. "We've got to find the Council and stop them," he continued quickly, glancing around the room for any sign of Ethos.

Before Aksell could reply, Ethos poked his head into the room.

"Aksell!" he ordered. "Come. We must evacuate!"

Aksell glanced back and forth between the pair, both of whom had stopped still at the sight of the other. The confusion and indecision were evident on his face as he stared at his father and his best friend.

Finally, Aksell spoke.

"Sorry, Tim," he said, producing a strange-looking gun from behind his back and firing it at Timothy. A beam of energy flew from the weapon, striking Timothy in the chest and freezing him in place. Unable to move or even to speak, all he could do was watch as Aksell and the rest of the Council fled the city, replaying Aksell's betrayal over and over again in his mind.

* * *

As the storm outside subsided, the blast from Aksell's weapon began to wear off, allowing Timothy limited mobility. It was then that Gearwire arrived with several of his crew members, weapons at the ready. But he was far too late. The Council was long gone.

Gearwire noticed the look on Timothy's face and immediately guessed the cause.

"Come with me," he said gently, leading Timothy outside, where he was immediately greeted by Samuel and Quill.

"You got my message!" Quill exclaimed, jogging over to him. "Samuel told me everything! What took you so long?"

Timothy forced himself to smile. "You could've given me a little better of a hint with that box of yours."

"The important thing is, you figured it out eventually," Samuel said, coming up behind the pair, a wide smile on his face. "I'm rather glad I'm not dead right now." He looked around. "Where's Aksell? I thought for sure he would have wanted to be here to meet us."

Timothy's face fell as he replayed Aksell's betrayal in his mind. "He - he chose the Council," he said at last, dropping his gaze to the floor.

A shadow crossed Samuel's face as he and Quill immediately grew somber. "I never thought I'd see the day when Aksell sided with Ethos against Kawts," Samuel said quietly. "But then again, I've been... incapacitated for some time."

"He'll be back," Quill said emphatically, although the look on his face contradicted his words. "As manipulative as Ethos is, Aksell is smart enough to see through his lies. It just might take a little time."

"Sure," Timothy said, not really believing it.

Gearwire approached the group, flanked by the remaining members of his crew. He put his hand on Timothy's shoulder.

"Listen," he said simply. The trio fell silent, looking out over the city of Kawts as dawn began to break. From somewhere in the city, the remaining musicians were playing a song, now a joyful melody as the people of Kawts celebrated the Council's defeat. The song was punctuated by shouts of joy as people reunited with family and friends they had long believed to be dead.

"You helped make this possible," Gearwire said softly. "Take it from an old soldier: you have to enjoy the victories while you can. Everything else can wait."

Despite all that had happened, Timothy felt a smile break out over his face. Regardless of the Council's escape, the fact remained that they had won. Kawts was finally free.

Epilogue

"Sir! There's a messenger here to see you!" Volker shouted into the library. Samuel groaned inwardly as he hastily tried to clear out the clutter from his temporary office.

"Send him in," he called back, dropping into his chair.

A lot had changed in the months following the liberation of Kawts. Long-lost friends and families had been reunited. Concerts and music classes had become frequent, as were classes on many other things that the Council had banned. Restaurants, libraries, and churches had sprung up all over the five cities as the people suddenly realized what they'd been missing out on for all those years. The Race had been immediately discontinued.

As for Kawts' government, Gearwire had appointed Samuel to lead the city. Samuel had objected at first, insisting that Gearwire, as the leader of the liberating army, should be the one in charge.

But Gearwire had just shaken his head and replied, "I've had my chance at leading Kawts. Look how that turned out." There had been a short pause before he added, "Besides, until yesterday, I was regarded as public enemy number one. The people need someone they can trust."

The messenger entered the library hesitantly, and Samuel could tell at once that he was one of the mutants from Alpen.

Draagetsew must've sent him, he thought as the man approached. *I hope his battalions made it home safely.* The mutant looked around nervously, as if not entirely sure he was in the right place.

"I'm only going to be here temporarily," Samuel said, gesturing to the rest of the library. "Just until we can build a new town hall. I can't very well run the free cities of Kawts from the Council's old lair."

The mutant nodded. "A message for you," he said, handing Samuel a ragged piece of paper. "From Draagetsew."

Samuel scanned the message quickly, a growing sense of dread filling him. This would be a job for the Guardians of Kawts.

"Thank you," he said to the messenger. "There's a boarding house down the street if you need somewhere to stay the night." The man turned to go, and Samuel added, "And send in Volker on your way out." The mutant nodded and disappeared into the street. Volker entered the room a few seconds later, and Samuel gave him his instructions. "Gather the Guardians of Kawts."

"Right away, sir," Volker said, jogging out of the room and leaving Samuel alone with his thoughts.

It had been Samuel's one condition when Gearwire had made him ruler of Kawts that some sort of group should be formed to advise him and to protect the city. To this, Gearwire had quickly agreed, and the Guardians of Kawts had been created. It was mostly composed of Gearwire's crewmembers, although there were a few of them who had only just recovered sufficiently to attend the meetings.

Idalbo had been found on the roof where he had fallen, riddled with bullets and barely alive. For weeks he had lain at death's door, but eventually, he made a full recovery, something that Gearwire attributed to nothing more than the grace of God and the remarkable healing capabilities of the people of Alpen. Jewel had also made a full recovery, the resistance's doctors telling them that if they had waited any longer to encase her in the crystal, she almost certainly wouldn't have survived.

In addition to Gearwire's crewmembers, Cedar Deeproot and Elmer Evergreen had also joined the Guardians of Kawts, representing the interests of the tree people as the cities tried to come together under one banner. Quill and Volker had been offered positions in the group as well, in recognition of their instrumental roles in freeing Kawts from the Council's clutches.

One by one, all the Guardians of Kawts filed into the room, taking their seats at a table they had 'borrowed' from Ethos' house. Timothy was the last one to arrive, out of breath from running all the way across town. Samuel nodded to his former protégé as he took his seat. After double-checking to make sure that everyone was present, Samuel explained the situation.

"I received a concerning message earlier today," he began. "It was from Draagetsew - the president of the Koalition der Alpen," he added for the benefit of Quill and Volker. "It seems that the Council has taken over Alpen, and he and those still loyal to him have been forced into hiding. He says that he suspects they're after the Weather Belt."

"So having lost one of the fail-safe devices, they intend to go after another," Gearwire murmured, shaking his head.

"We can't let them take over Alpen!" Idalbo said.

"We have to stop them!" Adalbo exclaimed at the same moment, his hand darting to the hilt of his sword.

Gearwire looked at both of them as he answered. "Then stop them, we shall."

Author's Note

If you've enjoyed this story, please consider leaving an honest review on whatever platform you purchased this book from. It really goes a long way toward my ability to continue to release new titles in a timely fashion. And remember, if you haven't already, sign up for my e-newsletter at weston-fields.com to receive a free digital copy of Crystal and Jewel's origin story!

Acknowledgments

This book would not be what it is today without the help and input of so many people who gave me support and advice throughout the process.

I would first like to thank my sister, Natalie, for reading through the early manuscripts for me on multiple occasions and allowing me to talk at her about the story when I got stuck.

I would also like to give a big thank-you to all the people who read and gave me feedback on this book: Laura Hughes, Aidan Almeida, Austin Funk, Melissa Hemling, Katy Gladd, Levi Huizenga, Emmett Lerwick, Henry Rittler, Janna Fields, and Gary Schmidt. I couldn't have done this without you all! A special thank-you is due to Aidan Almeida and my editor, Abby Davies, for pointing out the holes in my early drafts. A big thank-you also goes out to Uncle Timmy and Ken for helping to fund this endeavor.

A few more rounds of bonus thank-yous: Dad, for letting me name my main character after him; Natalie and Elizabeth, for allowing me to use the characters of Crystal, Jewel, and Madison in this story. I hope I did them justice.

Last, but certainly not least, I would like to thank God for giving me the abilities and the resources to complete this project and for providing such an amazing world for me to gain inspiration from.

About the Author

Weston Fields is a student at Calvin University, where he studies religion, philosophy, writing, and ministry leadership. When not considering adding yet another minor to his degree, he can be found working at the library or working on his latest book. *The Guardians of Kawts* is his first book.

You can connect with me on:
🌐 https://weston-fields.com

Subscribe to my newsletter:
✉ https://tinyurl.com/WFieldsnewsletter

Printed in the USA
CPSIA information can be obtained
at www.ICGtesting.com
LVHW090744030424
776150LV00002B/123